Gods Without Men

Gods Without Men

HARI KUNZRU

HAMISH HAMILTON
an imprint of
PENGUIN BOOKS

HAMISH HAMILTON

Published by the Penguin Group
Penguin Books Ltd, 80 Strand, London WC2R 0RL, England
Penguin Group (USA) Inc., 375 Hudson Street, New York, New York 10014, USA
Penguin Group (Canada), 90 Eglinton Avenue East, Suite 700, Toronto, Ontario, Canada M4P 2Y3
(a division of Pearson Penguin Canada Inc.)
Penguin Ireland, 25 St Stephen's Green, Dublin 2, Ireland (a division of Penguin Books Ltd)
Penguin Group (Australia), 250 Camberwell Road,
Camberwell, Victoria 3124, Australia (a division of Pearson Australia Group Pty Ltd)
Penguin Books India Pvt Ltd, 11 Community Centre,
Panchsheel Park, New Delhi – 110 017, India
Penguin Group (NZ), 67 Apollo Drive, Rosedale, Auckland 0632, New Zealand
(a division of Pearson New Zealand Ltd)
Penguin Books (South Africa) (Pty) Ltd, 24 Sturdee Avenue,
Rosebank, Johannesburg 2196, South Africa

Penguin Books Ltd, Registered Offices: 80 Strand, London WC2R 0RL, England

www.penguin.com

First published 2011

1

Typeset by Penguin Books Ltd
Set in Dante MT Std 12 / 14.75 pt
Printed in Great Britain by Clays Ltd, St Ives plc

A CIP catalogue record for this book is available from the British Library

ISBN: 978-0-241-14311-7

www.greenpenguin.co.uk

MIX
Paper from
responsible sources
FSC™ C018179

Penguin Books is committed to a sustainable
future for our business, our readers and our
planet. This book is made from paper certified
by the Forest Stewardship Council.

For Katie

Dans le désert, voyez-vous, il y a tout, et il n'y a rien . . .
c'est Dieu sans les hommes.

Balzac, 'Une passion dans le désert' (1830)

De Indio y Negra, nace Lobo, de Indio y Mestiza, nace Coyote . . .

Andrés de Islas, *Las Castas* (1774)

My God! It's full of stars!

Arthur C. Clarke, *2001: A Space Odyssey* (1968)

In the time when the animals were men

In the time when the animals were men, Coyote was living in a certain place. 'Haikya! I have gotten so tired of living here-aikya. I am going to go out into the desert and cook.' With this, Coyote took an RV and drove into the desert to set up a lab. He took along ten loaves of Wonder Bread and fifty packets of ramen noodles. He took whiskey and enough pot to keep him going. He searched for a long time and found a good place. 'Here, I will set up-aikya! There is so much room! There is no one to bother me here!'

Coyote set to work. 'Oh,' he said, 'haikya! I have so many tablets of pseudoephedrine! It took me so long to get! I have been driving around to those pharmacies for so long-aikya!' He crushed the pseudo until it was a fine powder. He filled a beaker with wood spirit and swirled around the powder. He poured the mixture through filter papers to get rid of the filler. Then he set it on the warmer to evaporate. But Coyote forgot to check his thermometer and the temperature rose. It got hotter and hotter. 'Haikya!' he said. 'I need a cigarette-aikya! I've done such a lot of hard work-aikya!'

He lit a cigarette. There was an explosion. He died.

Cottontail Rabbit came past and touched him on the head with his staff. Coyote sat up and rubbed his eyes. 'Honored Coyote!' said Cottontail Rabbit. 'Close the door of the RV. Keep it closed. Do your smoking outside.'

Coyote began to whine. 'Ouch-aikya! Where are my hands-aikya? My hands have blown off.' He whined and lay down and was sad for a long time. Then Coyote got up and made himself hands out of a cholla cactus.

He began again.

He ground the pseudo. He mixed it with the solvent. He filtered and evaporated and filtered and evaporated, until he was sure all the filler was gone. Then he sat down and began scraping matchboxes to collect red phosphorus. He mixed the pseudo with his matchbox scrapings and iodine and plenty of water. Suddenly the flask began to boil. Gas started to fill the air. It got in his eyes, his fur. He howled and scratched at his face.

He choked on the poison gas and died.

Gila Monster came past and sprinkled water on him. Coyote sat up and rubbed his eyes. 'Honored Coyote!' said Gila Monster. 'Use a hose. Stop your flask, fill a bucket with kitty litter and run the hose down into that. The gas will be captured. Trap it and watch it bubble and boil, there in the flask. Don't breathe at all if you can help it.'

Coyote began to whine. 'Ouch-aikya! Where is my face-aikya? I have scratched my face off.' He ran down to the river and made himself a face out of mud and plastered it over the front of his head. Then he began again. He crushed the pseudo and evaporated it. He scraped the matchboxes and bubbled the flask into the bucket of kitty litter. He mixed the chemicals and cooked his mixture and filtered it and added in some Red Devil lye. He watched his thermometer. He was careful not to breathe. He cooled the mixture down and added in some camping fuel and shook it up and jumped up and down for glee when he saw the crust of crystal floating on the liquid. He started to evaporate off the solvent but was so excited that he forgot to keep his tail out of the fire. He was dancing round the lab, lighting everything on fire with his tail.

The lab burned down. He died.

Southern Fox came past and touched him on the chest with the tip of his bow. 'Honored Coyote!' he said. 'You must keep your tail out of it! That is the only way to cook.'

'Ouch-aikya!' whined Coyote. 'My eyes, where are my eyes-aikya?' Coyote made himself eyes out of two silver dollars and started again. He crushed the pseudo. He filtered and evaporated it, he mixed and heated and bubbled the gas. He filtered and evaporated some more, and then he danced up and down. 'Oh, I am clever-aikya!' said

Coyote. 'I am cleverer than them all-*aikya!*' He had in his hands a hundred grams of pure crystal.

And Coyote left that place.

That is all, thus it ends.

1947

First time Schmidt saw the Pinnacles he knew it was the place. Three columns of rock shot up like the tentacles of some ancient creature, weathered feelers probing the sky. He ran a couple of tests, used the divining rods and the earth meter. Needle went off the scale. No question, there was power here, running along the fault line and up through the rocks: a natural antenna. The deal was done quickly. Eight hundred bucks to the old woman who owned the lot, some papers to sign at a law office in Victorville and it was his. Twenty-year lease, easy as pie. He couldn't believe his luck.

He bought a used Airstream off a lot in Barstow, towed it on to the site and sat for a whole afternoon in a lawn chair, admiring the way the aluminum trailer reflected the light. Took him back to the Pacific, the Superforts on their hardstands at North Field. The way those bombers glittered in the sun. There was a lesson in that dazzle, showed there were worlds a person couldn't bear to look upon directly.

He didn't sleep at all the first night. Lying under a blanket on the ground, staring straight up, he kept his eyes open until the blacks turned purple, then gray, and the wool was frosted with little droplets of condensation like tiny diamonds. The desert smell of creosote and sage, the dome of stars. There was more action up in the sky than down on earth, but you had to drag yourself out of the city to know it. All those damn verticals cluttering your sightline, all the steel pipes and cables and so forth under your feet, jamming you up, interrupting the flows. People hadn't fooled with the desert. It was land that let you alone.

He thought he stood a good chance. He was still young enough to take on the physical work, unencumbered by wife or family. And he had faith. Without that he'd have given up long ago, back when he was still a kid reading mail-order tracts in his lunch-break, making his first tentative notes on the mysteries. Now he wanted no distractions. He didn't bother about the good opinion of the folks in town. He was polite, passed the time of day when he went to pick up supplies at the store, but didn't trouble himself further. Most men were fools; he'd found that out on Guam. Sons of bitches never would let him be, giving him nicknames, making childish jokes at his expense. Took all he had not to do what was on his mind, but after Lizzie he didn't have the right, so he'd tamped down his anger and got on with fighting the war. Those saps had flown lord knew how many missions and with all those hours logged, all that chance to *see*, they still thought the real world was down on the ground, in the chow-line, between the legs of the pin-up girls they pasted over their rancid cots. Only person he met with a lick of sense was that Irish bombardier, what was his name, Mulligan or Flanagan, some Irish name, who told him of the lights he'd spotted when they were on their way to drop a load over Nagoya, green dots moving too fast to be Zeroes. Asked to borrow a book. Schmidt lent it to him, never did get it back. Kid went down with the rest of his crew a week later, ditched into the sea.

Little by little the place came together. The trailer was hot as all hell and he was trying to work out some way to utilize the shade of the rocks when he found the prospector's burrow. Didn't know what it was until he asked at the bar in town. Concreted over a few years previous when they flushed the old bastard out, some story about thinking he was a German spy. Crazy as a coot he may have been, probably starving to death since there wasn't a cent of silver or anything else on his so-called claim, but he knew how to dig. A whole room, four hundred square feet, right under the rocks. Cool in summer, insulated against the winter nights. A goddamn bunker.

After that it was all gravy. He graded an airstrip, sunk a gas tank into the dirt, threw up a cinder-block shelter and painted WELCOME in big white letters on the tin roof. Now he had a business. The café was never going to amount to much, but then he didn't need it to be General Motors. He felt he could have gotten along without another living soul, but his savings weren't going to last forever. He had another year, perhaps two, before money got tight, just about the right time for an enterprise like that to find its feet.

There weren't too many passing aircraft. About once a week someone would land. He'd serve them coffee, fry eggs. When they asked what he was doing out there he'd say just waiting, and when they asked what for he'd say he didn't know yet but it sure beat sitting in traffic, and that was usually enough for them. He'd never take visitors down into the bunker. After a few months the numbers increased. Pilots flying to and from the coast began to hear there was a place to refuel. He bought some chairs and Formica-top tables, laid in a stock of beer.

There were problems, of course. His generator broke down. There was a confrontation with some Indians he caught clambering about on the rocks, had to show them his shotgun. After they went away he found rock drawings up there, handprints and snakes and bighorn sheep. Another day a dust storm forced a plane down. The wind was blowing sideways across the strip at fifty miles an hour and the pilot did well to land at all – looked like it would pick up his left wing and flip him as he made his approach. Schmidt ran out to meet him, holding a bandana over his mouth. Without thinking he took him underground, the logical place to shelter.

The pilot was a young buck, twenty-one or so, head of dark hair, little dandyish mustache. Rich kid. As he stripped off his jacket and goggles, he looked around in wonder, asked where on earth he was.

By that time the project was well advanced. Schmidt had built a vortical condenser to store and concentrate the paraphysical energies flowing through the rocks. A crystal was set into a gimbal on the tip of the tallest stack, angled toward Venus. He was developing a parallel piezo-electric system, based on his study of Tesla, but for now was sending signals using an old Morse key, with an aetheric converter to transform the physical clicks into modulations of the paraphysical carrier wave. He explained all this to the pilot, who listened intently, taking in the machinery, the piles of books and notes. He seemed impressed.

7

'And what message are you sending?'

There was a question. Schmidt's message was love. Love and brotherhood to all beings in the galaxy. Two hours of redemption nightly, starting soon as the planet was visible over the horizon. Two hours of repeating his invitation: WELCOME. He didn't want to talk about it, not with a stranger, made some joke about higher powers, more things than were visible to the naked eye.

The pilot smiled. 'Hope you know what you're doing.'

'We'll see, I suppose.'

From then on the kid would land his Cub at the Pinnacles every couple of weeks. His daddy was some big farmer down in Imperial Valley, but Davis, that was his name, wanted more out of life than orange groves and wetback pickers. Though Schmidt didn't ask for a thing, he gave him money to buy books and equipment. Clark Davis was the first disciple, the first to understand the true nature of Schmidt's calling.

One night they flew over the Nevada state line, touched down at a ranch near Pahrump, a property with neon beer signs in the windows and a row of semis parked out front. Davis wanted to show him a good time, said it wasn't normal to be on his own so much. Against his better judgement – the whole escapade was against his better judgement – Schmidt found himself sitting nervously, drink in hand, as the girls lined up in their silky nothings, pouting and sticking out their behinds. Davis acted all man of the world, choosing a big-titted greaser and winking encouragingly as he followed her out, like Schmidt was some nervous teenager getting his dick wet for the first time. That got his back up. He downed his brandy, asked for another. He hadn't touched alcohol since that last night with Lizzie and soon he remembered why; though the little blonde scrap he chose was cute and gentle as could be, he just felt angry at her, at himself really, and she must have gotten scared and pressed a button or something because before too long he was outside with his pants in his hands, hunting for his other boot in the parking lot.

He tried to explain it to Davis. How he'd been a wild boy, too much for his broke-down mother. How he didn't care to know about school or a trade, just wanted a big canvas for his young life and air that didn't taste of sulfur, so he hopped a freight and never once looked back at the smokestacks of Erie, Pennsylvania. By seventeen he was working the line at a salmon cannery in Bristol Bay, spending his pay in the bars and getting himself into every kind of trouble, which eventually added up to Lizzie, who was all of fourteen years old, half-blood native and crazier than he was. Took him in her mouth in the doorway of a warehouse on the docks and it was like a band started playing inside his skull. Before too long she was pregnant and then he really was in the shit because she had brothers and her father was some town big-shot, more or less dragged the two of them to church just to save the family reputation. The old man hated Schmidt's guts for obvious reasons but to do him justice he tried to be decent, set them up in a little place, even gave money for the kid. Catch was Schmidt didn't like charity, and he certainly didn't like to feel trapped, and because the little boy's screams set him on edge and because he'd somehow lost his taste for her, he started slapping Lizzie around. Her menfolk warned him and each time it happened he cried in the girl's lap and swore he'd do better, but the arguments only left him feeling sore and cornered, and then one night he drank more than usual and she talked back and somehow he ended up tying a noose round her neck and dragging her half a mile behind his truck before he came to his senses and hit the brake.

She survived, though she didn't look the same after. In the lock-up some boys held him down and messed with him and he thought they'd kill him because they said they'd been paid by Lizzie's daddy, but they let up when they'd done their business and he pulled on his pants and lay down in a corner of his cell and was still lying there when the Russian came to bail him out. The Russian had owed Schmidt ever since he stopped him putting some guy out of a third-floor window at the Friday-night card game. Think of all the years, said Schmidt, and the Russian, whiskey-deaf as he was, took heed. He was dangling the whimpering cheat by his ankles, about drunk enough to drop him, but instead he lifted him back in and gave him a couple of taps on the jaw and no more was said on the matter. Next morning when he sobered up he thanked him, said if he ever got into trouble he'd be there. The Russian's two hundred bucks was Schmidt's first stroke of luck. Second was when the police chief turned up at the door and told him that if he left the Territory that same afternoon, Lizzie's old man wouldn't press charges. Reputation again. Worth more to him than his half-breed daughter, it appeared.

So Schmidt headed south, and though he tried to tough it out, told the story to men he worked or roomed with like it was some kind of joke, the guilt grew on him until it blotted out all happiness and he knew he'd kill himself unless he did something to get back right with the world. I'm just scum, he'd say to anyone who'd listen. Can't help it, always been that way. And he thought he always would be, thought it was impossible to change, until he found out that *impossible is a word found only in the dictionary of fools*, which was a quotation, his first, the second being *if you gaze for long into an abyss, the abyss gazes also into you*, a saying he picked out of an old copy of *Reader's Digest* and which gave him the notion, foreign to him until that time, that you could find truth in the written word. Thereafter he made a habit of seeking out such written truths and copying them down, first on scraps of paper, then in notebooks, until finally he realized he was working toward a system, such an understanding of the world as very few possessed. He read as much as he could, devoured books in every spare minute of his day, and never again touched liquor until Davis persuaded him into it, and only then out of some momentary wish to be like other people, a right he knew deep down he'd forfeited.

Davis listened to his story without saying a word. It was several weeks before he visited again.

Schmidt busied himself with signaling and watching the sky, plowing the furrow he'd started with those few scattered quotations. His search had led him first to the Bible, and then other books. He always suspected that any valuable truth would be hidden, that unless you had to dig for a thing, it wasn't worth possessing. A year or two passed and he'd found himself in Seattle, pushing a mop around the inside of a T-hangar as engineers worked on aircraft whose size and complexity seemed like a miracle. Watching the great machines take off and land, the way the earth relinquished them and gently welcomed them back, he felt that here was the secret made manifest. He decided to become a pilot, but when he went for a sight test, they told him he was astigmatic. That route was closed.

He went to the office and asked how to get a job as an aircraft mechanic. Technical school, replied the manager, and soon Schmidt was taking classes during the day and working nights as a security guard. By the time the war in Europe started, he had a steady job at Boeing Field and a bungalow full of books, their margins blackened by his spidery writing. The shape of his project was becoming clear: how to connect the mysteries of technology with those of the spirit. He knew the aircraft he worked on – with their tangled skeins of electrical cable, their hydraulics, their finely calibrated gauges that monitored fuel levels and engine power – were only half the story. There were forces greater and more intangible than thrust and torque and lift. It had fallen to him to unify them. Perhaps when he was brought before his maker, he would be judged not as a monster, but as a bringer of light, a good man.

After Pearl Harbor he was reassigned to the XB-29 project, rushing out a new long-range bomber for use against the Japanese. The schedule was punishing. The aircraft had all kinds of problems, over-heating engines, mysterious electrical faults that took days to trace. One day a test pilot lost control of a prototype, crashing through a power-line into a nearby packing plant. The ground crew jumped into trucks and cars and drove toward the burning building, trying to get close enough to the wreckage to see if anyone could be saved. Thirty people died.

The engine problems wouldn't go away, and once the bomber went into production just about every part the plants churned out was defective. The generals wanted the planes in China to start oper-ations, but on the date they were due to leave, not a single one was ready. Schmidt was posted to Wichita, working double shifts in a snowstorm, overseeing a crew performing final mods on the navigation system. They had to turn around every twenty minutes, because that was the longest anyone could stay outside before frostbite set in. At last the planes started flying East, only to be grounded in Egypt when the engines, which had more or less worked at freezing point, started malfunctioning in the hundred and twenty degree heat. Schmidt was sent out to retrofit new baffles and a cooling system, designed more or less on the fly by a team working out of a hangar at the Cairo airfield.

The B-29s limped on; Schmidt went with them. Cockpit temperatures climbed to a hundred and seventy, then fell to minus twenty over the Himalayas as the airframes were tested almost to destruction by violent downdrafts and side winds that threw the giant planes around like balsawood toys. He peered through the clouds and caught glimpses of valleys and gorges, rivers, villages, every so often the bright unnerving gleam of aluminum wreckage on the black mountainsides. Something protected him, and a week after flying over the hump he was standing on the tarmac at Hsinching. Peasants straightened up from their paddies at the airfield's edge, shielding their eyes to watch ninety bombers of the 58th Wing take off on their way to the Showa steelworks in Anshan. He was almost hallucinating with tiredness, having spent the previous forty-eight hours field-modding the big Wright Cyclone engines, trying to stop the cascade of horrors that unfolded when things went wrong in mid-air: valve heads flying off and chewing up the cylinders, tiny leaks of hydraulic fluid that could prevent the pilot from feathering a stalled prop, so that it started to drag and then sheared off, or worse, seized up the whole engine, which then twisted right out of the wing. The planes looked like huge white birds, like angels. He felt a sort of queasy elation. He was atoning; he was helping win the war.

In early '45 they moved forward operations to the Mariana Islands. On Guam, Schmidt spent his breaks sitting in a deckchair by the enlisted men's mess at North Field, reading *Isis Unveiled* in an edition he'd bought from a Theosophical bookshop in Calcutta. Beyond the perimeter, out in the jungle, were wild animals and half-feral Japanese who'd been stranded when the Imperial Army evacuated. He, on the other hand, was out in the open, in the clear. For the first time in years he allowed himself to feel happy. He heard from aircrew about the incendiary raids, and somehow that didn't touch him, but then he was transferred to Tinian. The 509th Composite acted like they were the second coming, strutting around as if they owned the whole Pacific and everyone else ought to pay them for the privilege of using it. Rumor was they were testing some new super-weapon; as he watched the *Enola Gay* take off for Hiroshima, Schmidt knew it wasn't carrying the standard payload, but that was all. Like the rest of the world he found out through pictures: the burned children, the watches stopped at 8.15. His beautiful gleaming aircraft, the harbingers of light, had been used to unleash darkness. He'd been betrayed.

By fall of '46 he was back in Seattle, but couldn't settle into the routine of civilian work. The world seemed to be sliding toward some terrible new evil. The spiritual promise of energy had been perverted: instead of abolishing poverty and hunger, atomic power would turn the planet into a waste land. Unable to face going outside, he began to neglect his work. The bungalow was cold and damp. In the evenings he sat in front of the fire and shivered until he fell asleep, imagining the tall conifers outside the window closing in and blotting out the sky.

He quit before they could fire him, withdrew his savings from the bank, packed his library and his papers into his '38 Ford pickup and headed for the desert. In his mind he saw himself as one of the prophets of old, an ascetic sitting cross-legged in a cave. He would mortify his body, purify his mind. The world had split in two, either side of the Iron Curtain. He would heal the wound. His intention was to summon the only force powerful enough to transcend communism and capitalism and halt the cascade of destructive energies. Since the dawn of history there had been contact with extraterrestrial intelligences. Ezekiel's wheels within wheels, the Mayan space pilots, the cosmic weaponry of Vedic India – the visitors possessed a spiritual technology far in advance of the crude mechanisms of earth science. It was time for them to manifest themselves, to intervene in the lives of men.

So he sent out his invitation. Two hours a night – two hours to atone for Lizzie, for the bombing raids, for all the misery of existence on earth. As he scanned the skies, he saw many things: meteor showers, bright lights moving in formation over the Tehachapi Mountains. Sometimes military jets flew overhead, threading vapor trails through the blue.

One hot night he was sitting outside, dozing after his usual dinner of canned franks and beans. In the distance a coyote was whining, and the sound penetrated his sleep. He opened his eyes and stretched, thinking about going down into the bunker to get a cigarette. That was when he saw it: a bright point of light hanging low over the horizon. The sky was hazy, loaded with dust whipped up by a couple of days of high winds, and it took a few moments before he was sure of what he was seeing. As he watched, dry-mouthed, the object got larger, approaching at incredible speed. There was no roar of engines, no sound at all. As it came toward him, he saw it was disk-shaped, featureless but for a ring of iridescent lights round the rim, like gem stones or feline eyes. His body began to tingle with electrical charge, the hairs on his bare arms standing upright. The huge oval hovered overhead, hanging above the rocks as if surveying the ground. Then it descended, stately and imperial, landing in front of him without raising the slightest eddy of sand from the desert floor. It was, he thought, the most beautiful thing he'd ever seen.

Once it had landed, the craft began to pulse – that was the only way he could put it – glowing pale green, then modulating through purple and rose, a gentle throb like a heartbeat. He couldn't suppress a gasp as a door opened in the hull and a ramp unfolded, like the tendril of a tropical plant. In the threshold stood two human figures, one male, the other voluptuously female. Their blond hair was agitated by some ethereal wind, though the night air was close and still. Their skin was so pale as to be almost translucent, and in each of their noble faces was set a pair of remarkable gray eyes, animated with profound compassion and intelligence. The pair were dressed in simple white robes, belted at the waist with bright metallic chains. They smiled at him, and he was bathed in a sensation of all-encompassing benevolence. *Come,* said a voice – not out loud but silently, in the depths of his mind. It was rich and sonorous. It resonated through him like a prayer. *Come inside. We have something to show you.* At last, he thought. Smiling, he stepped forward into the light.

2008

Oh baby oh what you want went down to the crossroads got down on my mojo black cat whatever. In Nicky's opinion, the whole Americana thing had gone beyond a joke. He watched the lads sprawled on the big leather studio sofas. Lol in his trucker cap. Jimmy trying to play slide on his shiny new National, making gravelly noises in his throat like he was some old bluesman instead of a skinny Essex electrician's son with a smack habit. You're all wankers, he told them. Uh huh unh unh, went Jimmy. Ned was on the phone to his accountant. No one looked up. Fuck it, he thought. Fuck this and fuck them.

Out in the car park the sun beat down out of a boring blue LA sky. Nicky smoked a fag and watched the Mexicans hanging about on the corner, same as every day. According to the engineer they were waiting for someone to come past in a lorry and give them a job. Gardening. Carrying stuff on a building site. What a life. Think about it, he'd said to Lol. One roll of the dice and it could have been us, know what I mean? Not me, went Lol. I'm too tall to be a Mexican.

What happened? Three years ago they'd been running round Camden, blagging into shows, doing crap speed in the bogs at the Good Mixer. Not a care in the world.

And now look.

Of course most people would sell their grandmothers to be in a band like theirs. If you get the big tap on the shoulder, hit singles and telly and that, then start moaning about how it's not all it's cracked up to be, you shouldn't be surprised if you get treated like a mental case. You're living the dream, right? So shut up. He'd learned pretty quickly to keep certain things to himself. Smile and talk bollocks to journalists. Don't tell them you lie awake at night wondering why you aren't more happy. Klonopin, Ambien, Percocet, Xanax. He ought not to point the finger at Jimmy. His own bathroom was like a chemist's shop.

He was leaning on Noah's car, a lovely old Merc convertible sprayed with multicolored hippie swirls. You could tell which one was the studio by the cars. All the buildings on the block looked the same: big gray bunkers with metal doors. Only one had this collection of motors outside. There was his own orange Camaro, rented back when they first arrived and he was excited by America; Jimmy's Porsche, skewed across two spaces, big scratch down the passenger side where he'd scraped it against a pillar in a parking garage. Jimmy couldn't drive for shit, even when he wasn't twisted. Nicky wasn't a hundred per cent sure he still had a license.

So what was he going to do? Go back in and be a good boy and try and write songs with the bunch of cunts who used to be his mates? He couldn't picture it, couldn't see the point. Oh there were millions of points, of course, about two and a half million ones for him alone if you counted straight up advance money, before you got into all the crooked record company arithmetic and everything vanished again. They were supposed to be in LA making their West Coast record, the one with Sunset Strip and Laurel Canyon good-vibes sprinkled over it like fairy dust. Instead, in three months, all they'd done was bicker and buy stuff and get wasted in bars full of people who looked as if they'd just been unwrapped from their packaging, all shiny and expensive, like audio equipment. People who came with curls of foam and polythene bags and cable ties.

Three fucking months. Break America? Other way round, mate. At first him and Jimmy thought all they had to do was drive up and down and absorb it and they'd suddenly channel the Byrds or some-one and make good music. They drove up and down. They made crap – worse – crap that didn't even sound like them. They'd have been better off in London, even with all the bullshit – Jimmy's dealer hanging about, Anouk, the tabloids. In LA Nicky felt like a tourist. What was he going to do, write a song about palm trees? About lawn sprinklers? Bikram yoga? He told Jim he was homesick, but Jim didn't want to know, went on about the nights back in Dalston when they'd got high, playing Gram Parsons and banging on to each other about cosmic American music. He was just beginning to get into the scene, he said. He wanted to shag actresses and go to parties in big glass houses where you could see the lights down in the valley. All Nicky really wanted was a kebab.

Sometimes he got wasted and went to bed with someone. He wasn't exactly chuffed with himself, but at the end of the day Anouk only had herself to blame. He wouldn't have done it if she'd been around. He'd told her to come over, but there was a job in Moscow. Then another one, a TV ad in Phuket. The next time it was Paris fashion week. It was always fucking fashion week.

Don't whine, she told him. She didn't like it when he whined.

Nicky had a rule: *never get sentimental about birds*. After all, half the world's gash, at the end of the day. But Anouk was different. She didn't fall for his act. In her funny, bored way, she saw right through him. He hated putting the phone down on her, but you had to play the game. Never let them get the upper hand.

After the fashion week conversation, he did what he always seemed to do nowadays when he had a problem – worked through the minibar. First vodkas, then gins, whiskeys, then whatever was left. He watched bad telly and looked at YouTube. He could feel himself spiraling into the dark place. Her voice had sounded so flat. Who was she with, over there in Paris? Most of the blokes in fashion were queer, which if you were going out with a model was a mercy, but there were always more than enough straight ones sniffing about. Photographers, for a start. Lecherous bastards all. And those fifty-year-old rich geezers you only seemed to see at fashion parties, the ones with orange tans and a thing for teenagers. Sick industry, when you came to think about it.

Not a good night. Not proud of himself the next morning. Terry gave him a lecture, said the hotel weren't happy and did he realize how much it cost to keep the police out of it. Nicky told him it was his fault for putting him in a crap room. He ought to have had one with a bigger balcony. The look on Terry's face. A day or two later he made it up with Anouk, but it was obvious he'd have to get along without her for a while. He sent flowers, wrote lyrics, thought about sending her the lyrics, tore them up.

LA was a nightmare. The place was so uptight. Everything seemed to be *inappropriate*. Sorry, sir, this is a non-smoking environment. Sorry, sir, we don't permit English people talking loudly or having a laugh with their mates in our poncey white-painted restaurant. He wanted to walk to the corner shop. He wanted to get on a bus. Valet parking? What was that about? How were you supposed to get home when you were pissed in a city where there was no such thing as a cab? No one could even understand his accent. I'll have the tuna sandwich. *Cheena?* I'm sorry, sir, what is *cheena*? One day he was trying to get a glass of water. Water, he said. Water. The stuff that comes out of the tap. The waitress was getting shirty. I don't understand, she hissed, what is it you require? Noah had to intervene. Water, he said. *Wah-dah.* They sat around repeating it. *Wah-dah*, not *wor-uh*.

He phoned Anouk.

'Drop everything. I'll tell Terry to put you on the first plane.'

'I can't. I can't just "drop everything".'

'I need you, babe. It's serious. I'm not pissing about.'

'I have a job.'

'Fuck's sake, Nookie, you don't work in an office. Turn something down for once, eh?'

'Nicky, you decided to go and be out there. You left me, not the other way round. It was your choice.'

'I didn't leave you.'

'You could have found a studio anywhere. It's just a room with a lot of stupid black boxes. Not even any windows. What does it matter where you are?'

'You don't know what you're talking about.'

'No, of course not. I'm so stupid. I'm just stupid and good for fucking and being on your arm to have your picture taken.'

'That's not what I meant.'

'You're a selfish asshole, you know that? A spoilt little boy.'

'So I'm a little boy? Who's the man, Nookie? Who's the real man in your life?'

'What?'

'I know you. You've got someone. Who is he? Tell the truth, Anouk.'

'You're being ridiculous. I don't want to talk to you if you're going to be like this.'

Click.

He stood in the car park and thought about Anouk and tried to work out if the sick feeling in his gut meant he was in love with her. He wrote love songs, or what passed for them. But what did he actually feel about her? When he wanted something he hated not being able to have it, that was all. He tried to think of reasons to go back into the studio. A pickup stopped on the corner beside the Mexicans. The driver gestured and some of them climbed on the back. He wondered what would happen if he got on too. Where he'd go. What kind of life he'd lead.

Maybe if he went for a drive. He leaned into Noah's car and tried the catch on the glove box. Not locked. He flipped it open. No keys inside, but there was a plastic bag full of little brown disks, like crinkly coins. He knew what they were, though he'd never actually taken any. One of Noah's favorite riffs involved finding your spirit animal and entering the crack between two worlds. Behind the bag of drugs there was something else, wrapped in a cloth. He reached in and picked it up. A handgun. A big blocky *gold-plated* handgun with ISRAELI MILITARY INDUSTRIES written on the side. The sort of item you'd find in an African military dictator's Christmas stocking.

It had taken Nicky a while to work out that Noah was a psycho. He was more famous than they were, at least in the States. A few years older, pushing thirty, he made freak-folk albums which sold by the truckload to hipster kids who wanted a little taste of freedom – the light filtering through the redwoods, sitting in a hot-tub under the stars – all the stuff Londoners like Nicky fantasized about in their damp basement flats. Noah channeled all that longing into breathy vocals and squeaky guitar strings, overdubbed some crickets in the background and then rinsed the lot in strange electronic quasi-sitar drones which made his songs sound like they'd just been radioed in from Mars. The band thought he'd be the perfect producer.

The first time they hung out was at his house up in the hills. It was exactly what Nicky expected: a sort of deluxe log cabin mummified in ethnic fabrics, with girls lounging around wearing beads and headbands, smoking spliff and looking like designer Red Indians. Noah was high on something that made him trip over his words and jig about irritably on the deck. You Brits don't know shit, he told them. You Brits still think it's like, the 1800s and you guys are in charge. Nicky didn't really give a toss. In a way, it was what they'd hired him for – the *Americanness*. But Ned was getting aerated and started to argue back. Nicky nudged him and told him not to bother; Noah wasn't listening anyway. Holding a sarong round his waist with one hand, he was toking on a joint with the other, stabbing it in their general direction while he made an incomprehensible point about destiny and the frontier and Jim Morrison. You want to see something, he said suddenly. You really want to fucking *see*, man? He took them into a backroom, made a performance of undoing locks and bolts and switching on the lights. Around the walls were glass cabinets full of guns. He had pistols, rifles, shotguns, old flint-lock things like out of a pirate movie. He had a chrome-plated AK-47 he'd bought off some special-forces guy in a bar.

They shot them off the back porch. Noah had his squaws line up bottles on a wooden bench, like the beautiful assistants in a game show. Don't you get it? he was yelling. 'Living free, baby! Living free!' Nicky didn't really understand what living free had to do with blast-ing the shit out of empty Coronas, but it was a laugh. Eventually the cops turned up, blue and red lights flashing in the street. Earl sorted it out. Earl was Noah's equivalent of Terry.

After that night Jimmy and Nicky decided Noah was cool. Lol agreed. Lol always agreed if Nicky and Jimmy did. Ned didn't like him, but then if Ned hadn't known Jimmy at school and been basically the only drummer in Billericay, he would have still been working at Phones4U, so his opinion didn't count. Noah became their guide, their guru. They bought clothes and instruments in the places he recommended. They did bongs first thing every morning, because he said they needed to loosen up. Jimmy even tried meditating. In the studio they pissed about with Tibetan temple bowls and rain-sticks and Jew's harps, chanting in darkened rooms, sitting on the floor writing tosh on bits of paper and cutting it up to make word associations. Burroughs did it, Noah told them. He was a pioneer of consciousness. 'Who's Burroughs?' whispered Lol, squirting glue on the rug. 'Some cunt off children's telly?'

Noah was impressive, but he wasn't good for the band. As far as Nicky was concerned, pop music ought to be instinctive: you just put your head down, made a noise, then stuck some lyrics over the top. Now here they were, throwing the I-Ching to find a rhyme for 'baby'. Everything they came up with sounded pretentious. Nicky couldn't even pick out a tune without second-guessing himself. Jimmy was the same. Whatever else happened, the two of them had always been able to write songs together. Now, because there weren't any songs, they began to argue. Words were spoken. Nicky moved out of the band house into one of the hotels on Sunset. He worked in his room, Jim in the studio. For a while they only communicated by fax, but neither of them could be arsed to write stuff down so they gave up and starting talking again.

If only Anouk was around.

One day Nicky thought of a lyric:

> *Oh go to sleep*
> *you're too much*
> *when you're awake*

It felt like the beginning of something. Noah was hunched over a four-track in a corner of the rehearsal room, chewing on his beard. When Nicky asked him what he thought, he just went *hmm*.

'What do you mean, *hmm?*'

'Nothing. It's just . . . Well, it kind of lacks bite.'

Nicky had always tried to act as if he could take criticism. The lyric was about a time when he and Anouk had been up for two days, speeding and ordering room service in a hotel in Berlin. Nookie was really tweaking, and he'd been on at Terry to get them some valium. Despite how it sounded, it was sort of a happy memory.

There was an awkward silence. 'OK,' said Noah eventually. 'I'll show you what I mean. I think it needs something more, um, *striking*.' He walked up to the mike and sang:

> *Go to sleep*
> *little frog*
> *you're too much*
> *when we touch*

'She's not a little frog. I don't think of her as a frog.'

'OK, man. Whatever. She could be, I don't know, a squirrel.'

'Or a leech,' said Lol bitchily.

Nicky walked out. What else could he do? He stayed away for a couple of days, spent the time drinking with some lads who had a custom-car place in Venice. He reckoned he had Noah's number. Geezer was third-generation hippie aristocracy. His grandparents ran some Hindu healing center up in northern California, sort of like the place the Beatles went to. His dad had been a singer-songwriter who'd OD'd after one album. According to Noah, he used to live in a dome out in the desert, just jamming with his band and looking for UFOs. Once he played them the LP, which had a picture of a pyramid on the front and was called *The Guide Speaks*. It was rubbish. All the stuff which once seemed so amazing about Noah was basically just him being a chip off the old block. Nicky's old man had given him a lot of solid information about Spurs and cavity-wall insulation. If he'd grown up doing Zen calligraphy and going on horse rides with Leonard Cohen, things might have been different.

He should have knocked it on the head after the night of the hot tub, should have got on a plane. They were over at Noah's, and despite himself Nicky had managed to get into the swing of things. There was this bird Willow and they were in the hot tub with the bubbles on and he was just beginning to get to a place where Anouk was totally off his mind when Noah bounded up, stark bollock naked, brandishing a pistol. Willow made a little noise in her throat, scrambled out and ran off to find her clothes.

'Now look what you did.'

'Fuck her, man. You and I need to talk.'

Noah leveled the gun, holding it with both hands like he was on a firing range. 'It's weird how it concentrates the mind. You can feel it, right? The prickly sensation on your forehead? Think: what would it be like if I actually got shot? All that mush spurting out. All my brains.'

'I'm not being funny, mate, but if you don't put that down I'm going to ram your teeth down your throat.'

'I'm not being funny either, *mate*. I'm serious. See my serious face? I'm not happy, buddy. I think you and your band might be wasting my time. You might be wasting my fucking *life*. Do you actually want to make a record, or do you just want to smoke weed and ball chicks in my hot tub?'

'You're off your nut.'

'Time for answers, Nicky. Clock's ticking. Seems to me like you don't have any ideas. Seems like you don't have any *creativity*.'

Willow must have told the others, because at that point Earl ran up and wrestled Noah to the ground. He was furious, shouting about how he was filled with cosmic pulsating life and Nicky was sucking it out of him, but eventually Earl got the gun off him and persuaded him to go inside and have a lie-down. Terry offered to drive Nicky back to the hotel, but he didn't want to talk to anyone. He drove himself, so high and freaked out that he was barely able to see the center line.

He rang Anouk. It went straight to voicemail.

That should have been him done, back to Dalston, kebab in hand, pack of Marlboro Lights, six Stellas for a fiver and LA just a bad dream fading in the rearview mirror. Turned out the bastards weren't going to let him off so easy. The next day he got soothing calls from Terry and Earl and the record company and the management in

London and a concert promoter in New York who had no business knowing anything about the situation at all. Then a courier arrived with a big cardboard box, supposedly from Noah but most probably from Earl, with a cowboy hat inside wrapped in tissue paper and a note saying Neil Young had been wearing it when he made up 'The Needle and the Damage Done' and Nicky ought to have it as he was the true inheritor of that spirit blah blah blah. Nicky didn't like to be soft-soaped. Twelve hours in the air and he could be having a pint in the George on the Commercial Road with the rain pissing down outside and some dickhead bending his ear about how Ronaldo wasn't worth the money. Sheer bliss.

He told Terry he'd had enough and Terry did something he very rarely did, which was to sit him down and say no. Nicky reminded him it wasn't his job to say no, his job was to say yes. Terry said he knew that, but sometimes what Nicky thought he wanted wasn't what he actually wanted. The record company needed a record, and if they didn't get one in LA, they were going to consider the band in breach of contract. Fuck it, Nicky said. Breach the contract. We'll go to another record company. Terry sighed. It didn't work like that. A lot of money had been flushed down the toilet. He asked Nicky to imagine men in little cubicles doing sums. Men in suits. Nicky imagined. He didn't see Terry's point. Terry put it another way. If they didn't make the album, the record company would take all their money. They'd be broke. Nicky asked if he had a choice. Not really, said Terry. Not having a choice was one of Nicky's pet hates.

He finished his cigarette and ground it into the hot concrete of the studio car park. Make the record or be broke. Or steal Noah's drugs and his gun, leave town and hope that by the time the others find you, it'll all be sorted out. There was always a choice, if you knew where to look for it. He got into his car.

Driving was almost the only thing that felt natural in America. It was traditional. It was *patriotic*. When you accelerated you could almost hear the crowd cheering you on. The Camaro managed about a hundred yards to the gallon and sounded like a tank invasion. It was a 1970s orange fireball of environmental doom and if he had to spend his globally warmed old age on a raft or trudging through the ruins of Billericay eating dog food, it would have been worth it.

LA faded away into a thankless dead landscape. You couldn't call it desert, really. It was waste ground, the city's backyard, a dump for all the ugly things it didn't want to have to look at. Warehouses and processing plants. Pylons, pipelines. Broken things. Junk. There were whole junk towns, San this and San that, fuck all to them except concrete: concrete boxes to live in, concrete lots in front of concrete malls for all the little junk people to go and buy things. He was happy to pass through without stopping, to see those places as blurs by the side of the highway. A water tower, a wall painted with the tiger crest of some high-school sports team. He didn't care that his phone was ringing every few minutes. He didn't care the radio had nothing on it but Bible preachers and dinner jazz. The road was white as a bone, the sky was airbrushed blue, and he was on his way to the emptiest square on the map. Nothing mattered except keeping it tight, slotting into a space between speeding cars, peeling off at a junction, swinging round and over and under and back, leaving disaster far behind.

How long did he drive for? Three, maybe four hours. He wasn't wearing a watch. The car didn't have air conditioning and the wind blasting through the open window was hot and gritty. His brain was starting to sizzle in his skull like an egg in a pan, so he pulled in at a petrol station, stuck another sixty dollars into the tank and bought a big jug of water, most of which he poured over his head. As his poor swollen gray cells relaxed back to their normal size, he looked at the phone. Eleven missed calls. Several from Terry, a couple from Jimmy, even one from Noah. He didn't bother listening to the messages.

Whatever he was doing, it wasn't about the band. The only person he wanted to hear from was Anouk. He willed the phone to ring again, for her number to appear on the screen.

Call me, babe.

Come and get me.

The gaps between the junk towns grew bigger. Soon the only signs of life were rows of giant white wind turbines and billboards advertising casino resorts. An outlet mall rose up at the roadside like a mirage. Then nothing. Miles of rock and scrubby bushes. Eventually the light began to fade. Sparks were darting about at the edges of his vision, little comets he kept mistaking for overtaking cars or bats flying towards the windscreen. He was coming into a town whose name he hadn't caught when he saw a motel sign. There were dozens of these shabby places along the route. Desert this and palm that. This one was called the *Drop Inn*. He was too tired to go any further.

Reception was no bigger than a cupboard, a little box with a desk, a bell, a rack of postcards and a clattering screen door. The woman who emerged from the backroom had bigger hair than he'd seen on a real person since he was thirteen and found his mum's cache of eighties workout videos. She was wearing a purple jumpsuit, which might have been hot (or at least ironic) on a twenty-year-old, but on her was sort of sad, an outfit fixed at the fashion moment when its wearer last felt beautiful. He couldn't tell how old she was. Forty-five? Her mouth had little lines round it. When she wasn't talking it shaped itself into a tired grimace, as if she'd spent too much of her life saying things she didn't mean.

She told him to call her Dawn and insisted on giving him the full tour. He said he was tired, hoping she'd just give him the room key, but she was having none of it. She chattered away as if he was the most exciting visitor she'd had in months (which might have been true), pointing out all the details, the 'touches'. The 'rec room' had a coffee machine, a shelf of dog-eared books and a board with take-away menus pinned to it. Outside, the 'landscaping' consisted of a few flowering bushes poking up out of the dust, sheltering some little plaster foxes and bunnies. All the animals were painted purple. The corrugated-iron fence which screened the kidney-shaped pool was purple too. So were the fraying covers on the loungers, the doors to the rooms and the tiles sunk into the dirt to make a border for the cement paths. 'We turn the spa pool on between five thirty and ten,' she told him, as if this was information which might influence his decision to stay. He nodded, trying to keep his eyes open.

As Dawn demonstrated the spa pool's various jets, he looked out beyond the peeling fence. It was hard to say where the motel property ended. It sort of petered out. Behind the pool was a shed and a couple of plastic lawn chairs lying on their side in the dirt. Behind the chairs, the broken ground stretched away into the distance until it hit a line of barren hills, a jagged black outline against the evening sky. He wondered what it would be like to climb them. Impossible during the day. Scrambling, panting, the sun beating down. It would be a penance, a quick way to kill yourself.

'We don't serve breakfast here,' said Dawn. 'But you can get coffee in the rec room any time you like.'

'Can I see my room now?'

'Sure.'

She didn't move, just stood there staring up at the sky, her arms folded across her chest as if she was suddenly feeling cold.

'You can see a lot out here,' she said eventually.

'The room?'

'Oh, pardon me. This way.'

Later he lay on a bed that stank of lavender-scented detergent, listening to the sound of cars going by on the highway. His body felt like lead. His stomach was growling and he had a headache. The room throbbed with purples of various shades and intensities. Mauve bedclothes, lilac carpet, violet curtains. It was like being trapped inside a bruise. He dozed for a while, the TV jabbering in the background, occasionally jolting him awake with canned laughter or sudden bursts of gunfire. He finally had to admit he wasn't going to sleep until he'd eaten. He peeled himself up, put on his trainers and went to the office. The woman didn't answer the bell. Eventually he found her out the back near the pool, sitting in one of the lawn chairs, peering up at the stars through a telescope.

'What are you looking at?'

'Oh, nothing in particular.'

He told her he wanted to get something to eat and asked where to go.

'There's a diner just a mile or two down the road. You can't miss it. It's all lit up.'

He didn't leave immediately. Her mouth hung open slightly as she screwed one eye against the telescope. She seemed tense, expectant. He had a sudden picture of what she might have looked like as a child. Happy, optimistic. She sensed him watching her and frowned.

'Tell me something,' she said. 'Are you out here looking for lights?'

'No. Well, yeah, I suppose. Maybe. I'm just trying to get away from things, you know?'

She gave him an appraising look and turned back to the telescope. He went to get his car keys.

Driving into town, he passed a sign marking the turn-off for a marines base. A grid of lights glowed in the distance, covering an area much bigger than the little strip of Main Street. A video shop, a 7-Eleven, an off-license, a couple of bars. There was a barber offering 'military and civilian haircuts' and a house with three neon signs in the front window, one saying 'nails', a second 'massage' and a third offering 'Chinese food'. The diner was easy enough to spot. Like Dawn said, it was lit up. She hadn't mentioned that it was also built in the shape of a flying saucer. He parked outside and went through the door, up a little concrete ramp that had once been painted to look like metal. The UFO Diner had seen better days. Its curved plaster walls were cracked, and sections were dark in the band of red neon decorating the saucer's rim. The leatherette booths and battered chrome stools must have been there for at least thirty years. On the walls were posters from sci-fi movies, faded by the sun to pastel blues and yellows. Darth Vader was a ghost, ET the faintest fetal outline. He was shown to a table by a fat teenager who handed him a menu and went back to chatting up some lads who were hunched up in one of the booths. Five of them, tattoos, buzzcuts, all staring at Nicky, and not in a good way. It was possible that lemon-yellow skinnies, a cut-off T-shirt and spray-painted eighties high-tops weren't a look most residents favored out in San wherever the fuck this was.

Nicky tried to act nonchalant as he sipped his Coke. He wasn't a fussy eater. On tour he happily scarfed down greasy-spoon meals that would turn most people's stomachs – fried eggs swimming in fat, sausages made from bits of pig they didn't even have names for. But however bad the food was in Britain, at least they didn't put sugar in everything. He'd ordered the 'Mothership Chicken Basket' and the whole lot – meat, bread roll, chips, salad dressing, even the lettuce, far as he could tell – was sweetened. No wonder the waitress was a pig. He got some of it down – he was hungry – then had to give in. He pushed his chair back and slapped a twenty on the table. The young marines gave him the evil eye all the way to the door.

There was a queue at Dee's American Eagle Liquor Store. More short hair, more tats, more staring. Two blokes even came out to watch as he got back into the car. A six pack of Coronas and a bottle of tequila – frankly it was going to take at least that much booze to calm his nerves. He drove round the corner and stopped in the car park of a Taco Bell. He would have gone in and got a sandwich, but there were more military nutjobs inside and he just couldn't face it. The paranoia had woken him up, and he didn't want to go back to his purple cave quite yet. Fuck it. He had everything he needed. He should just get on with what he came for. He could spend the night outside and wait for the sun to come up. It was still over eighty degrees. It wasn't like he was going to get cold.

So he drove on, and after a couple of miles found a turn signed NATIONAL MONUMENT. Up ahead the sky was clear, blue-black. As he swung round, the headlights caught the shapes of huge cacti at the roadside, reaching their hands to the sky. He followed the road for half an hour or so, then stopped and switched off the engine. The sound of insects rose up in the darkness, an industrial sawing and scraping. He sat on the bonnet and drained a beer, gradually feeling his heart-rate slow. He threw the empty bottle out into the darkness. It made a little thud as it hit the dirt.

He fished the plastic bag of peyote out of its hiding place under the passenger seat and ate a couple of the buttons. They were so bitter it was all he could do to keep them down and he swigged tequila to take the taste away. Bad idea. After he'd spent almost a minute trying not to retch, he had to give in and spit a nasty mess out on to the ground. Silhouetted against the sky was a rock formation, a huge rounded boulder that looked like the back of a big sleeping animal, topped with three teetering stacks of rock. It didn't seem so far away. He wiped his mouth, dropped a few supplies into a plastic bag and started walking in its direction. In the bag the gun clinked loudly against the bottles and he had an idea it might accidentally go off, so he fished it out and tried to fit it into the waistband of his jeans. His trousers were too tight as it was and with the gun in there he had to walk like a constipated person. If he broke into a run he'd probably shoot himself in the arse. He ended up just carrying it.

After ten minutes the rocks didn't seem any nearer. He hadn't brought a torch, and he kept stumbling. There were these little furry cacti dotted around, all at about knee-height. They were very hard to see and he kept walking into them, getting spines stuck in his jeans. Despite himself he was beginning to think about snakes. And weren't there wolves out here, or coyotes or whatever? Don't be a pussy, he told himself. You're the lead singer of a band. You've got a gun. You are Jim Morrison. You are the hero of your own adventure.

No one knew where he was. No one in the world. But then again, wasn't that the point of coming out to the desert? You had to get lost to find yourself. Which sounded like the sort of thing Noah would say. Fucking Noah, it was all his fault. Checking the ground carefully, he sat down and had another beer, following it up with a few shots of tequila. So what if no one knew? How did life feel when people did know? No one really cared anyway. He had another go at the peyote, swallowing big lumps of it, trying to chew as little as possible. Something bright and white raced across the sky. The stars were like pinholes in a cloth. You could believe you were seeing through to some incredibly bright world on the other side of the darkness.

But the thought kept going round in his head. No one knew. No one knew. He took out his phone. He still had bars. She probably wouldn't understand, but he called her anyway, just to hear her voice.

She picked up, sounding hoarse and sleepy.

'Baby? It's me.'

'Nicky, it's the middle of the night. I have to work in a couple of hours.'

'I wanted to talk to you.'

'I have a really early call. Phone me later, OK?'

'What's wrong with now?'

'I'm going to look like shit.'

'And that's all you care about.'

'It's my job.'

'Where are you?'

'Paris.'

'Again? Are you with someone?'

'Jesus, Nicky, not that. I'm asleep. Leave me alone.'

'What do you mean, leave you alone?'

'You sound drunk.'

'Not really. A little. I phoned to say I love you.'

'That's nice.'

'I need you, baby.'

'Mmm.'

'I mean it.'

'Nicky, what's going on? I had a call from Terry. He wanted to know if I'd heard from you. Has something happened?'

'I don't know. No. Maybe. I walked out of the session.'

'Why?'

'It's complicated. I didn't want to be there.'

'Where are you now?'

'No idea. In the middle of nowhere.'

'Where in the middle of nowhere?'

'The desert. Listen.'

He held the phone up so she could hear the insects.

'Isn't that amazing?'

'What desert, Nicky? What are you doing out there?'

'Thinking about you. I want you to come. There's nobody here for me, Anouk. Only you.'

'How can I come? I don't have a magic carpet. What about the others? What about Jimmy? Or Terry? Why don't you call Terry?'

'Because I don't give a fuck about Terry. It's all turned to shit, Nookie. You're the only thing that matters. I mean it. You have to come and get me. I'm near a place called San – something. Get on a plane to LA, OK? I'll let you know where to come after that.'

'Nicky –'

'OK?'

'You're not listening to me.'

'Just say you'll do it. Just come, Nookie. You're all I've got.'

'That's not true. You're just being dramatic.'

'Don't tell me what I'm being. I'm serious.'

'I don't understand you. Why do you always have to be this way?'

'Come. I want you to come. Just get on a plane. I'll meet you at the airport. I love you.'

'Why now, Nicky? Why are you saying all this now?'

'Because it's true.'

'You're only saying it because you're afraid. You think you're going to lose me, so you say these dramatic things.'

'I mean it. If you don't come, I don't know what'll happen.'

There was silence at her end. He could hear her sigh, shifting position in bed. He imagined someone else beside her, another man kissing her neck, stroking her hair.

'Anouk, I'm serious. If you don't come I tell you I'll do something stupid.'

'You're always doing stupid things, Nicky. You're a rock star. You get to do stupid things.'

'I'll kill myself.'

'No you won't.'

'I will. I've got a gun.'

'You're full of shit, Nicky. I'm hanging up now.'

'Wait. You think I'm full of shit? Listen.'

He held the phone up and fired the gun out into the darkness. There was a deafening bang. He didn't expect the recoil to be so strong. It jerked his arm up and he stumbled backwards. The phone went flying.

'Oh, fuck. Nookie? Nookie, can you hear me? Shout if you can hear me. Shit.'

He had no idea where the thing had landed. The screen had gone dark. He kept shouting her name, then listening for a reply, shuffling around on his hands and knees like a dog. What had he done? Fuck fuck fuck. He took out his cigarette lighter, scouring the ground in little five-second bursts, flicking the thing off each time his fingers started to burn. He wondered if the phone had gone under a rock, turned one over, then thought he saw a snake. In a panic, he jumped to his feet and fired at it. This time the recoil made him step backwards and he tripped over one of the squat little cacti. The pain was excruciating. The calf of his left leg was now covered in spines, some of which had gone in quite deep. Even if he'd been able to take them out himself, he couldn't see a thing. He had to get back to the car. At least in the car there was a light.

Keep your head, Nicky. Whatever you do, don't lose your head. Picking up the plastic bag of booze, he hobbled back in the direction he thought he'd taken, but after a few minutes he lost confidence and retraced his steps. He could still see the big rock formation. Logically he ought to walk away from it. He just wasn't sure. The ache in his leg made it hard to think. Under his feet, the ground felt spongy. Was he going to die? Mate, he told himself, you really need to get a grip.

His mouth was dry, but he had beer. Logically he could drink a beer. His hands were shaking as he fumbled with the top. Him and his plastic bag of booze, out in the desert, with all the stars smeared across the sky. The ground was breathing. That was odd. The whole desert was slowly inhaling and exhaling and he was just a little wounded animal standing on its back. The giant rattle of the insects pressed down on his ears and he began to sweat. Every rock, every grain of sand was pumping out all the heat it had taken in during the day. The cacti raised their arms up to heaven. He wondered about joining them, praying for forgiveness. He felt sick. Would Anouk forgive him? What about all the others? He got down on his knees. Sorry, he whispered. I didn't mean anything by it.

He vomited on the ground, clutching his sides. His head was throbbing. Oh God, he was all alone. He ought to have been with someone. He was a rock star. He could have anyone. The worse you behave, the more they want you. They humiliate themselves, lose the plot when you walk into a room. Men get jealous. Girls go down on you. It happened in toilets, in dressing rooms, in the little cur-tained beds on the tour bus. What they got out of it, he didn't know. It used to make him happy, until he realized they weren't really blowing him at all. Making it with a rock star – that was the point. Not Nicky Capaldi. When he came, they got points. They were blowing an idea, blowing fame. They were proving they could make fame come.

In the distance he heard his phone ringing. He stumbled towards the sound, which stopped as he got close. He used the lighter, tried to spot the place. Then, just by his feet, he heard a triplet of short beeps. Voicemail. His scooped up the phone and hugged it to his chest. His hands trembled as he called Anouk.

'Baby?'

'You're alive!'

'I'm sorry. I didn't mean –'

'You bastard! You selfish bastard!'

'It was an accident.'

'You think that's funny? You think it's a joke, pretending to kill yourself?'

'I didn't do it on purpose.'

'You're actually crazy, you know that? A crazy person.'

'I dropped the phone.'

'I've had enough, Nicky. I'm not doing this anymore. You stay out in the desert and play with your gun. I don't care. I don't want to know about it. It's over between us. Don't call me again.'

'You don't mean that.'

'Don't you dare tell me what I mean. It's over, Nicky.'

'But I'm hurt. I fell over.'

'Mummy, I fell over. I'm hurt. You're a little boy. A selfish little boy.'

'But I love you.'

'No, you don't. I'm sorry, Nicky. You don't love anyone but yourself.'

'That's not true. Nookie! Nookie?'

There was no reply. She'd hung up. He called back, but she didn't answer. He couldn't believe it. This didn't happen. They didn't leave him. He left them, they didn't leave him. His head span. His leg throbbed. He drank more tequila and the desert breathed and the ground sucked at his feet like quicksand. Now he really thought of shooting himself. The gun would split his head apart like a watermelon. How had it got like this? When did he start hating himself so much? It was a mystery to him how other people ran their lives. What if he'd done more normal things? Washing up, cooking? He had no clue what was in his bank account. Did he have savings? People had savings. They saved up for things they wanted, things they couldn't have straight away.

Little by little the heat went out of the air. He sat and shivered and held the gun out in front of him like a cross to ward off vampires and his mind skipped from one thing to another. His mum crying when she saw him on telly, Jimmy's dad driving them to their first gigs. His kid sister, who got all the backstage passes she wanted, who did all the gak and drank all the Cristal and hung around China White's trying to get off with footballers. Did she love him? What about his mum? He'd bought his mum a house. Finally dawn arrived, a thin sliver of orange that spilled over the hills, lightening the sky until he could see some way into the distance and realized he'd been just a few hundred yards away from the car the whole time.

He drove back to the motel very slowly, along an empty road which seemed to writhe beneath his wheels like a snake. By the time he got there the sun was over the horizon and his leg was broadcasting pain in great red waves. He limped to the pool and sat down on a lounger, still holding the half-empty bottle of tequila. When he shut his eyes, there was redness behind the lids, a hot sick heavy redness that smothered everything.

1778

*To His Excellency Teodoro Francisco de Croix, Caballero de Croix,
Comandante General of the Internal Provinces of the North*

Señor,

With due submission to the superior person of Your Excellency, I have, as instructed, made my way to the Mission at Bac and offer this confidential report on its condition and situation.

Misión San Xavier del Bac is located in an extensive valley, twenty leagues from the new Presidio of San Agustín del Tucson. Pasturage is scarce except in the vicinity of the spring. Around forty leagues to the north there is an abundance of pine, suitable for building. Mesquite, creosote and saguaro are found in the open country, along with quail, rabbit, hare and deer. As for harmful animals, there are none save the coyote. While the land furnishes all amenities needed to sustain life, the air is alkaline and constipating, and all who come here suffer from chills and fevers. As the northernmost of the Sonora missions, San Xavier del Bac is vulnerable to the depredations of the Coyotera Apache, who make frequent raids and sorties, and harass the Pimas and Papagos in their rancherías, as well as the Mission itself. With these qualifications, it may be stated that the area satisfies the requirements for new settlements, as laid down in the First Law of Don Felipe II, registered in Book Four, Title Five, of the Laws of the Indies.

The Mission is directed by Fray Francisco Hermenegildo Tomás Garcés, a wily old Aragonese friar who seems to have been fitted by Almighty God almost to perfection for the reduction of the savages to our Holy Faith and obedience to His Catholic Majesty. I have seen him squatting in the dust with groups of Indians, eating their food with the greatest appearance of relish, though to a civilized palate it is repulsive and unwholesome. He is fluent in several of their tongues and has become famous in Sonora for his entradas into the country of the warlike gentiles on the far side of the Río Colorado, during which he frequently traveled alone, without an escort of any kind. Fray Garcés shares the stubbornness and secretive nature of his Franciscan brethren, and is highly suspicious of my presence at Bac, which he sees as a possible prelude to the secularization of the Mission. I have been at pains to reassure him that Your Excellency has nothing but respect and solicitude for his holy work.

I am inclined to forgive Fray Garcés his temper, for he has, through faith and determination, transformed a wild and desolate place into a tolerable home for himself and his flock, and has suffered greatly in so doing. When he arrived at San Xavier, despite the Mission being almost a century old, it was unable to furnish even those things most essential for the celebration of the sacred mysteries. His bed was the bare ground, and for his food he had no purveyor but providence, the various temporal possessions of the foundation in the time of the Jesuits having reverted to the savages on their expulsion, and they, like children, having failed to maintain them, allowing the fields to lie fallow, the buildings to decay and the livestock to wander. It is to his credit that in the ten years Fray Garcés has lived in this remote outpost, the Mission has made such progress in agriculture. It now produces a sufficiency of corn, wheat, barley and beans, and in good years is able to generate a small income by selling food to the Presidio. Fray Garcés has also set his neophytes to work in producing candles, tallow, soap and other necessities. There are three looms, on which San Xavier produces a small quantity of sackcloth. This suffices to cover the shameful nakedness of the neophytes, but Fray Garcés also is in possession of several bolts of red-dyed linen imported from Castile. This cloth is much prized by the savages, and the friar uses it to reward and encourage his charges.

Fray Garcés has under his care four hundred Indians, including a small number of mestizos and coyotes, most of whom are the descendants of soldiers stationed here during the Jesuit times. For his own part, he maintains an absolute prohibition on the fraternization of Españoles and Indians, though this is hard for him to enforce. The Mission is guarded by a corps of eleven soldiers, under the command of a Captain Díaz. This young captain and most of his men are without wives, though they appear to be good Christians, on the whole.

The buildings of the Mission are in pitiable condition. The mean little church is nothing but a flat-roofed adobe hall, built by the Jesuits without a stone foundation, or even adequate leveling of the site. The barracks for the unmarried women, which is supposed to be locked and guarded at night for the preservation of their chastity, is sorely in need of repair, likewise the living quarters for the soldiers. The barracks for the male neophytes is in better condition. The Mission has, at this time, no blacksmith or farrier, relying on the workshops at the Presidio for these and many other services. Besides a small granary, a kiln and a few huts – one of which is occupied by Fray Garcés – a single bell on a wooden scaffold and a tall iron cross make up the remainder of the Mission's material fabric. The most defensible building is the church, and Fray Garcés and his flock have had frequent recourse to this sanctuary, there being no stockade, curtain wall or other fortification. Fray Garcés makes frequent reference to the relationship between earthly poverty and spiritual riches, and on this point of theology he is no doubt correct. However, for the greater glory of God and the accomplishment of our civilizing task in this country, one could wish things were otherwise. As I write, the good father is much exercised by the delay in delivery from México of a parcel of instructional engravings, which he hopes will excite the minds of the savages more easily than words. He hopes soon to send for certain liturgical items, including a candelabra and a set of hand bells.

The mean condition of Misión San Xavier del Bac is partly due to the Apache raids which have continued, almost unbroken, for the last forty years. The friar tells me a thousand reals would not suffice to replace the goods the savages have stolen in the time of his service alone, though in this I am inclined to believe he exaggerates. Concerning the Apaches, Your Excellency is doubtless aware that the problem is hardly unique to the Pimería Alta, this vagabond nation being astonishingly numerous, roaming unchecked across the Provincias Internas of Sonora, Nueva Vizcaya, Coahuilla and Nuevo Reyno de León. In an attempt to mitigate their hostility, the Captain of San Agustín del Tucson has allowed, unwisely in my estimation, a number of Apache to settle in the vicinity of the Presidio. They are given a ration of corn and tobacco and trusted to visit Fray Garcés and receive Christian instruction, which they do not, unless coerced. The good friar, who is a man of great though not infinite patience, does not appear to hold out much hope of bringing them closer to God. They are otherwise allowed to maintain their barbarous customs, including the performance of obscene dances and ceremonies and the contracting of polygamous marriages. Their minor transgressions are tolerated, even the theft of beasts from the Presidio herd. No attempt is made to persuade them to farm. They are, in short, disguised enemies being succored at the expense of His Catholic Majesty's Treasury.

Despite these difficulties, Fray Garcés has established his mission sufficiently enough to make visits to the outlying rancherías of the Papagos, Cocomaricopas and Gileño Pimas without running the risk that in his absence his parishioners will flee or change their beliefs. As mentioned above, he has also made entradas to the country of the gentiles on the far side of the Río Colorado, for the spreading of our holy faith and the increase of His Majesty's dominions. During these extended absences it is my understanding that the Father Guardian of the Apostolic College of Santa Cruz de Queretáro supplied another friar to take his place at Bac.

To mark my arrival, Fray Garcés assembled his neophytes on the plaza outside the church. I counted a hundred or so, the majority women and children. When I remarked on how few they were in number, the friar informed me bluntly that during the summer many of the neophytes were in the habit of leaving the Mission to gather food and visit relatives. He described this absenteeism as lamentable but necessary. The piñons and acorns they collect on their wanderings supplement the agricultural products of the Mission in times of hunger, and it appears, though Fray Garcés would not say so directly, that only the scarcity of food during the winter months ties some of the neophytes to the place. I asked whether it were not in his power to prevent straying through the use of incarceration or physical chastisement. He says this had been tried, but proved unsuccessful. Parties of soldiers are, however, sometimes sent out to the ranchería to bring back runaways. I asked how the work of the Mission was done when so many of its members were elsewhere, and he laughed, telling me that this was indeed a problem – sometimes there was not even enough firewood to prepare pozole to feed those who remain. I found his attitude remarkable, labor being, according to authorities such as Verger and de la Peña Montenegro, an effective means for the savage to achieve salvation. Fray Garcés conceded this point, and spoke of long roads and short paces. He displays a sort of ecstasy at the poverty of the Indians, which he views as holy, in the Franciscan manner.

Upon observation I found the Mission's neophytes little better than their gentile brethren, prone to libertinism, insubordination, idleness, lack of foresight, distrust and instability of spirit. There is a preponderance of old women and orphan children among them. It seems relatively few able-bodied adult men can be induced to leave the ranchería. I refer Your Excellency to my previous remarks about winter food supplies and suggest that in some cases only an inability to feed himself leads an Indian towards God. Whether or not they are sincere in their conversion, the neophytes are much afflicted with sickness and lassitude. According to Fray Garcés the women produce many still births, and neophytes of both genders tend to wither and die without obvious cause. He conjectures that to take them out of their own ranchería deprives them of some subtle vapor necessary to their life.

Though Fray Garcés appears unwilling or unable absolutely to control his charges, discipline is not altogether lacking. During my time at the Mission, I saw one soldier placed in the stocks as punishment for a bestial crime against one of the native women. Also a number of Indians were hobbled as they went about their business, as punishment for fornication, malingering or petty thievery. Though this is commendable, there is a general laxity and tolerance of unsatisfactory conduct among the neophytes. The one exception to this is during Mass, when a sergeant walks among the rows with a scourge, striking them if they talk or rise from their kneeling position.

Fray Garcés permits the Mission cross to be adorned with votive strings, though he forbids certain other idolatrous practices, such as hanging tobacco and deer meat from its arms. I confess, Señor, I do not see the divide between one thing and the other, and would greatly prefer not to see such offerings, but the friar disagrees, viewing the strings as a stepping stone on the road to true faith. It is my impression that the neophytes' understanding of the principles of our holy religion is primitive, but this is due to their deficiency of intellect, rather than any lack of zeal in instruction. Fray Garcés makes heroic attempts to teach them the catechism in their own languages, and I have spent tedious hours listening to him repeat in a variety of guttural tones that there is only one true God, who is the creator of all the things we see and do not see, that God is the Most Holy Trinity, that God the Son became man in the womb of Holy Mary, that he suffered and died, that heaven is where all good things abide and hell is fire and damnation and so forth. Some young boys (in whom the father takes a particular interest) are able to commit much of this to memory and repeat it on command, but it is doubtful whether they understand when he explains that not only do they have to show themselves obedient, renounce error and observe all the obligations of a Christian, but must believe with all their hearts. Fray Garcés admits that only a minority of the neophytes can be trusted to make a sincere confession. Few Indians confess voluntarily, and some show fear at the sight of the confessional, refusing to enter. It is rare, however, that Fray Garcés will deny the sacrament of confession to a man on his deathbed. All, he says, shall have food for the journey.

As strict as Fray Garcés may be in the conduct of marriage investigations, interrogating the prospective bride and groom and enjoining them to tell the truth or suffer the pains of hell, the nature of carnal sin is a profound mystery to the savages. This alone should be enough to justify the good father's use of that authority which God concedes to parents for the proper education of their children, to reprimand and chastise them with the rod. Like the beasts of the field, they have no sense of shame in their nakedness. I have seen a woman leaving the Mission, and when she thinks she is far enough away not to be observed, shucking off her sackcloth shift like a snake discarding a skin. Whenever Fray Garcés observes his charges in such conduct, he whips them soundly, though in his employment of the lash he is stricter upon himself than his children, taking the discipline daily, not merely on those days customary to his order. The Indians' ignorance of all things is unsurpassed. Having never seen women with the Españoles, the Papagos of the outlying rancherías first conjectured that the friar and his escort were the offspring of their mules.

While recuperating last year at Tubutama, Fray Garcés wrote an account of his wanderings among the gentile nations of the frontier, though, from hints he has given to me in conversation, I believe that, while accurate in most particulars, this manuscript omits much detail, particularly concerning the physical and spiritual trials inherent in such a journey. He claims to have found over twenty-five thousand Indians on the banks of the Río Gila and Río Colorado, and to have cleansed them, turned them towards repentance and prepared them for receiving the Word of God and vassalage to His Catholic Majesty Don Carlos III, may the Lord preserve His name. It must be noted that on these travels Fray Garcés was frequently alone, hundreds of leagues distant from any other person of reason. His exaltation in holy poverty notwithstanding, I believe that, being far from human sight, he became lax in certain of his observances, and it is perhaps for this reason that he has lately adopted the strictest possible version of the rule of his order, to the extent that the Father Guardian of the Apostolic College of Santa Cruz de Queretáro has three times denied him permission to undertake certain fasts and acts of self-mortification which, in the heat of his ardor, he fervently desired to perform, enjoining him to find other penitential exercises, less deleterious to his health and his ability to discharge his duties at the Mission.

Fray Garcés has declared himself astonished at the roughness of the country on the other side of the Colorado, and the great obstacles God has fixed therein. Water is scarce, and wells must sometimes be dug out of the sand. At one such place he was confronted by a hostile band of Jamajabs and, having no means to defend himself, was resigned to martyrdom, when God inspired him to display a painting which he carried with him rolled in a wooden tube, depicting the Blessed Virgin and child. At the sight of Our Lady, the Indians prostrated themselves in great wonderment and then departed, leaving him to drink his fill. In celebration of this moment, in which he grabbed his salvation by the forelock, he named the well *Kairos*. Another sign vouchsafed him by the Lord on his wanderings was a representation of the Trinity, in the form of three vast spires of stone, Father, Son and Holy Spirit rising up out of the desert floor as a symbol of divine mercy and grace. At this place he encountered an angel in the form of a man, who conversed with him and revealed certain mysteries. He appears troubled yet by this encounter, and having once told me the story, apologized for it, saying certain things ought to remain in silence. Though I bade him continue, he declined, and I am of the opinion that he is uncertain as to whether this apparition came from Our Lord or the Enemy. Though he is reluctant to speak of his own miraculous experiences, Fray Garcés has much to say of the famous religious Maria de Jesús de Agrade, who was transported by angels to preach to the heathen of Alta California. He himself has met and conversed with old men among the Jamajabs and Chemeguabas who claim to have heard of a flying priest who came a hundred years ago to bless their people in the name of Almighty God. On his wanderings, Fray Garcés became convinced that previous preachers had prepared the souls of the heathen for his arrival, and he has hopes for great conversions once we expand our territory and link the missions of Sonora with those of Alta California.

I have now remained two months at San Xavier del Bac, and will this day depart for the Presidio of Tucson, there to wait for your orders, Señor. Two small incidents have soured my relationship with Fray Garcés, and it is no longer possible to remain without strife. One of my muleteers had carnal knowledge of a young Indian woman, soliciting her with tortillas and a piece of ribbon. The friar holds me responsible for this, and for the excessive zeal of one of my escorts in flogging a neophyte who stole a piece of leather harness. Fray Garcés blames me for the surliness and unrest provoked among his peers by the fellow's demise. Though I placed the offending corporal on guard duty for eight successive days, wearing five leather cuirasses, a serious enough penalty in this summer heat, it did not suffice to mollify the good father, who has the typical arrogance of the Franciscan, feigning humility but alive to any degradation or abrogation of his powers. It is here as it is elsewhere. Every challenge to Franciscan authority is held to be an assault on their holy mission. At the Presidio, the captain complains that Fray Garcés refuses to send his neophytes to them to labor and so soldiers are forced to perform manual tasks such as working the mill and pressing adobes, contrary to their dignity as Españoles.

I have come to know Fray Garcés very well. A true mendicant friar, he trusts completely in God and derives great joy, if not always a true sense of Christian brotherhood, from his converse with the natives, whom he genuinely appears to love and calls his children. His frustrations are many, and he often likens his work among the Papagos and Pimas to grinding ore in an arrastra to extract silver. He wishes to remain in sole charge of his scattered flock, and shows no interest in expediting the advancement of the status of the Mission to a doctrina. In any case, the realization of this change is impossible to imagine, at least for several years. The natives are incapable of acting in their own best interests, and it will be some time before secularization is appropriate.

In the discharge of their Royal patronage, ardent desire for the prosperity of both Church and State has caused our monarchs to issue many wise pronouncements, not least of which, Señor, was your appointment to the exalted office you now hold. The high regard in which I hold the superior person of Your Excellency leads me to believe that you will be sympathetic to my request now to be discharged from my duties and to return to my wife and family in Vera Cruz, which place I have not seen this last nine months. It is my humble desire that Your Excellency may derive benefit from this report. I remain your most obedient servant

Juan Arnulfo de Flores y Rojas, Hidalgo de Vera Cruz
Presidio del Tucson, August 21st, 1778

2008

For a moment Jaz thought he'd disappeared. But there he was by the pool, trailing poor bedraggled Bah behind him, standing like a little sentry over a sleazy-looking guy sacked out on one of the daybeds. Jaz hurried across the courtyard, careful not to slip on the wet tiles. Raj was at his most withdrawn, rocking slightly, his fists balled, his neck twisted around in the painful-looking S which always made him look like he was trying to bury his head in his armpit. The man lolled sideways, one skinny arm thrown out toward an empty tequila bottle which lay on its side on the concrete. He was dressed in tight bright clothes, like the hipster kids you saw cycling round Williamsburg. He seemed to be unconscious. The more Jaz saw, the less he liked: the straggly beard, the tattoo snaking up one side of his neck, the spots of blood on his pants; there was dirt in his hair, a film of it on his skin, as if he'd been rolling about on the ground. Just then he woke up. He looked startled to see the two of them beside him. Jaz tried to put a more neutral expression on his face.

'I'm so sorry. Was he bothering you?'

'Uh, no.' He had an accent. He rubbed his face and sat up straighter. 'Just having a kip.' British. Maybe Australian.

'Come on, Raj.' Jaz spoke soothingly. 'Mommy's waiting.'

Raj didn't move, just rocked a little harder. The guy leaned toward him, showing a mouthful of crooked teeth. 'Awright, little man?' Of course Raj didn't answer. The guy sat back again and looked up, shielding his eyes against the sun. Jaz caught the stink of stale sweat. Was he actually a motel guest? Maybe he'd just wandered in off the highway.

'Shy, your lad.'

Jaz didn't want to get into the details of Raj's condition with this character.

'Sure. He can be like that around strangers.'

'Right.'

'OK, son, let's go. Come with Daddy.'

Raj made it hard. He wouldn't give Jaz his hand, and when he was picked up he used all his most effective protest tactics, going alternately limp and rigid, squirming in Jaz's grip like a fish.

'Stop it now. Come with Daddy. Daddy needs you to come along.'

The man watched them struggle. Jaz tried not to feel embarrassed. He'd never got used to this part of being Raj's dad; the scenes, the way they were always the center of attention. They could never blend in, be a normal family. Lisa was tougher than him, but then of course she had to be: she was around the boy all day without a break. At least Jaz could leave, go to work.

Every weekday morning for four years Jaz had felt guilty. Guilty as he closed the front door and headed for the subway, guilty as he bought his *Times* at the news-stand; it was always such a relief to be away from Raj's relentless tantrums. Lisa had a shitty deal and he knew it and she knew he knew, and that was the hairline crack in the bowl, the start of their trouble. Before Raj came along they'd been fine. A terrible thing for a father to think about his son, but it was true. Despite the craziness at the firm, the foul-mouthed traders, the pressure from Fenton to sign off on Bachman's latest apocalyptic scheme, work was an oasis of tranquility compared to what the child had waiting for him at home – the sinking feeling as he turned the key and called out hello and tried to judge from Lisa's face and posture just how bad it had been for her that day. When he was born Raj wouldn't feed. He hated to be picked up. Then, when he started teething, he ground at Lisa's nipples like an animal. He transformed her. She became a weeping hollow-eyed version of herself, a wan creature in thick socks and sweat pants, her lovely long blonde hair plastered to her scalp. This is not my son, Jaz caught himself thinking. My son would not do this to my beautiful wife.

Always the same routine. Putting his laptop bag down, trying to be helpful. *Come on, I'll do that, give him to me.* Hearing about what new punishment Raj had devised, how unwilling he was to be cuddled or consoled. He'd sit on the impractical white couch where they'd once tried not to spill red wine – the couch now stained by spatters of puréed carrot – and absorb Lisa's anger, sitting silently as she shouted at him. Because he was there. Because no one else would understand. Then he'd hold her as she cried, smelling her hair, its scent of milk and baby shit and that mysterious authoritarian note of licorice he'd come to hate, the smell of his son.

Raj wasn't a normal baby. That had been obvious from the start. He didn't sleep, just lay there in his newly bought crib in his newly painted nursery and screamed, full-throated continuous yelling, primal and fierce. He sounded so outraged at having to inhabit that brightly colored box with its mobiles and plush toys and mural of zoo animals. The worst of it was his refusal to let them calm him. It cut Lisa to the bone. *Jaz, he flinched. I went to hold him and he flinched.* He'd tell her it wasn't her fault. She was a good mom, a great mom. He'd say those things and stroke her hair and she'd insist it was impossible. How could she be a good mom if her own baby was afraid of her? He didn't have an answer. He wasn't used to that, to not having the answer.

The doula told them it happened that way sometimes. Raj would calm down soon enough. All babies were different. All parenting experiences presented unique and rewarding challenges. Jaz didn't think of Raj as a rewarding challenge. Those inhuman cries, like those of a fox or a cat; the feral horror he exhibited when Jaz brought his face up close. His mother had Punjabi village words for what Raj was, words Jaz forbade her to use in his house.

They wouldn't sleep for days at a time. They didn't go outside. By the front door stood a thousand-dollar stroller, unused, plastic wrap still sleeving the handles. All the images they'd had of their new life, walking in Prospect Park bundled up in scarves and hats, holding hands – a proper American family. They'd never even put him in the thing. Jaz extended his leave to a month. His boss sent technicians to install a VPN in the study: trading screens, a terminal connected to their trading engine. He'd sit upstairs, doing regressions on the latest cluster of datasets, and listen to the chaos downstairs. After two months they demanded he go back to the office. Lisa understood. Raj would be her job. It was a question of earning-power. She looked like a ghost.

They got a nanny, of course. She came from an agency, very expensive. A Jamaican church lady called Alice, middle aged and severe. She gave in her notice after three weeks. Elena was from Puerto Rico, young and curvy. She'd tune the kitchen radio to reggaeton stations and dance in front of the ironing board. Jana was a Slovak student. There was another one, a Dominican who left after a week. None of them lasted. Raj drove them all away.

That was how they lived for the first two years. Jaz had once been overturned white-water rafting. One minute he was clutching a paddle and squinting into the spray, the next he was spinning round underwater. That was what it felt like. The suddenness, the extremity. By the time Raj's diagnosis came, it wasn't a surprise. They took him to the pediatrician – a new pediatrician, the third – just before his second birthday. He tried a few simple questions, asked him to point to things, to pretend to make a call on a plastic toy phone. Soon enough Jaz was standing outside the clinic, oblivious to the December wind howling down Lexington Avenue, the midtown traffic, the people shouldering past on the sidewalk. He was the father of an autistic child. What were the odds? He knew exactly. One in ten thousand in the seventies. Now down to one in a hundred and sixty-six. Jaz made his living building mathematical models to predict and trade on every kind of catastrophe. And now this: an event for which he had no charts, no time series. An entirely un-hedged position.

In the glove compartment of their car was yet another packet from Jaz's mom, just the same as all the others, on the envelope the shaky handwriting that wasn't even her own – she couldn't write in Punjabi or English – and inside a little wrap of kajal and a locket and a letter, written by his aunt, Sukhwindermassi. It had all the usual crap in it, pleas for him to bring Raj home to Baltimore, to see an astrologer, to apply the black soot to Raj's forehead and put the charm round his neck and find an exorcist to ward off the nazar, the evil eye that had fallen upon the child and caused him to lose his mind.

Jaz's pagal son, so shameful. A problem the family needed to solve, not out of any compassion for the boy, or even love for Jaz, but because of the dishonor it brought on the Matharu name. If the older generation had its way, the kid would be locked up in an attic somewhere, away from prying Punjabi eyes and wagging Punjabi tongues, all those aunties and uncles who knew in their heart of hearts that no good could come of what Jaz had done, the stain he'd put on the family izzat by marrying a white woman.

Of course Lisa understood something of the 'cultural differences' (that glib dinner-party phrase) between her upbringing and his own, but she had no idea, not really, of the vast territories he had to straddle to keep both her and his family in his life. His mom and dad were straight out of Jalandhar, betrothed to each other at some improbably early age, their childhoods played out in small villages against a backdrop of wheat and yellow mustard fields. Three days after their wedding his dad set off for America to join Uncle Malkit, who'd made a life in East Baltimore. Together the two cousins worked in a body shop owned by a Pole called Lemansky. In their family legend Mr Lemansky was a typical white boss, greedy and tyrannical, cheating Malkit and Manmeet out of overtime, mocking their religious observances and their faltering English. Jaz suspected that in reality he was no worse than the next guy, struggling, bemused by the changes in his neighborhood, the dark-skinned men who were the only ones willing to work for the low wage he could afford to pay. After two years of car parts and engine oil, his dad left to work on a production line assembling power tools. Soon afterwards he sent for Mom, whose first experience of America was in a factory packing candy bars with hundreds of black women. She didn't mix with them, sticking to her own coven of Punjabis at a corner table in the canteen. Jaz could picture them, their long braids tucked into hygienic hairnets, eating their carefully packed lunches of dal roti and warding off the new world and its kala people with acid remarks and superstition.

This was how you did it. Work hard; keep away from the blacks; remit money home for weddings, farm equipment, new brick-built houses whose second or even third storeys would rise up over the fields to show the neighbors that such and such a family had a son in Amrika or UK. Wherever in the world you happened to be, in London or New York or Vancouver or Singapore or Baltimore MD – you really lived in apna Punjab, an international franchise, a mustard field of the mind. All the great cities were just workhouses in which you toiled for dollars, their tall buildings and parks and art galleries less real than the sentimental desi phantasm you pulled round yourself like an electric blanket against the cold.

All the aunties worked at the same place as Jaz's mom, except the ones who had jobs as cleaners at Johns Hopkins, or were on the line at the condom factory. The uncles drove taxis. By the time Jaz was born, the son his parents had prayed for after two disappointing daughters, the family had moved out to the country, near the Gurdwara, an anonymous storefront with curtains in the window and a hand-lettered sign on the door. This was the center of their social life, a round of shaadis and festivals; dozens of people squeezed into cramped apartments and row houses, sitting on the floor singing kirtans. White sheets stretched over patterned carpets, garlanded pictures of the gurus in plastic gilt frames. As a small boy wearing a new kurta-pajama, straight out of the box and scratchy on the skin, Jaz never imagined there was any other world. Running his fingers along the criss-cross cotton folds on his chest, he'd pick his way through ranks of chanting worshippers into kitchens full of frying smells and forests of silk-clad female legs which could be tugged at to produce henna-patterned hands that reached down to adjust his top-knot or give him a morsel of food. A safe bubble for a cherished little boy. As he got older he saw that for all the mithai and cheek-pinching, this bubble was also paranoid and fragile and small, sensitive to the slightest touch of the wider world, the appearance of a police officer or even the mailman at the door. His mom would shake her head, pull her dupatta over her face and call for the kids, the English speakers, to find out what the gora in the uniform wanted. Always the suspicion that he was there to take something away from them, some old-country memory of tax collectors, landlord's thugs.

Jaz could never understand why his mom and dad were so scared. He lived his life in B-more, not the Punjab. He went to a school ruled by black kids, Americans, not the other blacks, the Somalis and French-speakers who came from families as adrift in the country as his own. He spoke English, recited the pledge, knew the capitals of the fifty states. He met plenty of white kids, Americans and new immigrants from Slovakia and Poland and the Ukraine. He met Latinos. He and the other 'Asians', Vietnamese and Pakistanis and Iranians and Tamils, none numerous enough to form their own clique, counted for little in the school hierarchy, but even as a skinny brown kid with freakishly long hair, he felt American. He played baseball, not cricket. He listened to the top forty on his Walkman. He'd go to the park with his family and the big world would parade before them, the frisbee-throwers and joggers and sunbathers, the crazy old ladies and baggy-shirted skateboarders, all seeming so free and easy, sharing the open space. Meanwhile his mom and dad would be delineating their boundaries by laying down blankets, huddling with the children over tiffin-carriers and Tupperware containers of food, too timid even to bring a radio.

But Mom, why can't I go? It's just a rock concert, just music.

You have your studies, beta.

His studies. Always that. Luckily he was clever. Math and science were his subjects. He could make numbers do the things he wanted. And just as he could see the patterns in an exponential or a logarithm, he could see there were other kinds of life to be led than his, lives which involved going on foreign vacations, having piercings, keeping a pet dog or a garden or a boat in the marina, playing with your band on MTV, locking your bike outside the vegan coffee shop and necking with your dreadlocked girlfriend. In such a life you could meet gora girls with short skirts and long legs, who'd talk to you instead of holding their noses and pretending to be disgusted by the phantom odor of curry. For a while, these girls were the sole focus of his life, girls in his class, in the neighborhood. Becky and

Cathy and Carrie and Leigh . . . There were insuperable barriers to becoming their friend, let alone sleeping with them. His geeky Asian-ness. His hair. Above all, his hair. By fifteen he'd swapped the topknot for a turban, but even then he had a carpet of soft down on his chin and long black wisps snaking along his jaw, a mess of unruly and undeniably childish growth which made the hormonal chaos of his adolescent skin look even worse. He was a monster, a pariah.

Some of the other Sikh boys did the unthinkable. They went to the barber. They endured their dads' beatings, their moms' tears. As if to taunt their more compliant brothers and cousins they began to spend hours in front of the mirror, shaving complicated fades and pencil-thin beards, teasing out fierce patterns of gelled spikes. They dressed like gangsters, smoked dope, drove their pimped-out rice-burner cars down to bhangra dances in DC. They were the real Punjabi shers, the bravehearts, always ready to go after the dirty black bandars walking on their block, the sick slut who dated white boys. Jaz couldn't have copied them if he'd dared. He was a nerd, a mathlete. On the fridge in his parents' kitchen was a yellowing photo of him aged sixteen, standing behind his prize-winning statistics exhibit at the city science fair. He always noticed his eyes in that picture. Glazed, fixed on escape.

Everyone had heard of MIT. Uncle Daljit had even visited the campus on some kind of tour. It was a-number one, the best. Of course Jaz would need a scholarship, but his teachers said that wasn't impossible. He was an exceptional student, gifted. How good that sounded in his parents' ears. *Our gifted son.* So it was decided: Jaz would try for MIT. The household organized itself round the mission. The television was muted. Meals were brought up on a tray. His mother and sisters moved around like ground technicians on an immigrant moon-shot. He was too self-absorbed to wonder why similar weight had never been put on the ambitions of his sisters. What had Seetal dreamed of before the hospital laundry? Or Uma, who packed chocolate bars alongside their mom? Both girls had been married by the age of twenty-one. No scholarships for them, just uncles Amardeep and Baldev.

He worked obsessively. On the physical level, energy and matter were tractable; unlike higher-order phenomena such as girls, their difficulties could be tamed by formulae. His SAT scores were exceptional, and one day he found himself walking across the MIT campus wearing a wide batik tie and one of Uncle Malkit's old suits, expertly altered by Seetal so it had looked, to the taste-makers on the family couch, quite stylish. Whether it was his manic determination or his impeccable minority credentials, the admissions board was impressed, and amid family rejoicing he was offered a full scholarship, on condition he maintained his academic performance. The eagle had landed.

One September morning, with his waist-length hair wrapped in a bright pink turban, a garland round his neck and a tikka mark on his forehead, he was taken to the station in his uncle Inderpal's cab and put on the train to his new life. His mother was already putting the word out for a bride.

In Cambridge, the first thing he did – before looking for his dorm, before registering for classes – was find a barber. He was determined that his student ID would have a new person on it, the one who lay in bed that first night running his fingers over his buzzcut bristles, feeling the unfamiliar shape of his skull and trying not to cry. The next day he falteringly began to invent a different character, more suitable than Jaswinder Singh Matharu to inhabit the domes and towers of a university campus. As Jaz – no family name – he avoided the desi scene, stayed away from the speed-dating, the cultural societies – anything which might remind him of the shame he was trying to outrun. His roommate Marty took it upon himself to introduce him to activities he'd previously seen only in the teen comedies he'd rented back home in Baltimore. Together they shotgunned beer, smoked pot and went to rowdy parties where people dressed up in bed sheets or bathing suits and groped one another in upstairs bedrooms. At one of these parties Jaz lost his virginity to a girl called Amber, who was just like the goris he'd always dreamed about, except paralytically drunk on Red Bull and vodka. Afterwards he thought he was in love and followed her around for a couple of weeks, until she told him to stop, explaining that what they'd done was a 'one-time thing'. He asked Marty what this meant. Nothing good, bro, was the answer. Jaz told himself she was nothing but a gandi rundi, a filthy whore like all white girls.

In this way most of his first semester passed before he had to face his parents and show the Punjabi world what he'd done. His cousin Jatinder was getting married in Philadelphia. He had to attend. No excuses. At least, he told himself, it would get the whole thing over with in one shot. His arrival at the reception, held in a banqueting room at a hotel, was dramatic. Uncle Malkit, taking a call outside, didn't recognize him at first. When Jaz said hello, his eyes widened. His parents were literally speechless. Instead of hugging him, his mom held him at arm's-length, a stricken expression on her face. His father wouldn't even shake his hand. Later he followed Jaz into a restroom and grabbed his collar, his face contorted with anguish. For a long time he struggled for words. Jaz wondered when he was going to hit him. 'You look like a thug,' he whimpered, then let him go.

His sister's husband Baldev was deputized to give him the lecture. He hoped Jaz was happy. He hoped it felt good spitting in his parents' faces, who'd slaved every day, who'd made such sacrifices. So proud of him, but the minute he left home he'd thrown away his religion. He was a grown man; it was his decision. Baldev understood how hard it was to keep to one's culture, especially in this maderchod Amrika. But couldn't Jaz see how cruel he was being? He'd killed something inside his maa; he'd trampled on his father's honor. How could the old man hold his face up in the community now his son was no better than those black gaandus who ran around behaving like monkeys, fighting and making trouble? Jaz muttered something about finding his own path, a phrase much on his mind at the time.

After Jatinder's wedding, he threw himself into guilt-ridden study. He stopped going to parties, abstained from drinking and, apart from his weekly trips to the barber, tried to go back to being the good Sikh boy who appreciated his parents' sacrifice. His mother eventually broke the silence, phoning him to ask if he was coming back for the vacation. No, he told her. He had work to do. He promised to see the family as much as his studies permitted, but for the next couple of years his visits were few and far between.

Marty, never the most sensitive of souls, didn't really understand the change in his party apprentice. He and Jaz grew apart. In his second year Jaz found different friends. He read European novels and bought a lava lamp. Day and night, he wore a pair of John Lennon glasses with purple lenses. He'd sit under a tree, pretending to read, desperately hoping to be distracted. In this way he met his first real girlfriend, a gothy biology major called Lynsey who seemed to accept him as a tortured intellectual. They were together almost two years. The simple things they did – going camping, eating in restaurants – convinced Jaz there really was something worth while about the larger America, something richer than his hormonal fantasies.

The family found the new Jaz hard to understand. He was dimly aware he made everyone uncomfortable by reading the *New York Times* at the breakfast table, commenting acidly on Bill Clinton or Bosnia. If he'd been able to put it into words, he would have said he was trying to broaden their horizons. One summer he worked double shifts in his cousin Madan's convenience store, then got a passport and went to Europe with friends. When he came back, he drove home, and without thinking went downtown to a deli, bought a few things and stashed them in his mom's fridge. It wasn't just the strange food (a camembert and some sliced mortadella) that outraged her; it was the invasion of her space, the implicit criticism of her mothering. Her son was in her house: it was her job to feed him. Jaz was angry that she threw his stuff in the trash. Then he remembered where he was. Even heating a can of beans would have been a provocation.

He had his vacation pictures developed and showed his dad the Eiffel Tower, the Brandenburg Gate. He expected him to be interested, or at least proud that his son had visited such exotic places. He tried to make him laugh by repeating some mildly spicy Italian phrases he'd learned in Naples, but the old man just looked dejected.

At the time Jaz interpreted it as disapproval. Later he realized it was a kind of mourning; he was sad because he couldn't connect himself with this image of his smiling crop-haired son, wearing shorts and a T-shirt, clinking glasses with sunburned white boys over plates of steak frites.

Lynsey broke up with him. She wanted, she said, to be part of his life, but he kept shutting her out. He tried to tell her it wasn't like that. How could he explain the impossibility of taking a gori back home, let alone introducing one as his girlfriend? None of his friends had met his parents. The few times his mom and dad made the trip up to MIT, he hustled them off campus as fast as possible. He endured a torturous lunch and took them to see the sights in a rental car. They were polite and attentive, but the feeling of relief when it came time for them to leave was obviously mutual.

And so his compartmentalized life continued. He stayed at MIT for grad school, partly because it deferred the moment when he'd have to choose a career. He'd always been more interested in theory than experiment, and his supervisor steered him toward the field of quantum probability, where he worked on reconciling competing mathematical descriptions of the physical world, attempting to understand life at a scale where precision dissolved into indeterminacy.

As if, back then, he had any idea of what indeterminacy really meant.

The boy was now four. He didn't speak. He didn't make eye-contact. He wasn't toilet trained. And Jaz was wrestling with him by the swimming pool in a cheap motel, the kind of place they were condemned to stay in because even though they had money, money Jaz wanted to use to give his family the best of everything, the romantic inns he and Lisa knew from the old days wouldn't put up with the disruption. It was always the same. Calls from the front desk; the discreet suggestion that they find somewhere more child-friendly. They'd tried it on the way from LAX. A junior manager had knocked on the door of the room. Was everything OK? She was sorry to intrude but there'd been a complaint from another guest.

Some vacation. Raj kept them up all night. At 5 a.m., since they were both awake and angry, they'd decided to leave. They'd driven on until they saw the sign from the highway. *Drop Inn. Vacancy.* It was mid-morning. They'd had no breakfast. Jaz didn't think they could make it any farther. He figured that in a place like this no one would look down their noses. The woman at the desk was polite enough. She probably saw and heard worse on a regular basis. As a precaution, he took the two rooms at the end of the block: one for the family and the one next door for insulation. No one should have to endure the sound of his son through thin walls.

'Come on, Raj. Let's help Mommy unpack.'

He picked him up and slung him under one arm like a parcel. Raj began to scream properly, the full amplified monotone. For a moment Jaz fantasized about throwing him into the pool, watching him sink to the bottom. His angry face disappearing under the rippling water, the silence afterwards.

1958

Joanie had to shield her eyes against the glare. She'd scrambled up the cliff to get a better view of the site and boy, was it hot work! Her sundress was clinging unpleasantly to her figure and she could feel little droplets of sweat running down under the band of her straw bonnet. She didn't care. The place looked so magnificent! The gleam of cars and trucks and trailers, parked all higgledy-piggledy on the desert floor among the mesquite and creosote bushes, the people swarming past the tents and stalls – what a hive of activity! What a carnival!

It occurred to her that it was a couple of hours since she last saw Judy. Poor kid. It had been a long drive, and she'd been an angel the whole way. No whining, no are-we-there-yet, even when Mom got them both lost outside Pomona and had to ask directions from a farmer. A real little grown-up, her daughter. A fine young lady. So what time was it now? Quarter of five. Long shadows and late afternoon light. There had to be several thousand folk down there. Hard to put an exact figure on it. Six or seven, surely. Ten? All the motels for miles around were full, or so she'd heard, but she'd never even considered sleeping indoors. Why would you when you could camp out under the desert stars? Such a treat! Last night Judy had been so sweetly excited as they were putting up the tent. Manny Vargas lit a fire, and a whole crowd of the Cohort people had toasted marshmallows and sung songs. Later, as they lay snuggled up in their sleeping bags, Judy had tried to point out constellations to her, and she realized she couldn't name so many herself. Yet another thing to add to the personal improvement list. The Guide always said humans needed to have a better relationship with the higher planes – a more intimate relationship. So, star names it would have to be. And memorizing the rest of the Blessings and writing up her

Experience and finishing her poem to the Ascended Masters and – oh, so many things!

After lunch Judy had run off with some of the other kids – a little tribe of them – to explore the various wonders of the convention. Joanie wasn't worried. They were good people, the saucer crowd, and the kid knew where the tent was. It was hard to tell, but as she looked down, she thought she could detect a shift in the patterns of movement, a general flow toward the main stage. The Command had caused it to be built in front of the Pinnacle Rocks, specifying through the Guide that it should be decorated with white streamers and reflective disks. The disks were on strings, hanging from the pyramid frame, and they channeled energy to the various speakers, plus they spun round and caught the sun in a really neat way. There was still half an hour to go before the Guide was scheduled to give his address, but Joanie guessed it was time to go down and get herself gussied up. After all, she was of the Cohort and would stand behind him as he spoke, dressed in her green sash and tunic. She'd need to freshen up after her climb. She took the lens cap off her Kodak, clicked a couple of pictures (which she was sure wouldn't come out) and started downhill.

What a day! There was almost too much to take in at once: people selling things, promoting their theories, telling one another about their encounters, all in such an atmosphere of trust and goodwill as – well, it was humbling, you could say that for openers. She wished she could record the scene to show the skeptics back home. This was what real brotherhood looked like, not the phony kind the authorities tried to foist on you. Golly, it made her mad to think of the dirty tricks they used. The public had a right to know what was really going on, and their government, their *own government*, was preventing them from learning some of the most important truths you could imagine. At least out here she could be herself. There was no one like that awful Bob Rasmussen from the office. Always hanging around the typing pool. Here no one was going to mock her or belittle her researches. There were secrets that were going to blow everyone's socks right off when they finally came out. People out here in the desert knew something big was going on.

She wandered down the double line of stalls, marveling at how many vendors were patiently sitting under sunshades, waiting for customers to come and browse their displays of books and pamphlets and magazines. More organized folk had folding tables. Others had just opened up the trunks of their cars or laid things out on the flatbeds of pickups. One woman was selling statues of an entity she'd encountered in her backyard in Wisconsin, a little pointy-headed guy with slanting black eyes. Life-size, said the sign on the truck. Well, that would make him about a foot tall, which somehow didn't seem very likely to Joanie. She was as open-minded as the next person, but in her experience there was nothing small scale about our alien visitors. Contact was the grandest, most awe-inspiring event in human history. It wasn't something to get all cutesy about. Still, it was a free country, and maybe this woman saw what she said she saw. Joanie would be the last person to deny someone's right to explore their own personal truth.

An old couple in home-made clothes were offering free vegetarian food to passers-by. The man had straw sandals. Joanie ate a little muffin-type thing, which was apparently made out of beans. As she chewed her snack, she stopped to look at a stall selling books on all manner of tantalizing subjects – number vibration, psychic healing, mineral therapy, astrophysics, mental calisthenics, yoga, the dimensions of Solomon's Temple, telepathic communication . . . Apparently there had been not one but sixteen crucified saviors since the dawn of time, and most of the Bible was copied from ancient Irish druids. The stall's owner was rhapsodizing to a small crowd about the importance of the Pinnacle Convention. Such powerful energies! He felt as if he'd been transported to another dimension. There was an angel on his shoulder, a being of light and love.

Joanie gave him a big smile. Good for that man! She wasn't so interested in all the biblical stuff, and at the end of the day some of those other things just boiled down to numbers, which she found hard to care about, not being mathematically minded herself. In some ways, the book guy seemed kind of muddled, but when it came to love, she was right there with him. The convention was a loving place, put together by people who wanted to heal the dreadful wounds in the world. She'd come a long way to be part of it, and so far she hadn't been disappointed. It had taken three full days of driving to make it down from Olympia WA, staying mindful all the way so her rattly old Buick wouldn't overheat or get a flat or start leaking oil. She was on a tight budget and greedy mechanics had a way of knowing when a person was desperate, not to mention her being a woman alone. Luckily the car held up, and she managed to find motels that were cheap but not too sleazy, though the one outside Fresno had some rowdy party going on at the end of the block and poor Judy hadn't gotten much sleep that night.

A little group of Buddhist monks walked past, chanting and banging drums. Most of them were actual Orientals, but a couple were white men, taller than the rest, looking a little self-conscious, she thought, in their orange robes. She hadn't known you could become a Buddhist monk unless you were brought up to it. Didn't they choose them as children, just turning up to the parents' house to take them away? So cruel. On the other hand, she supposed it was probably considered a great blessing by the natives. Halfway along the line of stalls she found Bill Burgess, surrounded as usual by customers browsing his wares and asking him sycophantic questions. Bill was a big cheese in contactee circles. The Guide had invited him to speak from the stage. He'd been on early that morning, which probably wasn't the best slot, but it was still an honor and Joanie had found him very compelling. His Experience was taken seriously in the movement; there had even been a drawing of it on the cover of *Saucerian* magazine. Late one night he'd been driving along the New Jersey Turnpike when he'd spotted a fuzzy oval-shaped light. He followed it, and eventually it veered off into the distance, but not before it released two pods, which landed in a nearby field. When Bill got out of his car, he'd suddenly felt light-headed, and his skin became hot and tingly, as if he'd stepped into some kind of radiation field. Voices spoke to him from the landing craft, and subsequent correspondence with the Guide confirmed that the visitors were indeed Space Brothers, representatives of the High Command, though from a different sector to the ones who'd visited the Guide when he first started channeling from the Pinnacles.

Bill waved to her and she shouldered her way through the throng of admirers to ask if he'd seen Judy. He said she was with the other kids, playing over by the Mux tower. Relieved, she thanked him and headed back to the tent to change, not without a little tinge of jealousy at all the attention he was getting. Her own Experience wasn't as dramatic as his, of course. It was more a feeling than an embodied encounter, a beautiful feeling which had descended on her one time when she was out walking in the forest near her home. It was a winter evening and there'd been heavy snow and everything was perfectly still. Suddenly she'd been cloaked in it, enveloped, that was the only word, in the glorious sense that she wasn't alone in the Universe, that benevolent beings were keeping watch over her and guiding her path. She'd stood still for what might only have been minutes but could easily have been hours. Then she'd made her way home and sat in front of the fire, so overcome she was completely unable to make head or tail of things, until Jake came back from whatever bar he'd been propping up, asking about dinner and wondering aloud how come she still had her boots on and was dripping all over the rug.

It was in a diner, of all places, that she found a clue. Someone had left a dog-eared magazine on the counter and she picked it up and read an article about the Guide and the Space Brothers and the Ashtar Galactic Command. Instinctively she knew that was the type of consciousness she'd encountered. It seemed like a sign. She wrote off for a subscription to the Guide's newsletter, and soon enough all the hours she wasn't typing up invoices in that infernal lumberyard office she was using to find out about the hidden secrets of the Universe. Of course Jake wasn't happy, but he didn't have any claim on the moral high ground.

Back at the tent there was no sign of Judy, though her things had been rummaged through, which meant she'd obviously been back.

Joanie drank a glass of water and had a little sit-down. When she'd caught her breath, she wet a washcloth and gave herself a quick once-over, face and neck, underarms, between the legs. She changed her underwear and wriggled into her tunic. It was the first time she'd worn her Cohort outfit, and stepping out in it made her self-conscious. It was kind of short. Though she knew she had passable legs, she wasn't twenty-one anymore, and even in her high-school days she'd never been the sort who liked showing herself off. She shouldn't have worried; as she made her way to the stage, people smiled and nodded; one or two men even cast admiring looks in her direction. She patted her hair and straightened her spine. Well, when you came to think of it, she *was* someone special. She'd become a member of the Cohort when it was still known, slightly tongue in cheek, as the Welcoming Committee. You had to send money through the mail and you got back a certificate and a button and a little purple book of rules. Judy was small then, and Jake was still at home. The fights were getting worse, and Joanie was trying to hold the family together, so she missed the first few conventions, despite wanting to go more than anything she could remember since she was a little girl. Finally she'd made it down to San Francisco to hear the Guide speak to a crowded hall about the Mux and the latest messages from the Command. It was the first time she was ever with him in the flesh, and she'd never been near a man with such a strong presence. Afterwards she'd chatted to Clark Davis, the First Follower, and he'd invited her to eat dinner with the inner circle, shamelessly squeezing her thigh while the Guide cracked lobster tails and described an electrical computer that Ashtar wanted to incorporate into the Mux. She could barely follow the discussion, but just the same felt so darn happy it lasted her all the way back up to Olympia, kept her going for weeks. Ever since then she'd considered her life one long preparation for the day the Command considered humanity ready to take up the burdens of full galactic consciousness, the beginning of the post-contact era.

On her way to the stage she passed by the Mux tower and looked around for Judy. A bunch of the other kids were there, including

Artie and Karen's two girls and a little redheaded tyke who surely belonged to Wanda Gilman. They were playing in the capsule, which had been removed from the main structure and opened out so people could get a look inside. The kids were lying in the cavity, their little arms and legs not filling out the shape, which of course was made for an adult man. She asked if they'd seen Judy, and they looked solemn.

'She went off with the glow boy,' said a little girl.

'What's that, honey?'

'She was here and then she went off to play with that boy.'

'I don't understand. What boy?'

'The glow boy. The little boy from space.'

There was no time to find out what the girl meant. At that moment Manny Vargas came up and hustled her away. The Guide was about to speak; it was time to join the formation. Vargas looked rather wonderful in his sash and tunic. Grecian. Everyone was ready at the foot of the stage, milling around and smoking, all looking thrillingly space-age and exotic.

The Guide appeared from the control-room chamber under the Pinnacle Rocks, making his way up the steps with his wife, Oriana, at his side. He was as impressive as ever, his gray hair swept back from his strong forehead, two muscular forearms emerging from the folds of his silver robe. He looked every inch the Dr Schmidt of saucer legend, the ex-test-pilot and research scientist with the Heidelberg and Oxford degrees. Oriana looked as pale as usual, which was amazing considering she lived out here under the desert sun. Her long hair was held back by a metal band with a jewel set into it, a tiara that made her look like an ancient priestess. She sure was mysterious! She'd conjoined with the Guide ten years previously; according to the stories, she'd just walked out of the desert and announced that she was fated to be his companion. She was supposed to be an expert in languages, and to know several of the desert Indian dialects, as well as Sanskrit and Mayan. Her face was oddly flat, and she had a spooky way of looking about, as if seeing something quite different from what was actually in front of her.

She spoke smooth, almost robotic English, with just the hint of an accent. It was obvious that Oriana was extraterrestrial, or at least had some extraterrestrial blood, though Joanie had heard one or two people say cattily that she was just French Canadian.

The sun was low, a great orange smudge on the horizon. At the sides of the stage, members of the Cohort lit flaming torches and fixed them into brackets. Joanie took up her position in the front rank, her arms folded and her feet slightly apart. The power stance, the Guide called it. Rooted to the earth, ready to make contact with the sky. As the crowd surged forward she tried to stop herself from grinning, to adopt the stern expression of someone who under-stood the epochal changes about to take place on earth, who was prepared to play a part in the tumult which would inevitably follow the first moment of mass contact. It was so difficult! She was too excited. The desert floor had turned a soft peach color, with hints of cool watery blue, as if the sand were turning to sea before her eyes. She wondered whether the fluttery feeling in her chest heralded another visitation. Could it be that the Command would choose this moment to make themselves known to their terrestrial helpers? Oh, that would be too wonderful!

Just then the Guide and his consort took the stage. As they mounted the steps, they waved, receiving a rapturous cheer in return. Approach-ing the microphone, the Guide tapped a couple of times with his finger to check it was working, then began to speak. At the sound of his voice everyone and (so it seemed to Joanie) *everything* became silent, as if a giant bell jar had descended, shutting their gathering off from the normal noise of the world.

'Brothers and sisters,' said the Guide. 'Brothers, sisters, dearest friends – I bid you welcome. As you know, the human mind is the most powerful force in the Universe, and yet we use not a hun-dredth, not even one hundred thousandth of that power. I come before you this evening to talk of many things, but firstly of a number that is key to unlocking the potentials of this wonderful force. This is the sacred number four hundred and eighty-six. The latitude of the Pinnacle Rocks, where we're gathered, is precisely

2057.6215 minutes of arc north. The reciprocal of this value is 0.000486. The original height of the Great Pyramid was precisely four hundred and eighty-six feet. This means that the latitude of this powerful place is the precise harmonic reciprocal of the height of the Great Pyramid of Giza, an ancient communications device of unsurpassed importance in connecting humankind with the directors of the spiritual program for our planet. The number four hundred and eighty-six also plays a central role in the harmonics of space and time, connected as it is with the universal interdimensional constant *aum*. Four hundred and eighty-six is a key that will unlock the gateway to dimensions. It indicates the cycle of challenge and transformation on which we are about to embark. Remember this number. Hold it in your minds as you listen to what I am about to say.'

Joanie knew the rocks were located in a special place. Many of the Cohort talked about the lines of power which intersected at this location, and not a few of them had dowsed along those force-lines, but this was the first she'd heard of a relationship to the pyramids of Egypt. She tried to fix the figure in her head, muttering it a few times under her breath to help. The Guide asked the crowd to join with Oriana in chanting the hymn of welcome. She stepped up to the microphone, opened her arms wide and began to speak.

'O Great Ones! O Brothers of Light! We pour out our libations of love upon you!'

After each line she paused, and the crowd repeated her words. The effect was electric, and Joanie became increasingly sure that something extraordinary was about happen.

'We pour out our libations, knowing that every drop –'

We pour out our libations, knowing that every drop –

'Brings a blessing on the one to whom it is sent, and to the sender!'

Brings a blessing on the one to whom it is sent, and to the sender!

'Welcome! Welcome! Welcome!'

Welcome! Welcome! Welcome!

By the time she'd finished, the desert had changed from peach to lilac and the sun was shivering over the horizon, about to vanish.

The Guide took the microphone again, and started to tell the story of his Experience.

'I am here with you today,' he said, 'because of something that happened to me in this very place. Eleven years ago I was alone and friendless. I'd come out to the desert in search of an answer, a truth I knew I must find or perish in the attempt. One night, as I lay beneath the stars, contemplating my insignificance before the infinitude of space-time, I received a visitation. The craft was of a type which I know will be familiar to some of you, a silent carrier like a huge topaz flying through the starry night. It landed before me, its descent so perfect and soundless that as it touched the ground I could still hear nature – the insects, the wind, the distant howl of a coyote, a beast as lonely as I. My body felt charged with spiritual electricity, a feeling of excitement such as I had never known. Before my eyes, the hull, whose surface had appeared as a perfect flawless sphere, opened up to reveal a ramp. On that ramp stood two figures, human, or so they appeared to me, people of such noble aspect and bearing that I felt I was in the presence of demigods. They were of a pure Aryan type, pale skinned and gray eyed, dressed in simple white robes, like our fathers of old.

'"What do you want of me?" I asked. They told me not to be afraid, and bade me accompany them into their ship. They spoke not in the crude voices that you and I use to communicate, but in a speech of the mind, a mental telepathy. Language took shape in my brain, clothed in what I understood as voices, beautiful, clear and mellow. When I stepped aboard, I entered a realm of wonder. The inside was curved and bathed in a soft warm glow, a comforting and womb-like space. I realized I was very thirsty. As if in response to my craving, a long-stemmed crystal cup appeared in my hand, filled to the brim with a clear liquid, into which was immersed what looked to be a green gemstone. In my surprise I almost dropped it. *"Do not fear,"* said my hosts. *"Drink. You will be satisfied."* I looked closely at them. More perfect beings I had never encountered. I felt they knew everything that was in my heart. I trusted them implicitly, though at the same time I had the uncomfortable feeling of being completely transparent to them, a sort of mental nakedness quite as embarrassing as the physical kind. When I drank from the cup I found it contained the most delicious nectar. All my fatigue disappeared, along with all the depressive thoughts and negative feelings I'd been experiencing before these wondrous men landed at my cave. My hosts asked me to make myself comfortable, which confused me, as there appeared to be nowhere to sit down. However, at a gesture from one of them, an aperture appeared in the floor and a sort of padded booth rose up through it. The three of us sat, and I noticed that the upholstery of my seat was subtly moving and shifting to adapt to the contours of my body.

'"We are Merku and Voltra," announced my new friends. "We have come from a place which you may choose to think of as far away, but in another sense is no farther than the distance between your thumb and forefinger. We are representatives of a group known throughout the worlds as the Ashtar Galactic Command. The Command has had your civilization under observation since the dawn of recorded history. Our seeing disks have absorbed much information. Our auditory rods have monitored the psychic vibrations of humanity with profound attention. For many thousands of years we have followed a policy of non-interference on Earth. Occasionally humans have experienced fleeting contact with us, but this has happened mostly by mistake. Now, however, we have decided to break our own rules. You are living in a time of grave danger. Your race has discovered certain crude ways of manipulating matter, the technology of atom-splitting that you know as nuclear power. You have in your hands an energy source which is capable both of great good and of great evil. We are sorry to say that though your level of technological sophistication has increased, your moral capabilities have not. Humanity is still a primitive race, governed by savage emotions. You are ruled by anger and fear. Because of this, you have already succumbed to the temptation to use your new tools in war. Now, you have divided into two atomic-armed camps and risk the absolute destruction of your fledgling world. We of the Ashtar Galactic Command experience a deep sense of brotherhood when we contemplate you, O People of Earth! We undergo feelings of immense compassion and kinship, and we of the Command, who represent the highest flowering of the great civilizations of the galaxy, have made the decision to wade into the tide of human affairs, to try to halt the destruction before it happens.

'"You must cease all nuclear testing immediately. Your meddling with the forces of nature can bring only horror, unless it is carried out with love and foreknowledge. We have contemplated long and hard the best method of steering you on to a peaceful path. At first we considered taking over human communication systems and broadcasting a message to the leaders of all world governments, commanding them to make overtures to one another, to start talks to bring about the cessation of war. However, our calculators have determined that the sudden appearance of higher beings, and the trauma associated with the realization of the relative backwardness of your evolution, would have negative consequences. In short, we fear that within your leadership structures are many individuals with unstable mentalities, who would fear usurpation, and provoke nuclear auto-destruction rather than relinquish their grip on power.

'"Instead, we have determined that the message of change and redemption can come only from within humanity itself. We have chosen to make contact with certain gifted humans. We have identified a number of individuals whose mental vibrations are at a higher pitch than those of the majority of your race. This makes them more suitable for use as communication channels. You are one such individual."

'As you can imagine, I was most concerned to hear this. The possibility that the world would imminently end was, I admit, something I'd often considered. But to have it confirmed, and from such a source! I doubted I was strong enough for the vital task these alien visitors had entrusted me with. They told me that though they'd embodied themselves for this first communication, henceforth there would be no need to engage in physical travel as there would be a permanent psychic channel open between us. In effect I was to become a kind of living transmitter, a tool to bring their message to humanity.

'"You are a special one," they told me, "for you have dared to raise up your eyes, to look beyond the material world into the etheric. The etheric plane is where we have our existence, and your senses are not adapted to detect our presence. We are beings of the seventh density, and humankind *can apprehend only the first through third. However, through our advanced spiritual technology, we are able to step down our vibrations and the vibrations of our craft to the frequencies of the atoms on the physical plane."* I realized with a shock that this perfectly explained the reports of extraterrestrial visitors walking through walls and other so-called solid objects, as well as the ability of their vehicles to perform in a manner that seemed to contradict basic laws of physics.

'After that we talked further. They introduced concepts of extreme complexity, ideas which ought to have required many hours of conversation and hard study to explicate. Amazingly, these concepts flashed into my mind in seconds, placed there by some instantaneous process, a sort of mental imprinting like a stamp on a piece of wax. I asked them about this wondrous method of learning and they confirmed they could absorb and transmit huge bodies of information in the blink of an eye. All human history could be transferred from one entity to another in as little time as it takes to listen to an episode of a radio serial. And so began a new phase of my life, that part which has been dedicated to the mighty task entrusted to me by my friends Merku and Voltra. Since that fateful day eleven years ago, I have received hundreds more communications. This very evening, they informed me that they would be monitoring proceedings from a spaceship orbiting 2340 miles above the Earth. They wish you, my friends, to know that the crisis grows ever more acute, and they are actively looking for more humans to join with them in preventing it. Under the guidance of Merku, Voltra and the other members of the Command, including Aleph, Lord Maitreya, Sananda-Jesus, the Comte de Saint-Germain and on occasion Director Ashtar himself, I have worked tirelessly to spread the word, and to recruit and train a band of volunteers, men and women of higher mental abilities who will prepare the ground for the next stage of human history, the transcendence of war and the advent of the galactic age, when our race will take its rightful seat at the congress of the Federation of Light. Now I will introduce you to those volunteers. Please give a big round of applause for the Universal Cohort of the Green Ray!'

As the crowd clapped and cheered, Joanie felt as happy as she'd ever done in her life. She hoped Judy had a good view. She'd be so proud to see her mom standing there, to hear her spoken of as a person with higher mental abilities.

As they left the stage, Manny Vargas tapped her on the shoulder and whispered that there was to be a special additional conference in the control room. Only certain people were to be invited, and the Guide had specifically mentioned her name. She was flustered, and bombarded him with questions. By name? Really? Was he sure? Did she have time to go back to her tent? She wanted to check on her daughter. He told her to get Wanda or Michelle to do it. They were going to start in ten minutes. Joanie grabbed Wanda and asked her to be a dear. Wanda made a face, but squeezed her arm and told her not to worry. Joanie could tell she was jealous. Apart from anything else, she had the most obvious crush on Manny. Real schoolgirl stuff. Joanie wished she could set Wanda's mind at rest. Much as Joanie liked Manuel, there could never have been anything between them.

It was the first time she'd ever been down into the control room. It was a real cave, hollowed out right under the Pinnacle Rocks. Apparently it was very ancient. The Guide had uncovered it after being told in a dream where to dig. Despite being underground, and the only air coming from a couple of little skylights up near the ceiling, it wasn't dank or smelly at all. In fact it was kind of cozy, lit up with oil lamps and furnished with throw pillows and low benches set around the walls, leaving a space in the center. Apparently the Guide used to do all his inventing here, but now he'd built a little house some distance away, where he and Oriana lived and worked. There was only one device left, a complicated-looking brass thingummy, with lots of rods and disks, and a little handle to turn it round, and a sort of cage into which was fixed a big clear crystal. Attached to the machine was a wooden box, and from the box ran a length of wire, attached to a set of headphones, the sort of thing a telephone operator might use to connect calls.

The invitees filed in, to be greeted by a hearty handshake from the Guide, and a sort of Oriental greeting from Oriana, who pressed her palms together and made a little half-bow. There were only about twenty people present. Outside were ten thousand others who'd give their eye teeth to be in this room. Was she really worthy? Higher mental abilities or not, she didn't always *feel* very special. Touching her face, her fingers came away wet with sweat, and she knew from experience a fit of nerves was coming on. For a minute, she thought she might actually throw up. That truly would be atrocious: to get invited to a special audience with the Guide and then make a mess on his control-room floor. *Get a hold of yourself, Joanie Roberts. Breathe.* She was about to make a dash for it when the Guide stopped conversing with his lieutenants and sat down on a high-backed wooden chair, positioned in the center of the room next to the strange device. He raised his hands and asked for silence.

'Thank you for coming,' he said. 'I've asked you here because you're all special to me. You are Star People, ones whose souls have undergone many transmigrations, both here on Earth and on other planets. You are drawn to the etheric, because, unlike most earth-folk, you retain some knowledge of your past states, a radiance that opens you to impressions and experiences others do not share. You're all committed to the work we're doing, and for that I thank you from the depths of my heart. You experienced the intense energy in the crowd outside. This is a good sign. We're at a crucial juncture in our mission. The Soviet Sputnik is orbiting overhead and the world has never been closer to catastrophe. It's time to move things to the next stage. You, my dear and devoted friends, deserve to know more about the current state of affairs with regard to research on the Mux. Most of you will already be aware of the scientific principles behind the machine, but for those who aren't, or who have had trouble grasping it – I realize the technicalities may be daunting to anyone without a higher scientific degree – I'll explain something about it before we proceed. As you know, it's been my obsession for much of the last decade, and I consider it central to saving Earth from atomic destruction. My friends in the Ashtar Galactic Command agree. The principle of muxing, or multiplexing, is one familiar from the world of communications. It's a way of combining multiple messages into a single signal, then sending it over a shared medium. That medium could be a length of wire or even the very air, in the case of wireless transmission of radio waves. Our Earth telephone systems use multiplexing, combining many calls and sending them through coaxial cables. The principle of the Mux is analogous, but the signal is of a much higher order. You can think of the Mux as an etheric transmitter-receiver system. It accepts input from many individuals and generates a signal on a different frequency for each. This results in a complex signal containing many individual messages. Why is this important? You know many of the senior members of the Command as individual personalities. Ascended masters like Merku, Voltra, Maitreya and Kuthumi manifest themselves in a way that is recognizable to us on Earth. However, their notion of individuality is very different to ours. Each Space Brother is in constant communication with all the other members of their various civilizations. This is far more than we understand by communication. It is really a kind of mind-melding, a total communion with each other and with the cosmos. Unfortunately we humans are insufficiently evolved to experience such perfect bliss. In order to have such a communion with our fellows, we need the assistance of the Mux.

'As I mentioned in the public meeting, the Command is concerned that the message of universal peace should come through a human mouthpiece, in order to cushion our less open-minded brethren from the overwhelming shock of contact. Through our researches, both here and in the laboratories of the Galactic Fleet, we've determined that a single person will not suffice to do the job. After all, throughout history there have been prophets and seers, and almost without exception they've been ignored and even persecuted by the ruling powers. The answer is muxing. By using the Mux, a human transmitter can make himself the medium for the signals of large numbers of interplanetary entities of different densities, unifying many thousands of psychic transmissions into a single signal. It's conceivable that using this technology, a single transmitter could become the mouthpiece for the combined will and power of entire populations, entire planets, the pinpoint confluence of all their knowledge and healing force. On Earth, it will allow a new caste of communicators to be in total union both with each other and with the Command. That is to say, as soon as the first generation of Muxes is in operation, human loneliness will come to an end, at least for those lucky enough to be part of the grid.

'So far, I have been your Guide. When we switch on the Mux, I will sacrifice my individuality and transcend to the next stage of my personal journey. I shall become the first Oracle. I'd like to say at this point that this is not an egotistical desire. Rather the opposite. When I am muxed, I will lose myself entirely in the cosmic signal. Besides, as I mentioned, it will take more than one Oracle to persuade the powerful skeptics of our benighted planet to abandon their path of destructiveness. It will take a network of Oracles, all of us bathing in each other's minds. Imagine a global society, with members in China, Europe, darkest Africa, the jungles of Peru. Each Oracle will be plugged into a Mux, communicating etherically with the Command, and electromagnetically with all the people of Earth, using the upper atmosphere as a transmission medium, a technology outlined by the great scientist Nikolai Tesla. The Mux, in short, is a stepping stone to the next level of human consciousness, a way of expediting our evolution toward total harmonic convergence with the higher will of the Creator.'

Here he paused, and took a drink of water. Joanie looked around. The expressions on the faces of his audience were all pretty much the same. Impressed didn't begin to cover it. They were part of history, right there in the thick of it, like Signing the Declaration of Independence or Landing at Plymouth Rock. The Guide asked if anyone had questions. No one was more surprised than Joanie Roberts to hear words coming out of her mouth.

'Are there risks?' she asked.

The Guide nodded. 'Of course. This has never been attempted before. It's not impossible that the human mind, even my highly expanded mind, will find it too much of a strain to perform this kind of work. My colleagues at the Command think the danger is slight, at least in my case, but it's still there. However, personal risk isn't really a factor. The task is too important. If I fall, someone else will take up where I left off.'

Bill Burgess spoke up from the other side of the room. 'Can you tell us more about the design of the Mux? We've all seen the capsule, but what about the rest of it?'

'Well, most of the actual circuitry has been designed according to blueprints transmitted to me from the labs of Araltar, the Magnetician for this quadrant. The mechanism is located in a sealed wooden box housed beside the capsule. A full explanation would be too technical, but suffice to say it's based on the violet ray and the elemental ray, focused through a crystal whose tip penetrates the sheath of the chamber in which the Oracle is secured. The violet ray is the carrier of the multiplexed etheric communications. It is directed in such a way that the elemental ray intersects with it, decoding the signal into mental vibrations of a suitable level for processing by the human mind. Transmission between earthbound Oracles is achieved through a conventional microphone, placed in the chamber, and a type of high-powered radio transmitter-receiver, which bounces the signal through the ionosphere to the other Oracles in the chain.'

'Why is it so tall?'

'Ah, I'm glad you asked that. We determined that the Mux should be placed in a conical tower, so that the tip of the transmitting crystal is in a precise harmonic relationship with the dimensions of the Temple of Solomon.'

'It looks like a rocket.'

'I assure you, it's not designed for physical travel.'

Everyone laughed. The Guide good-naturedly called for quiet.

'Tonight, I can reveal something very special. In precisely one hour we will be making the very first test of the Mux.'

There were gasps, and a burst of spontaneous applause.

'As this is just a prototype, and since there are no other Muxes to network with human Oracles elsewhere on Earth, we won't test this aspect of the capabilities. For a short time, I will place myself in total communion with the Command and the wider cosmos. After the experiment, I anticipate having to rest for some hours or days. It's going to be physically grueling, and I have no way of knowing how it will turn out. In order to prime the Mux, we need to charge the battery, so we can direct energy into the system. That's the other reason I've brought you all here tonight.'

As he spoke, Clark Davis and Manny Vargas carried a heavy-looking wooden box into the center of the chamber and fixed it to a tall tripod. It looked like an old-fashioned camera, the sort of machine a photographer would use to take a high-school graduation picture.

'You are among the most spiritually powerful of my collaborators,' the Guide continued. 'The Mux works on a mixture of electrical and etheric energy to amplify the spiritual force of the user. This battery is an etheric storage unit, designed to hold prayer-energy in a fixed form. Now, Oriana will lead you in a mantra, and each of you will direct your prayers into the battery through the copper terminal on the front of the casing.'

They lined up in front of the device. Oriana took up a karate-like stance, side on, one palm held out flat a few inches from the surface. Led by Clark Davis, they all began to chant *aum mane padme hum, aum mane padme hum* . . . The pace was frenetic, urgent, and Joanie was inadvertently reminded of King Kong or one of those other movies where the heroine got captured by natives and was about to be sacrificed to the primitive gods. Oriana intoned a line of prayer. 'Blessed are the wise ones, for they walk through the darkness and ignorance of the world, spreading Light.' As she said the last word, she twisted her body and jutted out her palm, projecting an invisible force into the machine. Clark Davis went next, saying the same prayer, making the same pushing gesture. Joanie realized that most of the people in the room must have done this before. If it hadn't been obvious already, now it certainly was: there were inner circles within the inner circle – and she'd been found worthy of inclusion, of ascent to the next level! As she waited her turn she took care to memorize the lines, so as not to garble them when it came time to make her prayer. Standing in front of the box, she made the correct motion and was sure she felt something, some personal energy, transferring from her to the battery. They performed the ritual three times, each person stepping up, saying the lines and pushing their prayer into the box. By the end the chanting was going at a breakneck speed and she felt breathless, giddy.

During all this time the Guide simply sat and watched. At last he motioned for everyone to sit down. As Davis and Vargas removed the battery, he slumped down further in his carved wooden chair. He seemed tired, and Joanie found herself wondering how old he actually was. Almost as soon as the impression of age came, it was dispelled: he reached for the headset attached to the brass machine beside him and slipped it on; immediately his head was jerked violently backwards and his body tensed as if suddenly flooded with electricity. With much pain and effort he appeared to master the flow, lowering his chin toward his chest as if encountering huge resistance. Then he began to speak. Joanie was shocked. His voice was completely different, low and raspy, coming from somewhere deep in his throat.

'Salutations! I am Esola, Master of Magnetics, 8,600th projection, 525th wave. I am standing by. Discontinue.'

Again he spasmed and jerked back his head. He spoke again, this time in a high-pitched, possibly feminine tone.

'I am Kendra, Record Keeper of the 36th projection, 6th wave. I too am standing by. Discontinue.'

Then the Guide, in his own voice, asked the two presences for their assessment of the experiment. Esola answered first.

'According to my instrumentation, the battery is fully charged. Discontinue.'

'I have noted the transference of energy in the cosmic ledger,' added Kendra. 'All is cleared for you to test the multiplex device. Discontinue.'

The Guide thanked them, exchanged cordial salutations and blessings, then removed the headset. It appeared the Command had given the go-ahead. He stood up, took Oriana's hand and gestured for everyone to follow him up the stairs.

Outside the night was clear and crisp. The stars overhead were bright pinpricks of light in the blue-black sky. Joanie felt cold in her skimpy Cohort outfit and wished she'd brought a sweater. Out in the desert she could see campfires, people passing back and forth in front of them like wraiths. The distinction between earth and air was hazy. She felt as if she were already in space, floating free in the cold clear ether between the planets. Cooking smells drifted across the camp, fragments of conversation, shouts and laughter. Somewhere someone was playing a guitar. They made their way over to the Mux tower, a conical shadow almost obscured by the three large shadow-fingers of the Pinnacle Rocks. Some of the men started up a generator, which sputtered into life and began a regular chug-chug growl. A run of cable led from it into the body of the Mux. Someone else brought a large lamp, like a theater spotlight, and directed it at the tower. A crowd was beginning to gather round, asking questions and trying to see what was going on. Clark Davis directed the Cohort to form a circle round the base, as Manny and some others carried the prayer-battery up the tower and installed it in the capsule. Joanie peered into the darkness, trying to see if Wanda was among the onlookers. She hoped she'd had the sense to put Judy to bed. The technicians came down again, briefly conferring with Davis and the Guide. As the onlookers whispered and pointed, the Guide hugged Oriana, then grabbed the rungs of the ladder and began to ascend.

2008

Lisa had the cases open on the bed. The room was small and cramped, papered with an unpleasant pattern of purple flowers. As soon as Jaz got him in, Raj stopped crying, wriggled out of his arms and went off to flush the toilet. Jaz hadn't the energy to stop him. He was obsessed with toilets. Dabbling his fingers in the water. Sticking his head deep into the bowl to examine the flow. He tried the flush again, before the cistern had refilled. Jaz could hear the hollow thud as he pulled the handle. And again. He could do that for hours.

Jaz sat down in an armchair. The room stank of some kind of artificially scented cleaning product. Carcinogens and lavender.

'Do you need a hand?'

Lisa shook her head.

'You OK?'

'Sure.'

He tried to take over, pulling out one of his shirts and reaching for a hanger.

'Don't.'

'What?'

'You'll mix everything up.'

He sat down again. Raj came barreling into the room and tugged at Lisa, who tried to carry on unpacking as he violently twisted her T-shirt.

'Come on,' Jaz pleaded. 'Leave Mommy alone. Here's Bah.'

Bah. Once-white bunny. Bald patches, tufted graying fur. Bacterial Bah, sucked and wiped and dragged, spongy with goo and secretions. Raj threw him at his mother's head. She ignored the blow, mechanically sorting through their things, shirts and pants and swim shorts, diapers for Raj, who was now happily wrapping himself in the curtains. Lately Lisa's face had acquired a fixed cast. The girl Jaz first knew had been a flirt, a wearer of short skirts, a teller of dirty jokes. She liked to do things on impulse: grab a bag and head for the airport; check into the Mercer to watch TV. She once made love to him in the toilet stall of a Lower East Side sushi restaurant while their friends sat in a booth, thinking they'd gone to get money at an ATM. Jaz had known very few women in his life and none at all like her. She had amazed his senses. At heart he was still a typical immigrant's kid, nervous, on the lookout for social banana skins. She showed him it was OK to take risks, to allow oneself uncalibrated pleasure. He wanted to remind himself of that woman; she must still be there, locked away inside this new version of herself, the princess in the tower.

'Are we going to go visit the park?'

Lisa shrugged. 'I guess. It's what we came for.'

'We need a picnic.'

'Damn it, Jaz. I know we need a picnic. I'm unpacking here, I can't do everything –'

'I didn't mean it like that. I'll take the boss to the market in town. We'll pick up food, plastic plates, whatever we need.'

'Sure.'

'You could take a nap.'

'I don't want – OK, sure, I'll take a nap, whatever. Thanks.'

The boss. The young master. Those were their names for him. They'd become the serfs in his little feudal kingdom. Jaz chased him down, smeared sunscreen on his screwed-up face, collected car keys, dark glasses, the GPS device with its pigtail of black cable. They left Lisa sitting on the edge of the bed, robotically channel-surfing the TV.

The motel manager was hovering about outside the office. Jaz hadn't paid her much attention when they checked in. She was an odd-looking woman, with a mane of permed hair and a lot of turquoise jewelry.

'You all OK there?' she asked.

'Sure,' Jaz said, squaring up. 'We're absolutely fine.' Was she going to complain? Raj hadn't done anything. The boy slipped his hand, started examining something on the ground. The woman smiled.

'Room to your liking?'

'Everything's great. We're just going to pick up something to eat, get a picnic to take into the park.'

'That's nice. There's a market on your right as you head down the hill. You can't miss it.'

'Thanks.'

'You have a good day. Take plenty of water and don't sit out in the sun.'

In the time it took them to exchange these pleasantries, Raj had vanished. Jaz looked around, but couldn't see him anywhere.

'My kid. Did you see where he went?'

'Oh, no, honey. I hope he didn't go out front.'

Jaz jogged over to the corner of the building, where he had a view of the highway. He half expected to see his son playing in the traffic.

'Sir? Excuse me, sir?'

The motel manager was pointing. The British junkie guy was standing at the door of one of the rooms, a small pink towel around his waist. Without clothes, his scrawny body was alarming, pallid and inked with tattoos, like raw chicken drumsticks scribbled on with a ballpoint pen.

'Mate? You looking for your boy? He's in here.'

Jaz went over. The guy pointed him to the bathroom, where Raj was stubbornly pressing the toilet flush. 'Sorry,' he said, gesturing nervously at his towel. 'I was having, you know, a kip. Rough night last night. Heard the bog and there he was. Couldn't get him to budge.'

'I'm so sorry. Raj, you're not supposed to be in here. It's not our room. This is the man's room.'

'Don't have a pop at him on my account. It's just – you know – you don't want some little kid in your hotel room. Looks a bit Gary Glitter.'

He nodded, pretending he understood the man's accent, then

took Raj firmly by the hand, apologized again and headed for the car. Raj didn't make too much of a fuss, allowed himself to be placed in his booster seat and belted in. As Jaz settled himself behind the wheel, he tried to work out how difficult the shopping trip was going to be. They really needed a few easy days, so Lisa and he could remember what it was like to be decent to one another.

She had come along without warning, in his final summer of grad school. She was seated next to him at a potluck supper, gorgeous, blonde, just finishing up a Master's in Comparative Literature at Brown. She talked about Henry James and Marrakech and the Kosovo war and the films of Krzysztof Kieślowski, and he had to stop himself smiling from the sheer pleasure of watching her mouth move. When he spoke, which he did hesitantly and (as he later heard) with painful seriousness, she focused on him so intently that he felt as if he'd been caught in the beam of a searchlight. For a few moments he was the only man at the table, the only man in the building. By the time the main course was served, he belonged to her entirely.

Lisa was well aware of the impression she'd made. As people started to gather their coats, she wrote her number down on the back of someone else's business card. You need this, she said. He thanked her, flushing with pleasure. She smiled flirtatiously.

'Don't you want to know why?'

'Sure.'

'Because you're taking me to the theater next week.'

'What are we going to see?'

'Well, that's up to you. But make sure it's good. I get bored easily.'

That week, stochastic modeling took second place to frantic combing of the listings pages. It wasn't that he couldn't concentrate. The numbers themselves seemed to have loosened their bonds. His distributions were all improbable, his scattering patterns shoals of little swimming fish. He bought seats for a production of *The Seagull* and waited nervously for Saturday night.

It seemed incredible to Jaz that a woman like Lisa would want him, let alone fall in love. Yet the week after *The Seagull*, she returned the favor, taking him to see a string quartet playing repetitive Minimalist pieces that he pretended to like much more than he did. Afterwards they went for dinner and at the end of the evening he worked up the courage to kiss her. Soon they were seeing each other regularly. His life opened up like a flower. He was drunk with her, her ambition, her intelligence, her sense of entitlement. Academia wasn't for her, she'd realized. She wanted to move to New York, to become an editor at a publishing house. He marveled at the precise picture she had of her future: children, a house with steps leading up to the front door, shelves of first editions, witty and fascinating friends. She asked him about physics, and surprised him by exhibiting a real fascination with his research. She also asked about his family, and for the first time he risked telling some version of the truth. Her reaction astonished him. She wasn't mocking or disdainful. If anything, it seemed to make him more interesting in her eyes.

As their relationship grew serious, he realized he was going to have to work hard to keep her. She seemed to be friends with several ex-lovers. He found this intolerable; often he lay awake at night consumed by sexual images of her with these old boyfriends – positions, acts. He wanted to feel as if she'd come into existence the day he first saw her, that there had never been anyone but him. When he blurted something out, she had the good sense not to get defensive. He tried to explain that where he came from it was considered demeaning for a man to marry a woman who wasn't a virgin. 'Marry?' she said. 'You're very sure of yourself.' He blushed and spluttered, until he realized she was teasing him. 'You'll just have to accept it, Jaz. I'm not your veiled teenage bride. If that's what you want, you better look elsewhere.'

She would talk about feeling rootless. She was an only child. As soon as she left home, her parents severed all ties with the Long Island suburb where she'd grown up and moved to Arizona. 'So my dad could live on a golf course and my mom could get skin cancer' was how she put it, her voice dripping betrayal. Jaz had never felt anywhere belonged to him enough to feel strongly about losing it. He did his best to sympathize.

They flew to Phoenix for Thanksgiving. Mr and Mrs Schwartzman lived in a giant subdivision of identical ranch-style houses. They were kind and curious, asking questions about his family and his 'culture', a word they used as if it denoted something fragile that might break if roughly handled. Her father drove him to the store to pick up wine for lunch, showing off the neighborhood as if it were his personal property. The tennis courts, the swimming pool, the landscaping in front of the clinic, all of it was important to him; in all of it he had a stake. Jaz felt awkward. The things he'd done with this man's daughter! He felt he wouldn't be able to look the man in the face unless he said something. Later, Lisa told him it was the phrase 'honorable intentions' that made Mr Schwartzman erupt into laughter.

When Lisa announced that she was moving to New York, he felt like a sinkhole had opened up beneath his feet. By that time he was writing up his thesis and thinking about applying for post-doctoral jobs. He knew their life, commuting between rooms in shared houses in Boston and Providence, wasn't sustainable 'in the long term'. But that was the long term, not the short term, let alone now. He was happy. He didn't want anything to change.

'Jaz, I've been talking about it ever since we met. It's not like I'm springing it on you.'

'Sure, but I thought – well, I thought we'd at least talk about it.'

'What's to talk about? You know it's what I want.'

'But what about us?'

'It's up to you, Jaz. If you're serious about me, you'll think of something.'

'I am serious.'

'I'm not so sure.'

'How can you say that? I love you!'

'I know you think you do.'

'What's that supposed to mean? You don't believe I know my own mind?'

'Well, what about your family? It's hard, I get that. But if you won't even introduce me to them, what does that say about us? Jaz, deep down I think all you really want is a Punjabi girl. You'll string me along for a while because it's comfortable and – oh, I don't know – because you like the sex, but you'll never commit. And then you'll marry someone else, some girl who can make samosas with your mom.'

'Lisa, that's not true.'

'I think it is.'

'So you're going to do this? You're just going to leave?'

'Well, it looks that way, doesn't it.'

They didn't speak for several days. He lay curled up on the couch, watching whole seasons of a TV show about an alien invasion. And then she was gone, staying with a friend in Brooklyn while she looked for an apartment. He thought his life was over. A friend had to explain it to him.

'Go get her, Jaz. She's waiting to see if you'll come after her.'

It was the best decision of his life. He rented a car and drove to New York, getting horrendously lost somewhere in Queens. At last, late on a Saturday night, he found himself pressing a buzzer on an old industrial building in Williamsburg. There was no reply, and he hung around outside for over an hour before Lisa turned up, several cocktails into her evening, hanging on to her friend Amy.

'I want to be with you,' he said to Lisa, as Amy hovered indiscreetly close, covering her mouth with her hands and making little cooing noises. 'I'll live anywhere. I'll introduce you to my family, all the cousins, my aunts and uncles, so many relatives you'll beg for mercy. Just say you'll be with me.'

In later years Amy would tell elaborate, highly embellished dinner-party accounts of the scene, 'the most romantic thing she'd ever witnessed'. Lisa always blushed and made feeble attempts to stop her, but it was clear she enjoyed the tales. It had been a proposal in all but name, though Jaz saved the real proposal for after he'd fulfilled his promise. As he made arrangements for the trip, he hid how nervous he was, trying not to frighten her with too many instructions about what to wear and how to behave. He knew the meeting would go badly – it was just a question of whether she'd come away too scared to stay with him. As they drove down to Baltimore, he felt like a condemned man on his way to the chair.

His parents had taken the news of Lisa's existence about as well as could be expected. On the phone, his mother asked her family name, where her parents lived. When he raised the subject of a visit, she responded with a sort of icy neutrality. If God wills it, she said, you will come. His father was warmer. Your family misses you, beta. It's been too long. Jaz booked a motel room, so the question of sleeping arrangements didn't arise. Lisa wore a pant suit and a long-sleeved shirt, despite the humid summer weather. As they passed block after block of boarded-up row houses, she looked uneasy, and was visibly relieved when they pulled up outside his parents' place, which, though small, was at least not in a neighborhood that looked abandoned.

They ate lunch, which his mom had prepared with help from Seetal and Sukhwindermassi. There was none of the usual bustle, no running around, no jokes or high-jinks. For long periods the rattle of the elderly air conditioner was the loudest noise in the room. His dad offered Lisa a whiskey and was displeased to see she accepted. As she sat and sipped her drink, Jaz shuffled his feet and tried to keep the conversation from petering out. In vain he translated some of Lisa's approaches to his mother, questions about her house, compliments on the food. She wouldn't respond, just scurried back into the kitchen and pretended to busy herself with pots and pans. Bravely Lisa persevered through the meal, trying fruitlessly to make a connection, helping Seetal and Uma carry dirty plates, even attempting to take charge of doing the dishes; Uma led her politely back into the living room, where Jaz was chatting with his uncles about real estate. She looked thoroughly dejected. Discreetly he squeezed her hand, earning an extra look of disapproval from his father.

Later they sat in the car outside the house. Lisa fumbled angrily in her purse for tissues.

'It's not you,' he told her. 'You understand that, don't you? They'd be like that with anyone.'

'Anyone white.'

'It'd be the same with a lot of Indians.'

She smiled wanly, dabbing at her eyes. 'It wasn't so bad.'

'Yes, it was.'

'You're right. It was awful.'

She saw the look on his face and reached out to squeeze his hand. 'Don't worry, Jaz. I won't run away.'

A few weeks later he took her to an expensive French restaurant in the West Village and asked her to marry him. He was still half expecting her to say no, but she looked at the ring and grinned and kissed him and a waiter materialized with champagne and the other patrons clapped politely, inaugurating what he now remembered as the best year of his life. They moved into a tiny walk-up in Cobble Hill. He commuted back to Cambridge to see his supervisor and she started reading manuscripts for a small publisher. They bought flea-market furniture and went on long walks and made love so frequently and loudly that the crazy French woman downstairs began phoning the super. They cooked pasta and risottos for other young couples, drinking red wine out of ill-matched glasses and arguing about books and films. Once they roasted a chicken for Lisa's parents, the four of them squeezed around the little kitchen table, clamping their elbows to their sides as they cut up their food. His own parents never saw that apartment. They were too busy, they said, to come to New York. 'With what?' he asked. 'So many things,' said his father, his voice trailing away.

He complained to Seetal. 'How can they visit you?' she snapped. 'You aren't even married yet. And she's –'

'She's what? Go on, say it.'

'You chose this, Jaz. You knew what it would mean.'

Jaz successfully defended his thesis, then spent a thankless summer tutoring entitled suburban college applicants, while half-heartedly looking for academic jobs. Then he ran into Xavier, an old MIT friend. He and Lisa were eating in one of the new neighborhood restaurants that had sprung up all across gentrified Brooklyn, a place that served steaks and oysters out of a storefront that retained some of the fittings from the old pharmacy which previously occupied the site. Xavier came over to say hi, and ended up joining them for dessert. He'd been a particle physicist, but had left academia for Wall Street. He wasn't the first person Jaz had heard of who'd done this. The application of physical models to the financial markets was something of a trend. Banks and hedge funds were hungry for specialists in so-called quantitative finance, mathematicians and computer scientists who could tame the uncertainties of international capital flows. Xavier used words like *revolutionize* and *transformative*. There was serious money involved: he was earning more in a month than Jaz could expect to make in two years as a junior lecturer. He left behind a business card and a waft of personalized cologne. The next day he phoned to say his firm was hiring. Was Jaz interested? Sure he was. He went for an interview with no special expectations. He didn't think he'd get the job. Yet six weeks later he found himself in front of a screen, writing code that used the same modeling techniques he'd employed on quantum-probability problems to track fluctuations in the bond market.

Jaz tried not to feel angry that money brought about a reconciliation with his family. Nothing else had worked. Since 9/11 his parents had become increasingly paranoid. They displayed a big American flag in their front window in case anyone mistook them for Muslims; on his first visit after the attacks, Jaz had been furious to find his mother sewing a flag patch on to his father's work overalls, another charm against white malice. As the war on terror intensified, they seemed more sympathetic to their son's choices, his decision to 'blend in'. Jaz's rebellion was recast as immigrant cautiousness.

With his Wall Street salary swelling their joint bank account, he and Lisa made an offer on a duplex in Park Slope and began preparations for their wedding. He was so desperate for his family to be there that he resorted to bribery, paying off the remainder of his parents' mortgage and sending cash to Uma to finance long-deferred dental surgery for her younger son. Coincidentally or not, his mother and father finally found time to visit, a harrowing weekend which began with a two-hour wait at Penn Station (they'd missed the train and, because neither owned a cellphone, didn't call to let him know), then continued through a minute examination of their son's domestic arrangements, several excruciating restaurant meals (Italian food they refused to eat; Indian food his mom excoriated, dish by dish, in stage-whisper Punjabi) and sightseeing. The high point was a trip to the Statue of Liberty. Jaz took a photo of Lisa, standing between Amma and Bapu against the rail of the ferry, the three of them smiling bravely into the wind.

In the end they had two weddings: one in a synagogue in Prospect Park, attended mostly by their friends and Lisa's relatives, the second in the storefront gurdwara where Jaz had spent so much of his childhood. Jaz's close family went up to Brooklyn for the Jewish ceremony, where they allowed themselves to be shepherded around, listening politely to the explanations of the various prayers, the chuppah, the broken glass. In Baltimore, Lisa brought an Indian girlfriend for support, who helped her dress and provided a buffer against various aunties who'd appointed themselves to oversee her preparations. Her mother, father and a cluster of Brooklyn friends joined the crowd. At the reception, in a nearby community hall, the two sets of parents attempted conversation, using Uma as an interpreter, while the DJ (one of Jaz's cousins) span bhangra at ear-splitting volume, so the younger ones could dance. Jaz was glad none of their Brooklyn friends understood Punjabi; at the reception he overheard some drunken uncle making a remark about gori sluts and had to be restrained from throwing the man out.

Married life was good. Lisa got a job as an editorial assistant at a publishing house. Jaz swapped his first bonus check for a classic Mercedes sports car, a seventies model which Lisa pretended to dislike. Together they dove into the city, angling for tables at hot new restaurants, taking the subway to the outer boroughs on weekend excursions. They attended charity benefits where traders from Jaz's firm bid thousands of dollars for dive vacations or the chance to spend a day with the Mets, and book parties where Jaz felt the icy chill of being a 'Wall Street guy' among innumerate arty types who disapproved of the way he made his living. Little by little, the apartment silted up with books. They took a summer rental in Amagansett, bought mid-century modern furniture from design stores in Tribeca and hung over their fireplace a painting by a fashionable young artist, which Lisa had fallen in love with at a Lower East Side gallery. Looking at the collection of gestural swirls and neatly painted little skulls that gave his wife such inexplicable pleasure, Jaz felt replete.

Then Lisa got pregnant. She told work she thought six months off would be sufficient. On the scan Raj looked like a little white ghost, a rag of ectoplasm. Jaz phoned his parents to say it was a boy, and the joy in his mother's voice affected him so strongly that he had to hold the phone away from his face as he sobbed. Raj arrived, a beautiful little person with olive skin, a mop of black hair, a big Punjabi nose and brown eyes that would have been the delight of Jaz's life had he been able to see anything human behind them.

It felt like a long time ago.

He started the car engine and let it run for a moment, glad of the sudden blast of air. The Mojave sun was high in the sky, bleaching everything white, except for the black strip of the road into town. He reached into the glove compartment and fingered his mom's latest letter, addressed in Sukhwindermassi's shaky handwriting. On the back seat Raj moaned and wriggled in his harness. Jaz opened the envelope and took out the little locket his mom had enclosed, to ward off the evil eye. What could be the harm? He reached back and hung it around Raj's neck. The boy put up a hand to feel the string and for a moment Jaz thought he'd tear it off, but he settled down, staring at some object on the other side of the window.

Pulling out on to the highway, Jaz reflexively switched on the radio, then turned it off again. Lately music had begun to frighten Raj. The doctors said his hearing was abnormally acute. As a baby he'd cried at the sound of the vacuum cleaner. The subway was impossible, and it took a long time before he was comfortable in a car, but when he was a newborn music always used to soothe him. Another depressing thing, another loss. The drive from LA had been undertaken in silence, boredom filling the car like carbon monoxide.

They headed down the hill into town, past billboards advertising attorneys and retirement communities. The sun was fierce. Heat haze splashed mirages across the highway and for a moment Jaz wasn't sure if the thing he saw was real: a group of women walking by the roadside, swathed in sky-blue Afghan burqas. It was as if a shard of television had fallen into his eyes, a stray image from elsewhere. He slowed and checked his mirrors. There they were, incomprehensible cobalt ghosts, making their way from one place to another. Involuntarily he glanced around to see if everything else was still as it should be – the billboards and power-lines, the creosote bushes – as though he might find himself suddenly transposed, peering at a mud-brick village through the reinforced windshield of a humvee.

At the market they got a spot right by the entrance. Raj was docile and allowed himself to be led inside. They walked through the aisles adding items to their cart: sliced turkey, bottled water, crackers, all the things they'd need for a picnic lunch. Raj was fascinated by the shelves stacked with canned goods. He loved to make piles, putting one block on top of another or lining his toys up in a row, and here was an environment with just the regimented order he liked. He clicked his tongue and flapped his arms, expressions of pleasure which Jaz had learned to read and enjoy. When Raj started to fill the cart with cans of corn Jaz managed to divert his attention by handing him an orange, an object he always found absorbing and could carry around for hours, like a plush toy or a pet. There were a few tears at the checkout when he had to give up the slightly squashed fruit to be scanned, but otherwise their expedition went smoothly. On the drive back Jaz whistled and drummed his fingers on the steering wheel. Raj clicked and hummed. Jaz looked out for more sky-blue women, but saw none.

Back at the motel, they found Lisa sunbathing by the pool, her long legs splayed over a sun lounger. She looked good in her bikini and Jaz felt an unfamiliar moment of passion for his wife. He reached down and kissed her, running his fingers over her thigh. She smelled great, like suntan oil and fresh sweat.

'Hey.'

'Hey yourself.'

She sat up and felt Raj's forehead.

'You're so hot. Come on, let's get you into your swim things.'

Jaz kissed her again. 'It's OK, I'll do it. You lie down.'

In the room Raj made no complaints as Jaz put him into cloth swim diapers and rubbed sunscreen on his body, but when he tried to slip the locket over his head Raj let out a fierce yell and gripped on to it. Jaz decided the battle wasn't worth fighting. No big deal. The kid could keep it if he wanted.

'Come on, let's go find Mommy.'

Out at the pool, Jaz saw Lisa talking to the motel manager, laughing over some joke. The woman walked off as he approached, and Lisa propped herself up on one elbow, shielding her eyes against the sun.

'What's that?'

'What?'

'That piece of crap round his neck.'

'Oh, something my mom sent. He liked it, wouldn't take it off.'

'You put that on him?'

'Yeah. It's just a – a traditional thing. She sent it as a present.'

'Damn it, Jaz, I thought I'd made it clear. I don't want your mom's superstitious bullshit anywhere near our son.'

'There's no harm in it.'

'No harm? As far as she's concerned her family's been cursed because you married a white woman. She thinks Raj is our punishment.'

'Don't exaggerate.'

She pulled the boy toward her and tried to slip the locket over his neck. He grabbed at the string and began to wail.

'You're hurting him.'

'Raj, let go!'

Finally the string broke. Lisa swore and hurled the charm over the fence. Raj began rocking backward and forward, craning his head into his shoulder like a hibernating bird. Jaz sank down on to a plastic chair.

'Perfect. Good job.'

Lisa glared at him. He got in the pool and swam a few lengths, trying to control his anger. Finally he pulled himself up on to the side and sat with his legs in the water, feeling the heat evaporating the moisture from his back.

'Lisa?'

'What?'

'Could you – I don't know – just try to see how hard this is for me? She's my mom.'

'Jesus, Jaz. Sometimes I think you actually believe it. You think there's something wrong with him.'

'Well, there *is* something wrong with him.'

'The evil eye?'

'What do you want me to say? That my mom and dad are ignorant? That we're just poor brown-skinned immigrants who don't understand your big modern American world? Between you and them – God, you have no idea of what I have to do, how hard it is . . . I mean, look at him, Lisa! He's not normal. No amount of PC language is going to change that. And if you really want to know, yes, sometimes it feels like a curse. It feels like I'm being fucking punished.'

He knew he'd gone too far.

'Lisa –'.

'Don't.'

'I didn't mean that. I love him just as much as you do. But look what it's done to us.'

'What *he's* done to us, you mean.'

'We were never like this.'

'It wouldn't be so hard if you'd just support me sometimes, instead of behaving like I'm the problem.'

'Come on, baby. That's not true.'

'Yes, it is. You could at least stand up against your family. You don't think it's hard for me – to know what they think? According to them, this is my fault.'

'They don't think that.'

'Yes, they do, Jaz. And you let them think it. You've never stood up to them, not once.'

'We barely see them.'

'That's not the same thing. Running away isn't the same as fighting.'

'And what do you expect me to do? Disown them? I have a duty. They're my family. Family's everything to us – that's what you people never understand. I love my parents, and I love my son.'

She stared at him as if he'd just slapped her.

'You people?'

'You know what I mean.'

'Christ, now I'm "you people". Well, you know what, if you love your son so much, you and your wonderful Punjabi family can take care of him without me. Everyone will whoop for joy. Ding dong, the witch is dead! The nasty white witch has vanished and all the happy villagers can celebrate. You people? I don't fucking believe you, Jaz. Where are the car keys?'

'What do you want them for?'

'Just tell me where the fucking keys are.'

'On the table by the bed.'

'Right.'

Grabbing her towel, she stalked off to the room. Jaz sat with Raj, trying to work out what had just happened. A few minutes later she came out again wearing a T-shirt and shorts, a pair of owlish over-sized sunglasses screening her face. Without a glance over at the pool she marched around the corner to the car. He heard the starter motor squeal as the key was turned violently in the ignition. Then, with a screech of tires, she drove away.

1969

As kids they used to go out to the rocks and look at the site of the accident. The wreckage had mostly gone to salvage, but you could see the remains of the rocket or whatever it was, a sort of twisted, crumpled cylinder pocked with bullet holes. The boys used it for target practice, though Dawn couldn't see what kind of practice you got out of hitting something that size. It was more the sound, she supposed, the plink as the rusty metal gave way. There was a cracked concrete base, a burned patch; that was about it. Not much to see.

Everyone had different stories about how it had happened. Something electrical. Some kid lighting a firework for a prank. But the whole thing had gone up like a torch, in front of thousands of people, with the feller inside it. Communist, said the old guys at the store, who always knew everything about everything. An agent of hostile foreign powers. Still, getting burned alive like that, trapped in a tin can. No one should suffer so.

Frankie DuQuette had a beat-up Plymouth and they used to drive it out there, do skids and donuts, raise clouds of dust – just letting off steam, really, no harm in it. After, they'd sit up on the rocks looking out over the desert, or just lie on the hood, playing the radio and watching the sunset. When it got dark, they'd switch the headlights on; dust motes would dance in the yellow beams and they'd make out and Frankie would put his hand inside her shirt but never go further, because he was a timid boy and mortally afraid of his pastor. Her uncle Ray would do a lot of screaming when she got back home after those nights out at the rocks with Frankie. He'd remind her how grateful she ought to be for them taking her in, while her aunt held her hand over her mouth and made fish eyes.

Then the crazy lady came. She just towed a trailer on to the land

and started playing house, right there under the Pinnacle Rocks. Turned out it was privately owned, nobody even remembered by who. Everyone thought it was government land. She didn't bother anyone, only came into town when she needed supplies, driving an old Ford pickup that had been patched and filled and repaired so many times it was hard to say what color it might once have been. Mostly it was rust color. There were all kinds of theories as to why she was there and how she made her living. She must have had money from somewhere, for she didn't work. Heaven knew how she spent her time.

One day one of the boys at the store got up courage to ask. She told him she was waiting for her daughter. No one knew what she meant by that until Uncle Ray, who'd been there when the accident happened, at the meeting or whatever, reminded them about the little girl who'd gone missing. The guy had climbed up the tower in his silver outfit, and after it started burning a lot of wreckage had come down, killing three people. The kid must have been playing inside. There were a lot of kids around, apparently. She must have been burned right up.

Dawn sometimes worked at the store after school, and she got a good look at the crazy lady the next time she came in, at her greasy overalls, her sunburned arms and neck. Dawn wasn't afraid of her. She was trying to get a sight of her eyes; that's what you did, look at their eyes, except the crazy lady was staring at the floor. She counted coins into her hand and you could see she had dirt under her fingernails, in the creases of her palms. Working hands, like a man's. Lord preserve Dawn from ever having hands like that.

'You having yourself a good time out there?' She bit her tongue for asking it. Old Man Craw stopped working the deli slicer and shot her a look. The crazy lady glanced up and there they were, little brown chocolate-button disks like a rabbit or a deer, peering out at the world from under that nasty chewed-up straw hat. Dawn saw nothing in them, not really, but afterwards she told everyone in class how in her opinion the old bird wasn't crazy, not at all.

By the following year there seemed to be a few people out at the rocks. They set up a kind of compound, with a wire fence, a couple of tin-roofed shacks. The sheriff sent Officer Carlsbad out to check on them. He came back saying they smelled kind of ripe but far as he could see they weren't breaking any laws. The crazy lady started coming into town with an older guy who had an eye patch. Dawn couldn't hardly look at him. Under the eye his cheek was slick and pink, like it was going to slide down over his jaw.

So now she knew they were definitely saucer people come back. It was obvious. She told Uncle Ray and he said whatever they were she should keep away from them. That was sort of official policy. Everyone in town was to be polite, no more. The young ones were supposed to keep their distance. Of course that made them all curious. There was every kind of rumor. They did a lot of driving by.

Then one day she saw the girl, just walking by the side of the road in the heat of the day about five miles from town. Dawn pulled over and asked if she was OK. Thought she'd hear a story, most probably about being dumped there by some asshole boyfriend. Instead she said she was fine and her name was Judy and she was on her way home.

'Home?'

'Yes.'

'Just walking?'

She was blonde and wore a sleeveless white shirt and jeans and had her hair in braids like a kid or an Indian squaw, which was amazing to Dawn because that was the time when all the girls were going for that big high hair, bubble and flip, the kind that took hours with rollers and spray. She looked about nineteen. And beautiful, without any effort at all, crisp and clean as if she'd just showered instead of walking however many miles in that sun. When she swung the truck around, pointing into town, this Judy said oh no, she lived out there at the rocks. Dawn couldn't help but laugh.

'With them? You live out there?'

'With my mom and some friends.'

Who knew what to think about that? When they got to the compound Judy didn't invite her in, just said thanks, see you another time, which made Dawn feel kind of sore toward her. She did get to tell the news to the girls over floats at the Dairy Queen and that was some consolation, but as it turned out she didn't see Judy again until about a year later, when the girl made her real entrance into town life. By then Dawn had left school and was more or less just working at the store. She was there one afternoon, pretending to do something useful, when Judy walked in with the three freakiest-looking people you ever set eyes on. Dawn didn't even want to blink in case she missed some shimmer or glimmer or strange remark or taking on or off of a hat or pair of dark glasses or a feather. One guy had all this silver and turquoise on him and a big black Stetson with a beadwork band and snakeskin boots and a long Mexican mustache. The other seemed to be wearing a pair of green ballet tights through which you could basically see every-thing, which meant she tried to concentrate on the top half, where there was a rabbit-fur vest and a bare chest and a blond beard with little knotty braids in it – kind of disgusting, really – and if she didn't want to look at that and couldn't at the middle the only other option was his bare feet and they were just dirtier than hell. The other one was a colored girl, if you please, wearing a long yellow silk gown like a bathrobe, slightly torn and no bra underneath. Her hair was a big round afro bubble and she was stoned on something, you could just tell she was, and in the middle of them all was Judy, in her jeans and her neatly pressed white shirt, looking just the same as before.

'Hey,' she said.

'Hey,' said Dawn.

'Guys, this is Dawn. She's one of us.'

Mexican Mustache made a kind of growling noise in his throat and leaned over the counter, all toothy and attracted. Dawn blushed right away. She hated how she did that. The others fell about the place, except Judy, who just stood there, smiling sweetly, like she was about to recite a poem.

'I'm sorry,' said the colored girl, 'it's just your face, man, you should see your face. You got eyes like – kerpow – you know?'

Dawn didn't know and to be honest it was her first-ever conversation with a colored person apart from one time on a class civics trip to Sacramento when they were there at the state capitol with a school from a deprived neighborhood. She must have looked confused or scared or something because right then Mr Craw came bustling out of the storeroom and took a look at the customers and a look at her and put on his no-trespassers voice.

'Can I help you, young lady?'

Mr Craw kept a .38 under the counter, alongside of a baseball bat and a length of chain. He was positioned where he could reach it.

'I said, can I help you, young lady?'

Judy turned her big smile on him. 'Sure, brother. You can sell us some food.'

'What kind of food?'

'Noodles, rice, cheese. Food.'

'You'll have to be more specific.' He was flexing his hand under the counter like a Saturday serial gunslinger.

'I have a list.'

This set Mr Craw back some. A little more clowning around and he might have used that gun. Mr Craw had been a POW in Korea and now he liked to keep to himself. There was no Mrs Craw. That mostly said it for Mr Craw. Dawn just prayed those boys and girls didn't remind the man of anything he didn't care to be reminded of.

Somehow they got out alive with five big bags of groceries. She stood in the doorway looking after them. They had a school bus parked outside, painted all kinds of colors and patterns. The back half was stuffed with yards and yards of shiny fabric; there was so much, it was bursting out the windows. There was a sort of astronomy-dish item on top, and at least three or four more people hanging around outside, but she didn't get a good look at anyone except a guy in a cape and a football helmet, because Mr Craw pulled her back inside and told her to go and bag up the delivery orders for the veterans' home.

Soon after that Sheriff Waghorn found occasion to fly his plane right out to the Pinnacles. He landed it on the dry lake near the rocks and invited himself in for a neighborly tour of the property. When he got back, he held a meeting in the backroom of Mulligan's Lounge and Grill, just the usual half-dozen of them – the mayor, Mulligan, Mr Hansen from the gas station, the Rotarians basically – and soon enough the town knew the feller with the burned face was called Davis and had taken the sheriff around very politely, shown him a bakery and some kind of windmill thing, but the place was a nuthouse, there were easily over twenty of them living there, including a naked chick and two niggers, which detail made it officially the biggest beatnik outbreak in the history of the county and ensured that Dawn and her friends Lena and Sheri wasted no time in giving their respective boyfriends the slip and heading over to get themselves some life experience.

It was a Friday night and they'd seen some lights out at the rocks which suggested a party. After a lot of ebb and flow on the telephone to coordinate excuses they found themselves in Lena's truck having an argument which wasn't really about was it OK to like Tommy James and the Shondells, but was it OK for Lena to have let Robbie Molina put his hand inside her panties at the Methodist Barbecue and Dance when he'd so recently had his hand inside Dawn's panties and then been such a pig as to tell the basketball team after.

When they got to the compound, they sat in the dark for a while, fighting about what to do. Some kind of weird music was floating on the air. Dawn felt nervous. The three girls had finally screwed up their courage to get out of the truck when a pack of evil-looking characters pulled up beside them on motorcycles, gunning the engines and craning their necks to see into the cab. Right then they thought they were about to be victimized in some kind of chain-wielding greaser sex attack but instead the main one asked all soft and nice why they weren't heading on in. It was none other than the dark leaner-on-the-counter from the store, the good-looking one with the Mexican mustache. He said his name was Wolf and smiled to show his big white teeth.

They didn't really have a choice. They got out of the truck and followed Wolf and his buddies through the compound gate, trying to pretend it was the kind of thing they did all the time. Right away Wolf ran into some chick and started walking along with his arm around her, though Dawn was vaguely trying to walk next to him on that side. They were projecting colors on to the rocks, slides and oil-drops and such, and a whole bunch of people were sitting in a circle around a fire, playing drums and pipes and other instruments into this thing in the center, a sort of mound of microphones and boxy electrical devices.

No one paid much attention when they joined the circle. A few people nodded hello. The musicians just carried on playing. Dawn really dug the music, though it wasn't like anything she'd normally listen to. 'What do you call it here?' she asked the girl sitting next to her, who was wrapped in a Navajo blanket.

'This,' said the girl, 'is the prime terrestrial hub of the Ashtar Galactic Command.'

'The what?'

'Our secret Earth base. Our first one. There are going to be a lot more eventually.'

Dawn didn't know what to say to that, so she nodded and brushed her hair out of her face, to let the girl know she was interested.

'A lot more bases,' said the girl pensively. 'Maybe hundreds. When we break through a lot more people are gonna get reintegrated. More bases'll just naturally come then. Do you want to look through my glasses?'

She was wearing an odd pair of granny glasses, whose lenses were faceted like gemstones. Dawn put them on. The fire broke up into splinters of prismatic color.

'The Urim and Thummim,' said the girl. 'They show you the past and the future.' Dawn had no idea what she was talking about.

'How did you find out about all this?'

'About what?'

'Bases and such.'

'Oh, I can't remember. Feels like I've always known. I met Judy on the street in LA and she introduced me to Joanie and Clark and they asked me if I wanted to come and live out here. That's about it.'

'Joanie and Clark?'

The girl pointed to the other side of the fire. One thing was for sure: the crazy lady looked a lot less crazy out there at the rocks. She was wearing a flower-print maxi dress that made her seem old-timey, pioneering. Her hair was combed out long and straight, a gray curtain falling either side of her face. She and one-eyed Mr Davis weren't sitting cross-legged on the ground like the others. They were provided with high-backed wooden armchairs, sturdy things like countrified thrones: Ma and Pa, with Miss Judy at their feet, still looking All-American, bright and fresh, propping her head on her hands like she was at morning assembly.

Dawn smiled over, but Little Miss Judy stared straight through her like they'd never met.

Navajo Blanket Girl didn't seem to mind talking, so Dawn carried on asking questions. Turned out the old lady was called Ma Joanie, except you said it with a long aah sound, because it was from The East. *Maa* Joanie. *Maaaaa* . . . So was she crazy or wasn't she? Lena and Sheri, sitting on Dawn's far side, widened their eyes to show her she was being rude.

'She's seen a lot of things you and I haven't,' said the girl. 'She's very highly advanced.'

Which sort of sounded like a yes.

Lena mouthed *Let's go*. Dawn wanted to stay. There was all kinds of good stuff to look at, such as the light-show and the well-built young guy with no pants on dancing by the fire, just shaking his thing from side to side in a way that would not have come naturally to Frankie or Robbie or in fact any of the boys they knew.

'What about Judy? She seems kind of aloof.'

Navajo Blanket Girl lowered her voice to a whisper. 'Judy's the most important person here. Judy's the Guide.'

'To what?'

'Say, can I have my glasses back?'

Just like that, without saying goodbye, Navajo Blanket Girl got up and wandered away, humming to herself. Dawn was confused, but she had to recover quick, had to check she was put together OK and was acting cool, because Wolf stretched out beside her, propped himself up on one elbow and offered her a hit on a long skinny joint. The important thing was not to say or do anything stupid.

'Hi,' he said.

'Dawnie,' whispered Sheri. 'Let's get out of here. A person could get cooties just from the ground.'

Dawn was about to smoke her first pot and had no intention of leaving, for Sheri or anyone, so she shot her a shut-your-trap look and they listened to the music for a while. Dawn smoked some of the joint and handed it to Sheri, who didn't want any. Lena took a hit and then started to cough like a sick cat, which was kind of funny. Then Wolf asked if she'd like to meet some people and she said yes, and he helped her to her feet and she ignored the sight of Sheri pointing angrily at her watch and Lena holding up her car keys. She walked with Wolf, like in a procession or a dance, around to the other side of the fire.

'Dawn,' he said. 'You won't even have to change your name.'

2008

As she put the car into drive, Lisa saw her hands were shaking. She was on the verge of tears and somehow that made her even more angry, a vicious cycle which tightened her throat and blurred her vision as she drove down the hill toward the strip of fast-food restaurants. She muttered under her breath. Damn Jaz. So often he made her feel like this, playing Mr Scientist, the peer-reviewed voice of reason. No, darling, do it this way. Not like that, you'll damage the mechanism.

A truck pulled out in front of her, forcing her to brake. She swore and leaned on the horn, but even as she was giving the finger to the giant white shape she knew she was in the wrong. Come on, girl, she admonished herself. Sleep or no sleep, get a grip. What would happen if you got killed? Who'd look after the poor kid then? Not Jaz, that was for sure. He wouldn't know where to begin.

She pulled into the parking lot of a Denny's and sat for a moment, examining her hair in the mirror, putting on lip balm and checking her purse, conjuring up a routine to compose herself. Then she went in and ordered coffee.

So the 'healing family vacation' idea was a bust. By the time they got to Phoenix things between her and Jaz would be as bad as ever. Her dad would probably try to mediate, though he didn't understand the first thing about Jaz, was secretly a little afraid of him, treated him like some impressive but unpredictable exotic pet, an iguana or a kinkajou. Her mother would give her that terrible doe-eyed look of pseudo-sympathy, and Lisa would feel like tearing her eyes out of her discreetly worked-on face.

A group of boys was crammed into the next booth, so young that at first she thought they must be from the local high school, a club or a sports team. Then she took in the cropped hair, a certain coiled surliness in their manner, and realized they were from the marines base. One had his leg in a cast, stretched out straight into the aisle. A set of crutches lay beside him on the floor. A football injury? Or a war wound? Had these kids been in Iraq? She overheard some of what they were discussing. Not cars or girls, but the state of the nation. She caught the words *honor, decency, fags*.

She'd known more or less what her parents would think of Jaz before she introduced them. Her father was a simple soul: Poppy just wanted his little girl to be happy, for her to hug him sometimes and give him useless golf accessories on his birthday and to never ever stop calling him Poppy for as long as they both should live. So an East Indian was fine by him – he seemed to find it necessary to add the 'East', some tic he'd picked up since they moved down there, as if suburban Phoenix was confusingly full of Hopi and Apache who needed to be filed separately. Jaz was Educated, Polite, earned Good Money, was Kind to His Daughter. Check, check, check and check. Due diligence done. So Poppy had signed off and headed back to the den for the Sunday afternoon football. Mom was trickier, one of those women who made a picture in her mind of how things ought to be and then panicked when reality deviated. Jaz was a major deviation, an unknown unknown, and Patty Schwartzman's attempts to figure him showed her daughter an ugly side. She'd insisted on a 'girls' day out' at a spa right before the wedding. It was obvious she had something on her mind. So Lisa had sat through the manicure, the pedicure, the hot-stone massage; Patty waited to say her piece until they were slumped on loungers in matching robes, sipping fancy imported European spring water, a vile chocolate facial (chocolate, of all things) caking fecally on their skin. Within two minutes they were hissing at each other, Lisa raging, Patty feigning wounded incomprehension.

'They're different from us. That's not calling anyone names.'

'Mom, if you bring up Jason Elsberg now, I'm going to slap you.'

'You know he got engaged. Don't look at me like that. I'm just saying, when it comes to women, the men are very old-fashioned. They like things a certain way.'

'And you'd know because, what? You had a thing with an anthropologist? He's not Osama bin Laden. He wears polo shirts. All my friends think he's a Republican.'

'You always liked to make things difficult for yourself, even as a little girl.'

'You know, Mom, you look exactly like someone smeared your face in shit.'

Lisa would rather have died than admit she'd ever had doubts herself. Back when she and Jaz first met, she'd probed for signs that he was about to tear off his genial mask and reveal an Oriental Bluebeard who'd keep her cooped up in the kitchen and beat her for showing her ankles to other men. Of course all that turned out to be ridiculous, but at the same time there were things about him, sore spots – the pitch of his jealousy about her exes, a certain physical prudery – that you'd have to call Indian, or Asian, or Punjabi, or whatever. Or maybe not; maybe it was all just Jaz. By that time Lisa had long since worn herself out with such questions.

She had breezily assumed Jaz's problem with his family was more or less in his head. She was a good person, and she loved their son; surely anyone – anyone who got to know her – would be pleased to have her as a daughter-in-law? She'd even entertained one or two pleasant fantasies of being absorbed into an old-fashioned extended family, a sort of subcontinental version of *Little Women*, with meals around a big table and parties where she'd get dressed up in beautiful fabrics and silver jewelry, one of a crowd of giggling brown-eyed sisters. Then came the terrible trip down to Baltimore, the desolate neighborhood, the cramped strange-smelling house full of inscrutable angry people. She tried everything she could, every tactic to ingratiate herself, but it was plain they didn't want to know. To be *hated* just for who she was, and not to be able to do anything about it! To be hated behind a mask of dogged politeness, by people who ate off plastic plates and had a cabinet of cheap tourist tchotchkes and a decaying Tercel parked on the street outside, people who lived like *immigrants*. A shameful thought. An unsayable thought. That was the worst of it, the way those people made her feel like some red-state bigot, made her feel like her mom.

Lisa was too proud to let anyone know how much the visit scared her, and Jaz was so sweet and tragic that somehow it made everything OK. He wasn't his family; he wasn't a bit like them. As he drove her back to the motel, nervously making jokes about their terrible day, she reminded herself of the things she loved about him, his tenderness, his nerdy way of treating her problems like Rubik's cubes, puzzles that he could solve to be helpful. He was the kindest, most decent man she'd ever known. Their life together was beautiful. Of course she wanted to marry him.

The first wedding was the day she wanted. Surrounded by all their friends, she felt so charged with happiness that she coasted through the Sikh ceremony a week later, contentedly sitting in the gurdwara with her eyes lowered while her in-laws chanted hymns and adjusted the cloths covering their holy book. It was fun to have her old roommate Sunita by her side, squeezing her hand and helping her mother lead her in – yes, Patty Schwartzman, wrapped in a sari, goggling with concentration as she tried not to upset the natives. Poppy sat on the men's side, legs crossed, handkerchief on his head and camcorder in hand as if it were all no more strange than a luau or a ceremony at his lodge.

After that the two of them were married enough to please everyone who felt they had a stake in the matter. They went back to their life, cocktails and book parties and tasting menus and theater tickets, and everything was fine, family-wise, until she got pregnant and once again the whole world started acting like it had a right to interfere. Jaz would hunch over the phone for hours, listening to instructions from his relatives, saying nothing but *ji, haan ji*. Her mother angled to come and stay, 'just for six months or so', to help them get settled. That catastrophe averted, Jaz broke the news about the baby's name. Lisa had always expected a ceremony of some kind, but hadn't realized God would want such a say. She'd filed away names for her child – Conor or Lucas or Seth, if it was a boy, Lauren or Dylan for a girl – names she liked, that felt connected to her life. The idea that there'd be a lottery element, opening up the Guru Granth Sahib at random to find the initial letter, seemed like an imposition. It was one thing to dress up and get bored for a couple of hours to placate your in-laws, another to allow them to dictate the sounds you murmured as you held your infant to your breast. When Raj was born, rigid and screaming, they just called him 'baby' or 'the egg', deferring the question. Then Jaz let her know that circumcision was strictly prohibited in Sikhism and the full extent of their trouble dawned. She wished she and Jaz had been less good, more independent, had been happy to say to hell with family and tradition and God in whatever hat or turban or yarmulke he was currently wearing; but as they talked, she realized with a sinking feeling that both of them half believed, that in some sentimental way they both wanted to do right by their people.

'But what does it matter? It's just a piece of skin.'

'It's – I don't know, Jaz. It's about identity. We've been oppressed for so many generations –'

'Oh, so remind me who was oppressing you at your private school?'

'Don't be an asshole. It's a symbol. There was . . . the Holocaust, the pogroms. If I didn't do this for him, they'd have won. All the bastards who wanted us to disappear.'

'The Nazis.'

'Yes, the Nazis.'

'And the Tsar.'

'Actually, yes.'

'Listen to yourself. Do you even know how ridiculous you sound? You don't even believe in God. The only time I've ever seen you in a synagogue was at our wedding.'

'It's not about religion. It's culture.'

'And what about my culture? What about our Guru Arjan Dev, who was executed by the Mughals for refusing to change the words of our holy book? Or Guru Tegh Bahadur, who was so cruelly tortured that he had to be cremated in secret? Sikhs have been persecuted. The Muslims tried to convert us by force. They tried to circumcise us *by force*. Do you understand?'

'I thought you were an atheist.'

'Agnostic.'

'You used to rant about the death of God. You used to wave Nietzsche at me.'

'And you seem to be saying God wants you to mutilate my son.'

'*Our* son, Jaz. And there are health reasons too. Transmission of STDs, for example.'

And so it would go on. Round and round, for days, weeks. She looked up what the Sikh scriptures said. It sounded like a borscht-belt joke, a line delivered by a fat man in a ruffled tuxedo shirt. *I don't believe in it, O siblings of destiny. If God wished me to be a Muslim, it would be cut off by itself.* She read about the Mughal persecution of the Sikhs. She guessed they had as much right to memory as the Jews, though she couldn't say she felt it, emotionally. There was something special about the Jewish people. About Jewish experience. At least that's what she'd always been taught. Perhaps that was all she retained of her religion – a vague sense of election. She wondered if Jaz, for all his passion about the tortured gurus, felt anything deeper.

So they kept putting off a decision. There were other things to think about. She agreed to the naming ceremony, hoping Jaz would compromise on the other thing. Her son Raj (not Seth or Conor) was prayed over in that awful gurdwara, that dingy room that smelled of hair oil and feet. The women scowled at her as the baby yelled, as if she were doing something wrong. Look at the white bitch, who obviously didn't know how to raise a child. After the ceremony she locked herself into a bathroom and refused to come out. Jaz tried to talk to her through the door, his voice strained. She made him swear that nothing like that would ever happen again, that he'd protect her from those women.

'You have to stand up for me, Jaz. You never stand up for me against your family.'

'I will, darling. I will, I promise.'

He swore. And now he was giving in again, to all their vile super-stitions, their primitive crap.

★

She paid the check and got back into the car, where she sat for a long time, watching customers walk in and out of the diner, having no thoughts about them, barely seeing them as people, just moving shapes. Cars sped along the highway, pulled in and out of the parking lot, disgorging more meaningless forms. Later she found herself driving through town, past plate-glass storefronts. Computer supplies. Weight Loss Club. She turned on to a side street, then another. Cracked concrete and chainlink fences. A collection of self-storage units fronted by desiccated palms. A community whose landmarks were laundromats and 7-Elevens, trailer parks for the unlucky and for the slightly luckier, subdivisions of low, mean-looking ranches, bunkers with double garages and dead brown lawns strewn with children's toys. There were yellow ribbons everywhere, schematic loops on bumper stickers, forlorn sun-bleached rags tied to streetlights and fence-posts. *Support Our Troops*. Win the war. On the side of a McDonald's was painted a mural of marines fighting in the desert, men in goggles and helmets shouting and pointing, surrounded by helicopters and burning oil wells. Two soldiers helped a wounded civilian, carrying him between them, his arms flung around their shoulders.

She got out of the car and stared, then remembered she had a camera in her purse. Broken glass crunched under her feet as she walked forward to fill the frame. It was the first picture she'd taken in months. She'd brought the camera as a sign to herself that she was on vacation. She wasn't sure why she wanted to remember this mural, or if she really did. A shiny black truck went past, blasting bass out of the open windows. The teenage driver stared at her from behind a pair of dark glasses, then blew a kiss. She was startled. How long was it since someone put the moves on her?

Her stomach was growling. It was lunchtime and all she'd had was coffee. She thought about going back to the motel. It would be the right thing to do. But, on the other hand, fuck it. Across the street was a Mexican place with a fake Mission bell-tower and a pizzeria offering a three ninety-five dinner special. *Yes, we're 'open'*, said a hand-lettered sign taped to the door. 'Open' was obviously not the same as open. Trash was blowing about in the parking lot. The windows were smeared with soap. She drove back toward the highway and found the UFO Diner, a cheesy theme restaurant that looked like it had seen better days, probably during the Nixon administration. The place was pretty full. She ordered Chicken Caesar, dressing on the side. She watched the teenage waitress wobbling about taking orders, the Latino busboy. Shapes. The salad arrived. She'd just started picking out the croutons when two women in head-to-toe Muslim tents, hijabs or whatever they were called, walked by the window. One was pushing a stroller, the other leading a small boy by the hand. Slouching along behind them was an older boy in jeans and T-shirt, carrying a skateboard. The effect was jarring, like a transmission from Baghdad.

She needed to pull herself together. What would her father say? *Suck it up, girl. Put your troubles in your pack and hump them on down the road.* But Poppy, I can't. *Can't? No such word, baby.* When they first got Raj's diagnosis, her parents had been amazing. She'd sobbed down the phone and her dad, who never knew what to say, had said exactly the right thing, which was nothing at all, just *there there, baby girl, there, my little one.* Whispering it down the line; *all better now, all better.* At least she'd be with him in a few days, would be able to crawl into his arms and smell his comforting smell, that den fug of pretzels and old magazines.

To fall for that evil-eye crap! To put that nasty little string on her boy!

When they found out about Raj's autism, Jaz had seemed completely floored. For weeks he barely spoke, just hung around, listlessly watching as she tried to cope with yet another tantrum, another screaming fit. His passivity made her so angry. Why couldn't he man up? She'd been raised not to give in to a challenge. Her poppy had taught her to fight. Of course they both felt guilty; try as she might, she couldn't rid herself of the suspicion that they'd done something wrong. What rule had she broken during the pregnancy? Used a cellphone? Eaten a tuna steak? A couple of times when they were with friends at a restaurant she'd drunk a glass of wine with her meal. Jaz had never raised an eyebrow, had even encouraged her. They'd made their decisions together. So why could she deal and he couldn't?

Nothing happened without a reason. No problem was without a solution. If her husband wasn't going to provide one, then it was down to her. She started browsing support forums, reading posts from mothers who sounded just as desperate as she was. She took notes, ordered books on Amazon. One night she found details of a conference for parents of autistic children and booked herself a ticket. She told Jaz she had to go and see a friend; he'd have to look after Raj by himself. He stared at her like she was insane.

She wasn't sure why she didn't want to let him know where she was going; he wouldn't have stopped her. She could tell it crossed his mind that she was going to see a lover, but neither of them had enough energy to sleep with each other, let alone anyone else, and he knew it. He'd hovered in the bedroom doorway as she packed, a stricken look on his face. Stop watching me, she snapped. You're coming back, he asked. Of course I am, she stuttered. Don't be ridiculous.

The conference was in Boston. On the train up she stared out of the window and fretted. There was a thunderstorm and she took a taxi to the convention center, which was jammed with people wearing stickers saying *Hi my name is*, dripping water on to the carpet tiles. She walked down aisles lined by little stalls, each manned by someone, usually a parent, passionately promoting magnesium injections, antifungal creams, biofeedback, craniosacral massage, hyperbaric oxygen, Chinese herbs, antibiotics, vitamin B-12 . . . There were blood tests, eye tests, tests on saliva and hair and urine and brain waves. Some of these treatments were plainly ludicrous, and she found it hard to make eye-contact with their proponents, scared she'd find her own need reflected back in strangers' faces. She collected leaflets and tried not to feel the energy that filled the hall, the shared yearning for a magic bullet, a royal touch to ward off evil.

That evening she attended a seminar where a doctor with a headset and the breezy manner of a late-night television host claimed that autism was caused by thimerosal, the mercury-based preservative in vaccines. The answer, apparently, was something called chelation therapy, drugs which would cleanse the heavy metals out of a child's blood. The doctor's own son had been autistic. After chelation, the boy had smiled. The doctor knew the other parents in the audience would understand how this had felt for him personally. For the first time his kid had smiled and looked his daddy in the eye! The doctor spread his arms wide. He looked elated, transfigured. Lisa bought a copy of his self-published book. On the train home the next day, she gave in to her excitement. Could this be the root of Raj's problem? She and Jaz had dutifully followed the vaccination schedule imposed by their physician – hepatitis, polio, meningitis, diphtheria, MMR . . . What if they'd poisoned their baby? What if they'd hurt him through their very eagerness to keep him safe?

When she told Jaz where she'd actually been, she burst into tears. He asked why she hadn't told him before and she sobbed on his shoulder, trying to describe the horrible neediness of the other parents. She knew instinctively from the limpness of his arm round her, the tightness in his voice, that something had changed between them. By going up to Boston she'd taken the initiative. From now on it would be up to her to decide what they'd do for Raj. The next day she took a urine sample and sent it off to a lab with a check for three hundred dollars. Two weeks later she received a letter confirming that Raj's mercury levels were slightly elevated. By that time Jaz had been doing some reading of his own, and objected that the link between mercury and autism wasn't proven. It was, he said in one of his infuriating scientist-phrases, 'highly contentious'. This led to a vicious row. Had he given up? Was he really too weak to fight for his son? He seemed to have no answer, and she triumphantly entered his credit-card number into a website to buy a course of chelating drugs, which arrived in a UPS box a few days later.

Raj hated the treatment. It smelled foul and made his pee sulfurous. But she persisted, forcing it down his throat, even when he struggled, and Jaz claimed she was being too violent. And it seemed to make a difference. Raj was calmer. His concentration was better. She phoned girlfriends to exult. Yes, that's right. He played with his blocks for fifteen minutes without getting distracted. We were in the park and he held my hand.

Jaz was compliant, but she began to resent his lack of enthusiasm for the struggle. One evening she confronted him and forced him to admit that he didn't see much change in Raj's behavior. Are you blind, she asked. Are you actually blind? He shrugged and held up his hands defensively. The pathetic little gesture made her so angry that she threw a lamp at him. It arced across the bedroom, smashing against the wall. His face took on a strange look, a mixture of fear and pity she'd never seen before. In a gentle voice he told her he thought she was taking on too much. She needed a rest. That was when she attacked him properly, kicking his shins, beating her fists against his head and chest until he gripped her wrists and forced her down on to the bed. They were both in tears. She could hear herself yelling how dare you, how dare you. *How dare you tell me I'm taking on too much when you won't even try?*

It became a battle of hope against measurement. Jaz thought she was being irrational, and rationality was everything to him, his way of trying to limit the chaos that had overtaken their life. She got that. She wasn't stupid. But really? *Measurable improvement. Objective criteria.* Such tone-deaf, boneheaded phrases. When he talked like that she wanted to tear down his pomposity like old ivy off a wall. There was something so smug and unimaginative, so *stupid*, about his assurance that there was no alternative to the medical establishment's current theories. After all, how many times had they been wrong? Once upon a time people had swallowed radium as a cure-all and thought women's wombs were damaged by train travel. Glumly, Jaz accepted all this was true, and even began to help when it was time to get Raj to take his meds, but it was not enough to win him more than a truce. She could tell he was getting involved not because he believed in the treatment, but because he wanted her to realize for herself it was wrong. Somehow this made things worse. It was as if he didn't want Raj to get better. The drugs *were* having an effect. She was clear on that. Then, as a month became two, then three, she felt less sure. The early signs of progress hadn't continued. Finally she admitted to herself that Raj was as withdrawn as ever. In some obscure way she blamed Jaz. He'd contaminated the treatment. If he'd believed, *really* believed, maybe it would have worked. She knew she sounded like Peter Pan, but she didn't give a damn.

One night Jaz came home to find her emptying the kitchen cabinets, throwing cans and packets into the trash. GFCF. Gluten-Free, Casein-Free. Jaz asked if she really thought autism was caused by not eating organic. She told him to stop patronizing her. If Raj had allergies, a change in diet would at least alleviate some of his gastric symptoms. Jaz sat down at the breakfast bar and held his head in his hands. 'Are you really going to put us all through this?' he asked. Never had she despised him so much. Was she really married to a coward, a man so spineless he wouldn't even fight for his own son?

So the family embarked on a wheat- and dairy-free diet. Already, seafood was banned on the grounds of mercury contamination. Jaz absolutely refused to countenance vegetarianism, claiming that without meat, he'd feel he'd lost his culture altogether. Lisa scoffed. Did he really feel so threatened? They'd already put off the decision to circumcise Raj because of his cultural sensitivities. She put sneering air-quotes round the phrase. He began to find excuses to eat out, with clients or people from the bank.

She started researching other remedies. Could injections of an intestinal hormone help Raj with his bowel problems? What about sessions in an oxygen chamber? Increasingly, the particular treatments were less important to her than a stance, a hopeful habit of mind. She read books about self-healing, positive visualization. Former colleagues would sneak proofs to her from the publisher where she used to work, which had an imprint dedicated to New Age thought.

Be in the moment. Walk the path that leads in the direction of your dreams. Instead of imagining the worst, bring to mind the best. Go about your daily business with a light heart and a mind full of love. You have to learn to let yourself fully experience the joy each one of us has present inside them. Once you can let your joy bubble up to the surface you are halfway toward a new kind of consciousness, one which will bring to you abundance, happiness and material wealth. If you can emanate positivity out into the Universe, it will be returned to you a thousand-fold, a transcendent light with the power to totally transform your existence.

She read these books in a semi-clandestine way, like an Eastern Bloc dissident poring over samizdat copies of Havel or Solzhenitsyn. She derived something vital from them, something fragile she could never share with Jaz. *Visualize what you want to happen. That's the first step toward making it come true.* Soon she'd abandoned her old reading altogether, the literary novels with bleak endings, the books about environmentalism or human rights. Those things felt like luxuries now, baubles for people who had no battles of their own. She wasn't sure she had enough hope for herself, let alone Somalis or street kids or Yanomami Indians.

The midday light poured through the windshield, harsh and white. How long had she been circling the backstreets of the little desert town? It could have been hours, days. Sooner or later she'd have to go back to the motel. It was all lurking in wait for her there. The monstrous trap of her life.

On the other hand, fuck it. She turned on to the highway heading out of town. Dutifully the buildings fell away, leaving her in a basin pocked with Joshua trees at the head of a ribbon of blacktop that led off toward a mountain range. There was little sign of human beings. A hand-painted sign, bleached almost white by the sun, saying FEAR GOD, a few trailers and cabins scattered across the desert floor like loose change. She drove on. Soon even these remnants of life disappeared. It was just her, piloting her little craft through the void.

She pulled over and opened the door. A blast of warm air hit her as she stood up, shielding her eyes from the glare. Above her the blue shaded into purples and blacks, the colors of space. The atmosphere was thin, tenuous. She switched off the engine, but something in the car, the air conditioning or some cooling fan, kept running, a whirring sound like a long slow exhalation of breath. Finally it cut out and there was silence. She took a few steps into the desert. Plastic scraps in the scrub at the roadside. The tracks of some small mammal, a rabbit or a rodent. A few more steps. A few more. Now the car was a long way off, a white gleam in the distance. Up ahead, perhaps a mile or two away, was a peculiar rock formation, three stone towers like fingers pointing up into space. If I were to lie down here, she thought, I would die. I would step out of my body like a dress and float straight up into the blue.

1920

The man was Deighton, but the People called him Skin-Peeled-Open, on account of his burned face. No one could say why the other white men hated him so. He had money: he paid for stories with new-minted silver dollars. He even had an automobile. Perhaps it was because he was sick. On the nights he slept in the camp you could hear him coughing. Once Stone Apron couldn't sleep for the noise of it and got up to fix him rabbit-bush tea. Didn't help. He sounded like he was going to die.

He was a tall and ragged kind of a man, with an oil-stained coat and a week's growth of whiskers making his face lopsided, for they grew only on one half of his jaw, the half not smeared with smooth pink scar tissue. When he first came the young boys threw stones, then ran to hide down by the water. The men who turned out to drive him away were amazed to hear him speak. He told how he'd stayed at a camp on the far side of the Colorado and People there had taught him Language. His accent was strange and many times he used women's words or mistook one thing for another, but finding a white who could speak at all was a wonder. Two-Headed Sheep was another name for him. Freak of nature.

What did he want? He asked after old ones. Who was the wisest? Who knew the songs and could tell him the names of plants? The People were suspicious, but he was persistent and showed money, so they took him first to Thorn Baby, who was strong in English and could remember when mule deer still ran in large herds on the land. The man said Thorn Baby had too much white schooling and that was when they decided he was crazy, the kind of white who would always be trying to turn his own whiteness upside down. They wanted him to leave then, but he kept hanging around and somehow they got used to him. He gave presents to the children and said good day in his comical accent and finally they suggested he talk to Segunda, who loved to gossip so much the young men called her Empty Clay Olla, the kind that makes a hollow noise when you rap it with your fingers. She knew that was her name. They thought she was just a deaf old woman, but she knew. The crazy white man visited her and seemed happy afterwards. Everyone agreed: the two of them fitted, like a joint in a socket.

Soon a routine was established. Skin-Peeled-Open would drive to the camp and spend whole days watching Segunda weave baskets, listening to her talk about the time when the animals were men. He would listen and write in his book, which made some of the People nervous, reminding them as it did of the magic worked in courts and land offices, the kind that always fell out one way.

She grew comfortable in his company. They'd sit together under her ramada, looking out at the stand of palms by the waterhole, she cross-legged on a mat, he on the little folding stool he brought with him in a footlocker, along with his bedroll and the cans of corned beef that were a sore temptation to mouths bored with yucca and mesquite meal. The man pretended not to notice when food disappeared from his trunk. He could easily have put a padlock on it, if he'd wanted.

He complimented Segunda on her baskets. Who had taught her to weave? What materials did she use? How many different styles did she know? He watched her cut willow and grind yucca root and devil's claw into dyes. He made her feel proud of her baskets – most people had no use for them now they could buy basins and pails from the general store – so she let him follow her to the ditch to watch how she soaked the yucca fiber in guano. Above all he wanted to know if there were any old stories about basket-weaving. Of course there were, and when she got tired of his pestering, she told them. She told of the basket that Ocean Woman used to scoop up the sun, and the basket Coyote used to bring the People back from the west, carrying it on his back like a water-spider with its sac of eggs. She told other stories, such as the one about the time Dog and Coyote went their separate ways, Dog to the camp and Coyote to walk around. She told about the time when Coyote and his brother Wolf lived on Snow-Having and hunted bighorn sheep.

Then came a day when he wanted her to say disgusting words. She was upset and would not speak to him. After that she began to pick up her basketry and hide when she heard the sound of his machine coming toward the camp. She complained about it to her nephew. Little Bird sat the man down and explained, very slowly, as you would to a child, that it was forbidden to speak the names of the dead. The man took out his little book. Interesting, he said. So does the name die with the person? His speech made no kind of sense. If a name had died, there'd be no need to forbid people to use it.

Little Bird told him he wasn't welcome anymore. The man didn't understand. Little Bird just couldn't get him to see, not after he'd written so much down in his book. That was typical of them. He even asked to speak to Segunda. Little Bird blushed, and pretended not to know such a person.

Then the man did a strange thing. He sent his woman. She was young and pretty, which made the People laugh because he was such a stringy old thing. Under her big straw hat, her face was as white as salt. With her dusty skirts and her patched shirtwaist she cut a sorry sight. She had no jewelry, not so much as a string of beads, and when she sat down on the earth you could see the holes in her shoes. Then the People knew she was not rich, though the man Deighton drove an automobile. They said to each other: there must be trouble between them.

Salt-Face Woman tried to talk, but no one could understand. Then she spoke English to Thorn Baby and Charcoal Standing and those two told the People that her husband had sent her to the camp to be his mouth and ears. The other women felt sorry for her. They helped her build a shelter; Skin-Peeled-Open had already left and gone back to town.

One evening she came and sat down beside Segunda at the fire. Thorn Baby was embarrassed at having to repeat her words in Language. She was talking about dust. She was asking for the names of the dead. Segunda covered her ears. She was afraid. These people had death all over them. They were covered in death, like a hide. Segunda ran away. Thorn Baby came to find her in the arroyo to say that the woman had promised not to bother her again.

Salt-Face Woman stayed for a long time. After a while it seemed like she accepted the way of things. She was certainly a quicker study than her husband. Her voice grew louder. Segunda could understand some of what she said. But she made her afraid. Segunda didn't want to talk anymore. Salt-Face Woman had struck her dumb. Everyone remarked on it. Empty Clay Olla not talking? What could be the matter?

When a person is dead, it is right for them to go into silence. You should never call them back. Trouble for them and trouble for you. It was possible the woman wasn't human. She could have been wearing someone's skin.

Then into camp came Mockingbird Runner, who'd been away working as a hand for one of the cattlemen. Ever since the time when the whites fought their war for the waterholes, they'd hired People to watch over certain places. Mockingbird Runner carried a rifle and wore fancy boots, but he was also an owner of the Bighorn Sheep Song and People said he got his name because he knew how to run in the old way. His grandfather was a famous doctor who had a bat familiar that protected him from the cold. Though he was young, Mockingbird Runner had power. When he heard about Salt-Face Woman he went to take a look at her. The next thing Segunda knew, they were sitting together under a ramada and the little thing was writing in her book.

Segunda sidled closer, to listen to what they were saying. Mockingbird Runner was telling her a story of the time when Coyote was living with his brother Wolf at Snow-Having. They went to war with the Bear People and Wolf was killed. The Bear People took his scalp and Coyote snuck into the camp with his penis, the two of them disguised in the skins of old Bear women who'd been out gathering mesquite branches for the fire.

Mockingbird Runner was telling this story and the woman was

writing it down. Of course he didn't use the word *penis*. He called it
Coyote's *tail*.

Willie Prince, said the woman. That is only your English name.

Soon after that the man Deighton came back and took his woman
away. Segunda felt happy, but all the same she talked to Little Bird
about moving to another camp. There were many places they could
go. People were down in Imperial Valley, and on the riverbank up
near Adobe-Hanging-Like-Tears. There would be trouble at Kairo,
she was sure. The snakes were listening. They should go somewhere else. Little Bird had work driving mules at one of the silver
mines in the mountains. He had to go back to that place. He said
she could go to another camp if she liked. He would follow her
later. But she was an old woman. It was hard to bestir herself to
make a long journey on her own.

Then Deighton brought his wife back again. He left her with a
box of canned food and drove away. Before he left, he raised his
voice to her, saying she was wasteful and a poor worker. Salt-Face
Woman hid in her shelter, where she thought no one would see her
cry. That evening Mockingbird Runner sat beside her, telling her
words. The names of animals and rocks and stars. The types of
rain. Rain that slashes at the skin. Spring rain, as fine as palmita
seeds.

Willie Prince, said the woman. That is only your English name.
What is your real name?

Segunda had warned Mockingbird Runner about such questions.
He laughed and told her she was a foolish old clay olla, with a few
grains rattling around inside. That one was reckless. He didn't care
if the snakes were awake. He didn't care about telling stories to a
spirit. Segunda saw him show Salt-Face Woman the scars on his
back from the Mission school. She heard him sing one of the songs
they taught him there. When the woman asked a third time,
Mockingbird Runner told her his true name.

Who would leave a wife alone in a strange camp? It was obvious
to Segunda the man Deighton didn't care for Salt-Face Woman at
all. Everyone said so. That was why she cried so much. At night it

was cold. She had only a thin blanket. Segunda saw Mockingbird Runner bring her a quilt. She saw them talking in the firelight. She saw Mockingbird Runner lay down beside her.

I shall explain to her about death, said Mockingbird Runner, as he washed himself in the water the next morning. There is no need, Segunda told him. These people know more about it than you or I. But he would not listen. It was what Salt-Face Woman wanted to know, he said. He wanted to make her happy.

That afternoon the two lovers climbed the rocks together. Though it was years since Segunda had walked so far, let alone scrambled over boulders or up narrow paths, she followed them. She saw them sit down together in a sheltered spot. She saw Salt-Face Woman open up her little book. Segunda crept closer and strained to overhear. It was as she feared. Mockingbird Runner was telling the story of the time Coyote traveled to the Land of the Dead.

Coyote was wandering around, aimlessly as usual. He was feeling sad that so many of his companions had been killed in the war against Gila Monster.

'Haikya! I am lonely. There is no one to help me carry the game I kill-aikya! Where are my friends, the friends with whom I used to play the hand game and sing by the fire? Gila Monster and his people have killed them all.'

He asked his penis, who knew many more things than he. 'Penis,' he said, 'what shall I do-aikya! Once I had companions to help me dance the old dances, but Gila Monster and his people have killed them all-aikya!'

His penis thought for a while. 'If you want to see your friends, you must travel to the Three-Finger Rocks and look inside the cave beneath them. There you will find Yucca Woman, weaving a basket. She is blind and will not know what you are doing, just so long as you are quiet. Cling to a strand of devil's claw and hold on tight, because she is weaving together this world and the Land of the Dead. At the moment when she holds the willow wands open, there is a gap between the two worlds. You can crawl into the Land of the

Dead. But, whatever you do, never let go of the devil's claw strand. If you do you will be trapped.'

So Coyote traveled over the mountains and across the white sands and came at last to the Three-Finger Rocks. Sure enough, in the cave beneath he found old blind Yucca Woman, weaving her basket.

'Who is there?' asked Yucca Woman. 'Nobody is there-aikya!' said Coyote. 'Just an old dust devil, the kind the children beat with sticks.' And Yucca Woman went back to her basket-weaving.

Coyote made himself very small and flattened his belly against a strand of devil's claw, clinging tightly as Yucca Woman's nimble fingers threaded the weft through the willow wands. As soon as the strand passed beneath the willow, Coyote found himself in twilight. It was cold and gray. He looked across the land and saw many dim green lights, the glowing campfires of the dead. He squinted into the darkness. Finally he recognized the faces of his companions, the young warriors killed in the war against Gila Monster. He called out to them. 'Haikya! Hello, my brothers! How good to see you! Are you happy here-aikya? Do you have enough to eat?' His friends replied, but being dead their voices were very faint and hard to hear. Just then, the nimble fingers of Yucca Woman passed the devil's claw strand back through the willow wands and once again Coyote found himself in this world.

He felt frustrated, but remembered the wise words of his penis. A second time Yucca Woman passed the devil's claw thread beneath the willow and a second time Coyote clung on tight and passed into the Land of the Dead. Once again he saw his companions sitting around the pale campfires. Once again he called out. This time they beckoned to him, showing him they had made a place for him beside the fire. Still he couldn't hear their words. When he passed into the Land of the Dead a third time he couldn't resist and let go of the strand. He dropped to the ground and went to sit by the fire with his companions. 'Old friends, it is good to see you-aikya! Tell me the news. What game do you hunt down here in the Land of the Dead? Do you still wrestle and throw sticks to pierce the hoop?' His friends said nothing.

'Coyote!' said his penis. 'You have been very foolish! Look what you've done!' Coyote squinted up through the gloom and saw a young warrior climbing on to the devil's claw strand. 'Goodbye, Coyote!' shouted the warrior. 'Goodbye and thank you. You have saved me from the Land of the Dead. I've been here ever since I was speared in the war against Gila Monster. Now I shall go back and feel the sun on my face, and run and hunt and lay down with a woman.' Coyote shook his fist. 'Haikya! You tricked me-aikya! I'm sorry I ever came down here.' He wept and wailed as he thought about how he had been tricked. 'What a fool was I, to let go of the strand of devil's claw. Now I will have to wait here in this gloomy spot, until I can fool another person into taking my place.'

Segunda listened to this story and knew that, for all his power, Mockingbird Runner had fallen into a trap. She lay in the cover of bush and watched the lovers take off their clothes. She saw his red body next to her white body, and she knew there would be a baby, and it would be Coyote's baby, belonging half to this world and half to the Land of the Dead.

2008

'I suppose,' said Jaz, 'we'd better wait for Mommy.' Raj was standing at the foot of the lounger, staring at the sky and humming in a high-pitched wavering tone, usually a sign he was hungry. Jaz tousled his hair. Raj took a step back, out of range.

'Oh, to hell with it. I could use something to eat too.'

He fixed a lunch of tuna fish and rye crackers. They ate together by the pool. Raj stood, clutching his food in a hot little fist. Daddy perched glumly on a folding chair. Raj drank apple juice. Daddy had a beer. Daddy had another beer. He crushed red Tecate cans under the sole of his flip-flop and threw them at the painted metal bucket that served as a trash can. What the hell was Lisa playing at? She'd made her point. He was more than ready to apologize. If he admitted his faults, then maybe they could all go look at scenery or something. She was the one who'd wanted to take a trip out to this godforsaken place. And until she came back with the car, he and Raj were stuck at the motel.

An hour went by. He coaxed Raj into the pool and held him while he splashed, feeling his wriggling body twisting about in his arms, a little seal cub, a porpoise. Afterwards he smeared more sunscreen on the boy's torso and tried to persuade him to wear the floppy-brimmed hat Lisa had picked up at a Wal-Mart on the way out of LA. Raj didn't want to know about the hat. Even tying the strap under his chin didn't work; his fingers deftly picked open the knot as soon as Jaz's back was turned.

The more he thought about Lisa, the more the print on his paperback novel swam in front of his eyes. *You people.* Well, sometimes she *was* you people. A piece of string, for God's sake. That's all it was.

Another hour passed. Jaz took Raj's hand and went out to look at the road, in the magical hope that this would conjure his wife and their rental car out of the shimmering blacktop. The air had a pink haze. He considered walking down the hill into town. How long would it take? An hour? With the boy?

He always defaulted to work when stressed or angry. The sun was low and he was failing to concentrate on a pile of reports when his cellphone started to vibrate in his pocket, playing a trebly polyphonic 'Ride of the Valkyries'. Not Lisa. The ringtone was his bad-taste private joke on Fenton Willis, a man it was probably risky to make jokes about, even if he wasn't your employer.

'Mr Willis.'

'Jaswinder.' The firm's CEO was the only person in Jaz's life other than his parents who insisted on using his full name. He pronounced it *jass-whine-dur*, a mangled sequence of syllables he emitted with such ponderous formality that Jaz sometimes felt like the object of a hearts and minds campaign. *Step one: look him in the eye and address him using correct honorific. Step two: tell him why you regret calling in the airstrike on his village . . .* Watercooler gossip had it that in Vietnam Willis's job had been to clear Viet Cong tunnels, crawling along in the dark with a flashlight and a .38. Sometimes, on the subway or waiting in line for a coffee, Jaz found himself wondering how many of the men around him had done such things. Which of the guys strap-hanging on the F-train had been to war? Which of them, with their copies of the *Post* and their laptop cases, had tortured or killed?

'So, how's the desert?'

'It's just great, Mr Willis. We're all having a great time.'

'Glad to hear it. I stayed in a neat little place round there. Working cattle ranch. Help with the round-up, rope a steer, that kind of thing. I could get Linda to send you the details. Great place. You spend a night on the range. Eat beans out of a mess tin, Indian feller tells ghost stories. Mesquite fire, the whole nine yards.'

'Sounds awesome, sir. But maybe next time. Our itinerary's kind of set.'

'I see. Look, son, I wouldn't bother you on your vacation, but I had lunch with Cy Bachman yesterday, and he seems to think you aren't happy.'

'I wouldn't put it like that, exactly.'

'Well, how would you put it?'

'I think we're working well together. And Cy's a talented guy. No doubt about it.'

'But?'

'I think there's too much exposure. If it goes wrong there could be consequences.'

'That goes without saying. We've got a lot of chips on the table.'

'Not just losses for the firm. Systemic consequences.'

'You'll have to unpack that for me.'

'I just think we haven't thought through the logic of what we're doing with Walter.'

'Cy says you're risk-averse. He says you pitched him some kind of candy-assed moral argument, told him you thought taking highly leveraged positions based on his model was against your conscience.'

'That wasn't what I said.'

'So what did you say? If you think the model's no good, then you need to stand up and say so. I'm not paying you to spot problems and keep them to yourself.'

'Well, I –'

'And you need to tell me what in hell's name your conscience has to do with the price of rice.'

This was not a conversation Jaz wanted to have, not today. Preferably not ever, but particularly not today. He thought of asking Willis whether he could call him back, but that wasn't really an option. If right now was when Fenton wanted to talk about Cy Bachman and the Walter model and all the rest of the shit Jaz had hoped to keep in a holding pattern over the fan for another few days, then right now it would have to be. It was obvious what Bachman had been saying. Their relationship had never been straightforward, and now – after their argument – he wanted Jaz off the team. Fenton was doing him a courtesy, allowing him to defend himself, but it was probably a *fait accompli*. He assumed his security pass had been deactivated. They were probably boxing up his personal effects for the courier.

This had been coming for a while.

He'd first set eyes on Cy Bachman two years previously, over lunch at a steakhouse in the Financial District, the kind of place Willis favored for meetings, where you could eat eighty-five-dollar Wagyū burgers and wash them down with bottles of Opus One. Bachman turned out to be vegetarian, a fact Willis evidently knew and had ignored when making the booking. While the CEO told a boring story about a horse he was thinking of buying from a stable in Saratoga, Jaz had watched an elegant, fiftyish, shaven-headed man shoot his French cuffs and tackle an enormous bowl of arugula, whose size appeared to be the kitchen's consolation for the meal's total absence of protein. It occurred to him the salad was a joke – the place was known for the 'no rabbit food' motto emblazoned on its creamy letterpress menu. Bachman affected neither to notice nor to care.

When Willis finished the horse story, Bachman smiled at Jaz and complimented him on a paper he'd co-authored at MIT, outlining a simplified statistical technique for describing the behavior of certain assemblies of particles. Jaz was disarmed, but at the same time wary. Bachman had a reputation as one of the most talented financial engineers on Wall Street; it was an open secret that Willis had poached him from one of the big banks to head a new research team. He assumed the lunch was because Willis wanted him to work under Bachman. The comment was his new boss's way of letting him know he had prepared. Later he'd discover that this care and meticulousness was carried through to every aspect of Bachman's life, from his fastidiously stylish dress to his almost neurotic concern for the visual presentation of data. A trailing zero could drive him into a rage. He insisted his team was 'properly attired' even if all they were doing was writing code.

Willis seemed untouched by Bachman's aura, his WASP sense of entitlement and large personal fortune providing an effective shield against intellect. 'Enjoying your meal, Cy?' he chortled.

Bachman made a face. 'This is revenge,' he explained. 'I took him to a raw-food place in the Village.'

'Bastards made me a coffee out of pistachio nuts.'

Jaz laughed heartily. He knew better than to be fooled by Fenton's bluff manner. Behind the genial clubman's mask, the oak-paneled three-martini smokescreen he put up to fool the credulous, a ruthless tactician lurked. When it came to the acquisition of money, he was entirely pragmatic, prepared to act without prejudice or sentiment. In this respect, he was quite brilliant. Jaz couldn't help but connect this ability to suspend judgement, to take each new situation entirely on its own merits, with the image of a man crawling down a tunnel with a gun in his hand, feeling his way in the dark.

'So Jaswinder. Cy's taken a look at your work and he thinks he could use you on Walter.'

'Walter?'

'It's a new global quant model.'

'Goddamn theory of everything, isn't that right, Cy?'

'If you say so, Fenton. Everything would be kind of a large data-set.'

Jaz was intrigued. 'What stage are you at?'

'Personally,' interrupted Willis, 'I think it's just great already. If it was up to me I'd go live right now, start counting my winnings. But Cy says the bastard's got a half-life of about twenty seconds, and if we go off all premature we'll blow the chance of a bigger payday down the line.'

'But it *is* down to you, Fenton. Just say the word.'

'Cy. If you tell me I can have a dollar today or three tomorrow, I'll take the three bucks. Deferred gratification – it's what separates civilized man from chimps and children. We're getting OK returns on the established models, so I'm happy to wait. Just as long as Renaissance or those bastards at Goldman don't get there before us.'

'Fenton, I'd be very surprised if they had any interest in this strategy.'

'Well, I wouldn't. Probably bugging the damn table decorations in this joint, paying off the sommelier. Speaking of which, let's get another bottle.'

When Jaz presented himself at Bachman's office the following day, he expected to be shown some kind of formula. The Walter set-up was very cloak-and-dagger, a separate address, pin codes and biometrics to get through the door. Bachman had a view of the Hudson and a display case full of curios behind his desk that Jaz avoided scrutinizing too closely, in case it led to a conversation about basketry or ceramics or netsuke, topics which would quickly lead him out of his comfort zone. Luckily Bachman got straight to business. He told him the best way to understand the model was to work with it, which seemed sensible enough. When Jaz asked about its basic principles, he waved the question away.

Bachman's model was conventional in that it relied on discovering certain predictable behaviors in the market – regularities, trackable cycles – and using that knowledge to trade. But, as far as Jaz could grasp from the initial presentation, which took almost three hours and left him feeling like he'd been sparring with some kind of higher-dimensional gorilla, the type of regularities Walter sought were particularly fleeting and unstable. The model was being trained not simply to exploit some temporary price disparity, but to identify and track entirely ad hoc constellations of five, six, seven variables, brief but dazzling phenomena, lightning flashes of cor-relation. The math, Jaz thought, was some of the most beautiful he'd ever encountered. The problem that would come to tug at him like an importunate child was something else. Something about Walter's responsiveness, its voracious thirst for data. It was more like an organism than a computer program. It felt *alive*.

For the first few months he had little to do with Walter's guts, the software that identified patterns and executed trades. His job was to take certain datasets and hunt for statistical relationships, what Bachman called 'rhymes'. The material (prepared according to some arcane process Bachman refused to discuss) came in discrete clusters, little clots of seemingly unrelated numbers. Some of it was familiar: commodity and share prices, government bond yields, interest rates, currency fluctuations. But there was other data: on shopping-mall construction, retail-sales figures, drug-patent applications, car ownership; on the incidence of birth defects, industrial injuries, suicides, controlled-substance seizures, cellphone-tower construction. Walter consumed the most esoteric numbers: small-arms sales in the Horn of Africa, the population of Gary, Indiana, between 1940 and 2008, the population of Magnitogorsk, Siberia, for the same years, prostitution arrests in major American cities, data traffic over the TPE trans-Pacific cable, the height of the water table in various subregions of the Maghreb.

Some of the data was so bizarre that Jaz couldn't help but feel Willis's quip about a theory of everything was close to the mark. It was as if Bachman were trying to fit the whole world into his model. What was external to Walter? Was there anything it *didn't* aim to comprehend? When Jaz tried, hesitantly, to frame this question, Cy launched into a convoluted monologue, at the end of which things were no clearer than before. Walter, he said, pacing his office like a prisoner exercising in his cell, didn't rely on the opposition between external and internal. It wasn't some tin-toy simplification of the world, which chose a few variables and ignored the rest. Conversely, it didn't need to know the state of 'everything' at some initial time t in order to find the patterns it sought. Walter worked in a different way. 'It's like plunging your hands into a river,' he said, 'and pulling out a fish.'

Despite Jaz's skepticism, he soon had to admit that there *were* rhymes, and they existed in the weirdest places. One day he found a periodic cycle in a cluster of figures for CPU transistor counts since 1960, IQ test scores for African American boys from single-parent families and an epidemiological analysis of the spread of the methamphetamine drug ya-ba through Thailand and South-East Asia. Not only was there a strange harmony to the movements of this grab-bag of statistics, but it seemed to track a certain popular measure of volatility in currency markets. He checked and rechecked the figures. He hadn't miscalculated. Filled with an odd sense of foreboding, he presented his findings to Bachman, who nodded appreciatively.

'Perfect,' he said. 'I told Fenton you had the knack for this. I wasn't wrong.'

Jaz spoke carefully, not sure where his words would lead him. 'I'm not sure I understand, Cy. Surely this is meaningless coincidence. There's no link between any of these things.'

Bachman's hands fluttered to his neck, checking the perfect Windsor knot of his tie. He swiveled his chair toward the window and looked out at the river, a dull gray band between the sleek black faces of the towers. It was early February and rain was smeared against the glass, the outside world a barely recognizable blur.

'Get your coat. I want to show you something.'

They took Bachman's car uptown through heavy lunch-hour traffic. Bachman fiddled with his cufflinks, idly leafing through a stack of reports. Jaz sent texts, half aware of the rubber-booted pedestrians swarming the crosswalks, wrestling their umbrellas into the wind. It was a bad day to be selling gyros or hailing a cab. Trucks plowed furrows through the curbside puddles, sending waves of dirty water arcing into the air. Office-workers scurried for cover; die-hard smokers jostled for position in sheltered doorways. Any heavier and there'd be kayaks, people clinging to floating wreckage.

The driver let them out at a townhouse in the east eighties, facing the park. A discreet plaque announced the place as the Neue Galerie, a museum Lisa had talked about, but Jaz had never been inside. Bachman appeared to be known to the staff; the security guard greeted him by name as he waved them in. They climbed the stairs and entered a room hung with paintings. Bachman steered him past a flashy Klimt, ringed by tourists, toward a vitrine containing various small decorative objects, clocks, glassware and jewelry. Like a waiter gesturing at a particularly good corner table, he extended his hand toward a silver coffee set, sleek and plain and scientific-looking, pots and jugs with big geometric handles and rows of studs around their bases, arranged on a little tray, complete with a set of tongs and a spirit burner to keep the coffee warm.

'Do you enjoy the Wiener Werkstätte?'

Jaz would probably have used the word 'deco' to describe the things in the case. Bachman frowned, picking up on his discomfort. 'I'm sorry. I didn't bring you here to lecture you about art history. This was made in Vienna just before World War One by a man called Hoffmann. A very brilliant man, an architect and furniture designer, founded a sort of Viennese Arts and Crafts movement. I don't know why I find it so moving. It's such an unserious thing. What a lot of effort and skill to lavish on something as ordinary as making coffee! And when you think about when it was made . . .'

He trailed off, staring gloomily into the case. After a moment he shook his head in the abrupt manner of a sleeper trying to wake himself up. Jaz realized he knew precisely nothing about Cy Bachman, about how he thought, the things he loved. He had a sudden image of a man for whom the present day was no more than a thin crust of ice over a deep cold lake. Disturbed, he turned around, pretending to examine a painting on the wall behind him. Bachman touched his arm, gently repositioning him in front of Hoffmann's coffee set. He spoke under his breath, as though imparting a secret.

'When I come here, I always find myself wondering what happened to the people who owned this. I feel they must have been Jews. Wealthy Viennese Jews. How long did they survive? First their country vanishes. Then the Anschluss, the deportations. How many years could the family maintain a life that included such luxuries?'

He sighed deeply. Jaz wondered if he expected a reply.

'Have you ever been to Vienna, Jaz?'

'No. I haven't.'

'It's a very unsettling city. At least I find it so. The main cemetery is vast. They say it has a larger population of the dead than the city has living. All very well kept, very neat, until you come to the Jewish section, which has been completely neglected. There's no one left, you see. No relatives, no descendants, to tend the graves. All those families, with their possessions and their big houses and their servants and their *taste*, all vanished. Ashes floating out of a crematorium chimney.'

He went on, speaking urgently now, gripping Jaz's arm with one hand and describing little arcs and circles with the other, like a concert-goer following a score.

'As with most art, this is an attempt to stand outside time. That's perhaps its most luxurious quality – one could even say a sign of decadence. What a moment to deny history! When it was about to trample over everything, not just the ritual of coffee and cake, but everything! The whole culture! There's a tradition that says the world has shattered, that what once was whole and beautiful is now just scattered fragments. Much is irreparable, but a few of these fragments contain faint traces of the former state of things, and if you find them and uncover the sparks hidden inside, perhaps at last you'll piece together the fallen world. This is just a glass case of wreckage. But it has presence. It's redemptive. It is part of something larger than itself.'

'I see.'

'No, I don't think you do. Not yet. What if one were to want to hunt for these hidden presences? You can't just rummage about like you're at a yard sale. You have to listen. You have to pay attention. There are certain things you can't look at directly. You need to trick them into revealing themselves. That's what we're doing with Walter, Jaz. We're juxtaposing things, listening for echoes. It's not some silly cybernetic dream of command and control, modeling the whole world so you can predict the outcome. It's certainly not a theory of everything. I don't have a theory of any kind. What I have is far more profound.'

'What's that?'

'A sense of humor.'

Jaz looked at him, trying to find a clue in his gaunt face, in the clear gray eyes watching him with such – what? Amusement? Condescension? There was something about the man which brought on a sort of hermeneutic despair. He was a forest of signs.

'We're hunting for jokes.' Bachman spoke slowly, as if to a child. 'Parapraxes. Cosmic slips of the tongue. They're the key to the locked door. They'll help us discover it.'

'Discover what?'

'The face of God. What else would we be looking for?'

Perched on the lounger, pushing one of Raj's plastic toys around with his toe, Jaz tried to form sentences for Fenton Willis, trying to explain why he'd come to be afraid of Cy Bachman and the face of God. 'It's not a question of conscience, Fenton. I know you have no time for that – and of course neither does – well, yes, I am kind of going on my gut. No, Walter's robust. I'm not disputing that. It's a very powerful model.'

That was the problem: Walter's power. The power to affect the things it observed, to alter the course of events with its predictions.

It seemed impossible. After the visit to the Neue Galerie, Jaz started to suspect Bachman was a crank. He'd call Jaz into his office and initiate esoteric and largely one-sided discussions of recursivity, non-computability, the limits of mathematical knowledge. At times he was openly mystical, wanting to discuss the Fibonacci sequence, Kondratiev waves, predestination. He'd make gnomic pronounce-ments (*when price meets time, change is imminent*) and read aloud from books which appeared to have nothing to do with finance: the Bhagavad Gita, the Tao Te Ching. For a man who worked with computers he had a strong taste for pen and paper. His desk was frequently covered with hand-drawn charts, often hexagons, plotted with tiny numerals. Once he showed Jaz a graph plotting the Dow Jones Industrial Average against phases of Saturn, claiming that he was 'tinkering' with the idea that all significant cycles in stocks and commodities were either multiples or harmonics of something called the Jupiter–Saturn cycle. Occasionally he'd mention his house in Montauk, imagining his retirement there, or proposing to sell it and buy somewhere in Europe, possibly Berlin. 'I think that's the only place I could truly understand the past,' he said once. 'But what about the future? Is the future even possible there? Maybe Mumbai or Beijing?'

Why he chose him as his interlocutor, Jaz couldn't tell. There were surely other people in the firm better able to follow the fork-ing paths of his conversation. Sometimes he seemed manic, staring out of his window at the forest of lighted bank-tower windows like a cartoon supervillain in his mountain hideaway. At other times he could be despondent, slumped in his chair, muttering about the world being a hall of mirrors, a puzzle with no solution. Once Jaz found him at the window with his arms outspread, a silk-suited *Cristo Redentor* blessing Broad Street.

'Why do you do this work, Jaz? Strange I've never asked you before.'

'No mystery. I have a wife, a son. I want to give them a good life.'

'Is that all?'

'And of course because it's interesting.'

'Oh, come on, that's one of your dishwater words. A map of Brooklyn is *interesting*. A documentary on penguins is *interesting*. Not a life. Interesting isn't the reason you get up in the morning. Tell me, do you believe in God?'

'No, I don't think so.'

'You don't think so?' He paused. 'I see. Well, aren't you going to ask me the same thing?'

'OK. Do you believe in God?'

'*Interesting* you should ask, Jaz. I think the real question is whether God believes in me.'

He began to laugh, a shrill ascending scale. Jaz was irritated. Raj had kept him awake much of the night, and the previous day the latest in their long series of nannies had quit. He had no patience to spare for Bachman's metaphysical jokes.

'Look, Cy. You want to know why I'm doing this? Because with luck it'll make Fenton a lot of money, and he'll give some of it to me. Perhaps you're right. Perhaps Walter is profound, but you know what? I don't care. I just want to build a trading model, I don't need to save the world.'

Bachman sat down at his desk. For a long time he was completely silent, rocking slightly from side to side on his chair, steepling his long fingers.

'I'm sorry, Cy. I'm sleep-deprived. My son – I didn't mean to be rude.'

'Next month we're going to go live with Walter. Small volumes initially, but if it works as it's been doing in testing, we'll soon step up.'

'OK. Right.'

'That'll be all.'

Jaz left feeling angry. Why couldn't he have kept his mouth shut? That night he tried to explain to Lisa what had happened. Having never met Bachman, she'd formed a romantic picture of him as some kind of unworldly scholar, toiling away in his office like a medieval alchemist. Jaz would remind her of the custom-tailored suits, the handmade shoes, but she couldn't shake the image of a banker who wasn't primarily motivated by money.

'Did you really shout at him?' she asked.

'I told him I wasn't interested in his theories.'

'Oh, Jaz, why? He sounds like the most interesting guy in the place.'

'Interesting? Christ.'

'Are you going to get fired?'

'I don't think so. Maybe he'll just find someone else to rant at when he's bored. I'm not sure he's got any kind of home life. There's no wife, no kids. It's possible all he does is think up new ways to look for God in unemployment figures.'

Bachman didn't fire him. The stream of data continued. Gas volumes pumped through the BTC and Druzhba pipelines, racial assaults in Australia, coltan mining yields in the DRC free-zones, incidence of Marburg hemorraghic fever in those same zones, hourly volume of technology stocks traded on the Nikkei . . . Jaz was no longer analyzing these clusters himself, just feeding them into Walter, which was unearthing connections at an alarming rate. Everything seemed to be linked to everything else: the net worth of retirees in Boca Raton, Florida, oscillating in harmony with the volume of cargo arriving at the port of Long Beach, South-western home repossessions tracking the number of avatars in the most popular online gameworlds in Asia. At first Jaz had wondered whether the model was a hoax, something that existed only in Cy

Bachman's imagination. Now he found himself disturbed by its power. What would happen when they started trading? Like dipping your hands into a river and pulling out a fish, Bachman said. What ripples would Walter create?

Almost in passing, Bachman told him that he was already preparing for what he termed Walter 2. The firm had paid to install equipment inside the New York Stock Exchange, a necessity for high-frequency trading, in which a few milliseconds' lag could destroy competitive advantage. In what seemed to be a gesture of reconciliation, Bachman invited him to watch the technicians connecting their system at a high-security data center in New Jersey, which also housed the NYSE matching engines, the computers which sorted through bids and offers to complete trades. The wind-blown site was on a bleak industrial park two hours outside the city, a low shed whose anonymous construction was designed to prevent its becoming a target for terrorist attack. As the limo waited in the parking lot, they walked between racks of humming machines, accompanied by a nervous NYSE employee who would evidently have much preferred it if Bachman didn't run his fingers caressingly across the hardware as he passed, like a small boy trailing a stick along a fence.

He asked Jaz to imagine a Walter whose time horizons were in the order of milliseconds. A pattern could be identified on the first cycle, matched with others on the second or third, used to trade on the fourth and then would vanish back into entropy. The speed of light itself, the ultimate physical horizon, would be part of their daily lives as traders. As the data center manager hovered behind them, he began to talk about Walter's ability to split trades into thousands of pieces, to disguise the positions the firm was taking from their competitors. 'It has an effect we've not properly understood. We're inducing stable feedback in the markets, propagating the trends we want, dampening down the others. It's not just reacting, Jaz. We're *making* the market, creating our own reality. And when we use Walter at high speed, the effect will be profound. Of course, when the regulators catch up, they'll say we're gaming the system. And they'll be right. We *are* gaming the system. After all, there's no social value to it. Markets are supposed to allow us to allocate resources efficiently. They're supposed to be useful. But it's nothing to do with allocating resources anymore. We're not turning around container ships or varying toothpaste production at the speed of light. It's a glass-bead game, and I sometimes think I'm the only one who has a worthwhile reason for playing it.'

When Walter went live, Jaz had an attack of nerves. He wasn't sure what he was more afraid of: that the model wouldn't work, or that it would. He missed the first few minutes of trading, locked in a bathroom stall. When he came out everyone was celebrating. The rate of return seemed to surprise even Bachman. By the time the US markets closed, Fenton Willis could barely conceal his glee. The traders were high-fiving each other and opening bottles of Krug '95. Around him ties were being loosened and plans made to hit a new lapdancing club. He rang Lisa and told her he was on his way home.

That week people bought cars, ran up ten-thousand-dollar checks at Per Se. Jaz went to Harry Winston and chose Lisa a necklace, a delicate chain of platinum links which coiled in the hand like a very expensive snake. The returns continued to surpass everyone's wildest dreams, and without waiting for further risk analysis Willis authorized the Walter traders to make much larger bets. Jaz got caught up in the general enthusiasm. His worries appeared ridiculous, the effect of stress and overwork.

Soon afterwards, Bachman invited them out to Montauk. It was a beautiful May weekend and Jaz couldn't wait to get out of the city. The plan was to drive out on the Friday night, but at the last minute Lisa decided she couldn't leave Raj. Jaz told her she was overreacting, which precipitated a bitter argument.

'Don't you see?' he yelled. 'We have to have a life. We can't be shackled to him forever.'

'But we *are* shackled to him. He's our son.'

'A weekend. It's just one fucking weekend.'

He lay awake in bed, trying to control his anger; he could feel her body beside him, her back turned to him, walling off her space.

The next morning he finally persuaded her that the highly creden-
tialed new nanny was capable of looking after the boy for one night.
They threw their weekend bags into the car and headed out of the
city to join the unbroken stream of traffic on the Long Island
Expressway. Lisa checked her BlackBerry every few minutes, as if
willing some disaster to arise so they had an excuse to go home.

Bachman's house wasn't easy to find, even with a GPS. On the
third pass they spotted it, a narrow gravel drive leading off the Old
Highway, terminating in an automatic security gate, which slid
open to let them through. They parked outside an unremarkable
modernist villa, low and almost squat, as if it were trying to sink
into the earth beneath its sharply pitched roof.

The door was opened by a strikingly good-looking young man,
dressed like a J Crew catalog model, all linen and espadrilles and
sandy-blond hair. He introduced himself as Chase, took their cases
and told them that 'Mr Bachman and Mr Winter' were outside on
the deck. Lisa let out a little gasp when she saw the interior. Even Jaz
could tell there were some exquisite things: Bauhaus lamps, a plinth
displaying a piece of abstract sculpture that looked like it might be
a Brancusi. Most spectacular was the view. The house was built on
the cliffside, and the entire rear elevation seemed to be glass, a frame
for the gray Atlantic Ocean.

Chase showed them through to the deck, where a table was laid
for lunch. It was the first time Jaz had ever seen Bachman dressed
other than in a suit. He was wearing a pair of tennis shorts; beneath
them his legs poked out like two white twigs. With him was a con-
siderably older man who was introduced as Ellis, his partner. It was
clear Ellis was not in the best of health. With Chase's help, he stood
up to greet them. His handshake was a frail, featherlike thing, but
his eyes were alert and humorous. Jaz felt like a fool. Why would Cy
never have mentioned this man, his lover (apparently) of more than
thirty years? Was it because he expected him to disapprove? He
could almost hear the conversation. Yes, they're very prickly about
these things, very conservative.

Feeling sweaty from the long drive, they made a little conversation.

Ellis had been a plastic surgeon, doing facial reconstructions on burn victims and car-crash survivors. 'Never anything cosmetic,' he insisted. 'I was an idealist in those days.' Later, when they'd been shown their room, Jaz tried to explain to Lisa why he was annoyed. It wasn't that he had a problem – not even with Ellis being so much older, or with the fey boy floating about, smirking behind his hand. It was just that he hadn't known. He'd worked with Bachman for a long time.

'Well,' said Lisa, hanging her evening dress in the closet, 'you've never been the most observant person.'

They went back down to the pool, where Chase poured iced tea. Fenton Willis and his third wife, Nadia, made their way up from the beach, carrying towels and bottles of water. Willis looked slightly absurd in his weekend clothes – salmon-pink pants printed with a pattern of whales, a yellow silk ascot tied at the neck of his shirt. According to company gossip, Nadia, who was several years younger than Lisa, had been a hostess at some downtown restaurant when they met. She wore a sarong over a shiny silver one-piece swimsuit that looked like it wasn't really designed for getting wet. Jaz couldn't help but notice her gym-toned body, which was, he supposed, the point. Cy and Ellis greeted her like a long-lost sister, affecting to find her amusing, instead of trashy. This outburst of camp was another unexpected side of Bachman, and Jaz wasn't sure what to make of it.

Chase served a lunch of lobster rolls and chowder, accompanied by an excellent white burgundy. Jaz talked to Nadia about a foundation she was starting to benefit orphans in the Ukraine. She intended to host a gala in the fall, 'with many celebrities, an atmosphere for people to feel comfortable to open their check-books'. Music was piped out to the deck from a system somewhere indoors, a man warbling German songs accompanied by a piano. Lisa identified it as Fischer-Dieskau singing Schubert, which led her into a long conversation with Ellis about some Austrian director who'd used the music in a film. Lisa was clearly a hit with both their hosts. After lunch, Cy found her admiring a Schiele drawing hanging in the living area, and insisted on taking her on an art tour of the house. Jaz tagged along, mainly so as not to get stuck with Willis, who was telling some interminable story about a helicopter safari in Kenya. Each chair, each ornament, appeared to have a rich history. How long must it have taken to assemble such a collection? How much longer to gain the knowledge that lay behind it? Cy appeared particularly proud of an unabashedly sexualized painting of a young man dressed in overalls and an urchin cap, leaning against a brick wall in some kind of expressionist alleyway. Privately Jaz thought it was hideous, the sludgy greens and browns, the offensive bulge at the crotch. It was apparently the work of a noted 1930s black artist, a New York communist who'd worked with the WPA.

That afternoon he dozed by the pool, half listening to Cy and Fenton discussing America's trading links with China. Fenton had been spending a lot of time in Shanghai, and had developed a sort of obsession with the mutual interdependency of the two countries. Lisa and Nadia were discussing a new boutique which had opened up in SoHo. Jaz knew for a fact that Lisa had never shopped there, but she discussed it as if she were a regular. Back issues of *New York* magazine, he supposed. Ellis was swimming, bobbing up and down in the water with the aid of two polystyrene floats. Chase was helping him, supporting his legs, retrieving his sunhat when it slid off his head into the water. Jaz watched them from behind his dark glasses, the old man's frailty, the younger one's tenderness. There was something about the intimacy of the scene he found upsetting. Where did it end, this paid companionship? Where was the line drawn?

As they dressed for dinner, Lisa rhapsodized about their hosts, their culture, their esthetic sense. 'If only you'd told me!' she said.

'Well, I didn't know. We work together. We talk about work.'

'Oh, come on. You said he took you to see some Wiener Werkstätte silverware.'

'What? Oh, the museum. Yes, that's right.'

'You must have realized he's not like the others. Everyone else I've met from your firm is like Fenton.'

'Don't you think it's kind of strange, Ellis being so much older than Cy?'

'I think it's beautiful. They fell in love when Cy was in his early twenties. Ellis saw him in the street in Greenwich Village and followed him home. Cy was very handsome and very aloof. Ellis had to woo him. It was like a nineteenth-century courtship – flowers and fans and hand-written notes.'

'How do you even know this? You only met them today.'

'Cy told me.'

'My God, one afternoon and they're telling you this.'

'You probably never asked. Also – well, Jaz, I realize this is a little out of your comfort zone, but –'

'My comfort zone?'

'You might want to let your guard down a little. They know you belong to me. It's not like anyone's going to leap on you and deflower you.'

'What are you talking about?'

'You've been rigid with panic all day.'

'I have not.'

'Suit yourself. I just want you to have a good time.'

'Hello? I was the one trying to persuade you to come out here. By the way, have you phoned home in the last five minutes? How's Bianca coping with Raj?'

'You can be a real prick, you know that.'

'You're the one accusing me of being homophobic.'

'I didn't say that.'

'You implied it.'

'Let's just drop it, Jaz. And stop raising your voice. They can probably hear us downstairs.'

Two other couples joined them for dinner: a hedge-fund manager and his wife who were renting the house next door, and another gay couple, a well-known artist and his partner, who had a studio in East Hampton. The food was beautiful – Blue Point oysters, a whole fresh salmon, fine wines that Ellis had collected on various trips to Europe. Everyone except Jaz appeared to be enjoying themselves, particularly Lisa, who was radiating a social energy he hadn't seen in a long time, holding forth to the table about art and books and music, making everyone laugh. On another day he would have been proud of his wife, overjoyed to see her so happy. Now he just felt sour. The conversation had little to do with finance, though Fenton occasionally tried to turn things back in that direction. The artist described his latest work, which involved artificially distressing thrift-store paintings and mounting the results in wooden boxes. Cy told the story of an acquaintance who'd been conned by a dealer selling fake Joseph Cornells. There was a lot of talk about travel, trips to Italy, Iceland, the Maldives. Only then did Lisa fall silent. It had been a long time since they'd gone on vacation.

Jaz brooded on what Lisa had said upstairs. Could she be right? Was he a bigot? He had to admit he didn't really understand the way Bachman lived. There was the age difference. Perhaps it was no different to Fenton and Nadia, but Cy as a trophy husband? Surely he was the wealthier of the two? They certainly weren't a family, not in the way he thought of one. What was the purpose of all this wealth and culture if not to be passed on? Perhaps that was where Chase fitted in. A surrogate son? He wasn't sure why he'd taken such a dislike to the boy. It had something to do with his poise, the ease with which he carried his good looks. Chase looked somehow invulnerable, golden, as if the Long Island sun had warmed him right through to the marrow. Watching him languorously pour wine and serve salad, Jaz wanted to scream: *Get a real job! Stop being a parasite!*

Despite the evening breeze, the air on the deck felt close and humid. Jaz mopped the sweat from his forehead with a handkerchief. When the party left the table for liqueurs, Cy and Lisa slipped off to the study. Feeling like a spy – or a jealous husband – Jaz followed them, knowing he was making himself ridiculous, yet still irritated by his wife's look of surprise as he poked his head around the door. He clasped her proprietorially by the waist as Cy showed off yet more treasures, his collection of early printed books of Jewish mysticism. Here was a text of the *Zohar* printed in Antwerp in the 1580s. Here was Isaac Luria's *Tree of Life* in an eighteenth-century

Polish edition . . . Cy held the Luria open to a page of diagrams of interconnected circles, like molecules in an organic chemistry text-book. Lisa emitted little oohs and aahs of wonder. It was more than politeness; she seemed moved. Jaz tried to infuse his hug with meaning, hoping to transmit an intimacy he didn't feel.

'They're great, aren't they, darling?' he murmured. She didn't even nod.

Cy was talking with his usual fevered intensity. 'Of course there are so many things I don't have. I'd love to own a copy of the 1559 Mantua edition of the *Zohar*. I have a bid in at an auction in Moscow next week for an edition printed in Lublin in 1623. I already have printings from all over, Salonika, Smyrna, Leghorn – such evocative place-names, don't you think? A whole diasporic history.'

'It's a beautiful collection,' purred Lisa.

'Thank you. It's always nice to show it to someone who can appreciate it. When you talk about Kabbala now, people just think you mean Madonna and red strings. Even Jews.'

'Terrible.'

'I've been trying to persuade your husband that he's working in this tradition, but I don't think he believes me.'

Jaz shrugged, cautiously pleased he was being linked to a topic that impressed his wife. From behind, he couldn't see Lisa's expression, but it obviously amused Cy, because he arched an eyebrow and grinned. 'How much,' he asked her, 'has he told you about Walter?'

'Your computer program? A little. He says you're making the firm a great deal of money.'

'That's true enough. But I like to think we're doing more than that. You know we work with data, Lisa. We're in the business of comparing disparate things, finding links. For a Kabbalist, the world is made of signs. That's not some postmodern metaphor – it's meant literally. The Torah existed before the creation of the world, and all creation emanates from its mystical letters. Of course the modern world is terribly broken. Its perfection has been dispersed. But I like to think that in our small way, by finding connections between all these different kinds of phenomena, Jaz and I and the rest of our team are reading those signs, doing our part to restore what was shattered.'

'What a beautiful way to put it.'

'I'm not sure Jaz thinks so.'

'What? Sure, I think it's beautiful. I just – well – I prefer to think in more concrete terms.' He trailed off, furious at the look of scorn which flashed across Lisa's face. Sensing the complicity between them, he was reminded, for the first time since all the crap about circumcising Raj, that his wife was a Jew. This mystical hocus pocus was another thing she had in common with Cy. Absurdly, he felt as if this – this *queer* was excluding him deliberately, stealing her away.

He was sweating profusely and couldn't trust himself not to lose his temper, so he muttered an excuse and went back to the main room. At the bar he poured himself a large vodka, brushed off some bonhomous comment from Fenton and went out on to the deck to drink alone. His head was throbbing. The back of his shirt clung heavily to his skin. What was happening? Was he having a panic attack? He asked himself what he was doing there. He had nothing in common with those people – not really, not deep down. What did he have to stand against all their art and culture, all those books and paintings and bottles of Grand Cru Chablis? He was a single generation away from the village, mud bricks and country liquor and honor killings. He was nothing but a jumped-up peasant.

Convinced something terrible was about to happen to him, some-thing abject and physical, he followed the path down to the beach. The moon was almost full and it was easy enough to pick his way. The vodka was gone. He wished he'd thought to bring the bottle. Disgusted, he threw his empty glass out into the darkness, hearing a dull thud as Cy's expensive crystal hit the sand. Sure, there were the glories of the Khalsa, the Sikh heroes. But what was that to him? India wasn't his country. He'd only been there once, a family trip when he was fourteen, three weeks of heat and disorientation and stomach upset. The noise and smell of Amritsar; the homicidal confusion of the roads; the family village, just a few whitewashed huts surrounded by endless green fields. It was another planet. His cousins called him

Tom Cruise and tried to teach him cricket. As the family drank sweet tea and ate pakoras in his uncle's living room, painted a kind of undersea blue-green and decorated with cheap calendars and garlanded pictures of dead relatives, little kids jostled for space in the doorway to stare at his sneakers. He spent most of the vacation in that room, watching Indian movies on an old TV set whose wood-effect case was covered with a lace doily.

No, Baltimore boy, India doesn't belong to you. He slouched along the beach, trying to name one thing he really owned, one card to play against Cy and Lisa and their Schubert and their old books. Why did a woman like that even want to be with him? What did she see? Nothing, at least not anymore. She'd obviously finally worked out the truth. That's what it felt like. Palling around with his boss, making little remarks, talking all that intellectual Jew shit.

And there it was. The very bottom. A few drinks and out it came, a little diarrheic trickle of hate. Queers and Jews: he was no better than his uncles. A couple of years of college, a veneer of culture, but still just a boor, a frightened village boy with a chip on his shoulder. And so it went on, as he trudged all the way down to the rocks at the point, turned around ... When he made it back to the house, he pretended he was tired and went to bed. He could hear the others, talking and laughing downstairs. The sound of piano music filtered under the closed door. He wound the sheet about himself like a shroud, praying for sleep. Lisa came to bed very late. In the morning, as they packed to go home, he felt so worthless he could barely look her in the eye.

A few weeks went by. The Walter profits continued to mount. One day he was monitoring the system, doing risk assessments, when he noticed that several figures had deviated from expected values. Certain trades were becoming marginally more profitable. The deviations were tiny, barely noticeable, and he would have discounted them, but they came at the same time as a flurry of news about the currency and bond markets. For a couple of days Walter had been betting heavily against several small currencies in Asia and Latin America. It had shorted the Honduran lempira, which had now plunged in value, making the firm several tens of millions of dollars. Walter's position, disguised as it was in thousands of small trades which appeared to come from all over the globe, had led many other investors to think that something substantial was wrong. The Hondurans were now facing a national crisis, as offshore capital fled and debtors started to call in their obligations. As Jaz watched, they suspended trading and went into talks with officials from the International Monetary Fund.

We did that, thought Jaz. We went in there and turned it over, like robbing a bank.

That was the game, he knew. He'd always tried not to think too hard about that side of things. What was it Bachman had jokingly called himself at that dinner, replying to yet another sycophantic question of Lisa's? A *haruspex*. The priest who read the sacred entrails for the Emperor. The Emperor being Fenton Willis, who'd turned his thumb down with a regal flourish. *The slave must die*. The traders were celebrating their big win. Jaz went with them. There were jokes about quants and pointy-heads. They wanted to get him drunk and he let them. He called Lisa from a club on the Lower East Side, not realizing it was already one in the morning. The next thing he knew, he was waking up in a Midtown hotel room, mercifully alone. He headed straight back to the office to check the newswires.

Throughout the next day the lempira carried on sliding. The Honduran government looked shaky. People were on the street in Tegucigalpa. Jaz chugged coffee and looked over Walter's advice to the trading desk. The lempira didn't figure. It had turned its attention to another asset class, another region. Everything was now US mortgage-backed securities. He was relieved. At least Walter wasn't telling them to twist the knife.

In the following days Walter built up a huge holding of Australian mining stock, and made some obscure bets in the West African government bond market. Bachman ordered the team to plug in figures on financial institutions in the region, and Jaz's screens were filled with the activities of the Banque de Développement du Mali, Banque Internationale pour l'Afrique Occidentale, the Bank of Africa,

Banque Sénégalo-Tunisienne, Compagnie Bancaire de l'Afrique Occidentale, Ecobank . . . He wouldn't have noticed anything out of the ordinary, had he not opened the wrong file on his desktop and found himself looking at a graphic illustrating the performance of the Bourse Régionale in Abidjan. The pattern of rise and fall looked familiar. He compared it to a graph of the value of the lempira during the crash and found it tracked almost exactly. That was a coincidence, of course. There was no reason for those two things to be linked. But there also seemed to be no reason why stocks on the Abidjan Bourse should fall so catastrophically just at that moment. There had been no major announcement, no rumour of war. Unlike the lempira, recovery was quick. Three days later trading was at its old level.

He was developing a strange rash on his eyelids. Lisa was barely speaking to him. Though he was exhausted, he was having trouble sleeping: all night Walter's scatter-pattern visualizations pulsed behind his closed eyes like a swarm of malign insects. He spent several nights in front of the computer in his office upstairs at home, eating chips and salsa by the light of a desk lamp and running comparisons between time-series data on the performance of the lempira and every African variable he could think of – exchange rates, balance of payments, international liquidity, interest rates, prices, production, international transactions, government accounts, national accounts, population. When he was done with Africa, he moved on to East Asian countries.

He found it in Thai banking stocks. The same sudden crash. The same period of time. He couldn't help asking himself: *Had they done this?* It seemed contrary to reason, one of those ideas, like quantum superposition, that defied common sense. Was Walter having some kind of echo effect? Or was this something else, one of Cy Bachman's sparks, a trace of divine intellect? Jaz's neck was spasming. He riffled through the bathroom cabinet, looking for something to help him sleep.

The next morning, before he left for work, Lisa asked if he could take some time off. He stared at her as if she was insane, even as he realized he probably could. No one else at the firm was worried about the Honduran trade. It was only him. He told her he'd see what he could do and phoned Bachman's assistant, asking to be notified when he was next in the office and free to talk.

Bachman seemed to be in Bangkok. It was almost two weeks after the lempira crash when his assistant finally phoned to say Bachman could give him a few minutes. Jaz hurried over and found him staring out of the window, wearing noise-canceling headphones, big black cans clamped over his bald head like parasitic beetles. The sun had just set, and the skyline was performing the trick it had of dissolving, three-dimensional buildings becoming shimmering planes, then checkerboards of light. Jaz didn't want to startle him. He stood there for a full minute, waiting impatiently until Bachman swiveled round in his chair.

'Gershwin,' he explained, taking off the headphones. 'I do it every so often. You know, with the buildings? I'm sure I shouldn't. It's probably fattening. What can I do for you?'

'I need to talk.'

'So go ahead.'

'Cy, you once told me we were cheating, gaming the system.'

'Yes?'

'Well, I think we should stop. Walter's – well, it's very deep in the guts of the financial markets. I feel as if it has the power to – I mean – I don't know what I mean, Cy. But I've been thinking a lot. Walter has the potential to be very disruptive. I can't help being worried. About consequences, unintended effects.'

'These unintended effects being what, exactly?'

'Instability. Increased volatility.'

'We're properly hedged, Jaz. You don't need to worry about the firm.'

'I don't just mean us. I'm kind of tired, so I'm probably not expressing myself too well. Take the Honduran thing, for example. Walter crashed their currency. Just like that, in a morning.'

'Walter didn't do any such thing. Sentiment moved against the lempira.'

'We fucked their country.'

'That's a little dramatic, Jaz.'

'And at the same time, the BRVM and Thai stocks moved in the same way. If Walter can do that, what else can it do? And it's getting better. More sophisticated. What happens when we use the same techniques at high speed? Too fast for actors in the market to respond?'

'It's operating exactly as we built it to. It's a heuristic trading engine, Jaz. It's learning as it goes along.'

'I know Fenton is authorizing larger volumes. What if Walter does something else like that? What if it does something systemic?'

'Systemic? You think we're about to crash the global economy? And you get this from a medium-size win for our currency arbitrage strategy? When I last looked this wasn't the Fed, Jaz. We're a hedge fund, not the People's Bank of China.'

'I just think we should consider pulling back.'

Bachman laughed. 'Don't let Fenton hear you talk like that.'

'You're not taking this seriously.'

'Trust me, I understand. You feel a little queasy about that trade. On corporate social responsibility grounds, whatever you want to call it. But we didn't cause anything elsewhere. Shit happens, Jaz. If it wasn't us, it would have been someone else. You won't feel so bad when you get your bonus. I expect we'll soon be neighbors up in Montauk. Perhaps your wife could get on one of the museum boards.'

'What happened to the face of God? You usually talk as if we're about to discover the secret of the universe.'

'Are you alright, Jaz? Is everything OK at home?'

'Yes, everything's OK at fucking home. Why won't you listen to me?'

'Calm down. It's a model. It's not causing anything. You're mistaking the map for the territory.'

'We're trading on the model. We're acting.'

'Jaz, Walter won't even exist in two years' time. At least not in this iteration. The market is going to adapt. When that happens, we'll need a new tool. All we're doing is contributing to market efficiency, and as efficiency increases, our profits will drop. We'll move on. Life will go on.'

'Why don't you understand? I'm trying to say I believe you! I think I finally get what you've been trying to tell me all along. That it isn't about money. That we're messing with something – something fundamental.'

'I don't know what to say. You're talking like some villager waving a pitchfork in a Frankenstein movie. You want to burn the witch? Tie old Cy Bachman to a stake?'

And then he started using stock phrases. Take a few days. Get some rest. It was only when Jaz was riding the subway back to Brooklyn that he realized he'd just walked the plank.

The sun hammered down. The pool was glittering blue glass. Behind the roofline of the motel cabins, the sawtooth of the mountains rose up against the sky like a graph of profit and loss. Fenton Willis's braying voice came through his cellphone as a tinny rasp, as he watched Raj trying to stack plastic chairs by the hot tub. The sound of New York. You can run but you can't hide. Well, every blocked drain and pretzel vendor and gala fundraiser and overpriced apartment in the whole fucking city could go to hell. This was as much as he could cope with: an almost-empty world, a jumble of rocks and sand.

'I've got to go, Fenton. I'm sorry.'

He ended the call, stared down at his BlackBerry like a gun that had accidentally gone off in his hand. No one hung up on Fenton Willis. No one. So that was it. No more Walter. No more firm. That was him done. He felt, for the first time in months, a profound sense of peace.

1970

It was as simple as that. Step by step, she walked away from the town and into the Command, which absorbed her into its structure like a big soap bubble incorporating a little one.

Bubbles, said Wolf, were a good way to think about the future. Soon buildings would be more like them, soft and fluid, free to float away at any time and attach themselves to another cluster. At a moment's notice you could change your mind about how you lived. You could be part of a city, or a village, or stay on your own. Just untether yourself from your surroundings and go. That, he told her, was what freedom looked like.

Dawn didn't know much about freedom. All she knew was the life she wanted didn't include working at the store or grappling on the back seat of Frankie's Plymouth or her uncle running her over with his eyes all the time like she was something good to eat.

There were about ten of them. They lay out on the rocks by the Indian signs, climbing a route she'd known since she was a kid. The whorls and cross-hatched lines scraped into the red-black varnish. The white bed of the dry lake leading away toward the mountains. They passed a joint. Someone was tapping out a slow soft rhythm on a drum. Wolf laughed and stretched out flat, sunning himself on a ledge. Dawn peered over the lip at the construction going on below. Beneath the overhang, a hollow whose roof was about fifty feet off the ground, nestled the half-finished skeleton of a dome, like a broken eggshell. People were clambering over it, winching up metal poles welded into triangular struts, bolting them to the structure. Raggle-taggle freaks in Goodwill finery, spidering over a huge frame. Already the cluster of huts and trailers where they lived seemed small and temporary.

From one of the huts emerged a long tail of cable. It snaked its way under the rocks, where it disappeared into a hole.

'What's that down there?'

Wolf glanced down. 'Oh, that's my brother. He's probably under us right now, listening.'

'Listening?'

'That's what he does. He's sneaky that way.'

'Did I meet him?'

'I don't think so. You'd remember if you had. He looks like me, only uglier. Slant eyes, long nose?'

She laughed. 'I don't think I met anyone like that.'

'Like I said, you'd remember.'

As the summer wore on, Dawn spent most of her free time at the rocks, hanging out with Wolf and his friends. There were so many people to get to know. Pilgrim Billy and Floyd and Sal and Marcia and Yucca Woman and the Sky Down Feather Brothers. They were all older than her and about the most interesting and different personality types you could imagine. They were scary too, in a not-quite-good way with their weird talk about reintegration and the land of the dead and the community of the whatever-they-were planets. The person who freaked her out most was one-eye Clark Davis. He dressed like a fool, in a panama hat and Keds and a sort of biblical bedsheet robe. He must have been handsome once, in an old-fashioned Errol-Flynnish style. Before his accident.

Dawn tried to keep her distance from Davis, who was friendly in a manner she didn't care for. She never saw much of Judy, who was usually shut up in one of the caravans or meditating with Maa Joanie. The girl wasn't like anyone else at the compound. She never dressed up, always wore the same white shirt and jeans. She looked so neat and scrubbed it was hard to imagine she lived in the midst of all that dust and chaos. If you met her on the street, you'd think she was a secretary or maybe the nicer kind of student. A good Christian. She didn't sing or play music with the others. She never hooked up with anyone, though you'd find her beautiful, if you went for the wholesome type. She looked healthy but at the same time far away, like someone had unplugged something she needed to connect her to the current of everyday life.

Dawn made a friend called Mountain. She had a Southern-fried accent and green eyes that seemed to be looking at something just behind you, as if she could see what was coming up in the future. One night they went up on the rocks and Mountain told her the story of Judy and Joanie and what had happened back in the old days, when the First Guide had gotten himself killed trying to reintegrate the Earth into the Confederation. There was a terrible fire, something to do with the electrics in a machine he'd built to communicate with the Space Brothers. He was trapped inside a capsule and burned to death. Others were killed too. Clark Davis had been there, and lost his eye trying to drag people out. After everything was cleared away there was still one person missing and that was Joanie's daughter, who was only eight years old. Everyone thought she must have been killed, though they couldn't find her remains. Joanie refused to believe them. She always said that little Judy had been evacuated by the fleet, and sooner or later she would come back. She knew that if she waited patiently, the Space Brothers would return her little girl. So she came out to the rocks and that was exactly what happened. One day Judy came walking out of the desert, looking like she'd been out for a stroll. She was older, of course, because time had passed on the ships just the same as it had on Earth. But Joanie knew her at once. Judy had spent ten years in orbit being educated and infused with higher knowledge. Now she had returned to be the new Guide.

Dawn didn't know what she thought of that. She busied herself helping out with the earthly business of the Ashtar Galactic Command, fetching and carrying, chopping carrots and potatoes for huge pots of the tasteless vegetable stew that was all anyone seemed to eat. The food was one thing she found hard to get along with, but she was prepared to suffer a few hardships because her new friends turned out to be on a mission to achieve the salvation of Earth.

Here are some of the things Dawn wanted: to be herself, to live in a bubble, to make it with Wolf, to experience Divine Universal

Love. She diced onions and humped scaffold poles and stared into the fire and little by little the Pinnacles became more real to her than the dusty streets of town, more real than the high school or Hansen's Service Station or the Dairy Queen or even the General Store, though she still spent long hours dreaming behind the counter, tuning out old man Craw's lectures about morals and communism and the correct way to stack egg noodles. Wolf said the purpose of the Ashtar Galactic Command was to reintegrate the Earth into the Space Confederation. At first she just laughed at him and he laughed along with her, as if he didn't really believe it either. But he was serious. They were all serious. There was some kind of project, and thinking about it scared her slightly, but for the moment all she wanted was to be part of something bigger than herself, to clap her hands in the circle and sometimes get up to dance.

Soon the dome started to shine. The Command was cladding it in metal from car-tops, which could be had for twenty-five cents a time from a wrecker's yard in Barstow. The guys drove over in the school bus, and since they didn't have cutting torches they just chopped the tops out of the cars, standing on the roofs and swinging axes like giant can-openers. Back at base, they beat the metal into triangles, hammering them over the frames. The dome looked like a shiny ball trapped underneath the arch of a foot. The metal surfaces caught the sun like a beacon, which was the way they wanted it, except they were trying to signal outer space rather than town, and town was where people found they couldn't ignore it. At certain times of day, particularly late afternoon, the glare fish-hooked you, caught in your eye as you tried to go about your business. A lot of folks found it a provocation.

In town they grumbled. Out at the rocks, girls perched thirty feet off the ground, their bare breasts swinging back and forth as they swung a mallet at some nut or bolt.

'Our job,' confided Mountain one day, 'is to reconnect the Earth to the current of spiritual impressions.'

'Why?'

'Because we're surrounded by negative energy and it's beginning to tilt the Earth on its axis.'

'What'll happen when it tilts?'

'Tidal waves. Massive destruction. The devastation of almost all life on the planet.'

She must have looked freaked out, because Mountain stroked her cheek.

'You don't have to worry, honey. You're part of the Light now. The Command is monitoring us on all frequencies. If it happens, they'll evacuate us. It's the others we're worried about. There's not going to be enough room for everyone.'

Dawn tried to imagine a tidal wave rushing across the desert. Like a flash flood, only a million times greater. There were many things she had to learn. It turned out there were many sources of negative energy vibrations, including:

War
the H-bomb
cities
greed
artificial fibers
the financial markets
television
needle drugs
plastics
fear rays
other dark side weapons

Of all these the H-bomb was the worst. Not just because it was nuclear. Because it used hydrogen. Splitting hydrogen atoms threatened the life-force. It was in air and water, part of the Earth's very soul. Also, the burning of hydrocarbons such as coal and oil (whose atoms contained Earth-memories of the Ancient Times when dinosaurs roamed and man was unconscious of his inner truth) was combining with the modern-day projections of human negativity to produce smog, which lay over big cities and made it hard for Lightworkers to signal the fleets. That was one reason the Earth base was located in the desert. Pollution.

It was a beautiful thing, reconnecting the Earth. It was going to save billions of lives. So it was frustrating that Dawn's schoolfriends didn't seem to understand. Whenever she said a word about the Command, they treated her like a mental case. They couldn't see beyond the lack of air conditioning and the dust and the vegetable stew. She tried to tell them there was something wondrous about life in the Ashtar Galactic Command. Something real.

'What's not real about here?' asked Sheri. 'No one place's realer than another.'

They were sitting in the Dairy Queen. Dawn shrugged. From the look of Sheri and Janet Graves and Diane Castillo, surrounding her in the booth, it didn't seem worth trying to argue. She could talk all day and they wouldn't hear a thing.

Sheri was suspicious. 'Have they got you hooked on something?'

Another unanswerable question. Of course they had. Energy, Reality. Whatever you wanted to call it. There was stuff out there those girls had no idea existed, alien ships big as cities hovering invisibly a thousand miles over their town.

'It's about love,' she said. 'What can I tell you? It's about shining forth with the Light.'

'Oh my goodness,' said Sheri. 'Oh my.'

By the time the nights started getting cold, things had pretty much broken down with Aunt Luanne and Uncle Ray. Old Craw fired her from the store for running off with Wolf too many times and Uncle Ray told her she was going to have to find some other kind of work and quick, because he sure as heck wasn't going to carry freeloaders. He had a whole lot more to say, about decency and the young men fighting in Vietnam and the obligations that came with living under his roof. When she told him she was against the war and suggested he'd probably be less uptight if he was to get rid of his stupid roof and float free of the rest of town in a personal bubble, he got mad and slapped her face. He would have done worse had her aunt not intervened.

Dawn knew what really bothered the old bastard: the thought of her having 'sexual relations'. He'd come home from work (he drove a backhoe out at the borax plant) and start right in on lecturing her. It was sexual relations this and sexual relations that, and she had the idea that he sat there in his cab, pulling levers and imagining in fine detail who was or wasn't getting into the white cotton panties she pegged out on the line in the yard. He'd always been sort of touchy-feely, even when she was a little kid and first went to live with him and Aunt Luanne. He'd pinch her thighs and pat her on the tush in a way that always meant more than he was letting on, but in the last year or so he'd really let the cat out of the bag. If she was sun-bathing, he'd find some reason to be outside with her, fooling about in the rain gutter or tinkering with his truck. He had this whole routine of walking in on her when she was in the bathroom, pretending he hadn't heard the shower running. She'd taken to wedging a chair against the door, and even then he kept on trying the handle. She knew what he wanted, and he knew she knew. The idea of her making it with 'some greaser' was probably more than he could bear.

She'd have been out of that cramped little ranch house like a bullet if only she'd been confident she could support herself. She was half sure the Time of Tribulation was coming, in which case money wouldn't matter soon enough. The other half of her mind was full of inconvenient questions about where she'd be in five years' time and how she was going to pay for it. So she went to speak to Mr Hansen about a job, and he said he might have something because he was opening up a new location over in Morongo. She might be suitable, just as long as she kept up her appearance. He asked why she'd stopped doing her hair. She'd given up on the spray and tongs and was wearing it straight, or else tied up in a bandana like the other girls at the Command. Lena and Sheri had said flat out it was a cry for help.

Eventually Uncle Ray banned her from going out to the Pinnacles, and for a while she did as she was told. Then Pioneer Day came along and the folks from the Command drove into town in their school bus, which they'd freshly painted silver like a NASA rocket and wanted to run in the parade. Mayor Robertson and the other committee men refused to let them, though the parade was a small, drab affair, just the high-school marching band and the veterans and the fire department and the Cholla Queen and her cactus maidens waving from the back of a convertible. With their costumes and that great glittering dazzle of a bus, the Command would have livened things up, but those committee boys had some excuse about permits and applications needing to be made in advance and right then and there she decided she couldn't stand it anymore. It was time to pick sides. That afternoon, when the big silver bus drove out of town, she was on it.

Problem was she was under twenty-one. Uncle Ray must have infected the mind of Sheriff Waghorn with imagery of her panties, because the next day Waghorn was out at the rocks, purple-faced, bellowing about how he was going to commission a medical examination to check she was still 'intact' and threatening all kinds of legal consequences if she wasn't. 'Are you here of your own free will?' he kept asking, repeating the question when she said yes, thank you, as if putting it a third or fourth or God help her a fifth time might produce a different answer. 'Did they give you anything? An injection? Did you eat something made you drowsy?' She'd have laughed out loud if she weren't also scared to hell. When she refused point blank to go back with him, the sheriff got so angry he snorted the breath out of his nostrils like a bull.

She thought the Command would just put her out. She was bringing trouble on them. But Clark Davis took her over to Maa Joanie's shack for a meeting. It was one of the buildings on the compound that was kind of off-limits and she'd never had reason to go in there. The shack turned out to be just one room full of all kinds of books and papers and religious items, crystals and Buddha statues and candles and pictures of Jesus opening up his bleeding heart. Maa Joanie had hung it with electric Christmas lights, which made the whole place look like a cantina in Mexicali she'd once been to with Uncle Ray and Aunt Luanne. There was a little bed covered with a patchwork comforter and an old-fashioned washstand with a basin and jug and a big round mirror and a few photographs in frames that mostly seemed to feature groups of people in shiny uniforms, with sashes and tunics and little hats like tin soldiers or majorettes.

Maa Joanie was sitting in a rocking chair. Judy stood behind her, brushing her hair with a silver-backed brush. She was concentrating real hard, her eyes sparkling like it was some sort of treat.

'Hundred strokes before bedtime,' said Maa Joanie, who looked contented, half asleep. Clark Davis turned a wooden chair backwards and sat down heavily on it, rotating his hat nervously in his hands.

'Well, little Dawn, you've certainly put the cat among the pigeons.'

'I didn't mean to. I just want to be here, you know? Be part of the Light.'

'I can understand that. But, as Sheriff Waghorn was at pains to remind me, your uncle's still your legal guardian. He's got the right to decide what's best for you.'

'My uncle's an asshole.'

'That's as may be.'

'It might be best if she goes,' said Maa Joanie, who didn't even look over, just stared off into the distance with that dreamy expression on her face.

'Do you want to?' asked Davis.

'No! You don't know what it's like. My uncle's a creep, and my aunt doesn't do a thing about it.'

'What do you mean by that?'

'I – I don't know.'

'You're saying he's interfering with you?'

'Well . . .' She thought about it for a moment. 'Yes.' It was true enough. It was what was on his mind.

'I want to be clear. This involves touching and such? Sexual touching?'

'Yes,' she said more firmly.

'Clark, I don't like this,' said Maa Joanie. 'We've got a burden on our shoulders as it is.'

'But if what Dawn says is true, then her uncle's in league with the Dark Forces. Look at this girl, Joanie. She's a starchild! You can see the mark on her brow. We can't just throw her out. We have a duty.'

'They're going to come after her. They'll start hassling us, and we're too far along just to up and move to another place.'

'Then we'll fight. That's what we're here to do.'

'This isn't the Tribulation. It's not that time.'

'It's close. We all know that. We need to take guidance. We ought to contact the Command.'

While they were talking, Judy stood behind Maa Joanie, the hairbrush held limply in her hand. The faintest trace of a smile played about the corners of her mouth. Dawn didn't see what was so funny. This was her life they were talking about.

Maa Joanie got up and switched off the Christmas lights, leaving only a candle burning on the nightstand. Everyone settled themselves down. Not really knowing what to do, Dawn just followed the others, sitting with her hands in her lap, dropping her head like she was praying in church. It was clear that Judy was now in charge. She did some kind of strange breathing thing and began to speak.

'Calling Command! Calling Command! Beloved Commanders, are you monitoring my wave? Come in, if you are receiving this signal. We of Earth desire contact with the Light.'

There was a silence, then a deep male voice spoke. Dawn didn't dare open her eyes, but it sounded as if it was coming from where Judy was sitting.

'Salutations! I am Argus, director of Earth Missions, 325th wave. I am standing by. Discontinue.'

Maa Joanie spoke.

'Beloved Commander Argus! Greetings and salutations to you and your Supreme Commander Ashtar. In the name of Lord Jesus-Sananda, we need advice. Earth base is threatened by law enforcement operatives in league with the Dark Forces. We need to know if we should protect a young Lightworker, or if we should ask her to sacrifice her connection for the greater good of the mission.'

'I hear you, Beloved. Your emotions are imprinted on my soul. You are in doubt. I am sorry that it should be so. This is a complex problem. I will consult my colleagues in council. Please stand by.'

The silence seemed to last forever. If it really was just Judy using a weird voice, Dawn was sure the 'aliens' would tell them to send her back to Uncle Ray. Her thoughts drifted on to whether she should beg Old Man Craw to reconsider or just get on a Greyhound and leave town. Where to? LA? San Francisco? Then Judy did her strange breathing thing again.

'Beloved, we have met in telepathic council and all are in accord. The girl is a special one. She has the solar seal on her brow. You are to protect her from the Dark Forces. Use any means necessary. My blessings and the Blessings of all the Solar Hierarchy fall upon you. Dwell in the Light. I am Argus. Discontinue.'

Dawn looked up at Judy in wonderment. Judy smiled. And winked at her, she was sure. Maybe it was just a trick of the light.

And that was how Dawn found herself in a law office in Victorville with Maa Joanie and Clark Davis, who was wearing ostrich boots and a bolo tie and a new felt hat for the occasion. She said the things he'd schooled her to say, about how her uncle came in when she was in the shower and touched her inappropriately and made remarks, and how she feared if she stayed under his roof he would fall into sinful ways. Sheriff Waghorn sat and stared goggle-eyed and Ray cursed and waved his hands and the lawyer told him he didn't look kindly on such displays in the presence of a young lady. Then the sheriff told Ray flat out to drop it, said it wasn't worth his while to keep hold of her if she didn't want to stay. Ray looked like he wanted to strangle her with his bare hands, but settled for calling her a tramp. All the while Aunt Luanne cried bitterly. Dawn felt sorry for Luanne, who'd never done anything to deserve a pig like Ray.

Looking back, that was the real start of the war between the town and the Ashtar Galactic Command. Each side thought the other was in league with the Dark Forces, and each side was prepared to do whatever it took to ensure right should prevail. A couple of days later Sal and Marcia came back from town all covered in red house-paint, saying some boys in a green and white Mercury drove past on Main Street and threw it over them. Dawn knew exactly who it was. Frankie and Robbie and Donny Hansen and Kyle Mulligan and some of the other jocks had taken to driving out to the Pinnacles to hang around. They'd play music and lean on their cars, drinking beer and throwing the cans over the compound fence. If Wolf or Gila or any of the other guys came out they'd take off, but sometimes they shouted things about Dawn being a hippie slut and how they hoped she liked being fucked by niggers. Hurtful things, specially from Frankie, who always used to be so sweet.

Of course everything the good old boys at Mulligan's thought was going on up at the rocks really was, and more besides. It took a while for Dawn to cotton on to why people who were sometimes so talkative could spend whole days lying silently in the dome or trudging naked circles on the dry lake. At least some of the money for food and building materials was coming from the drug runs being made to LA and San Francisco, which seemed to be almost a full-time occupation for many of the Children of Light. Whatever was getting bought and sold wasn't really any of her concern. As for being 'intact', whatever that meant, the night of the Pioneer Parade Wolf had taken her out on the rocks and calmly stripped her of her shorts and halter-top and licked her pussy with his long tongue and then fucked her slowly and methodically until she whimpered and scratched his back. Afterwards she felt more intact than she'd ever felt in her life.

It wasn't all good, though, not by any means. She thought she and Wolf were together and he more or less acted that way until the night he took his bedroll and went to sleep next to some new girl from Wisconsin, calmly, like it was nothing. Dawn had been studying hard. She understood possessiveness was a kind of negative energy and true souls of Light shone their love indiscriminately on the world, but she still felt hurt and more or less followed Wolf around until he told her to stop. She said she loved him and he said he loved her too but his love was too big to be confined to any one person or thing. For a while she holed up on her own and even thought about leaving and going back to town, but Pilgrim Billy talked her out of that, and soon enough she was snuggling down next to him under a scratchy Indian blanket, while his big gentle carpenter's hands explored her body, making her feel the world wasn't so bad.

At that time they were all sleeping in the big dome, except for Judy and Joanie and Clark Davis, who had their own cabins. The metal skin made it stifling hot during the day, and even at night it was a sweaty, busy place, the air roiled by body-smells and mesquite smoke from the cook-fire and farting and coughing and the sudden flickerings of pipes and matches and the rake of flashlight beams as people hunted about for space to crash. They were naked most of the time, and though she was shy at first, she gradually got used to it, to the sight of bodies, to the hearing and the seeing of sex, which was natural and beautiful, not 'intercourse', full of fear and guilt. She thought about Uncle Ray, and Frankie and the red-faced sheriff, about how scared they all were, and to her surprise she actually began to feel a little sorry for them.

Further on down the line she found out nothing came for free. She was a starchild, a love-giver, but it was easier to shine your light on some people than others. After Billy there was Guru Bob and then Floyd, who she didn't really want to go with, because he had a skin condition, but it was hard to deny someone without generating negativity and giving aid to the Dark Forces. Then one night Mountain told her Clark wanted to see her. She knew what was coming. He'd let her know in small ways that she owed him, and though he was supposed to be with Maa, he liked to get laid and was persistent and paranoid about rejection and sooner or later everyone had to give it up, just to get some peace. You were only unlucky if he took a shine to you, was what she'd heard. Dawn made sure he got bored quick enough. She lay there like a dead fish while he did his business, thinking about how righteous and moral he'd been with Ray at the law office, and how he and her uncle were probably more or less the same age.

None of the bad stuff mattered. Not when you were in contact with beings from other stars, part of the earthly salvation mission of the Ashtar Galactic Command. Wolf and the others had a saying: *Music is the message.* That was to say, it was communication, a way of making contact with the Command. Almost everyone on the compound played an instrument, and those that didn't, like Dawn, knew how to chant or bang something or clap in time.

Listen. We repeat. Listen.

They'd meet in the dome, or just sit out under the stars. And it would start, the low bass drone of the Tronics circling round and round, opening a space for the drums to make patterns. Then the strings and pipes would add their lines and the great noise would swell and people would begin to chant *this is our message this is our message are you receiving us are you receiving come in* and soon they'd feel the presence of others, higher-density beings, contributing their beautiful overtones to the cosmic music, until all were one with the harmonic vibrations of the Universal Field.

We speak in the names of all sentient beings in the thirty-three sectors of the Universe, in the name of the Ascended Masters and the Conclave of Interdimensional Unity. We bring this music to you, the Star People, so that you may understand.

Of course there were sugar cubes and blotters and acid punch, and this was where she learned how to let her mind shatter without feeling afraid, how to open up to the wonder of existence and let the vastness of the Universe enter in. It altered her on the molecular level, changed her from little Dawnie Koenig into a true starchild, the substance of her body stretching out through time and space, making contact, bringing her closer to the celestial realms of Jesus-Sananda and the Ashtar Galactic Command.

It wasn't the drugs. The drugs were just a tool, a key to unlock the door. The other tool was the Tronics, built by Wolf's hermit brother, who spent his time alone in a room dug under the rocks, fooling about with wire and valves and solder. He made oscillators, tone generators. He made filters and processors. He took the sounds made by the musicians, transformed them into cosmic energy and sent them up into space. He was a scientist, Coyote, though Dawn suspected he stole a lot of the things he said he made himself. The Tronics looked too sleek and expensive to be cooked up in a dusty hole under a rock.

They timed the sessions to important cosmic events – solstices, the Perseid meteor shower. People would arrive days beforehand, on bikes gleaming with chrome, in beat-up buses, carrying instruments and amplifiers, eating and crashing together amid snaky tangles of cable in the dome. Ash-covered sitarists, Nashville junkies in soiled Nudie suits with pedal steel guitars. Once an old flatbed truck sputtered its way into the compound, disgorging the entire congregation of a peyote church from over the border in Arizona, solemn men in workshirts manhandling giant drums, their women following behind, carrying cauldrons of corn mush and foil-wrapped rounds of frybread. Here was some fat old poet, withered buttocks wrapped in a sarong, twanging on a Jew's harp and pronouncing the scene wholly holy. There was a tattooed vet, hair only half grown out, stalking around with a bedroll and a harmonica, looking for a place to dig a foxhole. All come to plug into the Tronics, to have their sounds converted into etheric waves. To feel the Universe unfolding, the drone sweeping them far away.

When the compound was full of strangers, setting up for the session, you'd spot Coyote flitting here and there, setting up microphones, adjusting settings. It was more or less the only time you'd ever see him out of his cave; he was so secretive that for a while Dawn thought Wolf was playing some kind of joke on her, and he didn't really have a brother at all. They weren't alike. It wasn't that Coyote was bad-looking, exactly. *Uncouth* would be a word. *Fleabitten.* He looked like someone who ate out of dumpsters. For ages you'd never run into him and bit by bit you'd start forgetting he existed. When he turned up it'd be a shock. Always, every time. You'd stumble on him doing something low and disgusting, flopping his cock out of his filthy jeans, rummaging through your stuff.

You'd try and avoid him, but suddenly he'd be everywhere, standing over the lunch table, grabbing food and chewing with his mouth open, making lewd remarks at you when you were getting ready to go to sleep. His teeth were mossy. His grimy hands were twisted back on themselves, the nails black with dirt. Amazing he could do anything with electronics. Dawn always thought you had to be clean for that. Before a session he'd rush through the dome with a damp joint glued to his bottom lip, splicing things, coaxing dead connections into life, sticking his nose in and upsetting everyone, but somehow getting it all together, making the thing happen. In a manic mood like that he'd electrocute himself once, twice a day. Plugging in the wrong cable, knocking over a bottle of water. Before a session, he always carried the stink of burned hair. He smelled like the onset of a migraine.

In the early days, before the paranoia set in, Clark or Joanie would lead everyone in the invocation. *In the name of the Great Master Jesus-Sananda and of Ashtar, Commander of the Brotherhood of Light* . . . They'd talk about the project, about the tsunami of negative energy emanating from the darkness and the certainty that, unless it was countered by an intergalactic union of Lightworkers, the Earth would tilt on its axis and human civilization would be wiped out. *Think of the libraries, the great repositories of knowledge! Think of the treasure houses of gold!*

All the works of all the hands.

We will not fear, says Clark Davis, as the drone of the Tronics cranks up into life. Worlds unfolding, vibrating deep in the body, sending waves shuddering through to the bone. *Forty million are with us, forty million souls!*

This message is going out to whosoever will listen and understand.

During the evacuation, explains Maa Joanie, *some will be lost, but others, who make it to the motherships, will undergo extraordinary experiences. Your minds will be quickened by the rays in which you bathe, the blue rays and the green rays and the violet ray and the elemental ray, the carrier of all our higher communications. Your cells will be regenerated. You will live for two hundred years.*

We will not fear

*Know that attempts have been made by powers on Earth to persuade you
that your reality as Star People is false. These powers, strongly magnetized
to the Darkness, must be resisted at all costs. They seek to destroy you, and
plunge you into the brute negativity of matter.*

We are pure spirit.

We are the high gods.

Do not fear

*Do not fear, Children of Light! Each of your names is punched into
record cards held in the brains of our giant computers! We know exactly
where you are!*

We know exactly where you are! Do not fear!

*Do not fear! Fifteen fleets of ships are orbiting the Earth. Millions of
vessels, each one assigned a quota of souls. Families separated during the
evacuation will be reunited. Special care will be taken of the children.
Release your hold on the ones left behind. They shall only be left behind
because something in the core of their being tells them to stay. Release those
souls into the infinite world-soul, the many-mansioned House that is the
body of the Father. The ships are beautiful. The ships are filled with joy.
Your children will play in huge soft rooms filled with light.*

*Remain calm when it comes. There are no accidents. There are no
coincidences. All is in the plan.*

The ships are beautiful.

The ships are filled with joy.

Remain calm.

Do not fear

Do not fear

Do not fear

Do not fear

Do not fear

Do not fear

Do not fear

Do not fear

Do not fear

Do not fear

Do not fear
Do not fear
Do not fear
Do not fear
Do not fear
Do not fear
Do not fear
Do not fear
Do not fear
Do not fear
Do not fear
Do not fear
Do not fear
Do not fear
Do not fear
Do not fear
Do not fear
Do not fear
Do not fear
Do not fear
Do not fear
Do not fear
Do not fear
Do not fear
Do not fear

Do not fear
Discontinue.

2008

Jaz surveyed his new perimeter, the afternoon sun, the pale blue lining of the motel pool. A tactical retreat. He smeared more sunscreen on his face and lay down on the creaky plastic lounger, listening to the traffic on the highway, waiting for the sound of their rental car pulling into the front lot.

He slept for a while, woke up dry-mouthed. The shadows were long, distorted black streaks thrown across the paving, ghosts of chairs and sunshades. He went out and stood by the road, holding the boy's hand. Raj was bored, twisting from side to side and making clicking sounds. They spent a while spotting trucks, the bigger the better. Raj liked trucks, though he covered his ears with his hands when they went by.

The manager came out of the office and stood watching them.

'You folks not been out today?'

She was wearing a striking outfit, shiny pants and some kind of tapestry vest woven with a wizardy pattern of stars and planets.

'Everything OK? Not sick or nothing, is he?'

'Just waiting for my wife. She went to run some errands. She'll be back soon.'

The manager pursed her lips around a skinny menthol cigarette, exhaled skeptically. 'Sure, honey. You just yell if you need anything. If you're hungry there's takeout menus in the rec room. Pizza place delivers.'

He dialed Lisa's cell. If she was off sulking somewhere it was time for her to stop. The phone went straight to voicemail. Ten minutes later he called again. The light softened to a pinkish-gold, tumbling over the pool like gauze. He and Raj played an interminable game: Raj fetched pebbles, placed them in an arc by his seat. Jaz moved them to the other side. Raj moved them back.

There was a system. Order. Cooperation. Every so often he hit redial.

Voicemail.

And again.

With a click and a buzz the motel lighting came on. The red glow of the sign leaped up. The string of Christmas lights tacked to the eaves burst out in a sudden scatter of multicolored points. What if she'd been in an accident? She was upset, she could have crashed the car.

As if summoned by the setting sun, the English guy emerged from his room, drowsily scratching his ass. Raj dropped his pebbles and ran straight toward him, skirting the pool in a busy arm-flapping run. He careered into his knees like a football player going in for a tackle. The English guy looked embarrassed.

'Well, hello there.'

'I'm so sorry. I've never seen him do that before. Raj, come here. Come to Daddy.'

'He's alright. You got the time, by the way? My phone's out of batteries.'

'It's ten after eight.'

'Fuck, I missed the whole day.'

He cracked a kind-of-smile, more of a leer, revealing a missing tooth. His accent was alarming, like something out of *Oliver*. Jaz was surprised. Raj never wanted anything to do with strangers. He only touched his parents under sufferance. Now he was suddenly cuddling up to some sort of scabrous cockney vampire. 'He doesn't usually do this,' Jaz said again.

The vampire looked confused. Jaz felt he ought to explain. 'He's kind of autistic. He doesn't find it so easy to deal with people.'

'I see.'

'I'm Jaz Matharu, by the way.'

'Nicky.'

'And that's Raj.'

'Awright, Raj? Come on, you can look at me, can't you? Don't be shy.'

Raj kept his face buried in Nicky's crotch. Nicky frowned. 'So he's like, locked away.'

'Yeah. You could say.'

'I'm sorry, man. That's bad times.'

Jaz shrugged. 'Bad times sounds about right.'

'Well, I'm just off down the Maccy-Dees.'

'Excuse me?'

'You know, get something to eat. A burger.'

'Oh, right. Good talking to you. Say, is that your Camaro parked out front, with the rims and the pearl finish?'

'Yeah. Goes like the clappers.'

'Nice ride.'

'Thanks. It's just a rented car.'

'A rental? Wow. I'm driving some piece-of-shit Dodge. Or at least I was, until my wife – well, she took off this morning. Family emergency.'

'You been stuck here?'

'Yeah. Raj is getting kind of cranky.'

'Probably wants his tea. So, you angling for a lift?'

'Sorry?'

'A lift. A ride. We could pick something up in town for the lad. Be no bother.'

'God, I didn't mean to – that'd be so kind. Are you sure? Hear that, Raj? The kind man's going to take us to get food.'

'I'll have to go find my keys.'

The night manager, a mournful Latino with heavily tattooed arms, took Jaz's cell number and promised to call if Lisa turned up. They sank into the Camaro's bucket seats, which were coated with a thin layer of dust and grit, as if the top had been left down in a sandstorm. Raj reluctantly disentangled himself from the gaunt young man and sat in Jaz's lap. As they gunned down the hill into town, the sunset's brief orange blaze subsided to a faint residual glow. The engine's throaty roar and the wind passing the open windows were enough to kill conversation. Raj was sitting with his hands firmly clamped over his ears, his mouth fixed in a stern frown, like a soldier heading off to war. Something hard rolled against Jaz's shoe. He looked down to see an empty tequila bottle in the foot well.

As they hit the strip, he thought he spotted their rental, but there were any number of white Dodge Chargers in the world, and this one was parked outside a grim-looking bar, not Lisa's kind of spot. Further down, in a lot between a Chinese massage place and a market, they found a Burger King. Nicky pulled in and peered suspiciously into the brightly lit restaurant.

'Last night this gaff was crawling with nutters. You know they've got a big army base here.'

'Marines, actually.'

'Like *Call of Duty*. Anyway, looks quiet enough tonight. Want to eat in?'

'Sure, we can try. Sometimes Raj doesn't get on too well in places like this.'

Raj refused his hand and attached himself to Nicky. He seemed completely content, placidly eating his fries like any other kid. One night only, screw the special diet. While Lisa wasn't around to oversee.

'So,' he asked Nicky. 'What do you do?'

'I'm a rock 'n' roll musician.'

'Oh yeah? What's your, uh, instrument?'

'I play guitar, sing.'

'That's so cool. And you make a living?'

Nicky smiled. 'I do OK.'

'I'm in finance.'

'That a fact? Merchant banker?'

'Well, kind of. I devise trading strategies.'

'Bet you're loaded, you merchant banker.'

They both laughed, though Jaz wasn't sure if it was about the same thing. Nicky had the type of hipster cool that always made him feel like he was failing an exam. It was soothing to find out he was a musician. It was somehow easier to think of the weird hair and clothes as a sort of uniform.

Raj yawned and flapped his hands.

'He OK?' asked Nicky.

'Yeah, he's happy.'

Lisa wasn't going to believe how well Raj was behaving. She'd think he was exaggerating, making it up to get on her good side. Lisa was the sole expert when it came to their son. Anything he told her was treated as provisional, as if he were some kind of assistant whose work had to be double-checked.

He and Nicky made small talk as they finished their food, mostly about cars. Nicky was cagey about the details of his career, so presumably his band wasn't that big of a deal.

They drove back to the motel. Still no sign of Lisa. Raj was sleepy. Jaz put him straight to bed, thankful that he didn't seem to be fretting. When he was sure he was down, he went over to the office and asked the tattooed night manager for the number of the county sheriff's department. The switchboard passed him on to some deputy who said there'd been no traffic accidents, and no other reports of anyone matching the description of his wife. If Lisa hadn't checked in by morning he should call again and they'd register her as missing, but until then it was too soon to get involved. The guy's tone implied he'd heard the story a million times. Give her time to cool off, he suggested. Buy her flowers.

He made sure Raj was comfortable, and carried a chair outside. Should he start phoning hospitals? Nicky was standing by the pool, smoking a cigarette and looking up at the sky. He called over.

'Want a beer?'

'Sure.'

He opened the bottles with a plastic lighter, popping the caps on to the ground. They clinked necks. Jaz picked up the caps. Nicky drained most of his beer, and held his cigarette out to Jaz, who realized it was actually a joint.

'No, thanks.'

'Suit yourself. So, if you don't mind me asking, why are you staying in a place like this? Doesn't really seem like your scene.'

'Oh. Why?'

'Well, look at you. You're not exactly the typical fifty-dollar-motel-room guest.'

Involuntarily Jaz glanced down at himself – his polo shirt, his expensive loafers. He shrugged. 'It's mainly because of the boy. He can be – kind of a handful.'

'Seems like a nice enough lad.'

'The way he was tonight – I'll be honest – it was unusual. We've been asked to leave places a couple times.'

'Yeah?'

'People complain. He gets so frustrated. He can be aggressive.'

'I would be.'

'Aggressive?'

'Frustrated. You know, if I was locked up inside that little head, trying to get out.'

'It puts a lot of pressure on my wife, him being the way he is.'

'So she does a runner once in a while?'

'She's on a family errand.'

'Don't worry, mate. She'll come back. They always do.'

They sat in silence for a while, then Nicky said he had to make a call and loped off back to his room. Jaz watched the stars. They were so bright, they seemed to illuminate the scene in a way that wasn't entirely physical.

Though it was late, the heat was still oppressive. He went inside and lay on the bed with the a/c up high, trying to read a book. The text swam in front of his eyes. Though the room had cable, most of the channels were snowy, and there didn't seem to be much on except reality shows and telenovelas, so he opened up his laptop and connected to the motel's patchy wireless. He surfed newsfeeds, stock tickers, a car site, some stupid blog of pictures of people dressed as Star Wars characters. It all led eventually to porn. Clicking through the forest of plastic vulvas just set him on edge: the relentless ramming of the animated tongues and penises, the wound-like holes. It looked like work, like a production line. Banner ads flashed migraine pink. He foraged half-heartedly under the waistband of his shorts, then slapped the laptop shut, unable to stomach another woman's drugged sideways look to camera as another disembodied cock spurted over her face. He switched off the lights and tried to regulate his breathing, step himself down.

Come on, Lisa. Come back.

He closed his eyes. Sometime later he slept.

He woke up into a low-contrast world. Shades of gray, a room he didn't recognize. The door handle turned. Trying to move quietly, a figure knocked against the door frame, making it vibrate.

'Lisa?'

She swore under her breath. 'I'm tired. Let's talk in the morning.'

'It is the morning. Where the hell have you been?' Sitting up now, trying to marshal himself.

'Shush. We'll talk, but not now. OK? I can't. Not now.'

'What do you mean? Just tell me where you were. I called the cops, Lisa. I was worried to death.'

'I need a shower.'

He got up, stood beside her, touched her bare shoulder. Up close she was an animal presence, sweating and shaky.

'Don't,' she said, flinching.

His anger flared. 'You stink of cigarettes. And booze. Were you in a bar? Christ, it *was* you. I thought I saw the car outside a bar downtown.'

'Don't shout,' she hissed. 'You'll wake Raj.' She stepped into the bathroom and closed the door. He heard the sound of the shower. It ran ten, fifteen minutes. He began to wonder if she'd passed out and was about to get out of bed to check when the door opened. Without a word, still wrapped in a towel, she flung herself face-down on the mattress beside him.

'Lisa,' he said. 'Talk to me.' It was no use: she'd passed out. He propped himself up on one elbow, ran his hand over her damp naked flank. Her breathing was heavy and regular. He lay back down. After a while she turned on to her back and began to snore.

Not long afterwards, Raj woke up. Jaz let him crawl over Lisa, who moaned and raised her hands in feeble defense. Grimly satisfied, he pulled on a T-shirt and ambled over to the rec room to get coffee. The sun was already fierce. Back at the room he put a paper cup within reach of his wife, who'd rolled herself up into a cocoon of covers, a featureless hump which made a dull thud as it was battered, rhythmically and relentlessly, by their son.

'Coffee,' he told her. 'On the side. Don't knock it over.'

Her clothes were puddled on the floor by the bathroom sink. He picked them up, sniffed them. They didn't smell like her. They were covered in sand.

He showered, going about his routine with defiant correctness, choosing a shirt and long pants, combing his hair. Businesslike; that's how he wanted to be. Present without being present. When he was done, he cracked open the door, letting the full force of the heat fall on the bed.

'We need to get out of here.'

Blearily, Lisa sat up. Raj was pawing at her, cooing with pleasure. Jaz ripped the curtains open, forcing her to shield her eyes. She swung her feet to the floor and sat there for a moment, breathing in gulps of air. Then she pitched toward the bathroom and slammed the door shut. From inside came the sound of vomiting. Jaz hefted their cases on to the bed and began to toss in clothes and shoes. Lisa came out and pushed past him, retrieving underwear, a pair of shorts. 'What are you doing?' she asked.

'Well, you don't actually want to stay in this dump, do you?'

'What about the park?'

'What about it?'

'Don't you want to go?'

'You're asking me if we're going sightseeing? You have to be fucking kidding.'

'Please don't shout.'

'Oh, have we got a sore head? Heavy night, was it? Where were you, Lisa? Where the fuck were you?'

'We should go to the park. We're here anyway. I think we should go to the park.'

'I called the cops. I thought you'd had an accident. Raj and I were stranded here all day. We had to get a ride with this junkie-looking musician guy so your kid could get something to eat.'

'You called the police?'

'Of course I called the fucking police. You were gone all night. What were you thinking?'

'I'm sorry.'

'And there we have it, ladies and gentlemen. That all you got? Where were you? I want you to tell me right now where you were.'

'You're overreacting. I needed some time to myself. I was losing it.'

'I'm overreacting? Is that what I'm doing?'

'You seem to have forgotten what happened yesterday. I was angry with you. I *am* angry with you. That fucking string thing. Bringing your mother's bullshit into our world.'

'Oh, so you're punishing me? By going out into a bar and getting wasted? Go on, what else did you do?'

Just for a second, a stricken look passed across her face. Just for a second, but he caught it. His throat constricted. His voice sounded different to him, whiny and shrill.

'What happened, Lisa? Where have you been?'

'Nowhere. And get off my back. Nothing happened.'

Raj was hovering by them, picking up their agitation, flapping his hands. Lisa squatted down, cupping his head in her hands, trying to get him to focus on her. Gradually he calmed down. Jaz sank into a chair and watched them.

'Look,' she said. 'I was furious with you. I drove around all day, ate lunch in a diner. Then – I don't know. I drove out into the desert. I needed to be alone.'

'And after that?'

'Yes, I went drinking. I sat in a bar and got drunk.'

'And you drove back.'

'Sue me.'

'Oh, very mature. God, sometimes you can be unbelievably irresponsible.'

'You know what? Fuck you. How about that? Mommy did something irresponsible. Bad Mommy, take her baby away. When was the last time you looked at yourself, Jaz? When did you turn into such a self-righteous prick?'

Raj began to wail. Lisa knelt down again. 'Sorry, sorry, sorry. I'm sorry, OK. Yes, darling, Mommy's here. We're going to go and get some breakfast. Yes, I know, I know you're hungry. I'm hungry. I'm sure Daddy's hungry. We'll go get some nice breakfast.'

She looked up at Jaz, imploringly. 'He needs to eat. Let's go get something, OK? Please.'

They gathered their things in silence. As they were walking out to the car, they ran into the manager, who was showing a room to a middle-aged couple wearing identical sun visors.

'You OK, honey?' the manager asked Lisa. To Jaz's surprise, Lisa nodded and gave her a hug.

'That's good, dear,' said the manager. 'That's a relief.'

Jaz pointed the key at the car. The locks thunked open. They put Raj in his seat and belted themselves in. Lisa waved at the manager, who raised a hand as she walked back to the office.

'You were with *her*?'

'I ran into her at the bar.'

'That figures. Old freak.'

'Don't call her that. She's a kind woman.'

'In what way?'

'For two minutes could you stop interrogating me? I need a coffee. I suppose there's nowhere we can get something less revolting than the stuff at that place.'

'This isn't Park Slope.'

He sped down the hill, ignoring her appeal to slow down. He pulled in at a Denny's. They sat inside, silently watching the road through the window. Most of the other booths were filled with young marines, scarfing down eggs. Jaz ate pancakes, watching Lisa nurse a mug of thin coffee. His self-righteousness was fading beneath a rising conviction that some disaster had occurred and he would be the last to know what it was.

'Did you meet someone?' he asked.

She knew what he meant. 'Dawn,' she said. 'I met Dawn, from the motel.'

'Who else?'

'I talked to people.'

'What kind of people?'

'I don't know, Jaz. People. Men. I got drunk and talked to men. Now chop my head off with your curly sword for staining the family honor.'

'You just talked.'

'We just talked. I played some pool.'

'You didn't come home until six. The bars round here don't stay open that late.'

'Look, I know I should have phoned. I was angry. Let's just try to deal with this. I'm sorry. I'll make it up to you. Let's go take a look at the park. That's what we came here to do.'

'You seriously want to do that?'

'Yes. Before it gets too hot. We don't need anything from the motel. I just want to be outside in the open. I can't breathe in that room.'

'We haven't got a picnic. The water's in the room.'

'We'll get more water.'

'We haven't brought his hat.'

'There's a bag in the trunk. I don't want to be in that room. Let's just go, OK? You don't have to talk to me.'

'That's a stupid thing to say.'

'You know what I mean.'

They took the turn for the park and drove to the ranger's station, where they paid an entry fee and got a map and a ticket to display on the dash. They sped on through a moonscape, cliffs and ridges strewn with shards of broken rock. The road climbed up to a gap, through a field of rounded boulders, haphazardly piled up into mounds and turrets, weathered into fantastical shapes. The light was dazzling. Below in the valley the concrete pavement shimmered on the straight and it looked to Jaz as if he was hurtling down into a phantom lake, set in a huge flat plain of Joshua trees. The lake broke into pools and streams. The pools and streams dried into flat white salt. All illusion, all fake.

'Make a left,' said Lisa, as they came to a junction.

'Where are we going?'

'See those rocks? I want to take a look at them.'

Jaz turned the wheel.

'Why? What does the guide say?'

'I don't know. I saw them yesterday. Off in the distance. I tried walking toward them but they were too far.'

'You were here yesterday?'

'I think I must have been on the other side. I didn't come into the park.'

They drove toward the three spires, which rose up out of the dust like skinny arms lifted up to the sky. On every side the horizon was marked by mountain ranges, a jagged, absolute border to the world. The country opened up, until only a few tortured Joshua trees broke the endless flat. Lisa watched the rocks intently, as if they were about to do something – start moving, sprout hands and fingers.

They left the car in a little graded lot by the road and took a path toward the rocks, pushing Raj along in his stroller. The ground was rough and the boy was a dead weight. Lisa handed over to Jaz, who felt like Sisyphus as he maneuvered his sleeping son onward. The path passed over a wash and climbed a gentle slope, pocked with creosote bushes. There was no sound but the crunch of their feet, the stroller's squeaky bearings. Jaz could hear a faint high-pitched whine, almost at the edge of consciousness, and searched the sky for contrails. The clear ceramic blue was broken by high lenticular clouds, a formation of perfect little disks, like fluffy spaceships. He removed his sunglasses to get a look at them and was hit by a wall of light. The world was bleached out. Every scrap of color – Lisa's green halter-top, the stroller's red nylon hood – had been subdued by the intensity of the glare. It was like walking through an over-exposed photograph.

Finally they reached the rocks. They stood in their shadow and drained most of a bottle of water, decanting some into a plastic beaker for Raj. The three vast towers teetered on a flat plinth, stained black with desert varnish. They seemed to be straining directly toward the sun like heliotropic plants. Jaz looked at his watch. It was midday. He could see the car in the distance, a lone silver glint on the desert floor. Raj fell asleep again, so they parked the stroller in the shade and followed a path around the base to take a look at the country on the other side. A barren basin scrolled away toward the mountains, at its center the blown-out white plane of a salt flat, almost too bright to look at.

All about them on the ground were signs of recent occupation. Footprints, spent cartridges, a couple of crushed beer cans. They walked on, making a circuit. In one sheltered spot they found the remains of a poured concrete platform, a base for some kind of structure. Its crumbling surface was blackened by fire.

'I've been here before,' said Lisa. 'Except I've never been here.'

Jaz kicked a can. 'Looks like someone had a party.'

He saw a yellowy glint on the floor and poked it with his toe, expecting broken glass. A rock, shot through with bright flecks. He picked it up and held it out.

'We've struck it rich.'

Lisa turned it over. 'Is that gold?'

'Pyrites.'

Suddenly there was a huge crack, as if the sky had been broken open like an egg. Involuntarily they both ducked, putting their hands up to shield themselves. The crack became a long rolling roar and a fighter jet screamed overhead, just a few hundred feet above the desert floor. Within seconds it was just a dot, heading away over the mountains.

Lisa exhaled. 'It felt like he was aiming for our heads. Are they even allowed to do that?'

'They can do what they like.'

'I bet Raj hated it.'

'He's not making any noise.'

As they walked back to check on him, Jaz saw something wasn't right. The stroller's red hood was pushed back. The harness was undone.

'He can't have gone far.' He said the words instinctively. Magical thinking, making it true. Lisa was already shouting for him. 'Raj? Raj!' He joined in. 'Raj? Raju? Where are you?'

Hoping to get a better view, Jaz climbed a little way up the big rock and shielded his eyes, trying to spot movement among the bushes. Lisa was heading to the far side of the rocks, cupping her hands to her mouth as she called out Raj's name.

The emptiness was vast, inhuman.

'Jaz, over here!' He responded preconsciously to the tone of Lisa's voice, scrambling down to the ground, running toward the sound. He found her on her hands and knees, peering into a crack in the earth, a kind of hollow which led down under the rock.

'Is he in there?'

'I'm not sure. Raj? Raj?'

Jaz got down on to his belly and wormed partway into the hole to peer into the blackness. All he could see was a broken bottle and a tangle of rusty fencing wire. The hole seemed to be choked with loose stones and brush.

'We need a light.'

'I don't have anything.'

'There must be one in the car. A flashlight. Isn't there an emergency kit or something?'

'I don't know. I don't think so.'

'Well, go check!'

'It's a half-hour back down the trail.'

'Raju! Raj! Damn, I can't see a thing.'

'Raj! Come to Mommy.'

Jaz tried to crawl farther into the hole. There was nothing to be seen, just rocks and beer cans and a bad smell, as if some animal had made it a lair. A coyote? Too late, he thought about snakes and came scrambling back to the surface, breathing heavily.

'I don't think he's down there. It doesn't go very far. It's full of rubble.'

Lisa stood up and ran a few paces, shouting Raj's name. Then she turned and ran in the opposite direction. Jaz couldn't see her eyes behind her sunglasses. A sick feeling descended over him like a shroud. Something had happened, something that wasn't going to come right.

They walked and shouted and walked and shouted, turning wider and wider circles around the rocks until their voices were hoarse in their parched throats and their clothes were coated in fine white dust. Even as his head span and sweat soaked his back, Jaz felt as if an IV were pumping cold gel through his veins. The world was far away; he was trapped somewhere else, somewhere dead and bone-white, outside time and space. He thought perhaps he should look for prints, the ridged soles of a child's sneakers, but any trace had been obliterated by his own tracks, crossing and recrossing the same ground.

1871

His hands quivered and the skin under his eyes burned and above him a whirlwind came out of the north, a great yellow cloud with a fire infolding itself from the heart of it. Inside, hidden from view, were the air-ships, shadowing him as always, and inside them the cloven-footed airmen, their bodies sparkling like burnished brass. He turned his face upwards, in case there should be a message or a hand tugging at a lock of his hair and lifting him up to Heaven, but there was no message and no hand, just a pull from behind as one of the mules in the train briefly lost its footing on the narrow path. He turned in the saddle to watch it right itself under its load of charcoal. The lead mule, the one he trusted with the fragile alembic and the flasks, fixed him with a yellow eye. He spat its curse right back in its long face and kicked his heels into the flanks of his nameless horse. Reluctantly the spavined beast walked on. At length the cloud of light receded, and he was alone in the desert again, his skin prickling with little stars, the tips of his fingers throbbing as if held in scalding steam. Cry and moan, he muttered to himself. Cry and moan, Nephi Parr, for your God is a devouring fire.

Below him, the salt flat's blinding white had softened to amber. The Panamints were scored by deep shadows, the flanks of the distant range the color of ripe peaches. It was, he thought, a lying color. There was no sweetness out there; the nearest water in that direction was thirty miles. The fine white dust coated his clothes and skin, silting his eyebrows and the wiry hair on his arms. The whole plain had once been ocean and this was the origin of the great spectral sailing ships that plowed over it, lost souls eternally on the flood. Ghosted by the dust, he'd crossed before first light and started slipping and climbing over talus, and by the time the sun was overhead he'd made it up on to ancient dry land and was following the trail towards the notch of the pass as the metals in the rocks sang to him in their high glittering voices.

Another hour and the sun would dip. By God's grace he'd reach the Lost Promise before dark. Not that the night held any terrors for him, teem though it did with every form of creeping thing, for he was the moon's representative in that still country, ambassador of change and transformation. The day he first rode into it, following Porter Rockwell the Danite, Christ's blood had streamed in carmine ribbons across the sky and the sun had hammered inside his skull, and there had been great wrath and majesty and many deceptions of mind and eye. He'd been a young man, one of nine, covenanted to pray and never cease to pray to Almighty God to avenge the murder of their Prophet upon the Nation, all sworn that they would teach the same to their children and their children's children unto the third and fourth generation. They had ridden down out of the Sierras like a terrible swift sword, their hearts filled with love.

He took a swig of warm water from his canteen, as a figure appeared on the ridge and raised its hand. It wasn't long before he could see the shacks and the pile of tailings by the mouth of the mine. The older of the two German brothers took the horse's bridle and asked him in his halting English if he was well. He nodded and started to unload his gear, carefully lifting the iron flasks of quicksilver and stacking them in rows. The younger brother was working the arrastra, whipping four bony mules as they dragged the heavy grindstones over the crushed ore in the circular bed. He peered at the blue-black grit. It was the consistency of fine sand. They must have been walking the circuit several days to grind it down so far.

'You add water today?'

The young German shook his head.

'You ought to. It's dry.'

Over in the shade of the mine car was a third man, squatting on his haunches beside the rails, chipping at a lump of ore with a hammer.

'What's the Chinaman doing here?'

The German shrugged. 'Working.'

'Damn yellow ape.'

He did not give way to anger, though for a moment there came a noise of wings, like the noise of great waters. The Chinaman paused in his task and peered at him from under his wide straw hat.

'Don't you dare look at me.'

The Chinaman turned away and took up his hammer again. Least it wasn't a nigger. Parr was very clear on niggers. The Lord God had caused a cursing to come upon the Lamanites, a sore cursing because of their iniquity. They had hardened their hearts against Him and He had caused that they should be loathsome unto his people's eyes. He'd used up more than one of the devils during the war between the States and it was on account of such a killing that he'd lost his wives and been cast out to wander in the desert. That one had been got up as a preacher no less, a light-skinned buck who'd taken a high and mighty tone as he proffered his coin at the ferry crossing. If there was one kind of coon Parr hated harder than all the others, it was a yellow. Boy, he'd said to that monkey of a preacher, shall I tell you the law of God in regard to the Negro Race? If a white man mixes his blood with the seed of Cain, the penalty is death on the spot. The nigger said he never heard of such a law. He shot him in the face.

The German brothers fell to lighting a little pot-bellied stove and he sat and ate with them and afterwards they smoked and the older one asked if he would perform a divination as to the quality of the coming amalgamation. It was a trivial matter but he felt agreeable and so he took off his hat and placed the Urim and the Thummim over his eyes and overhead the sky cracked and it was as if a wheel stood before him, comprising seven wheels, one turning into the other. The seven hubs in the middle were like one hub eternally giving birth to the rims and the spokes of the wheels, and this divine air-ship manifested itself in the way it had for many months and years, emerging out of groundlessness to guide him on his spiritual path. In the light of the air-ship he saw every moment of his life, as if the whole was presented before his sight like a tapestry, from the time of his birth at Ambrosia on Marrowbone Stream, to the present instant in which he sat with the twin gems over his eyes, speaking prophecy.

He saw his mother lifting him up in his swaddling clothes to show him the true site of the Garden of Eden, there in Jackson County, Missouri, and saw himself climbing trees and fishing in the water and recalled that place as his own Eden, with orchards and ponds and hives of honey and full cribs of corn. He saw the Gentile mob tarring and feathering his father and the cabin burning and the oxen lying shot in the field. He saw the Saints run off their land and the militia riding in to Far West with their soot-blackened faces. He saw the rope and the rim of the well and the tangle of limbs at the bottom, and as all things arise from one by the mediation of one, he saw that all things in his life had their birth from this one thing by adaptation. The sun was his father, the moon his mother; the wind had carried him in its belly, the earth had been his nurse. He spake words of prophecy and afterwards all was silence and darkness and void.

The next morning he awoke and began the work of amalgamation. As the older brother drove the mules, he and the younger poured water. When he judged the consistency of the paste in the arrastra bed to be right, he directed the brothers to stop while he made an assay of the mud, turning it over in his hands, noting the way it slid through his fingers; not too watery, but slick, rich, the trapped silver singing loud to him, begging for release. Helped by the younger brother – he refused to let the Chinaman anywhere near the work – he sprinkled rock salt and magistral into the mix, and made another assay. By that time it was late afternoon. They rested the mules and sat down to wait for moonrise. They smoked and drank coffee and when the white moon appeared over the mountains, waxing gibbous, he stood and turned to them and raised his hands.

'In the name of Jesus,' he testified, 'I tell you this is the very Spirit of Truth. From the world's beginning all the Saints have desired to behold its face.' The Germans looked up, tin cups gripped in their fearful hands, two mustached faces silvered by the moonlight. He showed them a flask of Almadén quicksilver, mined and purified in the Sierras, unscrewed the stopper and poured the precious fluid out into an iron tub. There it lay shimmering, paradoxical and mysterious. 'As Christ is my witness, I am telling you no word of a lie. What you see is the very light of Jesus, flowing down into the darkness of matter. It dwells in fiery form in the sky and leads Earth up to Heaven. It is the Secret, hidden from the beginning. I tell you, it transcends both life and death.' And then, as always when he spoke in this manner, he was broken up by emotion and began to weep, for, in his own evocation of the threshold, he saw again the rim of the well, the rope, the feminine arms and legs in their slop of blood and calico. Three raped sister-wives, stuffed in there by the Gentiles. He was the smallest, twelve years old. They'd lowered him in a sling while his brother Jed cut the husband down from a tree. It was too much and he'd swooned and he never saw his home country again after that, for when he came round they'd crossed the river and were already in Illinois.

Together the German brothers looked upon the quicksilver and under his direction helped to pour it into a canvas bag, and he walked round the arrastra, squeezing and kneading it so that little drops fell on to the mud like fine metal rain. As he seeded the mud, he was moved to school the brothers in the Mysteries, and whether they understood or not or cared or not and whether the Chinaman overheard or not was of no importance to him, for he told of the One out of which proceeded the Three, which are Mercury, Sulfur and Salt, and how out of those three proceeded all the many substances of the World, which are truly one substance, infused and inspirited with God's luminous love. And that was how it was for the next days and nights while they incorporated the ore pulp and drew it off and spread it out under the scorching sun for Apollo's fire to work its influence. He preached and testified and the quicksilver sought out the precious metal in the mud and bound itself to it, drawing the comely light of the Lord out of the base nigger darkness of matter.

Every morning he made an assay, rubbing the silvery mud between his fingers, shaking sediment in a glass flask and watching it fall. They had ten mules and the Chinaman walking through the cake of ore-pulp to mix it through, and sometimes its body was hot and sometimes cold, and he added quicksilver and magistral as needed to balance the two principles. Little by little, the amalgamation progressed, and they washed and rinsed and purified and reduced and daily there was less gray offal in the swirling flask and the shining globule of amalgam that sank to the bottom was fatter and more solid and shone brighter than before. And on the twenty-third day it seemed to Nephi Parr that the final work should begin and he gave the order to light the furnace.

While the brothers waited for moonrise, he took a spyglass and climbed the peak above the mine. The sun was setting and the desert was washing its robe in red, as if preparing for some nocturnal orgy. As he climbed he wondered if death was finally overtaking him, for he thought he heard a flapping of great wings and above his head the firmament was like a sapphire throne, studded with agate and beryl and porphyry and chrysoprase. His whole left side was numb and under his shirt the skin was peeling away from his back. Do not call me to judgement, Lord, he begged. Not until I have completed this last work. He surveyed the land through the spyglass. At his feet the cliff tipped away into the void and he knew himself for a sinner whose bones would bleach out on the sands and whose disfellowshipped soul would never enter the Celestial Kingdom, clutching its scrying stone, for the light that played across the desert's white body seemed not the singular and steadfast light of God, but the mutable light of Mercury, laughter of fools and wonder of the wise. And then he dropped the spyglass and saw it shatter on the ground, for a sign had been given him: until their magnified appearance before his squinting eye he had not known the Lost Promise mine looked down on Three-Finger Rocks, where once he had felt ease of heart and certainty of purpose, waiting with Porter Rockwell to enact salvation upon one Lyman Pierce, who had traveled very far from Illinois to atone for his sins.

The Three that arise out of the One. He had been young, unschooled in the Mysteries. Now he saw the true meaning of the place. All things had birth from one thing, and his own destiny had always been to return here, to the place of death and generation, the very cradle of the Secret.

They had ridden for weeks to reach those stones. Precious blood was crying out under the altar, begging for retribution, and Brother Rockwell had received testimony concerning the man Pierce, who was said to be at Santa Fe, preparing to lead a party of emigrants over the Spanish trail. Atonement had been Rockwell's trade even while the Prophet was alive, and though the California goldfields had lured him away from Zion, he'd never broken fellowship with the Saints, and was known as far as San Francisco to be the Samson of their faith. Joseph Smith himself had laid a hand on his shoulder and prophesied that as long as he cut not his hair, neither bullet nor blade could harm him; and so it had proved. Port Rockwell was called the Destroying Angel by his enemies and Lion of God by his friends, for he had put aside many sinners in the name of Jesus Christ and pulled more than one young Mormon off a barroom floor and set him to the Lord's work. So it had been with Nephi Parr, who had not prospered on the American River and found his way to the camp at Murderer's Bar, where Rockwell supplied whiskey and whores to the Gentiles. The man had loomed over him, looking like a mountain and speaking consoling words in his strange high voice. So of course Parr had followed and learned the secret signs and sworn with the others that he would disembowel himself and slit his own throat if he ever broke silence about the work for which Rockwell had chosen him, which was to use up this hateful Pierce, who five years earlier had blacked his face and howled and cavorted outside Carthage jail, and was said by witnesses to have kicked and spat upon and in other nameless ways defiled the Prophet's dear corpse after he was shot to death by the rioters.

So they had ridden eastwards out of the mountains and entered the great desert, where their lips cracked and their eyes were dazzled by the whiteness of the land, which at midday seemed to breathe and palpitate, so that Nephi came to understand he was riding upon the white breast of the living earth and felt his mind overcome with dread at the immensity of the Most High. And after many days they came to the Three-Finger Rocks, planted by the Father in that desolate place as a sign of his blessing on their enterprise. Under the rocks was camped a ragged band of Paiutes, and Rockwell, who spoke their language, seemed to expect the meeting, greeting their chief and sitting down with them to smoke and parlay. He told the savages that the Mormonee were at war with the Mericats and enlisted their aid. The chief accepted a present of rifles and the two parties set to waiting, during which time Hosea Doyle, younger even than Nephi, fell sick with fever and the brethren laid hands on him and rebuked his disease in the name of the Lord. After that he was well again, which all took as a further sign of favor.

Following many days of idleness the emigrant train was sighted and they clad themselves like savages, in paint and feathers, and fell upon it by night and the Lord God delivered his enemies into the hands of his servants. Lyman Pierce died hard and slow up on the Three-Finger Rocks, begging for mercy until they relented and turned him off, and of his companions a third part fell by the sword and a third were scattered to the wind, women and children alike. When it was done they laid the bodies out on the sand, scalping and stripping them to give further semblance of a savage raid, and though Nephi Parr went back to Deseret and tried to live a settled life on the Green River, sealing to himself two good wives who hearkened to his counsel and were in every way ornaments of his kingdom, he could not forget the Three-Finger Rocks or the heathen markings scratched upon them. He would sit and brood outside his cabin at the ferry, watching the passengers assemble, and it seemed to him that the world outside the Celestial City was a wicked place, full of sorcerers and whoremongers and murderers and idolaters and those who loveth and telleth a lie. And soon enough all turned to dust and ashes in his mouth, for there was blood and war and rumors of war and politics or tricks as he preferred to word it, and instead of standing firm his brethren stole his wives and property and cut him loose to wander the earth, betrayed and disfellowshipped.

*

He left the shattered spyglass lying on the ground and trod the path back down towards the mine. The rising moon lit his way and as he neared the main shaft he saw the German brothers had lit the furnace in readiness for the last purification. Together they heated the amalgam in the fire and trapped the vapor with a copper hood, and the quicksilver renounced its subtile form and dripped back into a flask, and behind in the crucible was left pure silver. In the sky were signs and wonders and he lifted up his hands and saw the serpent with its tail in its mouth and for a moment he stood on the threshold between two worlds, bathed in an aura of violet and green and yellow. Through his art he had released the light of nature, and before his eyes this light suffused the whole world with knowledge of salvation, redeeming it and making it once again entire.

The next day he woke to find his limbs swollen and a great hammering behind his eyes and he could not understand the words the two brothers were speaking any more than he could the Chinaman, for the Lord had stopped his ears and made him deaf. By signs, the brothers gave him to understand that he had fallen into an ecstasy and they had been obliged to hold him down as a spirit rent his body, and at last it had come out of him and he had been as one dead. While he lay in his swoon they had poured the silver into molds and they showed him the fruits of the labor, of which he took two bars by way of payment and packed them in his saddlebags and got up on to his horse.

He rode in the direction of the Three-Finger Rocks, leaning low over the horse's neck, for he could not sit upright. Above him circled the air-ships and all about was change and transformation. As he rode he raised his hand to his face and saw the bones glowing inside it and a coyote howled and the sun shone through the palm of his hand like glass. And by this he knew his body was shrugging off its animal nature and it would soon come time to make the crossing. Oh God, he whispered, hear the words of my mouth; and the whole jumble of his life wheeled round him, bare running feet cut bloody by winter stubble, a cutlass and a fiery wheel and a camel and a steamboat bolted together on the floodplain of the Colorado. He saw men compelled to eat the flesh of their sons and daughters and Rockwell's unshorn hair and at last the air-ship came down and the Angel Moroni and the gods of many worlds appeared, calling him up to exaltation.

2008

Nicky's leg was throbbing. He spent most of the night sitting on the bed in his underpants, picking little black splinters out of his calf and watching old movies on cable. Men lit women's cigarettes. Soldiers sacrificed themselves for their buddies. Cowboys raced the stage-coach, watched by Indians on the ridge. It all circled round and round until he couldn't follow anymore and drifted off to sleep. When he woke, the room was too hot. The sun backlit the curtains. Someone was running a vacuum cleaner on the other side of the wall. He supposed he had to make a decision. Should he go back to LA? He just didn't have the heart for it. The explaining. Rehab. The self-righteous shit Jimmy would come out with at band meeting.

Someone knocked on his door and called out in Spanish. He shouted at them to wait. Breakfast. Never get into anything heavy before breakfast. He limped about looking for shades and car keys, then drove down the hill to the diner, the run-down one shaped like a spaceship. At the counter, he got in a weird row with the waitress about bacon. It's not supposed to be burnt to a cinder, he told her. It's bacon, she sneered. Bacon is crispy. If you didn't want crispy you should have ordered ham.

He came out of the place brushing bits of food off his clothes and decided to have a gander round town. The only place that looked at all enticing – in fact the only place in walking distance that wasn't boarded up or selling fast food – was a bunker-like thrift store. Toys and furniture were piled up on the pavement outside. Two supersize women reclined on unplugged massage chairs either side of the door, like a pair of obese ornamental lions. Both gave him the evil eye as he walked up. Inside, the place was a consumer graveyard. The wreckage of every cultural fad since the late seventies had been piled up on long metal shelves. Games cartridges, Barbie dolls, VHS tapes, dusty framed posters of cars and airbrushed Coke cans. A slurry of *Reader's Digests* spilled out of a cardboard box in one aisle, blocking the way to the crockery. The rear opened out on to a large back lot filled with appliances and laminate furniture and racks of paperback books bleached pale yellow by the sun. A jet-ski was sur- really beached in front of a row of fridges marking the yard's back boundary. A rack of clothes, mostly desert fatigues, had a marine's dress uniform at one end. Nicky slipped on the jacket. Nice. Team it with some glitter and it'd look fierce on Brick Lane. Still wearing it, he wandered back inside, half aware of someone hovering about behind him.

Finally he found the vinyl, stacked up in milk crates in a corner. Usual crap. *Herb Alpert's Tijuana Brass: Two Hundred Million More Yuletide Classical Faves Sung by a Tit in an Orange Tie*. There were a couple of good sleeves, eighties people with neon clothes and flam- mable hair. Then he turned up something with a hand-drawn cover, featuring a dog-headed figure with cartoon lines emanating from its body. It was standing beside a Joshua tree in front of a weird, organic- looking thing that was probably supposed to be rocks. It looked somehow familiar, though he couldn't remember where he'd seen it before. Seemed to be a Krautrock record. *Time of Transposition / The Ashtar Galactic Command*. That certainly sounded German.

It was hard to say whether Time of Transposition was the name of the band or the album. He flipped it over and reflexively slid the inner out of the sleeve. The disk was a bit dusty, but otherwise in good nick. The center label read 1971, and it was obviously some kind of private press thing. On the back of the sleeve was a track listing (two long tracks, 'Time of Transposition', 1 and 2) and a blurb, which was written in blurry purple type that was impossible to read.

Probably worth a bob or two.

Even so, it was exactly the kind of hippie crap Noah had been waving at him for months and he didn't feel inclined to buy it. He took the marine jacket and a couple of the eighties records to the counter, waiting for one of the enormous women to rouse herself and make it over to the till. He had a feeling she didn't like selling him the jacket. Not that he gave a toss. He put it on as he walked out of the door, flashing her a tin-soldier salute. He sauntered down the block, feeling quite fuck you; he was peering through the window of something called a Weight Loss Center, trying to see if it was full of fat people doing exercises, when some kid came up behind him and said hey. He looked about thirteen and kind of Pakistani and was dressed as your standard-issue mini gangsta – everything two sizes too big, baseball cap with the sticky label still on the brim.

'Bro, are you Nicky Capaldi?'

'Yeah.'

'Awesome! I knew it was you! She said it wasn't, but it was. Laila! Laila! It's him.'

A girl was standing halfway down the block, looking mortified. Her black hair hung in a curtain over her face. Despite the heat she was dressed in full emo black. Dress shirt buttoned up to the neck, jeans, ten-hole steel-toe Docs, silver jewelry. She trudged forward and raised a hand in a weak greeting.

'Sorry,' she said. It wasn't clear what she was apologizing for.

Nicky was over meeting fans. It always got weird. They gave you stuff: knitted portraits, poems written in their blood. It was better if they were hot, but that came with a whole other set of problems. More than once he'd had to call for Terry after getting himself cornered in a dressing room or toilet cubicle by some girl who was now threatening to cut herself/him/cry rape/not eat/tell their boyfriend/brother/dad if he didn't do whatever it was he no longer felt like doing. This one was clutching a record behind her back.

'Do you want me to sign that?'

'Whatever,' she said. 'I saw you looking at it. That's all.'

It was the hippie album he'd left in the shop.

'Oh, right. I thought it was one of ours.'

'No. Sorry.'

The boy piped up. 'Laila tried to go see you when you played in San Diego, but our uncle wouldn't let her.'

'Shut up, Samir.'

'He brought her back from the bus station.'

'He strict, then, your uncle?'

The girl shrugged and flicked her hair. As she tilted her head to the side, he saw the dark skin of her throat. She'd powdered her face chalk-white. He figured her for about seventeen.

'Yeah,' she said. 'Compared to Americans.'

'Where you from, then?'

'Greatest nation in the world!' butted in the boy. 'US of A!'

'Iraq,' said the girl. 'Though my ADD brother tells people he's American. I'm Laila, he's Samir. Not Juan-Carlos or Scarface or whatever he told you.'

'Eat me.'

'You are so fucking lame.'

Nicky was confused. 'You're Iraqi. And you're out here – what – on holiday?'

'We live in this shithole. Our uncle works on the base.'

'So, he's in the army?'

'Let's talk about something else, OK?'

'Laila has a picture of you inside her Spanish grammar book,' Samir mentioned confidentially.

'Well,' said Nicky, eyeing the distance to his car. 'That's great. I'm glad you're feeling the music and everything. It makes it all worth while.'

Laila looked stricken. 'Don't go,' she said. 'Just one more minute. My brother's a retard, but you have no idea how fucked up our world is. If I could have made it to that show, I would have. Your music's about the only thing that keeps me sane.'

'Thanks,' said Nicky. 'I appreciate it. You take it easy.'

She pointed to the records in his hand. 'You have a record deck, right? What am I saying? You're probably staying in a fancy place, with like a widescreen and a pool.'

'I'm just in a motel.'

'Because we've got one at our place.'

'Right.'

'And Uncle Hafiz has all this cool old Egyptian pop music.'

'Sounds like cats,' said Samir. 'No bass at all.'

'I'd love to, but you know how it is.'

'Sure.'

'But it was good to meet you.'

'You too. It's the best thing that's happened to me all year.'

Samir jumped back and took a couple of pictures with his phone. Automatically Nicky smiled, putting his arm round the girl's shoulders. She molded herself to his side.

'OK, guys, I should get on.'

He walked back towards his car, the high collar of the marine tunic rubbing at his neck. When he turned round, he saw the two kids were just standing there on the pavement, watching him.

On the way to the motel he stopped off at a market and bought toiletries, booze, a pack of white vests and a pair of surf shorts with a picture of a palm tree on the arse. Back at the motel he put on the shorts and went for a swim, sculling on his back and blinking into the sunlight. He thought about the band and about the album and nothing much good came to mind, which made him start to think about drugs. A nibble on one of those buttons might help take the edge off. He could sit out by the pool, watch the sunset, then drive to get a pizza once the rush had worn off. Plan. He was air-drying on one of the loungers, smoking a self-congratulatory fag, when a policeman came and started talking to the big-haired motel manager. Dude was actually wearing a cowboy hat, which reminded him of how many movies he'd seen the previous night. Mentally he tallied up what he'd done lately. He couldn't think of anything particularly illegal, unless somehow they'd found the gun. If they'd found the gun he'd have to call Terry. But the cop just talked to the manager and went away again, didn't even look in his direction.

He went to the room for a beer and flopped back down on the lounger. A few minutes later two more cops turned up, a man and a woman, with Jaz's wife in tow. He was pleased to see her and waved, forgetting he didn't actually know her except through Jaz's description. She gave him a strange look – more blank than puzzled – and disappeared into their room.

He decided against eating any peyote.

Jaz's wife came out, sort of leaning on the woman. The manager hurried out of the office and threw her arms round her. All this was happening over by the office, and Nicky couldn't hear what they were saying, but it looked like she was really spazzing out. He hated stress at the best of times, and hearing about really dark stuff – war-dark, news-channel-dark – tended to trigger a desire to self-medicate. He'd once tried to explain to a reporter about the three-day bender he'd gone on after the invasion of Iraq. It hadn't been a protest exactly. More a nervous reaction.

The cops left with Mrs Jaz. He decided to find out what was going on. Leaving his towel on the lounger, he went over to the office and knocked on the rattly screen door.

'Hello? Hello?'

The manager came out from the back. She looked a wreck.

'Sorry to bother you, but is everything OK?'

'Sure ain't. It's that couple and their little boy. He's lost some-where out near Pinnacle Rocks. They're searching for him now.' She lit a cigarette. 'Police, Park Rangers, they're all out. Parents turned their back and he was gone.'

Standing there in his swim shorts with the air conditioner blow-ing down on his neck, Nicky felt cold and damp. Jaz's kid. Christ. He was about to thank the woman and go back to the pool when a gravelly voice spoke through the screen door.

'Dawn? You in there?'

He turned to find himself face to face with the cop in the cowboy hat. He was a middle-aged man, whose large doughy face was set on top of a surprisingly thin body, as if two totally separate physical types had been mashed together to create him. Between the bristly mustache and the aviator sunglasses, he might as well have been wearing a mask.

'Afternoon, son.'

For a moment, Nicky caught his own twin reflections in the mir-rored lenses.

The cop scanned his tattoos and curled his lip in distaste. Nicky crossed his arms self-protectively over his narrow chest. He felt naked, talking to a man who had so many accessories – a hat and shades and a badge and a big black leather belt with pouches and cuffs and a baton and a holstered gun – when he had none. Dawn leaned on the counter and jabbed her cigarette in his direction.

'Tom, gentleman here was just asking about the kid.'

He turned to Nicky. 'That a fact? Deputy Sheriff Loosemore, San Bernardino County. And you are?'

'Nicky Capaldi.'

'Where you from, son?'

'London. England.'

'I know where London is. Went there couple years back. Can't say as I cared for it. What happened to your leg?'

'I fell over on to a cactus.'

'Looks infected.'

'It was just an accident.'

'So what about the kid?'

'What's happened to him?'

'You tell me.'

'Sorry?'

'You have any dealings with the child?'

'Dealings?'

'You talk to him? Dawn says you had him in your room.'

'He doesn't talk, as such. I gave him and his dad a lift to the Burger King last night. Jaz's missus'd gone off with the car.'

'The mother had the car.'

'I told you about that,' put in Dawn. 'I ran into her at Mulligan's Lounge, making nice to the boys.'

Jaz couldn't be too pleased. He didn't seem like a bloke who'd be overly flexible about that sort of thing. 'Do you think someone took him?' he asked. 'I hope nothing bad's happened. He's a sweet kid.'

The sheriff looked him up and down again. 'So you like kids, son?'

'Sure,' he replied carefully. There seemed to be an atmosphere in the room.

'That so? Got any?'

'No.'

'I got three.'

'That's nice.'

'Two girls and a boy. I'd hate like hell to see anything to happen to them. Now, you're telling me you got friendly with Mr Matahari and his son last night?'

'Mr Mat – uh, I didn't catch the name. Like I said, they needed to go and get food, so I gave them a lift.'

'He was real intimate with the boy,' interjected Dawn. 'I was kind of surprised. Kid's shy.'

What was her game? All hair and fag and green eyeshadow. 'He's autistic,' he explained, throwing her a poisonous look. 'It's a condition. His dad was glad he was responding to someone.'

'And you responded to him too, I expect. Sweet kid like that.'

The sheriff took off his sunglasses. His eyes were small and pale and bedded, top and bottom, in dark puffy pouches, like maggots on spoiled meat. Nicky suddenly had a very clear vision of the down-side of his situation. He made a silent vow to get rid of Noah's gun. And the drugs. And then to enter rehab. Or a monastery. Whatever it took to get away from those maggoty eyes.

'Bit parky in here, what with the air conditioning. I'll just go get a shirt.'

'Hold up a minute. I got a few more questions.'

'I'll come straight back.'

The sheriff turned to Dawn. 'Where's his room?'

'Number five, middle of the block.'

'Alright, son, I'll walk over with you.'

'No need, honest.'

'Just lead the way.'

The twenty paces to his room felt like a trek across open country. He was pretty sure he'd stashed the drugs, but where was the gun? It was possible that he'd been mucking about with it while watching a Bogart movie. There'd definitely been gunplay in that movie. It could be lying there on the bed. He opened the door gingerly.

Nothing obvious. The sheriff stood in the doorway while he found his jeans and a T-shirt. If he went into the bathroom to change out of his swimming shorts, the guy might look through his stuff. He undid the string and stood with his thumbs inside the waistband.

'Do you mind?'

'You go right ahead.'

Reluctantly he turned his scrawny buttocks towards the sheriff, who lit a cigarette.

'Tell me, son, you in a gang?'

'No, a band. Musician.'

'You one of them white rappers?'

'No.'

'I see. You probably feel happier now you got your pants on. Less nervous, I expect.'

Another cop came over and said something to the sheriff, who stepped outside, holding up a hand in Nicky's direction as if to freeze him in place.

The sheriff stepped back in. 'Now, son, looks like I got to be elsewhere, but if you'd be so kind as to give your particulars to the deputy here, no doubt I'll see you later. I'd much appreciate it if you didn't go anywhere until I say so. You may be able to help us out.'

Without waiting for an answer he strode off. The deputy, a young Hispanic woman with a braid and the same reflective sunglasses as her boss, took out her notebook.

'Mind showing me some ID, sir?'

He found his wallet on top of the TV. She peered at his driver's license and handed it back, a quizzical smile on her face.

'Should I know you? You look kind of familiar.'

A helicopter swept overhead, the roar of its rotors filling in for his response.

Twenty minutes and an autograph later, he was on his own again. He flushed the peyote down the toilet, drew the curtains, put the chain on the door and sat against the foot of the bed, smoking and watching a local news channel's eye-in-the-sky feed of the desert. A scatter of parked cars. A straggly line of deputies sweeping the area.

The situation was fucked up.

He watched TV until the sun went down and he felt safe enough to walk out behind the motel and look for a place to drop the gun. A big fuck-off gold pistol. It would have to be the flashiest cunt of a gun in the whole world. He knew he ought to drive somewhere further off, but was scared he'd get pulled over. He stood out in the open for a long time, feeling the last of the heat radiating out of the sand and listening to the distant sound of rotors. Some miles away, a helicopter was directing a floodlight at the ground. He watched it hover, a matchstick of light.

In the end he just walked back to the room and switched on the TV. All evening there were comings and goings outside. Voices, car engines, the crackle of police radios. He could still remember, very distinctly, the pressure of the little boy's hand gripping his.

He was woken early the next morning by a loud rap on the door. He struggled into his jeans and squinted through the spyhole. It wasn't a cop. Some guy in a suit and tie. The guy kept knocking for a while, then gave up. Nicky took a shower, dressed and checked the spyhole. No one there. When he stepped outside he saw suit-and-tie just down the block. Behind him stood another guy with a video camera.

He shut the door quietly and walked off as quickly as he could without breaking into a run, skirting the pool so as not to draw their attention. Suddenly the office door clattered open and the manager came running out of the office.

'Get off my property. Go on. Right now. You're trespassing. You're not guests of the motel and you didn't sign in, so get the hell out of here.'

'Ma'am,' said suit-and-tie, 'we're just trying to do our job. We'd be happy to get your point of view also.'

Dawn told them to leave her customers alone and suit-and-tie said something about the First Amendment and Nicky tiptoed round the corner to find that the whole front lot was full of cars. There were police vehicles and outside-broadcast vans and station wagons full of local teens hoping to see some action. Cops were drinking coffee out of Styrofoam cups. News presenters were climbing on boxes to get the motel sign in frame. There was a peculiar carnival atmosphere.

He heard his name being called and turned to find a boy ambling towards him. Seventeen, maybe. White-framed dark glasses and directional hair.

'Nicky Capaldi? I blog at *Sounds West*. What are you doing here?'

'I'm trying to get some breakfast.'

'Are you something to do with the missing kid? I mean, like a relative or something?'

'What are you on about? Shit, my car's boxed in.'

'Well, it seems like too much of a coincidence that you're here, like, with this kidnapping going on? I mean, are you here to do a televised appeal?'

'What have you heard?'

'Just that there's this kid and he's missing?'

In his peripheral vision, Nicky saw Deputy Sheriff Loosemore. Apparently the blogger was even more unnerved than he was; he immediately made himself scarce. The sheriff leaned against the nearest Crown Victoria and looked him up and down. A few teenagers sidled closer, taking pictures of them talking.

'Deputy Alvarez said you were famous.'

'Any news on the kid?'

'None. We got every available man out looking, so any leads would be appreciated. You met the boy. I'm sure you understand.'

He gestured towards his car, like a salesman. Nicky got in and tried to look nonchalant for the kids sticking their phones up to the passenger window.

'Looks like you're a regular pied piper to the young folk,' said Loosemore, dropping the sentence on to Nicky's lap like a rattlesnake. They drove in silence to the station, where in a small act of mercy Nicky was given a coffee and a rubbery Danish which gave him a momentary sugar rush he mistook for optimism. In an interview room, with a tape-recorder running, he told the story. The kid running into his room, the trip to Burger King, the chitchat with Jaz. So why had he got up so late? Where had he been during the day? He told the sheriff about the kids at the thrift store, the argument with the waitress at the diner. The interrogation went on and on. In a break, he said he needed to go to the loo, locked himself in a cubicle and phoned Terry.

'Where the hell are you, Nicky?'

'Come and get me.'

'Where are you?'

'Just fucking come, right now.'

'Nicky, listen to me. Are you OK?'

'No. I'm in a cop shop. You've got to come and get me.'

'Have they arrested you? Did you get arrested? It says on the internet you kidnapped a kid.'

'It says I did what?'

'You didn't do it, right?'

'Who says? Who says I did?'

'Nicky, you need to get yourself together.'

'How did this even happen to me? Right now, Terry. Come. I mean it.'

1920

The Indian was up on the rocks. He must have watched them riding across the salt flat and decided to make a stand. When the posse men started to climb, he fired a couple of rounds, sending them squirming on their bellies for cover. They came back down, cursing. He couldn't last forever. Food, ammunition or water: one of them would run short. Then it'd just be a question of who'd go up and get him. Until then, they'd have to sit and wait him out.

Deighton looked up at the sky. Though it wasn't yet nine in the morning, the light was fierce. It fell on his head like a curse, a reminder of the guilt he bore. Without him and the lie he told, there would be no manhunt. He knew he ought to put a stop to it, to tell them he'd made a mistake, suffered an hallucination – whatever it would take. But they weren't going to listen. The professor, the Boston Brahmin. Out here he was the lowest of the low, the lowest a white man could be.

He knew the place. That was what scared him most. Not by sight. From the last story Eliza had transcribed. *You must travel to the Three-Finger Rocks and look inside the cave beneath them. There you will find Yucca Woman, weaving a basket.* It was where the old Spanish friar had gone, during his missing days. *She is weaving together this world and the Land of the Dead.* It was the secret place, the womb of the mystery.

Death was in the sky, in the bone light hurting his eyes. Death was coursing through the sand under his feet.

He could taste it in his mouth.

He wasn't even sure what he'd seen. But if he'd invented it, if it was some fragment of his unconscious mind, he should have been able to explain. A perception in the absence of a stimulus. A trick of his war-disordered brain.

★

It had begun in the Indian camp at Kairo, when he drove out to check Eliza's work. She was sullen, as she usually was when he drew attention to her habitual sloppiness. He'd taught her his method of notation, and in the field she'd learned the value of rigor when checking grammar and pronunciation, yet she persisted in making elementary mistakes. He had every right to speak sharply. If there were to be any record of the desert Indian culture, it would have to be made now. The Indians were dying out. They were already impure, both culturally and in terms of blood. Take the informant, this Willie Prince. He admitted to a white grandparent. He'd grown up at least partly in a civilized context and had huge gaps in his tribal knowledge. And he was one of the more useful ones. There were at least two people in the camp who appeared to have some level of Negroid admixture. They were all far from pristine.

Unexpectedly, Eliza started to cry. He told her not to behave like a child. She'd known what marriage would entail. It wasn't as if he'd sugar-coated the thing. He'd made clear when he proposed that if she didn't feel she was cut out for the work, she should go back to New York and find herself some schoolteacher. She'd sworn she loved him. Still, she was a woman, and he had the impression she expected to be coddled. When he first left her out at Kairo, she'd utterly failed to see the logic. The two of them could gather twice as much material if they worked separately. Of course there was a certain amount of discomfort involved, but her objections were grounded in selfishness.

Checking her work took time, and he stayed at the camp longer than he intended. He had business in town, letters to write and send to Washington, and now it was too dark to drive across the desert. He told Eliza to find a spot by a fire and went to the car to fetch his bedroll. The cold was bitter. A fierce wind was blowing across the basin, the kind that cut through clothing and made its way deep into the bones. His hands already felt cramped, and he had no expectation of sleep.

When he came back, he was surprised to find that Eliza hadn't waited for him. It took a few moments to spot her, just one shape among the dozen or so huddled inside the largest wickiup. He shook her and asked what she thought she was playing at. She told him flatly to go away. The figure lying next to her propped itself up on an elbow. It was Willie Prince. Deighton was taken aback by the frankness of the man's stare. Indians usually avoided one's gaze. This buck looked impassively out of his broad flat face, entirely unafraid of being caught lying next to a white man's wife.

Deighton's first instinct was to strike them both, but he mastered it. He was not about to have an argument in front of a research subject.

'Come outside, right now.'

Reluctantly Eliza got up, but not before a look passed between her and Prince that was unmistakable in its import. Deighton felt physically sick. Eliza was a half-educated girl. He'd worked hard on her, made her fit to assist him in his labor. He'd shown her every consideration. He expected if not gratitude, then at least a recognition of the distinction he'd conferred on her by asking her to be his wife.

They stood opposite each other, shivering in the cold.

'What in heaven's name is going on?'

She shrugged. 'Something's happened.'

'Your vagueness is always infuriating. Now tell me precisely and clearly. I don't want to hang about all night.'

'I can't be your wife anymore.'

It was unthinkable. He couldn't in good conscience call the man a savage, for he had too much respect for the People's culture. *Primitive* would be the term, a consciousness whose horizons were limited in unimaginable ways. He had always considered himself tolerant, but now that he was forced to contemplate miscegenation as a real physical act, a wave of disgust rose up in his throat. She might be (what had his mother written in that foul letter?) a 'little shopgirl', but she was still a white woman.

While he struggled for a response, she told him she was going back to bed. They would talk properly in the morning. He rubbed the smooth scar tissue on his chin, unable to marshal his thoughts.

He commandeered Segunda's ramada, spreading out his blankets as close as possible to the dying fire. Whether it was an effect of stress, or his general poor constitution, he felt a sudden need to evacuate his bowels and walked out into the desert to find a spot. Before he squatted, he looked warily around. As expected, several of the camp dogs had followed him and were sniffing about, waiting to eat the fresh excrement. He'd never been particularly bothered by the squalor of Indian settlements, but this he always found supremely disgusting. There was one animal in particular, a big black mastiff which sometimes tried to knock him out of the way even before he'd finished. Thankfully, it didn't seem to be among the pack, and he threw a couple of stones at the others, which trotted out of range and loitered, waiting their chance.

He exhaled, trying to relax his sphincter. There was just enough light to see the little plume of his breath before the wind snatched it away. He'd been squatting a few minutes when he caught sight of something moving out in the desert. It gave off a faint greenish-white glow, and he indulged the momentary fantasy that he was on an ancient seabed, fathoms deep, watching some eerie bioluminescent fish. He stared, unable to decide what it was. Curiosity aroused, he buttoned himself up and set off to find out.

He walked into the teeth of the wind, shivering and wrapping his arms ineffectually over his chest. When he got closer he was amazed to be confronted by an Indian walking along hand in hand with a white child, a boy about five years of age. Neither seemed to be carrying any luggage, and though both were dressed in light clothes they didn't look as if they were feeling the cold. They weren't making for the camp. There was no settlement in the direction in which they were heading, nothing but barren desert for at least a hundred miles. Strangest of all, the child appeared to be the source of the glow.

The pair paid no attention to him. They didn't even seem to register his existence. Hypnotized, he followed in their wake. Afterwards he wouldn't be able to say why he didn't try to speak to them. Something prevented him. Not fear or shyness exactly. The feeling that he would be intruding. He trailed behind, trying to match their easy stride across the flat moonlit sand. He was walking quickly, fast enough to feel sharp stabs of pain in his chest, but he never seemed to gain on them. There was only one credible explanation: he was dreaming. The glowing boy and the Indian were just fragments, shrapnel thrown out by his restless brain. He slackened his pace, and the strange couple disappeared into the darkness.

The glow. Deighton couldn't be sure. The moon was bright. Perhaps it was just reflecting off the child's pale skin.

As he walked back to the camp, the world started to feel real again and with the return of normality he began to be afraid. Every few paces, he felt compelled to look behind to check if he was being followed. At the edge of camp he found Pete Mason carrying a load of kindling. Had he seen anything? Pete shook his head. Joe Pine was passing a bottle with Serrano Jackie. As Deighton came up they hid it. He waved his hands, trying to show he didn't care about the whiskey. An Indian and a white boy? No, sir, no one like that.

Finally he shook Segunda Hipa awake.

'Segunda, there was a man and a boy here.'

'Go away!'

'A man, and a little white boy.'

'I didn't see anything. I'm sleeping.'

'Yes, yes. But you must know something. Who has a white child?'

'White mothers have white children. Go away now.'

'I saw them, Segunda. The boy was glowing.'

She muttered irritably and rubbed her eyes. 'Go to bed, you Two-Headed Sheep. You didn't see anything special.'

And she pulled the blanket over her head. He swore under his breath and put his head into the fug of the large wickiup. Picking his way over grumbling bodies, he found Eliza. The space beside her was vacant.

'Where is he? Where's Willie Prince?'

'Go away. Please leave me alone.'

She rolled over. Exasperated, he went back to his spot under the ramada. Around him the camp was silent. He filched a few branches from Pete Mason's kindling pile and sat up for a while in front of a desultory fire, trying to work out what he'd seen. After a while he gave up. It was just too cold to think. He wrapped himself up in his blankets and tried to go to sleep.

He was back in the Bois de Belleau. It was early in the morning and he was standing in a trench on the northern edge of the woods. It was a shallow trench, recently and hastily dug, and water was seeping through its unlined sides, pooling in a deep puddle at his feet. Across the field floated long white scarves of mist and the dawn chorus was in full swing, though when he looked up he couldn't see any birds, just the charred, broken branches of the trees. High overhead hung a German observation balloon, a bloated eye looking balefully down on him. As he walked along the trench, the mud sucking at his boots, he realized he was completely alone. His unit had abandoned the position. Afraid, he watched for movement among the trees, signs of an advance. About the blackened stumps flowed a disembodied luminescence, an eerie algal glow.

At dawn he endured a shattering bout of coughing. His chest felt like it was on fire, and there was blood in the filthy handkerchief he tugged out of his pocket and pressed against his mouth. He'd known for a while that the desert air wasn't having the effect the doctors had hoped. In his firm opinion, good health was largely a matter of mental attitude; he refused to become one of the prematurely aged, neurasthenic scarecrows he'd seen hobbling about the veterans' hospital in New Jersey. They were men who'd left the best part of themselves in France.

He found Eliza brewing coffee. Wordlessly, she handed him a tin mug. They drank together companionably, and it was like the early days when he first brought her out to the desert, when he thought he'd found a companion.

'What now, Eliza?'

'I don't know.'

'I have to go back to town. Will you come?'

'No.'

'I see. And what do you propose to do out here in the wilderness?'

'I will shift for myself, I suppose.'

'That's not a practical suggestion, not for an unprotected white woman.'

'That never seemed to concern you before.'

'You're under my protection.'

'Really, David? I've never felt very protected.'

'Where will you go? How will you live?'

'Does it matter to you?'

'I must ask. Are you – this Willie Prince . . .' He couldn't make the words come out.

'He's a good man, David. A kind man. You were many things to me, but you were never kind.'

He could, he supposed, have talked to her about love, tried to woo her back. But that sort of thing had always seemed ridiculous. He'd never been able to play that character, the stage-door Johnny. Even when he still had all his face.

He went to the car, only to discover that the rest of his food had gone. There'd be nothing for breakfast, and it would be early afternoon before he made it back to town for a hot meal. A little gang of children watched him rummage in his footlocker. He knew they were probably the thieves, and though it broke all his rules – about decorum, about maintaining a good relationship with one's informants – he found himself screaming at them, calling them degenerates, street-Arabs, nonsensical insults that diminished him even as they came out of his mouth. Of course they just stared impassively until he'd worn himself out and collapsed into another fit of coughing. Angrily he cranked the starter on the Ford. The car was unhappy in the cold, but caught after a minute or two, the chassis juddering as he hunched in the driver's seat and released the brake. He headed out of the camp, watched as he passed the communal trash-heap by a little girl clutching an open can of corned beef, spooning out greasy chunks with her fingers.

He bumped his way along the track, following twin ruts he'd made more or less entirely himself in the months he'd been coming to Kairo. Gradually he picked up speed, his journey punctuated by evenly spaced creosote bushes. He'd often wondered about the grid-like regularity of their growth, something to do with the limited water supply; each kept the same considerable distance from its neighbors, like homesteaders on forty-acre plots. As he drove on, the circulation returned to his face and hands. The morning was crisp and bright, the hills the color of honey. He began to feel better, and regretted he'd lost his temper with the children. By the time he reached the main road and the first of the new cabins, he was humming snatches of doughboy marching songs, honking the horn for emphasis: smile! – smile! – *smile!*

He reached town earlier than expected and ran the car up in front of Mulligan's Hotel, grunting a hello to the rheumy-eyed old clerk, who was sitting in his usual guard-dog position on the porch, studying a newspaper with the aid of a magnifying glass. As usual his room smelled like something had died under the floorboards. Deighton accepted full blame; the chambermaid, a timid Mexican girl of fourteen or so, had refused to touch it since he'd shouted at her for disturbing his papers.

He gulped down a cup of lukewarm water from the jug on the washstand and stripped down to his underwear, throwing his clothes over the pyramid of boxes which took up most of the floor-space. Their contents, thousands upon thousands of index cards, some covered in his tiny backward-slanted handwriting, some in Eliza's loops and whirls, represented the fruits of a year's hard labor. Most of them were notes on the group of Uto-Aztecan languages he'd been studying, a card for each word or word-stem, each distinct element of grammar. Others dealt with the People's material culture, their philosophy, the fragments they still remembered of their old songs. His employer, the Bureau of American Ethnology, had given him a six-month grant to write a preliminary report, with a vague promise of more money if the findings were interesting. So far, through extreme frugality, he'd managed to make the money last twice the scheduled time. Eliza had complained about the poor rations and his absolute prohibition on fripperies, but he thought she'd grasped the importance of their sacrifice. It really was too bad that she'd fallen by the wayside. The time and effort he'd invested in training her had gone to waste.

Though Washington had little real interest in the ethnology of the Mojave, they liked the idea of sending a decorated veteran to a place where he might recover from his injuries. Before he volunteered for France, Deighton had worked with coastal tribes in Oregon and Washington State (it was his proud boast that he knew more about the mythology of salmon than any white man alive), but the doctor at the veterans' hospital had told him the Northwest was out of the question. 'All that rain and fog? You'd be dead within a year.' Deighton had worried the man would tell him he'd go blind. At the field hospital in Château-Thierry he'd spent a week in darkness, his weeping eyes like two rotten eggs beneath his bandages.

He trudged down the hall to the bathroom, got into the tub and crouched in a few brackish inches of water, scrubbing off a crust of sweat and dust. Then he went back to the room and rummaged around for something clean to put on, watched dolefully by the devotional print of the Virgin of Guadalupe he'd tacked up by the mirror. The image was a private joke, a dig at the Congregationalism of his youth, with its even temper, its puritan disdain for idolatry. Agony and redemption and lace and gold leaf. That, in his opinion, was a real religion.

He stood for a moment, holding a shoe, then knelt down to retrieve the other from the mess of reeds and willow-twigs under the bed, relics of an attempt to teach himself some of Segunda's basket-weaves. Dressed at last, he ran a hand over his chin and realized to his annoyance that he'd forgotten to shave. There was always something. He couldn't be bothered to go through the rigmarole of taking his shirt off, warming water, stropping the blade. Besides, there probably wasn't a man in town who'd either notice or care.

He walked across the street to the Chinaman's and sat down at a table as far away as possible from the chill draft blowing under the door. The Chinaman's daughter served him a plate of some mess which tasted slightly of chicken. As usual, he tried out his few phrases of Cantonese on her. As usual, she giggled and pretended not to understand.

Back at the hotel he cleared the desk of some rubbish of Eliza's, lit the lamp and tried to work on his latest batch of notes. It was impossible to concentrate, and for the hundredth time he found himself leafing through the *Itinerary* of the Spanish friar Garcés, the first white man to travel through the high desert, or at least the first to write an account of his journey. Deighton would very much have liked to converse with the old Franciscan, who'd had the privilege of seeing so many things as he wandered, carrying little but a cross and a picture of the Holy Virgin. He had the book in Professor Coues's translation, which, though copiously anno-tated, was a source of great frustration. The Spaniard, intent on evangelizing the Indians, had recorded little about their language and culture. There were strange gaps in the narrative, periods of days or even weeks with no entry. One in particular bothered him. He suspected Garcés had been at the spring at Kairo, and from there had traveled back toward the river. But the *Itinerary* was silent, and Coues had provided no elucidation. All the country with which Deighton was most familiar was missing from the narrative. It was as if Garcés had just vanished and reappeared in another place.

At last he flopped into bed, dropping seamlessly out of conscious-ness and into the Bois de Belleau under heavy night-time bombard-ment. Blue lightning flashes outlined splintering trees; shell bursts silhouetted running men and cascades of rock and earth. He was standing at the edge of a crater, shouting words of encouragement to troops that were no longer there. The whole scene was taking place in silence. He could touch things, see things – the vibration of the ground, the tangled undergrowth – but the only sound was a high-pitched insect whine. He woke into a blaze of winter sunlight, not knowing where or even who he was. For a few blissful seconds he was just a consciousness, a presence in the clean white flare, there to apprehend it for its own sake, without story or purpose or lack of any kind.

He dressed and went over to the Chinaman's, where he found a table of local worthies setting the world to rights over plates of greasy eggs. Among them was Ellis Waghorn, the Indian agent. Deighton had never been able to fathom why Waghorn worked for the Bureau of Indian Affairs. He spent as little time as possible on the reservations under his jurisdiction. Local rumor had it that his interests lay more with redrawing reservation land boundaries to the benefit of the Southern Pacific Railroad than with the welfare of native people. He was talking to the pharmacist and the owner of the general store. They nodded a greeting. Waghorn smirked, his mouth full of cornbread.

'Morning, professor. Caught yourself any interesting diseases out there at Kairo?'

Deighton shrugged. For months Waghorn had been insinuating that 'some squaw' was the real reason for his interest in the Indian band at the oasis. As furious as the suggestion made him, he never took the bait. Waghorn pressed on.

'We were just discussing the lights Old Man Parker saw a few nights back. You see anything out where you were?'

'Lights?'

'Floating lights. Bill Parker said they was just hanging there like Edison bulbs.'

'I didn't see anything of that sort.'

'So what are you up to out in the desert if it ain't watching the stars?'

He ignored the other men's hearty laughter. 'Same as ever. Language work mostly. They have a very unusual grammatical structure.'

'That a fact?'

'Actually, Mr Waghorn, I have a question for you. Do you know of any recent intermarriages among the Indians out at Kairo?'

'What do you mean?'

'Well, Indian men and white women?'

'No, sir, I should say not. They keep themselves to themselves.'

'It's just – well, I saw a white child.'

'Half-breed, you say?'

'No, white. Very white, as a matter of fact. Boy about five years old. Walking along hand in hand with an Indian man.'

By now, people at neighboring tables were taking an interest.

'Hear that, Ben? Some Indian's got hold of a white boy.'

'What do you mean got hold of?'

'Professor saw him.'

'You sure about this?' asked Waghorn. 'Where was it?'

'I don't think it was – that is, I don't think there was anything untoward about it. The boy seemed happy.'

'I ain't heard of no one losing a child,' said Tompkins the pharmacist.

Waghorn looked puzzled. 'Me neither. And this was out at Kairo? Who was the Indian?'

'It was – hard to say. I didn't see his face.'

'Probably weren't nothing. Just some breed. Lot of them are light-skinned.'

That seemed to be the end of it, but, as Deighton pushed his food around his plate, he regretted bringing the matter up. All day he went about his business with the nagging sense that he'd set something in motion which would have consequences. He wrote his letters – to the Bureau, asking for more funds, to his sister, declining an invitation to spend Christmas with her family in Boston – then picked up a parcel of books from the post office and dropped off his dirty clothes with the Chinaman's brother, who ran a laundry next to the feed store. That night he stayed up late with the Spanish friar's book, trying to imagine how it must have felt to walk through the high desert, utterly alone.

The next morning he was woken by a noise outside the window. He raised the dust-smeared sash to see a ragged group of People, among them Joe Pine, being marched toward the sheriff's office. He pulled on his pants and rushed down, joining a considerable crowd, all jostling to get as near as possible to the door.

'What's going on here?'

'Kidnapping. Sheriff's pulled in them Indians to ask about it.'

'Who's been kidnapped?'

'Little boy from round Ludlow way.'

'Kairo, so as I heard.'

Deighton shouldered his way through, brushing aside a deputy who tried to bar his way. In the office Joe and his friends were lined up in front of Sheriff Calhoun, who was marching about in front of them, barking out questions like a drill sergeant. Waghorn was in the room, as well as a man he recognized as Danville Craw, the owner of the Bar-T Ranch, which bordered BIA land out near Kairo.

'Professor.'

'Mr Waghorn. Sheriff.'

'We're kind of busy here, Deighton.'

'Professor's the one first saw the kid. Three nights ago, weren't it?'

'That's right. I was at Kairo, a little after sunset. I saw a small boy walking along with an Indian man. Lord knows where they were headed. You say he'd been kidnapped?'

Sheriff Calhoun wiped his bald head with a handkerchief. With his bull neck and a drinker's complexion, he made a sharp contrast to the Indian agent and the rancher, both of whom had a lean, scavenging look. 'Well,' he said. 'We don't know exactly what's gone on, but that's how it looks. Mr Craw here saw them on his land last night.'

'I rode after them, but they must have hid themselves. It was rough country, out near Paiute Holes. A lot of boulders and such. Anyways, I lost them.'

'Isn't the Bar-T west of Kairo?'

'That's right.'

'When I saw them they were headed east.'

'Must have doubled back.'

'Are these men suspects?'

'We ain't got round to questioning them yet. Mr Craw found them camped out in the same spot just after. None of them could say what they were doing on his land, so he and his boys brought them in.'

Joe and his companions were all stolidly looking at the floor. The others didn't look familiar. Deighton thought they might be from one of the bands who worked the cattle ranches on the other side of the Colorado.

'Can I speak to them?'

'Professor knows their lingo.'

'I'm not sure. This is police business.'

Deighton was fairly sure he knew what they were doing at Paiute Holes. Segunda had once named it as a site on the Mule Deer song. In the days before disease and dispossession, the songs used to function both as hunting routes and as a way of organizing esoteric clan knowledge. The songs were narratives, and when one of the People died, it was traditional to chant them in their entirety, starting at dusk and ending at dawn, sending the soul of the departed on its way to the Land of the Dead via the places that meant most to them when they were alive. This system fascinated Deighton; so much of it had collapsed. The elders died without transmitting their songs; family groups were scattered. Joe and his friends had probably walked out there to sing for a dead clansman. It would have been a matter of indifference to them that it was Craw's land, the idea that anyone could actually *own* land being more or less meaningless in their culture. But there was no way they would or could explain any of that to Calhoun, particularly with Waghorn present.

'Ellis,' said the sheriff. 'They're your boys. You think they had anything to do with this?'

'I couldn't say, Dale. Joey, why don't you explain to the sheriff what you were up to skulking around Mr Craw's watering hole.'

'We got lost,' said Joe. 'Thought we was still on government land.'

Craw spat on the floor. 'Bullshit!'

'And what about this kid? Which of you's going to tell me what you all was doing with a white child?'

No one volunteered.

'Who is the child?' asked Deighton. 'When was he reported missing?'

Calhoun sat down heavily in his chair, which creaked under his weight. 'Well, we ain't actually had a report yet. I've sent a wire to Victorville, and one of my deputies is over in the valley, asking around.'

'You mean no one's even made a complaint?'

Craw turned on him furiously. 'Godammit, professor! This ain't no time for splitting hairs. Some brave's dragging a poor mite round the desert with him. Who knows what he's about to do – '

'Do? What do you mean, do?'

Craw jutted his chin at the Indians. 'Weren't so long ago they used to eat our livers. Lord only knows what purposes they got in their black hearts.'

'Look, professor,' interrupted Calhoun. 'I hold you partly responsible for this mess. You saw that child and you didn't do nothing about it. Authorities wouldn't even have known if it weren't for Ellis here, who saw fit to mention it after Mr Craw brought in them boys.'

'I don't understand why you're making such a deal out of this.'

Craw looked genuinely astounded. 'My sweet Lord, will you listen to him? Some poor little Christian child's going to be eaten alive unless we make a so-called deal out of this.'

Calhoun looked at him sourly. 'Chances are it's one of the boys from Kairo. Professor, you were the one saw him. You sure you didn't recognize him?'

Deighton thought for a moment. And then he committed his great sin.

'Well, there was one man who seemed to be missing from his place.'

'What man?'

'His name is Willie Prince.'

'I know him,' said Waghorn. 'Arrogant son of a bitch.'

'Looks like we ought to take a drive out to Kairo. Professor, you'll take us.'

As they left the office the crowd pressed forward, trying to find out news. The mood was ugly. As Calhoun confirmed that they were holding the Indians in custody 'pending enquiries', someone at the back yelled out that they ought to string the red bastards up from a tree.

The journey out to the oasis seemed interminable. The car complained as it climbed the grade up into the high desert, past an area of new claims marked by half-finished cabins and piles of building lumber. Deighton took the turn toward Kairo at speed, juddering down the frozen track toward the distant mountain range, which on that day looked dull and lifeless, a jagged iron-gray strip on the horizon. A grit-laden wind was whipping out of the north, stinging his cheeks and making him glad of his driving goggles. Mercifully neither of his passengers wanted to talk. They sat, hunched down into their jackets, hats pulled down low over their eyes. Waghorn had his hands jammed into his pockets, Calhoun's on the carbine laid across his lap, like a musician waiting his turn to play.

When they saw the camp up ahead, Waghorn and Calhoun shifted impatiently in their seats. Deighton squinted ahead.

'Doesn't seem to be anyone there.'

Calhoun grunted and lit a cigarette. They pulled up in a cloud of dust and stepped down, stamping their feet and rubbing their hands to bring back the circulation. Calhoun and Waghorn strode around, pulling open covers and peering into wickiups. The embers of the fires were still warm. A few dogs were nosing about in the trash; as the men walked about, they came forward inquisitively, hoping for food. Waghorn aimed a kick at one, which trotted a little farther off. 'Now we know they're up to something,' he said.

'Where do you think they're headed, Ellis?' asked Calhoun.

'Into the Saddlebacks, I reckon. Any number of caves up there. They'll be easy enough to track. You think they've got the boy with them?'

Calhoun stuck his head through the doorway of another wickiup and rapidly withdrew it. 'I think we got someone. Jesus, it stinks like shit in there.' Deighton crouched down and looked through the opening. It took a moment for his eyes to adjust to the darkness. The stench was overpowering. Excrement, vomit and something else, something familiar to him from the war: the smell of a body in extremis. An elderly man lay on the ground, swathed in blankets. His breathing was labored, rattling in his chest like a bead in an empty box. By his side sat Segunda Hipa. He spoke to her in the People's Language.

'Segunda. Are you sick?'

The old woman's eyes were wide with terror.

'It's alright. Nothing's going to happen. Why did they leave you behind?'

She named the man she was sitting with. 'He's dying. It's not proper to leave him alone.'

'Segunda, where is Eliza? Where is Salt-Face Woman?'

'Gone, where you can't find her.'

'Is she with Willie Prince?'

Segunda said nothing.

'What's going on?' asked Waghorn, trying to see past Deighton into the gloom.

'Just a moment.'

The old man groaned. Segunda took a rag and wiped his face.

'Segunda, tell me about the boy. I know you know something.'

'Why did you bring them here?'

Waghorn pushed past Deighton into the gloom, his foot crunching through something on the packed-earth floor, probably a basket.

'Come here, old woman. You need to talk to us.'

With one hand pressing a handkerchief over his mouth and nose, he took hold of Segunda's arm with the other. When she didn't immediately get up, he tightened his grip, dragging her toward the doorway. She began to wail, a high-pitched ululation that cut through the fetid air.

Deighton was appalled. 'For God's sake, leave her alone!'

'Get out of my way.'

Deighton tried to break Waghorn's grip on Segunda's arm and all three of them ended up outside in the dust, Segunda in a heap on the ground, the two men swearing and scrabbling to pick themselves up.

'Christ, Deighton, I said get out of my way. And now, you flea-ridden old cunt, you're going to tell me what's going on here. Where's the kid?'

Deighton pleaded with Calhoun. 'Sheriff, do something, or I will.'

'Ellis –' said Calhoun. 'Lay off her, Ellis. This isn't helping none.'

Waghorn let go. Segunda sat in the dust and lowered her face into her shawl. Deighton stepped toward the Indian agent, his fists clenched. 'Professor,' warned Calhoun, 'you better back up there.' Deighton glanced over and saw the carbine in the sheriff's hands, the barrel leveled at his stomach. Part of him, the detached, externalized part, wondered how the situation had gotten so out of hand. He took a pace back. Waghorn's hand was on his own gun, a long-barreled revolver holstered under his battered leather coat. The three men looked warily at one another.

'What kind of fool are you?' Deighton asked Waghorn. 'She didn't want to talk. Now she never will. The others obviously heard what happened to Joe and his friends and ran away. I can't say as I blame them.'

'Oh, can't you?' Waghorn wiped the back of his hand across his mouth. Calhoun lowered the carbine and squatted effortfully down on his haunches, the breath whistling out of him like a deflating bladder.

'Come on, old woman. Don't pay him no mind. No one's going to harm you. Why don't you tell me what's happened here? We're just trying to find a child who's gone missing. Little boy.'

Segunda said nothing, staring fixedly at the earth in front of her. Waghorn kicked the ground in exasperation.

'Tell us, or your scrawny ass is going to find itself sitting in jail right alongside them others.'

The old woman sat in stubborn silence. Deighton felt sick.

'Please, let's just go. She can't help us.'

'Well,' said Calhoun, raising himself to his feet. 'If she can, she's choosing not to.'

'Dale, you ain't just going to let her get away with this?'

'Ellis, I don't know how you get anything done at all with these people. You're worse'n a rabid dog.' He looked at his watch. 'Too late to make it back into town now and besides, I don't think my butt'll stand any more of riding about in that damn bone-clanker. I told Mellish and Frankie Lobo to ride over to the Bar-T if there's news. We'll stay the night there and work this thing out in the morning.'

Waghorn and Calhoun started walking back to the car. Deighton crouched down next to Segunda.

'Are you alright? Are you hurt?'

She didn't speak. He made an ineffectual attempt to brush the dust off her shawl, then held out his hand, offering to help her stand up. She ignored it, keeping her eyes firmly fixed on the patch of dirt in front of her. Finally he walked away. As they drove off, the dogs trotted after them, their tongues lolling out. They looked as if they were laughing.

At Craw's ranch, Deighton refused dinner and went straight to the bunkhouse, where he lay awake for some hours, his face to the wall. Much later he heard others come in. A man climbed into the bunk above him. He pretended to be asleep.

At dawn, two deputies and an Indian policeman from the large reservation near Victorville arrived in the town's official car, a four-door Studebaker. Sometime in the night, Union Pacific employees working at a depot thirty miles north of the Bar-T had sighted an Indian running through the desert, carrying a young white boy. They said he seemed to be heading for a range of mountains known as the Saddlebacks. When Deighton heard this, he wondered how a couple of men standing outside in the middle of the night could see so far into the distance.

'Did they by any chance say anything about a light?'

'What kind of light?'

'From the boy. Did they say the boy was giving off light?'

Everyone looked at him like he was insane.

There was more news. A family of homesteaders down near the mineral pool at Palm Springs had lost a boy two months previously.

Ten years old, he'd last been seen climbing rocks in the vicinity of an old mine working. For most of the men gathered round Danville Craw's scarred pine table, that clinched it. There was a missing boy and a kidnapper. The only question was how to proceed with the manhunt. Once again, Deighton spoke up.

'There's no way the boy I saw was ten years old. He couldn't have been more than six, seven at most.'

'Professor,' said Calhoun carefully, 'thanking you for your concern, but I reckon it's time you got back to your books. I'll handle it from here on in.'

'You're sending riders up into the Saddlebacks?'

'I imagine that's how it'll pan out.'

'I want to go with you.'

'What?'

'You heard. I want you to deputize me.'

'With respect, professor, I don't think that's such a good idea.'

Craw, drinking coffee with his feet up on the table, laughed scornfully. Deighton turned on him. 'I know the language. I'm certainly a damn sight better at dealing with Indians than that fool Ellis Waghorn. And I have the Ford. I think I'd be very useful.'

Calhoun shook his head. 'You reckon on tracking him in your automobile? That Indian ain't sticking to no roads. He's somewhere out in the Saddlebacks, climbing for all he's worth. Your flivver ain't gonna be worth shit once we get past the rail depot.'

'I can ride.'

'You got a horse?'

'I'll borrow one from Mr Craw here.'

'Hell you will.'

'Then I'll buy one. I'll give you a fair price.'

Calhoun thought for a moment. 'Well, we do need every man we can get. But what about your health, if you don't mind my asking? If you can't keep up we ain't gonna be able to wait on you.'

'Let me worry about my health.'

'Alright, then. I'll swear you in.'

'Thank you, Sheriff Calhoun.'

'One thing, professor, before I do. I've seen how you rub people up the wrong way. You come along on this and you're under my authority. I know about how you was a college man and an officer in the war and heaven knows y'all got the scars to prove it. But you ain't no officer now. You're just a deputy. So you do as I say and keep your mouth shut, specially around Ellis Waghorn. I won't stand for no more incidents like yesterday.'

The speech made Deighton furious, but he nodded assent.

'OK. Raise your right hand. Do you swear to keep and preserve the peace in the county of San Bernardino, and to quiet and suppress all affrays, riots and insurrections, for which purpose, and for the service of process in civil and criminal cases, and in apprehending and securing any person for felony or breach of the peace you may be called upon at such time as needed?'

'I do.'

'By the authority vested in me, I appoint you a temporary deputy of this county. Get the man a horse, Danville.'

Deighton walked with Craw to a corral near the bunkhouse. The place was a mess, crates stacked up in teetering piles against a tumbledown shed, bits of tack hanging higgledy-piggledy from the hitchrail. In the pen, five half-wild mustangs stepped and kicked, shying away as the men drew near. Craw unpromisingly described them as 'green broke'. Privately Deighton thought that was an overstatement.

'Don't you have any properly trained horses?'

'Well, listen to him. Yes, sir, I do, trouble is my men took them. You want to try out one of these or have you changed your mind?'

A few hands drifted over to the rail to watch. Deighton pointed at a bay which seemed marginally more docile than the others. Craw ducked under the fence and slipped a hackamore over its head, then walked it around with a lead rope as it stamped and shied. Deighton stuck with his choice. It was impossible to say if it was considered good or bad by the authorities leaning on the rail. The horse skipped from side to side as he mounted, turning its head and eyeing him angrily. He trotted it a couple of times around the corral without incident, then tied it to the rail. Deighton had learned to ride English-style back East. This was different; even the tack was strange, the big square-skirted saddle with the high pommel, the unfamiliar bridle. Craw looked appraisingly at him and started to talk money. Once they'd agreed a price, an exorbitant amount which Deighton secretly knew he had no means of paying, he joined the other posse members getting ready, filling a canteen, retrieving his bedroll from the car, packing a leather bag with some tinned beans and franks, a razor, a bar of soap, Friar Garcés's book. All about him, men were cinching saddles, slipping carbines into scabbards. He saw Ellis Waghorn watching him, his lip curled. For a moment Deighton imagined him being hit by a howitzer blast, leaping high in the air.

They rode out an hour later. As the sun rose higher, they followed the line of barbwire fence that demarcated the Bar-T from the BIA reservation. A fine cloud of white limestone dust rose up over the horses, settling on the riders like sieved flour. Ahead of them the desert stretched away in the direction of the Saddlebacks, a serrated ochre ridge rising abruptly from the white plain. As they headed away from Craw's land, they climbed up through fields of rounded boulders, dipping down again into wide sandy washes, a rhythm that began to vary only as they neared a formation of dunes. Around noon they sighted a line of telegraph poles. Half an hour later they hit the railroad track and followed it until they came to the adobe buildings and big metal water tank of the railroad depot.

As Calhoun and Waghorn pored over maps and planned their route, Deighton lined up to refill his canteen from a big clay olla. When it came to his turn, he drank from the tin dipper and laved a little water over his head. The tracker Francisco Lobo was smoking and looking out at the mountains. He was a tiny man, barely five feet tall, with a hooked nose and a smooth round face that made it hard to tell his age. He wore his hair short, with a crumpled pinstripe suit jacket and a straw hat crammed down low over his head, an ensemble which gave him an oddly formal look. Deighton walked over and stood beside him.

'Who do you think it is?'

Lobo looked blank.

'The fugitive. Who is he?'

'Just a man, I guess.'

'I've heard of Indian tribes raising up white children, but that was a long time ago. Pioneer days. I don't understand why he's got this boy.'

'I ain't even sure there is a boy.'

Just then Calhoun blew a whistle, shouting at everyone to gather round to get their orders. Some men would ride a handcar to the next station east, where they'd pick up horses and try to cut the fugitive off on the other side of the range. The others were to head for the mountains, trying to pick up the Indian's tracks. They dispersed to saddle up, then rode out in two lines, each group heading for one of the old mining trails that ran through the mountains. They were barely an hour out from the depot when Lobo held up his hand. The men dismounted and gathered to look at what he'd found. To Deighton it was barely visible, an insignificant oval displacement of sand. Lobo walked on. He found a second print, then a third.

'He was running fast,' the tracker said. 'Very fast, heading for the mountains.'

Calhoun shook his head in disbelief. 'Look at the length of his stride. It's what, six, seven feet? That's incredible.'

Craw was skeptical. 'It ain't real. He's doing something, disguising his tracks.'

'I don't see how.'

'I've heard of this before,' said Lobo, 'but I never saw it for myself. The man's a true runner. He knows how to run the old way.'

'The old way?'

'Not like ordinary men.'

Lobo shielded his eyes and looked toward the mountains.

'I don't think we'll catch him.'

Calhoun was irritated. 'I don't care if he's an old-running Indian or a young 'un, he can't keep that pace up forever. Besides, there's no food up there. He can't have picked up anything to eat between the Bar-T and here. He'll be tired and hungry and he'll slow down. We'll get him.'

Lobo shook his head. 'I don't know, sheriff, sir. There's more to eat in the mountains than you think. And some of the People hide food up there for when they're hunting. Piñones, jerky. Maybe he knows a place.'

Calhoun didn't like being contradicted. He spat on the ground, then pulled out a pocket mirror, which he used to signal the second group of riders, some miles to the south. When he saw them change their course, he gave the order to saddle up. They rode on, following the footprints toward the mountain range, making their way across a plain of round rocks scattered with ocotillo and sage. Gradually the shadows lengthened and the warm evening light softened the land-scape, turning the white rocks honey-yellow. By the time the heat had gone out of the air, they were at the foot of the mountains, and hadn't found any sign of the fugitive for an hour or more. At dusk they were following the only plausible route, a narrow trail up a steep ridge, watching the last orange glow recede from the desert below. As they notched the pass, they saw it led down into a natural shelter formed by two steep walls of rock. Shepherds had built a paddock and a crude stone hut with a horse's skull nailed over the doorway. The hut was in ruins, and must have last been used many years previously, but there was wood stacked inside and water in an old stone tank. They made camp there. By the time the second posse arrived, they had a fire and coffee on the go. The hobbled horses nosed about for fodder, while the men ate beans and tortillas. Deighton took his plate and sat down next to Lobo. Though no one else was paying much attention, he spoke in a lowered voice, aware that the tracker might not want to speak openly. 'Why did you say we're never going to catch him?'

'Like I said, he's a true runner.'

'What does that mean?'

'In the old times, there were messengers who could cover two hundred miles in a day. True runners. They knew there's more than one way to run.'

'I don't understand.'

'When I was a boy we lived over on the other side of the river. There was a band of men who ran together. Not to get any place. Just for the joy of running. One of them was a young feller name of John Smith, though he had other names. When he was with his friends he ran ordinary, but on his own he ran another way, the old way, least that's what people used to say. There's a story about John Smith, how he and his friends are camped by Paiute Holes and he says goodbye and gets up to go to a camp way upriver, place they call Adobe-Hanging-Like-Tears. His friends watch him run off, running easy like he always does. They're curious about how he runs when he's alone, so they decide to follow him. At first they find his footsteps, long footsteps like we just saw. But they keep getting longer and longer, ten feet, twenty feet, until they just disappear. John Smith's friends run upriver, following the path. After some days they come to Adobe-Hanging-Like-Tears and they say to the people there, did you see John Smith? And the people say yes, he was here on such and such a day, just as the sun was rising. It was the same morning he left Paiute Holes.'

'So this John Smith was a shaman?'

'No, no, he never carried a stick, never had visions. He was just a man.'

'But he had a magic way of traveling.'

'Not magic. He never used magic. He just knew how to run.'

That was the end of Lobo's story. As Deighton lay by the fire, his head propped uncomfortably on his saddle, many things seemed to collapse into one: the runner disappearing and reappearing instantaneously at his destination, the wandering Spanish friar, Coyote clinging to the reed and weaving his way into the Land of the Dead. Was this where Garcés had journeyed in his lost days? Was this where the running Indian had led them? He fell asleep listening to the horses shifting about in their hobbles, and dreamed of Eliza, instead of the mud and confusion of the Bois de Belleau. The cold was fierce, and he woke up sometime before sunrise with a stiff neck and a hacking cough which wouldn't go away, however hard he tried to suppress it.

All that day he was in pain. He felt cold right down to his bones, and the sun was high overhead before he stopped shivering. He was unused to riding. The muscles in his back and legs felt sore, but more serious was the pain in his chest. Something about the motion of the horse seemed to aggravate it, and he began to wonder if Calhoun was right. Maybe he wouldn't be able to keep up after all.

High in the mountains they came upon an abandoned silver mine. The shaft had caved in, leaving a set of iron rails disappearing into a pile of rocks, like a conjurer's illusion. By this stoppered mouth a crude stone arrastra stood by a pile of tailings. Someone had camped there the previous night. Amid the ashes of a fire were lizard bones. Lobo knelt down beside them. Calhoun prodded them with the toe of his boot.

'Well, Frankie, that puts paid to your theory that our boy had food up here. Can't have been much of a meal, that chuckwalla. You ever eat one of them things?'

Lobo said he never did. His people were from the river. Only desert people ate lizards. They followed the mining track until it emerged at the head of an escarpment overlooking a vast empty basin that stretched away at least thirty miles, before the next range rose up to block its way. He'd never been in that country before, and was awed, as he often was in the desert, by the sheer absence of human markers, of any kind of recognizable scale. He didn't doubt it now. This was the silent space, the land of Garcés's missing days. The sun was setting, turning the whole expanse red, darkening to a sinister black at the base of its only feature, a cinder cone which rose up out of the flat gravel like a pimple. Calhoun took out a pair of field glasses and spent several long minutes scanning the scene.

'Well, I'll be damned,' he said at length. 'There he is.'

They passed the binoculars from hand to hand. There wasn't a hint of moisture in the air. Visibility was perfect. Deighton took a while to pick it out, a little wisp of dust in the emptiness, a flicker of blue casting a long shadow. It seemed impossible. How far away was it? Ten, maybe fifteen miles? A running man wearing a blue shirt.

On his shoulders a bundle of some kind. A child? It was impossible to say.

The mining track ran out and they made their way down a talus slope, picking a path as carefully as they could, the horses placing their feet with the care of tightrope-walkers. This was where Deighton's mount threw him. For two days the nameless bay had been docile; its show of temper in the corral seemed to vanish once they were out in the desert. Deighton was daydreaming, trusting the animal to find the best route down in the gathering darkness, when suddenly it reared up, sending him backwards out of his saddle. Instinctively he broke his fall with his hand, twisting his arm beneath him as he landed. The horse kicked out, narrowly missing his head, then skidded some way down the slope, almost falling as the loose gravel slipped under its hooves. There were yells from farther down, as the lead riders saw rocks bouncing down toward them. The panic spread to animals either side. A burro, laden down with firewood and provisions, slipped its halter and bolted.

Deighton got to his feet, flexing his wrist, expecting to find it broken. It seemed only to be sprained. A few cuts and bruises and a torn pair of pants was the worst of the damage. He was fixed up by one of Craw's hands, a grizzled oldster named Silas Henry, who grinned at the world through a set of shiny teeth he claimed he'd crafted himself from gold he'd mined at Skidoo, before the panic wiped him out.

They camped at the foot of the slope. It was a sorry, exposed spot. As the heat fled from the land, a bitter wind started to whip across the plain, picking up sparks from the fire which raced through the air like little comets. The burro's load of mesquite branches burned quickly, and after a hurried meal everyone made ready for bed, jostling for position near the embers of the fire.

In the violet haze of the early morning, as Deighton drank his coffee and ate his scoop of beans, Waghorn passed by and aimed a kick at his boots.

'I didn't get no sleep because of you. Goddamn coughing.'

Deighton was too tired and sore to talk back. He thought he was running a fever. The handkerchief stuffed into his inside pocket was soaked with blood.

As dawn broke they put on speed, riding fast over the plain until they were slowed down by the lava field, with its fantastical twists and bubblings. They kept stopping to look through field glasses, but there was no sign of the running Indian. 'There's nowhere for him to go,' pronounced Calhoun, as if by saying it he could make it true. They were low on water, and the horses were tiring. No one was looking forward to another climb. Deighton was glad of each break, pain and fatigue overcoming his fear of what lay at the end of the chase, the resolution to the thing he'd set in motion.

The sun was over the mountains when they saw a mirror flashing many miles to the south. They turned the noses of the horses toward the signal. As they rode Deighton could feel his head dropping forward, lights twinkling in his mind. He wasn't sure if the country he was seeing was real anymore. It seemed tentative, mutable. First he found himself on a salt pan, bright white and perfectly flat. Then in high country, where huge boulders rose up between the draws, their shapes like children's clay models. An elephant. A gas mask. A skull. They passed through a garden of cholla cacti. A hawk flew overhead. When, at last, they stopped, some of the men dug out a creek bed, looking for water. A few feet down they struck it, a brown brackish trickle, then a steady flow. The horses drank.

He could taste death in that water. That was when he knew they were close.

Soon there were other men. Handshakes and low voices. The second posse had a city fellow with them, a Hearst journalist out of San Francisco, with a camera and a tripod strapped behind his saddle. It's a big story, he told them. You got yourselves a crazed Indian. Nothing the readers back East like better than a little taste of the wild frontier.

Deighton had no recollection of lying down or going to sleep. The stars overhead formed a inverted bowl, a crystal dome over his head. Almost at once he was shaken awake. It was still dark. Around him, men were loading guns, saddling horses, making ready.

'We seen his fire. He can't be more than five miles away.'

They rode across the dry lake through a gray half-light, neither day nor night, but something in between. He felt delirious, ethereal, as if he were no longer completely inside his body. In the distance he saw the three spires of rock and knew that he had come to the threshold, the opening between this world and the Land of the Dead. Up on the rocks was a glow. It didn't look like firelight, but something else, something spectral and strange.

Oh Lord, he prayed. If you exist, make something happen. I have brought this about, out of jealousy. Lord, save me from the guilt of what is about to happen here.

They sat and they waited. The sun rose high in the sky, but the chill stayed in the air. Deighton watched the sky, and thought he saw things written in it. Secret trails. Wisdom. He wondered who was up on the rocks with Willie Prince. Not a child. How could he have taken a child up there? But Eliza? Please Lord, he prayed again. Let her not be with him.

The gunfire sounded like boys throwing fire-crackers.

The posse had gotten tired of waiting. They moved forward in a crouching run. The figure up on the rocks fired shot after shot. As Deighton watched, Danville Craw went down, clutching his leg. After that they crawled, taking cover as they climbed. It was an unruly, ill-disciplined advance. None of them would survive a minute in the face of those German guns. Do you need me to cut the wire? he asked. No one answered. Unless someone cut a route, they were going to get tangled up in the wire. Up in the sky a pale eye looked down on him. God's German eye.

That was not where he was. Why had he thought so? That was not where he was at all.

Waghorn was screaming, a continual high-pitched wail.

Deighton stood up. He opened his arms wide to show he was unarmed. He shouted out a greeting.

'Garcés! Fray Garcés! En nombre de Dios!' He repeated it as he walked forward. 'Get down, you fool!' yelled Calhoun. Ignoring him, Deighton climbed the path, stepping over Craw, who was lying in the dust, pressing his palms into the bloody wound in his thigh. A bullet ricocheted off the rock at his feet. Then someone tackled him from behind. He sprawled. The ground was ice-cold.

He lay for a long time, straining to catch his breath. He felt as if he were drowning, his lungs filling with sludge, each inhalation coming in a little, whistling rasp. He did not know where he was, why he was there. After a while he realized the firing had ceased. From up on the rocks came a ragged cheer.

As slowly as an old man, he stood and trudged his way upwards, stopping every few moments to rest. The others had all gone on. Up ahead, at the base of the tallest spire, he saw a sudden flash of magnesium light. Men were clustered around a corpse, laid out on the ground.

'I shot him!' exulted Waghorn. 'I got him! A clean kill!' Silas Henry capered about, grinning his big gold grin.

The Hearst man was taking trophy pictures. Waghorn and Calhoun with their rifles crossed, boots on the corpse's chest; Craw supporting himself on someone's shoulder, keeping the weight off his bandaged leg. Deighton looked down at the body, its clawed hands, bare feet. It was impossible to tell who it was. The face was blown clean off.

'Who is it?' he asked.

Francisco Lobo looked at him strangely. 'No one I ever saw before.'

'Where's the boy?'

'There weren't no boy.'

Around them, tired deputies were slapping each other on the back, passing round a bottle. No one seemed to care they'd chased a man for days across the desert, then murdered him without cause. They were victorious hunters. Once the photographs were done, they started to cut brush and pile it over the corpse. Deighton tried to pull it away. He wasn't sure who was beneath it, but he knew they ought to carry him down, give him a decent funeral. Two of Craw's hands dragged him off and laid him on the ground. It's just an Indian, sneered one. He don't care.

They stepped back and lit the pyre. Deighton watched the circle of unshaven haggard faces staring avidly into the flames.

Covering the grid. The make-up girl was professional, and moved around her without speaking. Neither personal nor impersonal. Just some powder. Mirror-Lisa, framed in bulbs. *Make you look like a person who sleeps.*

Q. Why did you do it? Why would a person behave like that?

Because she wanted to. Not long enough as an answer. People want more. They want explanations that *feel* like explanations.

On the first day they'd flown vectors over the park. Flown track-lines, expanding squares. Walking, they'd swept the area. Go on, said Dawn, out of the shadows. Ask her a question. Judy, sitting in that rocking chair under the bighorn-sheep skull on the wall. Back and forth, back and forth, Navajo blanket on her lap like an old woman. Ask her anything you like.

Impossible to cover all that territory.

Just some powder.

Ma'am, we stopped vehicles, questioned hikers. Everything by the book. At a certain time you have to conclude. At a certain time you have to. At a certain time.

You conclude that this was an abduction and it's possible the child has been taken across state lines.

There you are. All done.

The land and aerial searches.

The host came in and said hello. She looked older in real life. She looked like a real person. I am so sorry, she said. Jaz was getting made up in the next chair, a white napkin tucked into his collar. Awkwardly, he craned around. Lisa looked at the two women in the mirror, the one leaning over the other. My heart, said the presenter. My personal anger. The mirror made it easier to see her. It made it easier when she said why don't we all join hands.

She liked to do that before a special show. A show where we are dealing with life in its rawest form.

Judy rocking in her chair. Had Lisa ever really been in that room, with its triangular windows, its animal-skin rugs and polished floors? Under the dome of the stars. Only the stone hearth and the rocking woman had substance. Everything else dissolved into the shadows.

Side effects may include drowsiness, skin irritation, severe allergic reaction. Stop taking the medication and immediately seek medical help if you have any of the following:

The people in the hallway were her people. She had people. Victim support, Park Service media relations. Her parents had hired a lawyer or maybe an agent. He acted like an agent. His name was Price and he wore western boots under his double-breasted silk suits. He wore monogrammed shirts and talked to her like they were both in a Lifetime movie of the week. When they interviewed him on television, he was described as the 'family spokesperson'. Her mother took her aside and started acting strangely and eventually she worked out that she was trying to explain why they'd hired a goy. You don't know how it is out here, she said. They need to deal with one of their own.

There was a ribbon campaign, briefly. There was a website with a counter and a PayPal button.

In a moment she'd have to speak. The headset girl said they were almost ready for their segment. The girl leaned in very close. Her breath smelled of strawberry-flavored gum. It was strange how they all came in so close. It was like being pregnant, everyone wanting to rub your belly for luck. The little squeezes, the hugs. The holding of the wrists. When you're making up each step through force of will, creating ground on which to walk, it takes faith. Faith and an atmosphere of silence. People touching or talking to you can throw you off.

Her people. Really they were just there to wheel her about, like a patient on a gurney. She never said a word if she could help it.

Perhaps she could blame the pictures. There'd been a collage of photos behind the bar, groups of smiling young marines, arms thrown over each other's shoulders or fiercely squeezing girls. Over the bar were more photographs, framed black-and-white portraits of heavy-jawed men on plain backgrounds. Down below, everyone had a world – a fragment of counter, stark and shiny in the flash, a car hood, a beer poster, a table and chair. Up there, the heroes floated in the milky-white amniotic fluid of their heroism, safe from harm. The bottles against the smeared mirror, the tangled string of Christmas lights; the place reminded her of a roadside shrine she'd once seen in Mexico. She'd taken pictures while Jaz read out the names on the votive candles. *Nuestra Señora de Guadalupe. Contra el Mal de Ojo y Para Atrear La Fortuna.* How many of these red-eyed bottle-wavers were dead? Or had no legs? That was the difference now. Wonders of modern medicine. All coming home with chunks blown out of their brains or PTSD or missing limbs, as if by failing to die they'd also failed to complete a mandatory process, hadn't followed the correct procedure for their transformation into black-and-white floating heads.

And that was when he came up and asked if she'd like to play a game of pool. It wasn't complicated. She could already see him as he would be in the future, wheeling himself around. The sideways glances at the mall. The screaming eagle decal on the chair. It was strange. She'd never had a premonition, but she saw this very clearly.

Maria Dolorosa.

She thought about the sand in her hair, her sweaty clothes. She took a gulp of her vodka soda.

He repeated his question.

Swelling of the lips, face, throat and tongue. May impair your ability to drive or operate heavy machinery. Some people taking this medication have engaged in activities such as driving or making telephone calls and later have no memory of these activities.

It was time. She gave herself up to the strawberry-gum girl, floating along with an arm to rest on, a guiding hand in the small of the back. Her own hand was placed in Jaz's. It lay there, a damp fish on his papery palm. He was talking to her, using a warm tone, his trying-to-reach-you tone. Go toward the light, said the strawberry-gum girl, and launched them on set.

There was applause. The host hugged, patted, performed the holding of the wrists. She smelled of some powerful lilac deodorant. She smelled like an office bathroom. They sat down on the couch.

We're so glad. Our hearts. Such a difficult. Tell me.

Well Sally he reminded me of my cousin Nate made me feel beautiful like a woman you know how important that is for a mom well Sally I'm glad you asked because it was a cry for help you have to appreciate autism affects everyone parents carers we all live with my levels of stress were through the roof Sally I know your viewers understand how hard understand how very hard understand it's hard for me to come here today and admit alcohol drugs obesity gambling abuse has been a problem in my life but now with the grace of God and my husband by my side. My husband. My

Jaz shifted in his seat. The host said something. He said something. The host said something else. All eyes were on her: the witch Lisa Matharu, the woman who didn't cry for her son.

That was why they were there, after all. For the apportionment, the magical assignment of blame. Bad things do not happen without a reason. It is preferable, when thinking about bad things, to make them happen to bad people. We think of bad things all the time. Our thoughts have to go somewhere. If the bad people do not seem properly Bad, we must make them so, unless we can make them Good, but for that we apply the most exacting standards.

Q. You must feel terrible. What do you want to say to the person who has Raj?

We need everybody's help to find him and so I'd like to say to anyone out there if you know what happened please say just pick up the phone bring him home he needs to be with his family.

The camera silently swooping forward on its trolley. Zooming in to catch the tears. So many TV appearances and no tears. It was against nature. She'd watched two women discussing her on this very show, women she'd never met, who were giving their opinions of her dress sense, her mothering, her mental health.

If you fear you have experienced this, talk to your doctor about another course of treatment. This medication may impair your ability to

He was only a boy. Twenty-two years old. A baby. He had sandy buzzcut hair and ran corny lines on her and leaned into the bar in a way he'd probably seen in a movie. He told her all about himself, just spilled it out like he was interviewing for a job. The town with the water tower painted in the colors of his high-school football team, the times they used to drive out to the old quarry to swim. So generic, so stupid, it made her feel heavy and old and sad. The kid hadn't seen a thing. Not a single goddamn thing in his whole life. When he stood behind her and adjusted her shot, she felt like crying. Instead she rubbed the side of his face. It was like petting a cat.

His breath falling on her neck, his middle-western voice murmuring in her ear, putting the moves, putting the moves. Then she saw his friends watching them from a booth and she was nineteen again, on a road-trip she took with a college girlfriend through the South. Tennessee, Mississippi, Arkansas. Opening the door and feeling the men's eyes on her, her cut-offs suddenly too short as she walked the gauntlet to the bar.

The table erupted into laughter.

Don't pay them no mind, the boy said. They're just jealous. She asked herself, then, what the hell she thought she was doing. She needed to get herself together. She needed air. Putting down her cue, she walked around the table, supporting herself as she went. Then she launched across the room and pushed open the bar door. Outside, the night air was cool, the stars holes drilled through the blue-black sky. Was she hungry? Maybe she should put some food in her stomach. There was a Chinese place next door. She could get chow mein, soak up some of the booze.

A light breeze was blowing. She was walking across the parking lot toward the divider when she felt a hand on her arm and turned to find him standing there. He didn't say anything, just looked at her, and he was so blank and young, so unwritten-on by life, that she let her body go slack and put her face up to his.

He slammed her back against someone's truck and he had a fistful of her hair and she was kissing him hard and as she dug in his pants for his cock he pushed her T-shirt up to her armpits and started to suck on her nipple like a baby, cupping her ass in his two hands, sliding his fingers into her shorts to graze the seams of her panties. They paused for a moment, breathing in and out and in and out, and then he was tearing at her zipper and she wrapped her legs around his hips and just tried to hang on. There was some fumbling and he was inside her and she could feel the muscles tight in his back and the clench of his buttocks and she bit down hard on his shoulder to stop herself from crying out. He winced and wriggled his shoulder free, then put a hand on her throat, moaning oh fuck oh fuck as he came, shuddering against her like a patient with a fever. For a moment she hung there in space, stroking his hair as he shook, buried deep in his private dreams. Then they sank toward the ground, two separate people again, kneeling in the dust.

She could see figures lurking about in the shadows. Had his friends come out to watch? It didn't matter. None of it was real. Whatever had just happened, it meant nothing, stood for nothing beyond itself. She was a thousand miles from her normal life, floating far out in space.

Price told them they needed to stay in the Los Angeles area to maximize what he called the 'tail' of the coverage. The trick, he said, was to keep selling twists. Each day with no new development meant there was a chance an outlet would pull its reporting staff and put them on another story. He placed his hand on her knee. But you've got a good story, he said. A very good story. That's one thing in your favor. He had his hand on her knee and Jaz did nothing. He didn't even look in her direction. The boy was panting like a dog. She pushed him away. Did you come inside me, she asked. Yeah, he said. It was great. Older women are so fucking hot.

A story every day.

They moved to a hotel in Riverside. On the fifth morning Price organized what he called a 'walkabout'. They went to the park, followed by cars and vans packed with journalists. There seemed to be more than before. They were wealthy New Yorkers, lost out West.

There was a high level of human interest. When the media described Jaz, they used phrases like 'financial wizard' or 'Wall Street high-flyer'. She, on the other hand, was nothing. She was just the mother. Price gave directions, set up shots. A helicopter circled in the sky. They walked down the path toward the rocks, holding hands. At least no one expected them to smile.

Where was her boy? Would he walk out from behind one of the round white boulders? Was that what they'd arranged for her? A surprise?

Afterwards, in the back of their minivan, Price performed the holding of the wrists. Sugar, he said. You did well. I'm proud of you. Back at the hotel, Price and her dad and the doctor argued about her medication. They stood over her as she sat on the edge of the bed, trying to watch TV. They were in the way.

You have black onyx, twenty-eight diamonds, very dramatic, if you took just the center of this it would be quite classic, but if you throw in the black onyx it's something totally different so beautiful deep colors all natural not heat treated you've got the gold a beautiful beautiful setting, don't forget about our interest-free pays six pays half a year and it's yours look at how dramatic it is look shipping handling taxes on top how dramatic let's move on

One morning, when they were still at the motel, she opened the door to a young Hispanic woman. The woman had long curly hair which was falling over her face. She wore big gold hoop earrings. She shook her fist. He's my son, she screamed. Not yours. You stay away from him. Lisa didn't understand. My son, repeated the woman. He was the one who vanished out at Los Pináculos. My son, not yours. And then she scratched Lisa's face. She just reached out and clawed at her with her nails. Jaz sprang up and pushed the woman, who staggered back and sprawled on the ground. Then he slammed the door shut and stood with his back against it. His eyes were filled with tears. She remembered that very distinctly, the tears. What the hell's going on, he asked. As if it were her fault. When she touched her face, the tips of her fingers came away bloody.

The woman hammered on the door, shouting in Spanish. I've never seen her before, said Lisa. Jaz nodded. The woman hung around outside until the police came and took her away in a patrol car. They said they expected such things – a side effect of the media exposure. Lisa wanted to know if it was true. Had the woman's son really disappeared? She wished the two of them could sit down quietly together and drink coffee and talk.

I like your earrings.

Thanks.

So is that his picture? He's a beautiful boy.

In the parking lot she could hear the muffled sound of the juke-box. The air smelled of something dry and bitter. One by one his friends came out from their hiding places, hands jammed in the pockets of their baggy jeans. They'd seen the whole thing. They'd seen her getting fucked against a truck. For a moment the boy looked at her, then back at them. He grinned and lit a cigarette. She pulled on her panties, picked up her shorts out of the dirt. Step aside, she told him. And he did. His friends made no move to follow. She walked away, zipping her shorts. Her rubber sandals made soft little thwacks against her heels.

Q. And how about your relationship? How's it holding up under the strain? You've been dealing with this in the spotlight and there's been a lot of speculation, which must be hurtful.

She couldn't pretend. She'd wanted it to happen. And while it was happening it felt good. She'd enjoyed fucking a total stranger. She'd enjoyed it and afterwards she was punished. There were things on the internet. Things that had reduced her. The thickset man screaming insults into his webcam. Things that had

The 1 pic of Raj holding a dinosaur in his hand, and the one where Raj is wearing his blue shirt being held by his grandma as they show him the cake, I believe are two distinctly different Raj, they can't both be 3 yrs old!

yes a lot of chromosone abnormalities IS caused by interbreeding, along the generations. Thats why I believe, that we are seeing so much of these complaints unheard of 50 years ago b4 miscengation. But u gotta remember – lot of babies with genetic probs wd have died at birth or shortly after in those days, and no1 knew what had wrong. Same with most cancers and MS – people simply dint realize it what was wrong, and never went to doctors but

i some how dont buy their bullshit story, which parents in thier right mind would BRING A DANGEROUS SICKLY ill child to a remote desert

@TruFree2oo!! Thx for this extra background on the Matharus!! Really appreciate it. We need more enlightened citizens such as yourself to help transcend the masses above the filthy propaganda spun by the Jew York Media

Everybody! Please notice the way they are both laughing at 1.25 when they think the cameras are off!! A clear sign the two are remorseless and lying!!!

Each time she woke up there was a moment before she remembered. Then the helmet was lowered over her head. She tried to stay alive inside it, to remember there'd been a time *before*, but it took all her strength. She had nothing left for them, the reporters, the TV anchors, the strangers who'd begun to blog and tweet and post comments about her family. One day she found she'd forgotten the face Raj made when he liked something. The more she tried to call it to mind, the worse it got. She listed things that gave him pleasure – *raw carrot, trucks, his plastic dinosaurs, empty cardboard boxes* – and tried to picture him with them, but something had gotten muddled up, and she couldn't form a clear image in her mind. Her son was receding, slipping away. She began to panic. What if it was a sign? Was this what happened when someone died? Or worse, a precondition for death: was he slipping away *because* she'd stopped imagining him properly? If he died now it would be her fault. It was all her fault anyway, her punishment. Jaz found her on the floor of that hotel bathroom. He thought she'd taken an overdose and started yelling into the phone. She couldn't find the words to tell him what had really happened, just couldn't make the shapes with her mouth. I don't want him to die, she whispered. Jaz couldn't hear. She was disappointed. She thought he would be able to hear. The paramedics shone a little flashlight in her eye. They asked questions. She told them: *I don't want him to die.* It seemed to be the only important thing to say. She didn't want Raj to die and God shouldn't think she did.

By then he'd been gone three weeks.

Price tried to tell her things. You're holding it together real well, he said. Too well, in a way. People are confused. Now I know you're a classy lady. You got poise. But you're selling yourself short. You're not showing them the real you.

How did a person do that? How did you show them the real you? She'd tried so hard, reading out the talking points, looking at the camera lens when they made that sign, the two fingers pointing to their eyes. She'd tried to stare straight through the lens into the world, into the heart of the man who had her son. Bring Raj back. If you have any information, phone this number. Complete anonymity. All we want is our son. But the viewers didn't seem to like her. They didn't like her clipped voice, her thin-lipped mouth. They preferred Jaz, who could say the words they expected in the tone they expected, words like *these last days have been the most harrowing of our lives* and *we'd like to thank the police and the public for all the support we've received in this difficult time.* Jaz seemed to be able to sleep. She started to wonder if he was really feeling it, really missing Raj in the way she was.

Then there was the confusing business about the rock star, Nick Capaldi. She'd never heard of him or his band. On TV he looked like those boys you saw cycling up and down Bedford, scrawny and bearded, their pumping legs sausage-skinned in tight jeans. Jaz swore he'd had no idea Capaldi was so famous. He'd found him asleep on one of the loungers by the pool and thought he was a homeless person. Raj had run inside his room. She couldn't understand. There was nothing about this man that she could connect with her child. He was feral, faintly repulsive. Jaz said he was pretty sure he was on drugs.

They showed video of a concert, this Capaldi wrapped around a mike-stand in a forest of outstretched camera phones. It was a surreal experience, he said to the interviewer. I was out there just trying to think, you know? Commune? Like, with the desert? I was trying to get away from stuff and somehow I just got more involved.

The local police had held him overnight. Then a whole phalanx of lawyers had arrived from LA and the cops realized they'd made a big mistake. The internet went crazy. No one seemed to think it was a coincidence. There had to be a *reason*. Sent by Jesus, the devil, the banks. He was back in England now, with his own TV special, saying how *harrowing* he'd found his *detention*, how the *not knowing* had been *the hardest part*. Raj had hugged him, held his hand. She stared into his blank eyes and saw nothing human in them at all.

The public would find that ironic. They liked Capaldi. It was her they had trouble with.

For the first few weeks they'd tried to find a label for her. The suffering mother, holding up with dignity *in this difficult time*. The change came without warning, a sudden reversal of polarity that took her completely by surprise. She said something sarcastic to a journalist, a woman with pearl earrings and frozen blonde hair. This woman seemed to think Lisa should cry for her, to fit in with the images of Raj she wanted to show on her local news program, the scanned family photos, the video from his birthday party cut to a sentimental pop song. She asked questions, digging hungrily, scrabbling away like a dog. Lisa wanted to know why she thought she deserved to watch her break down. I don't even know you, she said. The woman looked at her with open hostility. Mrs Matharu, she asked, don't you think you bear some responsibility for what happened to your son?

After that they shouted at each other. How dare you. You took him out there. Unprofessional. Irresponsible. Inadequate supervision. All on camera.

The clip went viral.

The logic of the story demanded something new. A twist. LISA MATHARU SHOWS HER TRUE COLORS!!! Never rise to the bait, said Price. You might think it's intrusive, but you got to make it work for you. You got to keep bringing it back to your agenda.

Someone's kidnapped our son, she reminded him. He's not an agenda, he's our son.

Blowing out candles. By a swimming pool. Swinging on a swing.

There was something sinister about it. About what they were doing to him. They were making him a little saint. Every day he became less real. Her suspicion grew that it was only her own effort of will that was keeping him alive. She was the anchor stopping him from drifting across the border into death. That was when she stopped speaking. No one was really listening to her anyway. She focused on trying to remember what he was actually like, particularly in the bad times, two, three hours into a tantrum, when she hadn't slept and his animal screaming began to sound like the cawing of a crow. The times she'd change his diaper, wondering if he'd still be shitting his pants at ten, at fourteen.

well I hope so, and whoever did this shd be brought to justice. I still don t believe it was Jaz – as for Lisa, I dont trust them. Also Lisa had said that Raj was impossible. Btw did u read anything about Raj having learning difficul-ities/asperger s syndrome. In the photo of him holding the tennis balls he looks def asperger

NickyLUVLUVLUV if you love Nicky C and see all these comments saying crap like 'he took that kid' he is evil a vampire etc. u need to fight back he is an amazing artist and these ppl are pathetic with nothing better in thr life. They never give reason for their sick suspicious cuz they know nothing about music. Labels are misleading

You believe that Raj is autistic, when I believe it's another Vatican Bullshit to make it look like children get their father's and grandfather's diseases, as in their sins are passed on down to their children to the 9th generation, but really, the sins of the father's is autism, which is a child born of incest from father to daughter, cystic fibrosis is brother and sister, these are the sin's of the father's!

If you're so delusional, you'd probably kill anyone that speaks up of the fakery of the Matharu's, and cover it up like the Matharu's covered up Raj's murder! You should be ashamed of yourself!!!!!!!

One day teh bitch will be in PRISON where she is belongs, killing her ownly child and buried the body in the dessert helped by drug addicts

Take a picture of Raj's eye, put it in photoshop, take out the color and you get the Black Sun, known as Sonnenrad SUN WHEEL, the image taken from Raj's retinal scan image in his medical records

This couple are frauds and their campaign to find dear Raj is also a fraud. They're trying to portray the FBI as incompetent to cover up their blood guilt. If you don't expose them, or get them to expose themselves, they'll hide until the time come's when there truth is for all to see

I don't think they will, the only thing that will reveal the truth about Raj RITUAL SATANIST MURDER is when there is evidence against them, then they'll try to hide out on some distent island somehwere with all the money they've scammed off the public till they die from their greed

How they hated her.

A month passed. She felt trapped in Riverside. She felt trapped by the hotel. By the shiny curtains and the smell of the carpets and the voice of the Asian man who answered the phone when you called room service. Jaz asked, gently, if she wanted to go home. Maybe it would be easier. Not without Raj, she told him. He didn't push. Several times he flew back to New York. There was some situation at work, but he didn't want to talk about it. She watched TV and took her pills and waited for the police to call, but they came up with nothing, no leads, no credible sightings. They'd been over the sequence of events again and again, and neither she nor Jaz could remember anything useful. Jaz found some site on the net and talked it over with Price and her dad, some conference between men to which she wasn't invited, and one overcast morning they were driven to Pasadena, to a suite of treatment rooms above a Whole Foods where a shaven-headed guy with a ski tan and a lemon-yellow polo shirt spoke for ten minutes about what he called forensic investigative memory enhancement techniques – a speech which sounded like it had been delivered many times, usually with a PowerPoint presentation. Lisa stared at a collection of cycling trophies that occupied a shelf behind his desk. When he twirled shut the venetian blinds and asked her to sit back on a lounger and breathe regularly, she thought he was going to ask her to focus on one of the shiny metal figures, but he didn't. Nor did he use a pocket watch, or ask her to look into his eyes, but spoke in a soft lulling voice, about beaches and relaxation and her body being heavy, putting the moves, putting the moves . . . After half an hour of free association and word games, she couldn't remember anything useful, and he showed her out to the waiting room, where she took a seat and flicked through six-month-old fashion magazines without seeing the pictures, or anything very much at all, just listening to the quick tiny sound of the pages turning over, liking it for its repetitiousness, its predictability. *This is what happens when you turn a magazine page.* The place was warm and quiet and the receptionist didn't stare or make sympathetic faces, just ignored her and took calls and typed on her keyboard. She felt peaceful sitting there on the couch next to the rubber plant, peaceful for the first time in weeks, and, since she was without expectation, free of any thought or stimulus but the swish-swish of turning pages, it was jarring when Jaz and the hypnotherapist came out of the treatment room with their phones in their hands, gesturing and talking excitedly. When Jaz hugged her, she couldn't understand what it signified, thinking that through some scientific voodoo they now knew where Raj was. She grinned and hugged him back and when he told her what he'd remembered it seemed so small and pathetic that she pushed him away. A second car. There'd been a second car parked beside theirs, which hadn't been there when they started walking up the path to the rocks. Under hypnosis Jaz had remembered looking back and seeing the car roof, a square of glinting metal that he thought was white or silver, a light color certainly, and somehow this absurdly small thing was enough to infuse him with hope and fill his eyes with tears.

It was a twist for Price, and the media were given the new tidbit, and the public was asked again if it had any information and the police liaison assured Lisa that in some office somewhere trained people were looking through hours of CCTV footage from toll booths and gas stations. Of course it came to nothing. The following week they were right back where they'd been before.

Jaz said he wanted to go home to New York. They could fly out to California if there were developments. If, she asked. What did he mean, if? He was angry. Why did she insist on twisting everything? Did she think she was the only one who cared? She told him she was going to stay. He said it wasn't a good idea. Who'd look after her? Her mom and dad were back in Phoenix. If she wanted to be closer, why didn't she stay with them? He seemed to want to get rid of her. It was as if they were on twin moving walkways, separated by a partition. Moving along side by side, unable to touch.

Well actually Sally we don't speak to each other much. Though I've never told him, he's not stupid. He knows something happened. Often I think – I have all the time in the world to think, since, as I believe I told your viewers, I suffer from insomnia and even with the cocktail of drugs I take every day I often find myself alone in the dark with hours of solitude to kill, and I kill them by thinking about my broken relationship with my husband – yes, I think he knows the shape of what I did, and because he knows I suspect that even if our son is given back to us, that miracle probably won't be enough to hold us together.

The lights were making her sweat. She could feel her dress clinging to her back, a pool collecting between her breasts. Price said the interview was to 'press reset on her public image'. She wondered if the public still cared. The Matharus were an old story now. They wouldn't be renewed for another season. Her face itched under the make-up and she wondered if she was going red. Her body rebelled against her a lot these days. Hot flushes, rashes, breakouts. At quiet moments, she could feel herself trembling. Her hands were folded in her lap and they were quivering now, as if they had an independent life, as if they were birds about to take off into the hot studio air and fly away. Jaz was saying words, sticking to the talking points. How was he able to do that? She imagined her hands, panicking birds, beating themselves against the lighting rig, searching for an exit.

She did sleep sometimes, stretched out on her back like a corpse wearing a mask and ear plugs, fathoms deep under a sea of sleeping pills. Sometimes she had confused dreams about the rocks, and about a dog-headed man, neither threatening nor friendly, who was holding Raj's hand. She would be playing with Raj in the dust, the three spires outlined in the darkness, because it was always night in these dreams. She'd be trying to make him use the potty, doing all the things the books said you had to do – showing strong encouragement, praise, never punishing – and she would turn to the dog-headed man and say this is a very stressful time

this is a very stressful time

and the dog-headed man would scoop up Raj and for a moment he would stand there looking at her with his unknowable black eyes and then he would turn and run away.

Q. New York is sympathetic to you, but elsewhere people have been less understanding. How do you feel about the image of you as rich city slickers who got into trouble?

She was walking away across the parking lot, her rubber sandals flicking against her heels, and she could feel semen slick on her thighs and she realized she was drunk, really drunk. Suddenly she was dazzled by headlights, raking her like gunfire as a car swept past, then reversed, the window winding down.

'You OK, honey?'

It took her a moment to recognize the driver as the woman from the motel. She looked behind her and saw the men from the bar, hands in pockets, fanned out in a ragged line. Waiting.

The woman leaned over and pushed open the passenger door.

'You better get in. You ain't got a bag or nothing? Nothing at all?'

Then there was the road, rising up in the headlights, the smell of perfume and cigarettes, the radio playing mournful country music, fading in and out of static. They didn't talk much.

'Call me Dawn,' said the woman. 'That's not such a good place for you to go drinking.'

She asked where they were going.

'Not far. To see a friend of mine. After that I'll take you home.'

'I don't want to go home.'

They turned off the main road on to a track and stopped outside a house shaped like a dome. A fairytale house. The front door wasn't locked. She remembered that distinctly. The unlocked door. Dawn called out as they stepped over the threshold and the woman came down and together they held her under her arms and lifted her up because her legs wouldn't move and inside it smelled of woodsmoke and there were baskets and clay jars and Indian rugs. It felt good to lie down.

They put a blanket over her.

Q. We're seeing a new side of you. A very emotional side. Is this the real Lisa Matharu?

. . .

Q. What do you think of the theory that a wild animal, possibly a coyote, could have taken your child?

1971

The raid, when it came, was sudden and brutal. They arrived at four thirty in the morning, a convoy of trucks and Crown Victorias bumping up the dirt road in the pre-dawn. Two girls were awake, coming off a trip, sitting up on the rocks and waiting for the sunrise. Afterwards they told how they'd seen it go down, the dull gleam of rifles and shotguns, the men rousting people out of the dome, lining them up on their knees in the dust.

Amerika.

Dawn was inside, snuggled next to the older of the Sky Down Feather Brothers. The cops burst in kicking and clubbing people, no warning, no time to react or do anything at all except try to keep hold of a blanket to cover yourself as they pushed you out the door. They were dragging guys by their hair, shining powerful cop flashlights on naked girls, grabbing tits and ass as they took them out for the line-up. Sheriff Waghorn stood up on the kitchen table, which creaked under his bulk as he yelled orders into a bullhorn. You could hear crashes as the pigs searched, the shatter of glass. They were making sure nothing stayed in one piece.

They were searching for drugs and weapons. They found them. Knives from the kitchen, a hunting rifle, pills and grass. There was other stuff too, but that was all safely buried out in the desert.

They arrested thirty people. Six went to jail. Turned out the town had gotten themselves Donny Hansen, all six-foot cornfed octopus-handed QB1 of him, as their star witness. Donny was one of the beer-drinkers, the cat-callers, big butch high-school heroes who felt like shut-out little boys when they looked over the fence at all the lights and singing and pretty girls on the other side. His dad owned the gas station, the hardware store and a few hundred acres of range to the south of town. He'd hated Dawn ever since he tried to get his thing into her mouth at the drive-in and she fought him off and went to sit in Robbie Molina's truck.

One night Dawn had found Donny inside the dome, dressed in some kind of 'undercover' fringed buckskin jacket, picking his way between groups of people, trying to score. He was patting shoulders, offering handshakes. *Hey man. Got any stuff?* No one was biting; he sounded like an actor in a public-education film. She ran to find Wolf and Floyd, who agreed he was behaving like a narc and threw him out. Donny swore he was on a dare from some of the other football guys. They didn't believe him, but what could they do? When nothing happened for a week or so, they told themselves they'd dodged a bullet.

Turned out he'd been sent by the Rotary. She could picture the scene. The boys in the backroom of Mulligan's, working on a bottle of Four Roses and a big bowl of chips, throwing out names of who to send on their dirty little mission. Donny looked up to all those guys, those Rotarian guys. He cared about their good opinion. He'd eventually go and get himself killed for it over in Vietnam, but that was a couple of years later.

Donny said on the stand that he'd bought LSD from Floyd, and that was how they got the warrant. At the trial there were a few photographers around, trying to get pictures of the crazy hippies in their crazy outfits. The Command tried to get the underground press on their side, but none of them would bite. Those so-called hip assholes. Either they couldn't be bothered to get in their cars and drive out of town, or for some reason they didn't dig the Command's thing, which kind of weirded Dawn out, since she'd thought most everyone was on their wavelength. Wasn't it what the counterculture was about, working for the Light? And here they all were printing words like *cult*.

She sat on the public benches with six other girls, dressed in home-sewn silver mini dresses, with tabards saying the names of various Ascended Masters who were acting as celestial witnesses for the defense. *Korton, Cassion, Soltec, Andromeda Rex, Goo-Ling, Blavatsky* – she was *The Count of Saint-Germain*. Everyone was staring at them, but that was the point. They were an official protest against the court for not recognizing the Masters and allowing their channels to testify as to how Floyd was set up by Donny and the Rotarians. She looked down at all the suits and ties and thought to herself, well, Dawnie, here they are, the Forces of Darkness. Here they are in the flesh.

Floyd's sentence tore the heart out of her. Ten years. Ten years because Donny Hansen said so. What a good day for the boys at Mulligan's! Oh, they had right on their side! A good day for Mulligan's, for bastards who pushed people around by saying they built stuff and others were lazy, when actually that was just a barefaced lie and they didn't build a thing, not a damn thing, just balled their fists and made their backroom deals and planned how to keep hold of what they or their daddies or their daddies' daddies had stolen from everyone else.

They went to all the trials, not just Floyd's, and it was a horrible time. Seemed like they were always on the bus going into the city, watching the buildings get closer together, the concrete spreading over every patch of open ground. It was exhausting, heartbreaking. Walking up and down with placards, sitting through hours and days of Dark Side agents reciting so-called evidence. A couple of defendants drew five years, the rest two to five. Turned out Marcia had an outstanding federal warrant and she ended up back in New Jersey on some kind of armed-robbery charge. It was political, so Dawn heard; seemed she'd been in a branch of Chase Manhattan with a sawn-off and a bunch of black radicals wearing luchador masks.

A lot of people didn't want to be out at the Pinnacles anymore. Every day, one or two more packed up and moved on. Hugging and kissing and making her friends promise to write, Dawn felt scared. The rocks *were* the people, and if they all vanished she'd have to vanish with them, because otherwise it'd be her against Donny and Uncle Ray and the sheriff and Mr Hansen and Robbie Molina and all the other bastards, young and old, a whole town of men who wanted to put her down. She'd lose that fight, didn't take a genius to see it.

There was so much broken. They'd have to fix up the kitchen and the workshop almost from scratch. They'd a guard posted now, day and night. No weapons, just a lookout, give them a chance to run if the town came for them again. Clark and Maa Joanie had gone into their cabins and weren't coming out. Judy was marching about with a strained grin on her face, saying positive uplifting things like a person who'd temporarily lost her red shoes and yellow-brick road. Pilgrim Billy said they should dissolve the commune, just become nomads. You can live off the desert, he said. He was a city boy. Boston, as she remembered.

Wolf had an answer. We should hold a session, he said. That's the way to cleanse this place.

It was the one time she ever saw the inflatables in use. They belonged to an art collective who'd abandoned the air for the sea and gone off to commune with dolphins; for some reason they'd left their prize possessions with Coyote. Wolf took everyone out to the middle of the dry lake. The light was blinding. They formed a ragged procession, their feet crunching over the crust of salt. They blew up the inflatables with giant pumps, two fifty-by-fifty-foot silver pillows, a soft city tethered six feet off the earth. They were the most beautiful things in creation, the most beautiful things Dawn expected ever to see.

For twenty-four hours they stayed out there, naked, hooked up to the Tronics, playing music to rid themselves of the raid's negative energy. When they were tired they climbed on the bubbles and lay looking out at the flat white world. It was clear now: they were living at the end of time. Dawn would remember being high above the ground with the Sky Down Feather Brothers, crawling over a gleaming surface, her vision a mess of reflected light. It was a world of pure beauty, the holy beauty of Light, and afterwards, when she went into the darkness, it was this memory she tried to hold on to of the Ashtar Galactic Command: the great drone of the Tronics spiraling up into her body as she tumbled over the holy beauty of Light.

A couple of days later she was squeezed into an orange VW bus and driven to LA. They called it a fishing mission. They sent her and three other girls, with a tall Texan, name of Travis. Officially he was there to make sure nothing bad happened to them, but he had another thing going, which she wasn't supposed to know was a heroin deal. He talked to Clark on the phone at least once a day. But she wasn't to worry her pretty little head, oh no. Fill up the bus, Clark said. Get them to come. We need to grow again.

To her dying day she'd wish she'd never even seen Sunset Boulevard. She was just dumped there, right on the sidewalk outside Tower Records. Walk up and down, Travis told her. Talk to people. Travis made the girls dress sexy, hotpants and halter-tops. They'd stand on the corner and cars would go by honking their horns. The point was to meet prospects, boys mainly – going in and out of the record store, hanging outside the Whisky or Sneeky Pete's. If you got one talking you had to try to sell him the LP and engage him in conversation about the Light. *Have you ever thought about smog?* That was one of her openers. *You know smog's negative energy, right? It's not a question of believing me or not believing, because you can see it up there, right above your head. What else is it if it ain't negativity?*

'You could say you'll go with them,' said Travis, 'if you think it'll get them to come out to the rocks.'

'Go with them?'

'Don't act dumb.'

If one bit, you could take him to the house. It was a rotting Victorian in Echo Park. It had a lot of bedrooms, but they all smelled of dead things, and the neighborhood was full of junkies and Mexicans who made obscene gestures and called out after you in Spanish. She got followed a couple of times. At night she'd sometimes stop by a diner and take out a hot black coffee just to have something to throw, maybe give herself a head start.

If they needed to crash, you let them stay. You cooked a meal (mac and cheese, said Travis, something homely) and introduced them to the others. All four girls were young and pretty and they never had trouble finding men to sit on the ratty couches in the living room and listen to their pitch about the Command. She fucked some of the guys she brought back. She fucked some of the guys the others brought back. Travis would usually be upstairs. Sometimes you'd have to go up and be with him.

It was like time stopped when you were in that house. It was exactly the same, day or night. The sound of top-forty music on a transistor radio, the swish of the plastic-bead curtain leading into the kitchen. Her room was painted dark red, lit by a bare bulb on the ceiling. Someone was always talking to someone just outside the door, telling them about the evacuation. *Think about it. About earthquakes. You want to run the risk? The Command have been monitoring the West Coast for generations. They can evacuate the entire population within sixty seconds. They know where every one of us is at any time.*

Fuck me you little bitch come on fuck me.

the ships are beautiful

the ships are full of joy

Clark wanted money. It wasn't just that you had to go find recruits. You had to sell them the LP. Every afternoon, before they left to go to the Strip, Travis drummed it into them. How many would they sell that day? Think of a number, visualize that number. One night, Travis sat her down and made a suggestion. 'Selling the record's one thing,' he said. 'There are others. I ain't asking you to do nothing you ain't already doing for free.'

The LP had seemed like such a wonderful idea. It was made from a tape taken off the desk at one of the sessions. Somehow Clark had persuaded Coyote to hand it over and announced in a meeting that from now on they were going to reach out across the airwaves of the world, bringing news of the coming crisis to anyone with an enquiring mind and five bucks in their pocket. At a joyous meeting in the dome, the remaining Lightworkers sat down together in a spirit of unity to put forward their ideas about how the sleeve should look and what should be written on the cover. They were disappointed when Clark played the tape. It sounded like it had been recorded through a sock. Coyote wasn't around to shout at and Clark argued that sound quality didn't really matter, because the Command's message was coded into the carrier wave of the music. People would get it without having to get it. That was cool, but the record didn't give a shadow of the real feeling of the Tronics. They'd hoped for more.

She never could explain how Coyote got on the sleeve. Everyone assumed there would be a picture of Judy looking positive, or Clark and Maa Joanie in their robes. The drawing was by a girl called Kristel, who liked to call herself *ChrisTele*, which she said meant 'The Vision of Jesus-Sananda'. She drew Coyote getting electrocuted, standing in front of one of the Command's spacecraft. Clark didn't put up any resistance. Perhaps he was trying to get everyone to think he was sharing the Light.

Clark wanted them to sell the LP, so they sold it. Whether anyone ever listened to it more than once was another thing. The boys who paid their money and came back to eat the homely mac and cheese and liked the sound of a place out in the desert where sexy girls wanted to make it with you all day and night got put on Travis's bus, or else were trusted to find their way on the Greyhound, carrying parcels wrapped up carefully by Travis with the promise of a special thank you at the other end. Dawn would wave to them as they set off with their kit-bags and backpacks, like circus performers getting into a cannon and being shot up into the air. Yes, baby. I'm coming in a few days. Don't you worry. The ships are beautiful.

the ships are full of joy

She got gonorrhea, and Travis took her to a clap doctor, who gave her antibiotics and a lecture. At night she stumbled along the Strip, joining the swarm of kids trying to get in to see bands, eating from food trucks, tripping on the sidewalk outside the 76 station and looking up at the billboards. *Come to Where the Flavor Is*. There was a giant statue of Rocky and Bullwinkle and Bullwinkle's shirt changed color depending on the outfit of the girl on the casino billboard on the other side of the street. At the co-op, she lined up dirty and barefoot, paying with the food stamps Travis gave them in return for the LP money. After a while she lost track of time. To the store, back from the store, to the Strip, back. She watched crabs crawling over a stained mattress like a platoon of soldiers, counting them off, counting them off; she went with Kristel and Maggie to score at an all-night drug store and noticed the dealer had a wooden hand. They couldn't stop laughing. She was sitting in someone's office doing her first blow, saying have you heard of the evacuation and remembering the dealer's wooden hand and laughing laughing laughing and going to the store and back to the Strip and taco stands and coffee shops and topless bars and passing cars and passing cars and passing cars and passing cars . . .

She stayed three months, through the spring and early summer of 1971. Though she didn't think so at the time, it took something out of her. A freshness. She rode back into the desert sitting on the floor of Travis's VW bus, bumping shoulders with her latest pickup, a red-haired boy from Iowa who didn't know he was carrying almost half a pound of Laotian number four heroin in the lining of his bag. Through the smeared little porthole windows the Ashtar Galactic Command's primary Earth base looked meaner, more beat up than she remembered. The dome still loomed over it, but its panels were rusty and dull. Maa Joanie's shack had caught fire, burned right down. It was all anyone could talk about: who'd set the fire, was it the FBI or the town or the Forces of Darkness operating through an agent in the compound. Far as Dawn could see, it could have been anybody. The place was full of strangers. She and the other fishing girls had sent maybe twenty pickups out there, but there seemed to be all kinds of other people who didn't look like they were passing through. A lot of tattoos. One or two obvious runaways, at least three guys walking around with Gypsy Joker patches. The first night all she could hear was the sound of bike engines, people smashing bottles, raising hell. Round about two in the morning some girl started screaming. No one sleeping near Dawn in the dome seemed bothered by it. No one even sat up. She went outside and poked about with a flashlight, but the screaming stopped before she could find where it was coming from.

The next morning she saw the red-haired boy thumbing a ride by the side of the road. He had a black eye. When she said what's up, he told her to go to hell. You promised me this place was cool, he said.

A lot of faces were missing out of the old crowd. That night at dinner (which had gotten worse, if that was possible – a scoop of rice and a slop of flavorless lentils served in institutional metal trays) Dawn caught up on the news. None of it was good. The town had been tightening the noose. People from the Earth base got refused service in most of the stores. They had to drive twenty miles to get gas. The boys from Mulligan's had hit them with every legal trick they could think of. Building code, sanitation. They'd declared the dome a hazardous structure, wanted to send in the bulldozers and clear it away.

Clark wanted her to come see him. He made her kneel down and once she was finished told her to be careful because walking among them were some who were not part of the Brotherhood of Light. 'They are emanations of the Left Hand, little Dawnie. Their rays fall upon us as a weight, a kind of depression. If you feel such a weight, you let me know the name of the person. The Command will send help. You just tell me right away.'

Afterwards, she picked her way up on to the rocks. As she sat, thinking and smoking a joint, she heard someone climbing the path toward her. A figure wrapped in a jellaba came into view, the pointed hood pulled down low over its face.

'Is that you, Dawnie? It's me. Judy.'

Judy rushed into her arms like they were long-lost sisters, hugging her and covering her face in kisses. It was a clear night and the moon was full. Dawn was shocked. The girl looked a thousand years old, her sunken eyes twin boreholes in her face, as if someone had pressed two thumbs into white clay.

'What's the matter? What's going on?'

'I don't know, Dawnie. It's all falling apart.'

Judy had a way of saying things like she believed them and didn't believe them at the same time. When she got emotional, you'd suddenly feel part of her was completely detached, watching herself being happy or crying or interested in your day. Sometimes it seemed like she was just copying other people, as if she hoped that going through the motions would supply the feelings she didn't actually have. That night was different. Her hands were freezing. She was quivering like a cornered animal.

They climbed up to the base of the tallest of the three Pinnacles, where there was a circular hollow, like a dry hot tub, in which you could sit and be sheltered from the wind. Judy pulled her knees up to her chest and rocked backwards and forwards. She shook her head when Dawn offered her the joint.

'Dawnie, they're going to kill me.'

'What?'

'I know it. They're going to do away with me.'

'What do you mean, kill you? Who?'

'Maa and Mr Davis. They're working themselves up to it. They pulled me out of the flow, now they're throwing me back.'

She had that strange tone again, that sarcastic tone. Dawn fitted the roach into a clip and hunkered down, trying to light a match.

'I don't understand you, honey. I don't think anyone's out to get you.'

'It's all such a worry, what with the town hating us so much. Mr Davis is looking into getting proper sewage laid, but that isn't going to hold them for long.'

'Judy?'

'You don't know. You haven't even been here.'

'Try and keep your mind on one thing. Talk to me.'

'I was her little girl. They said that, over and over.'

'Judy, they worship you. They hold you up on high. You're the one's been to the ships. They wouldn't harm a hair on your head.'

'Mr Davis has got guns, you know. Stashed out in the desert. He's got people training.'

'You're scaring me.'

'You should be scared. He's giving out radiation badges.'

'Clark's doing this?'

'So you can detect it. It's colorless and odorless. You have to wear the badges.'

'Is there something radioactive here, Judy?'

'Must be. Mr Davis wouldn't lie about a thing like that.'

'Judy, has Clark got something radioactive?'

'It's the Dark Forces, Dawnie. The Left Hand. You can feel it, can't you? It's all over this place. Mr Davis keeps talking about sacrifices. How we need to make them. For the Light. He goes on and on. It's like he can't think of anything else.'

'And you think he means you?'

'Why would he kill me, Dawnie? When he found me and took me up and looked after me for so very long?'

'I don't know. I can't believe he wants to hurt you – wait a minute. You said he found you?'

'In Salt Lake. That's all I remember. I was just a little kid. He picked me right up off the floor like a shiny penny.'

'I thought you walked out of the desert. Maa Joanie waited for you and you came back to her.'

'I was the answer to her prayers.'

'Are you saying you're not her daughter?'

'Dawnie, there are things that are over and done. We don't like to talk about the things that are over and done.'

She leaned forward and hugged Dawn tight, pressing in, molding herself to her body. Help, Dawn thought. If you're out there, Ascended Masters, help me. This is my distress call, my beacon.

No one came. No higher presence, no lights in the sky. Do not fear, she told herself.

do not fear

Rumors. You had to look out for the cigar-shaped craft, the ones with the insignia on the side. They were the dark ships. If they were invisible you'd still feel their energy, the negativity directed at the Earth base in a great black beam. There was radiation everywhere, in the menthol cigarettes, the purple aum blotter acid, the water, the lentil stew. There were people who couldn't be trusted, aligned to the Left Hand. They'd buried sources around the compound. Pellets of uranium. They were signaling to their masters using infra-red.

She found Wolf and Coyote in a wickiup, singing rebel songs. The air was full of mesquite smoke. They'd sewn rainbow patches on to their clothes.

Everyone knew there'd soon be another raid. FBI, CIA, some clandestine government agency without an official name. Didn't matter: the government was at the bottom of it. They were rolling up the Brotherhood. Ultra-low mental frequencies. Secret offshore prisons. Lightworkers tortured, disappeared. Plausible deniability. COINTELPRO. How much radiation? Terrestrial or etheric? Who could say? They were in a remote area, free from the psychic vibrations of major cities. Maybe the Pinnacles had been chosen as an experimental site.

By whom?

'What are you doing?' she asked Wolf.

'I'm cleaning my gun.'

'Why?'

'So it can speak.'

Coyote slumped down next to her and held a Zippo lighter over the crotch-seam of his jeans. He farted loudly. A little greenish puff of flame spurted out.

'It only takes a spark,' he said, 'to light a prairie fire.'

'You're disgusting.'

He laughed, showing a mouthful of yellow teeth. 'You know there aren't any ships, right? No ships filled with joy?'

Rumors. There were agents up on the rocks with masks and protective suits, sweeping, searching, combing the area. Clark was collecting the dosimeter badges for testing. The darkness coiled its way through the camp, rising up between people, causing fights. Coyote built a Geiger counter. A little box with a handle and a microphone on a rubber cord. When he held up the mike, a needle jumped across the dial and clicks and pops stuttered out of the speaker. In our food, our skin, our blood, the marrow of our bones. Everyone with their own decontamination regime. Scrubbing and gargling. Rose crystals, aluminum foil, lemon verbena tea. Was the whole site infected? In the chickpeas. Sprayed into the air from crop-dusters. Fine droplets. Microscopic scale. Coyote, throwing lumps of quartz, snickering about background radiation, cosmic rays. Ten, twenty parts a million. The Tronics were broken. Sabotage? They had no protection. The darkness, getting into the circuits. The violet ray, the green ray, the black ray of despair.

Every day more people left, others arrived. Drifters, bikers, informers, agents. Every morning Dawn woke up and looked for Judy. Until she saw her she couldn't relax. The camp had split into two factions. The radiation freaks clustered around Clark and Joanie; the others were with Wolf and Coyote. You saw people carrying rifles. A new phrase, a new philosophy.

Armed love.

Off the pigs! Strike terror into their plastic hearts. Clark and Joanie walked about dressed like Christmas trees, shouting at people about the Command. The Ascended Masters were looking down on them in horror. Wolf and Coyote were taking their orders from the black ships. Kill their gods, whispered Coyote. Rise up and be free. It was a declaration of war. Angry scenes in the dome, rad-freaks versus armed lovers, shouting, finger pointing, clenched fists punching the air. Clark tried to bring order. The hierarchy existed for a reason. Not everyone could send messages through the sacred channel to the sky. The fate of the Earth was in their hands. Unity was everything! His voice was high and cracked. No one seemed to give a damn. Coyote squatted down and pissed up against his throne. Wolf called out from the floor. Armed love! Only one division, one barrier – between the living and the dead. Time to break it down. Time to storm heaven.

Great liberation on hearing. The dead were tunneling through, slithering under the wire. Where were the ships, the beautiful ships filled with joy?

Now death was inside the dome, a skeletal communard breaching the citadel of the living. Clark was brandishing a pistol. Shots were fired. People ran for cover. Dawn didn't know the name of the young man who fell. Blond hair. Death's blue-eyed boy, clutching his chest. We aren't settlers, he'd said, rapping round the fire. We are unsettlers. We want to learn water, learn animals fire sun moon edible plants. We want to be a drop-out nation, living wild and free. Rattle the bones. Bones and stones. Ancient, futuristic. Red rose blooming through his shirt. Just a boy, shivering, bleeding out. He couldn't speak. He was heading into the bardo. How it was decided,

Dawn would never know, but instead of taking him to a doctor, they all gathered around with their instruments. Coyote was scurrying here and there, dishing out squares of blotter, connecting cables, getting mixed up in the paths and flows. And so they hooked the boy up to the Tronics and began the final session.

This was the bardo of the moment of death.

There was no chanting, no prayers. Just the drone, unfolding, opening up a doorway between the lands of the living and the dead. Merge with the Light, urged the drone. Know that you are part of the clear light of reality. Let go of all else.

There were guns. There were knives and machetes, duct tape, a saw. There was a car battery, jumper cables.

The dead boy was pulled down to the second bardo.

It was the scariest night of Dawn's life. It was like finding yourself at the bottom of a cold dark well. How long did it last? Days? Weeks? She fell away from the Light into visions of hell. Blood and darkness. Writhing snakes, like intestines. The boy's body was wrapped in a tarp and carried out into the desert. Figures digging a hole, throwing him in.

When the sun rose over the mountains, and a wedge of watery orange daylight started pushing its way through the doorway of the dome, Dawn wept with relief. That morning, as people stumbled, blinking out into the light, she packed a bag and headed to the highway junction. She didn't say goodbye to anyone. Not Judy. Not anyone. All she could think of was getting away.

She thumbed a ride from a trucker who was going to LA, and, like water heading downhill, soon found herself back on the Strip. She spent a few nights on the street, a few more nights with a pickup, then found a job dancing in a cage at a bar where the girls served drinks in superhero outfits. She crashed at a place in West Hollywood, then another in Santa Monica, owned by a Hasidic Jew who had a chain of dry cleaners and was happy to take favors for the rent. Time passed. She made the glitter scene. She never talked about Ashtar or anything like that. Ancient history. She wore hotpants and five-inch space boots and hung around with nymphet girls and faggoty boys outside the English Disco, trying to meet musicians. For a while she followed bands, fucked roadies and booking agents, trying to get close to Bowie or the Stones. One of them took her to Vegas, where she got raped by three guys in a hot tub to the sound of the Doobie Brothers and things kind of slid from there, five shifts nightly, topless, full nude, no touching, touching, until she was giving head in the bathroom at an all-night coffee shop in return for food, her arms and legs a mass of bruises, her mind shot to hell. One night she headed down a rabbit hole following a line of cocaine and by some miracle emerged alive to find it was 1986 and she was sitting on a bed in a Miami hotel room with a hundred and eighty thousand dollars cash and a lot of smashed furniture and the memory of something bloody and violent she'd promised never to speak about again.

She bought the motel with that money, and only when she was painting the place, using healing lilac and purple, did she start to have doubts. Had that last session in the dome ever really ended? Was the life she'd led just another bardo, another intermediate state? Waking consciousness was a bardo, between past and future existences. Dreaming was a bardo. Was she dreaming? Or was this one of the bardos of death? She could feel herself falling away from the Light. She could feel the drone, still working inside her.

2008

No one except Laila seemed to think it was a good idea to take the record deck.

'Why you need this?' asked Uncle Hafiz. 'You have iPod, everything you want for music.' Uncle Hafiz was a big fan of modern things. If he had his way, they'd all be living on a space-station, eating food that came in tubes.

Her aunt worried about the dust. 'It's mine,' Laila reminded them. 'I know how to look after it.'

'Leave her,' said Samir. 'She's *loco*.' Lately he'd started talking Spanish. He'd been telling kids at school he was Salvadorean, swaggering around and throwing hand signs. He told horrible stories about revenge killings and severed heads rolled on to dancefloors. She thought he might be getting bullied.

She packed the record player into the station wagon, carefully coiling up the long tails of wire which hung from the back of the speakers, wrapping the units in towels and wedging them between her suitcase and the cardboard box containing her uncle's mayoral props. She carried the records on her lap so she could look at the covers on the way. Her collection had been more or less dictated by other people's taste – what they'd once liked but didn't anymore. For over two years, since Uncle moved them from San Diego, she'd been making regular trips to the thrift store to riffle through dusty crates of marching-band music and nineties pop. It had started as a necessity; there was pretty much nothing to do in town unless you had a car. It soon got to the stage where she had to limit the number of times a month she'd go in, so at least there'd be a chance of finding some new stuff. Mostly she looked out for hair. A band with good hair, or at least big hair, was probably worth risking a dollar to hear. She liked eighties power ballads, synth pop, old-fashioned

Jheri-curled rappers. New stuff she found on the net, same as every-one, but with old records you got more than just music. You could put an album cover close to your face and smell garages and attics, trace with your finger the ballpoint-pen signature of the previous owner on the inside of the gatefold. Digital things were just what they were. They had no atmosphere.

She replayed, for the hundredth time, the way she'd gushed at Nicky Capaldi. The best thing that'd happened to her all year? Oh God. And he just stood there and stared, looking all British and bored. He'd been kind of a jerk, actually. A while back she'd had this breakthrough that was probably more to do with a new level of English, some tone she was finally catching, than with music or philosophy or God or anything, but America had suddenly made much more sense to her and she'd felt happier than she had since – well, for a long time – and it was all wrapped up with his band, particularly this one song. She'd even wanted to get the chorus as a tattoo, in a coil round her arm:

Got to have faith in believing in faith in believing in faith.

But that was a year ago and lately the tattoo idea had begun to seem sort of lame. It was only a dream, of course. In reality she'd never be allowed to get a tattoo.

Now that she came to think of it, she'd always thought the guitarist was cuter than the singer.

Her uncle started the car. Samir and Auntie Sara waved at them from the porch. Weakly, Laila waved back. She felt as if she was looking out at the world from inside a plastic bubble. *Imagine if the only thing keeping you alive is this car, because outside the atmosphere is unbreathable for a creature as delicate and advanced as you.* Auntie Sara adjusted her scarf to protect her honor from the rapacious gaze of the neighbors, then waddled indoors. Samir gave her the finger. She stuck her tongue out at him. She was just a visitor in this world, a stranger. She looked through the pile on her lap until she found the Ashtar record. It wasn't a roller-disco compilation or some strange soul album with fat black men in nasty-colored tuxes on the cover. It was even better than that. She'd already looked it up on the internet. Nothing. No mention, not a single hit. She wasn't used to invisible things. It was like finding something out of Harry Potter, something with secret powers.

There was the jackal-headed man, the lines of force. There was a spaceship.

The crackle, then the first tone.

music is the message

The back of the sleeve had writing on it, the purple type so smudged that it had taken her ages lying on her bed to decipher it.

Listen. We repeat, listen. This is the voice of the Ashtar Galactic Command. We speak in the names of all sentient beings in the thirty-three sectors of the Universe, in the name of the Ascended Masters and the Conclave of Interdimensional Unity. We bring this music to you, the Star People, so that you may understand more fully your place in the cosmos. The AGC is an ensemble comprised of humans and higher-density beings. As Children of Light we employ electronic instrumentation and processing modules that allow us to tune our output to the harmonic vibrations of the Universal Field. Know that attempts have been made by powers on Earth to persuade you that your reality as Star People is false. These powers, strongly magnetized to the Darkness, must be resisted at all costs. They seek to destroy you, and plunge you into the brute negativity of matter. This message goes out to whosoever will listen and understand. In the name of the Great Master Jesus-Sananda and of Ashtar, Commander of the Brotherhood of Light, Adonai!

Uncle Hafiz drove, singing along to the *Beverly Hills Cop* sound-track. The heat is on, he sang, pounding the steering wheel. He'd drunk a lot of tea before they left. He was excited about the new rotation. 'I promise you,' he'd said, more than once. 'You gonna have the greatest time.' In some ways Uncle was sweet, but he was also an insane person. Packed in the trunk with his other props was a complete faux-leather Franklin Mint edition of 'The Timeless Novels of Charles Dickens', which he was going to use to decorate his office. There was also a sword and a Perspex award she'd found for him at the thrift store. It was actually for something called Excellence in Network Marketing, but it was shaped like a pair of wings and he was very pleased with it. An excellent gift, he pronounced it. A thoughtful gift.

Laila doubted she was going to have the greatest time, but she needed the money. If she didn't make it to college next year, she would definitely slit her wrists. Or walk out into the middle of the I-5. One of the two. Sure, it was kind of Uncle Hafiz to get the job for her; she just wished he worked somewhere else. They wouldn't be at the base for another few minutes, but she was already feeling nervous.

The clearest symptom of Uncle Hafiz's insanity was his cheerfulness. Laila could see little to laugh about in this life; he seemed to find everything hilarious. He'd been in San Diego twenty-some years, since before Desert Storm, and maybe that was part of it. In a lot of ways he and Auntie Sara lived in a dream-world; some things you never brought up in front of them. Leaving Iraq was the best decision of his life, Uncle always said. 'I weep for your parents because they never listen to me when I beg them to get out.' He'd been a happy young man in Baghdad, playing soccer for a college team, hanging around in cafés with his friends. The family had money, but then came the fighting with Iran and air-raids and shortages. In those days Saddam was America's ally, so it was possible to get a green card. He had a speech which started with 'California is like a beautiful woman,' and rarely got any farther because it scandalized Auntie Sara. When Laila finally heard it in full she was disappointed to discover it was just a series of cheesy anatomical comparisons featuring LA and San Francisco as the breasts.

Uncle Hafiz loved California. He loved its rivers and forests and freeways and red carpets and smog. He was the proudest American she knew. If anyone expressed doubts in front of him about the wisdom of the Bush family or the beauty of capitalism or even the superiority of a McDonald's hamburger over any other food item one could buy for a dollar ninety-nine, he would simply wave his hand at the Happy Gold Cash and Carry, if it was in waving-range, or if not would produce the laminated picture he kept in his wallet, thus (as far as he was concerned) winning the argument at a stroke. To Uncle Hafiz the Happy Gold Cash and Carry was a sort of cross between Mount Rushmore, Arlington National Cemetery and the Alamo. It represented all that was profound and noble about his adopted country – opportunity, struggle, never paying retail. The name had been given to the business by its previous owner, a Chinese guy who'd gone back to China to buy a shoe factory. Hafiz had thought of changing it to something more truthful and self-evident, perhaps in honor of his favorite president, Ronald Reagan, whose strange nickname he always used (it sounded like 'the jeeper'; Laila had never seen it written down), as if the two of them were old friends who read the newspaper together and played backgammon. But *The Jeeper*, all agreed, was a weird name for a Cash and Carry, whereas Happy Gold made some kind of sense, so Happy Gold it remained, though it now had a red, white and blue paint-job to help it carry its load of patriotic significance. He'd left his son Sayid in charge. I have my duty, he told the family when he announced the move. We are at war. Every evening he phoned for a report on the takings.

Sayid, who regularly shook his fist at CNN, but knew better than to mention the war in front of his father, was happy to be left to run the business without daily homilies on the righteousness of the American cause in Iraq. His wife, Jamila, would often roll her eyes and mutter at her father-in-law, even though Sayid had ordered her expressly not to contradict the old man. 'It only causes *us* pain,' he told her once, while Laila was in the kitchen, trying to make herself invisible. 'Him? He hears nothing. Water off a duck's back.' They had a lot of arguments like this. Sayid would tell her not to waste her breath. Jamila would cry. She'd had family in Fallujah. Three cousins, all gone. When Hafiz was talking about the war, she'd try to carry on quietly with her work. Laila, stirring while Jamila chopped, would sometimes see her freeze for a moment, the knife quivering in her white-knuckled hand.

They drove up the long straight road that led to the base, which was much larger than the little town next to it. At night it lit up the valley, a parallel world that Laila could see from her bedroom window, with traffic and fast-food signs and a grid of streets. The main gate was like a checkpoint at home, a slalom of concrete crash barriers and bored marines bending down to peer into the car. Involuntarily she began to fidget as they came closer, her eyes flicking to the speedometer. Uncle was approaching too fast. He didn't seem to know how dangerous it was to spook these people, how quick they would be to fire.

A marine crouched down beside the window. Uncle Hafiz greeted him like a long-lost relative. The marine scowled and took their IDs. After a few minutes he came back out of the office and instructed them to drive through to a shed, where the car was searched. Laila was allowed to get out; she walked around, scuffing her sneakers across the concrete. There wasn't much to see. It was just a shed. Hafiz kept up a steady stream of chatter, mostly about the presidential election and the heroism of the Republican candidate, who'd been a POW in some past war. Laila wished he would be quiet. He was trying too hard, making a fool of himself. No one wanted to talk to him. She needed to go pee, but was told she'd have to wait until they got to the reception center. One of the young marines doing the search kept trying to catch her eye.

At last they could drive on. They passed barracks and hangars and basketball courts and a big box store with SNEAKER SALE NOW ON written in the window. Then they parked in front of another office and went inside. There was a whole crowd of Iraqis waiting in the hallway. Uncle Hafiz seemed to know them all, and started hugging and kissing cheeks. When she came back from the bathroom, he showed her off, putting his hand on her shoulder and saying how proud he was that she was doing her duty for her country. She didn't bother pointing out that it wasn't her country until the immigration case was settled. Everyone was introduced as her auntie or uncle; they were all going to look after her. This was what she'd been afraid of – a whole new crowd of busybodies reporting on what she did, who she spoke to, offering opinions on how she dressed, like they knew the first thing about fashion. They were a motley crew, dressed in American clothes, except for one very old man who Uncle referred to as Abu Omar, in yashmagh and dishdasha, clicking his prayer beads and blithely ignoring the No Smoking sign on the wall.

She grimaced through the introductions and put her earbuds back in. Eventually someone nudged her and told her they were calling her name.

A woman dressed as a soldier registered her and made her sign an indemnity form. From now on, anything that happened was basically her problem. Then the woman took her photo and made her a pass. Laila wondered what it was like for her, working with so many men. Did they behave themselves? Or did they pester her, opening the door when she was in the bathroom, making stupid remarks?

She was told to get her stuff and wait with everyone else in the parking lot. They stood in a long line, holding their passes, until they'd all been checked off by a marine with a list. There were more people than she thought. Easily over a hundred. Batch by batch they were loaded on to trucks and driven out into the desert.

The sergeant who rode with them shouted instructions and handed out bottled water. The name of their village was Wadi al-Hamam. It was located 'fifty clicks' away. No one was to move from their seats while the vehicle was in motion, due to considerations of health and safety. They drove across a flat plain, dust kicking out behind the back wheels of the truck and masking the vehicle behind. The passengers sat facing each other, bouncing and sliding from side to side on the benches, their luggage piled between them like the worldly goods of refugees. The afternoon light made everyone's faces glow golden-yellow. The thin-faced man with the bad teeth, the two women trying to read a celebrity magazine. It was a freak-show. This was going to be her world for two months?

Wadi al-Hamam was weird. The village looked exactly like one of the little towns where her mother had family. Walls of cinder block and cement and mud brick, a whitewashed minaret. Poking up over the roofs were wooden telegraph poles carrying a tangle of wires. The desert stretched away in all directions. They'd parked beside a row of shuttered stores with one-room apartments over them. Signs hand-painted in Arabic: TAILOR. AUTO SPARES. The sky was peach and lilac; it looked hand-painted too.

'See,' said Uncle Hafiz. 'This is for me.' He was pointing to a building with an English sign fixed to it: MAYOR'S OFFICE. She looked around more carefully. All the buildings were actually shipping containers, with false fronts to make them look like houses. As they walked toward the hall for their induction, she realized that the telephone wires didn't go anywhere. The bricks and cement were sheets of molded plastic, tacked to wooden frames. It looked like what it was, a stage-set for an elaborate play.

Know that attempts have been made by powers on Earth to persuade you that your reality as Star People is false

That night everyone sat up late and sang songs. It was like a wedding back home; the women congregated on one side of the room, the men on the other. They ate snacks and sipped glasses of sweet tea. It was good to be surrounded by a crowd gossiping in Arabic. It felt as if a weight had been removed from her shoulders. At first she enjoyed herself, laughing and making jokes with the rest. Then, like a tower collapsing inside her chest, all her pleasant feelings crumbled. It was no use. The singing, the hands clapping – everything led back home, to her old life, to the good things and the bad and eventually the worst thing of all, the corpse lying on the garbage heap by the airport. She slipped out and hid in the dormitory, pulling the sleeping bag over her head so she didn't have to hear the music.

She knew it would feel strange to be surrounded by soldiers, but since Uncle had moved them to the desert, she'd seen enough of them – hard-faced young men driving about in trucks, buying cases of beer at the supermarket – to be prepared. So she was ready for that part, but not for this, not to feel as if she were actually back in Iraq. She tried to make the picture cute, to add a soundtrack of passionate guitars and surround it with pretty bleeding hearts and flowers and color the scene in romantic black and white, but still Baba lay there, broken and dead. He'd been all alone. He must have been so frightened. It was worse, somehow, because they'd never let her see him. That only made his ghost more powerful.

There were a few memories that came back time and again. An evening at some uncle's house. How old was she? Nine, ten? Everyone was sitting outside because of the heat and she was playing with Samir, a chasing game that was making them both giggle and scream. Her father was talking around the brazier with the other men, smoking, wearing a dishdasha instead of his ordinary suit. He was relaxed, enjoying himself, playing at being back in the village. She had a flash of herself at that age, her feet tucked underneath her as she read a book on the swing-chair.

They used a drill on him. She overheard Sayid say it, only a few months ago. No one had ever told her that part.

There were nights just after the war started, when there was bombing and everyone had to sleep in the main room, laying their bedding down on the tiled floor. It was a large room, but they all ended up close together, because it wasn't safe to be near the windows. Who could sleep on such a night? The children went crazy. Even the adults would act hysterical, her mother and the other women bickering about stupid things, raising their voices, bursting into tears. Sometimes the men would go up on the roof and look over the river toward the ministries, smoking and watching the shock-and-awe. She always begged to be allowed to go up too, but she never was. It was one of those nights, when everyone was staying over and the electricity was cut so the whole apartment was like an oven and the family was tense because someone had gone out and not come back. She was dancing with Samir in the candlelight, making up the songs and music herself, from fragments of the pop videos they showed on state TV:

Sexy sexy!

Sexy sexy!

The two of them were hopping about, singing the naughty words and screaming with laughter. Then her father came in. They thought he was going to scold them but instead he started dancing too, wiggling his hips and singing along.

Sexy sexy!

Sexy sexy!

Her mother and Auntie Amira came in, asking what all the noise was about. At first they stood in the doorway looking stern; then they started to laugh. Baba raised his arms in the air, scrunching his lip and making his mustache wiggle from side to side. He took her hands and danced around the room.

Round and round. Her daddy. All hers.

But he would keep getting involved in things. She remembered him crying – actually crying – about what had happened to the treasures in the National Museum. He went to ask the Americans to do something about it, waiting all day in the sun in a line of other men, as if he thought he'd be invited to sit down in an office with a glass of tea and say to some sweaty pink fellow in a uniform, *Look, my dear, I happen to be a professor of history and unless you people smarten up you won't achieve a passing grade*. As if he thought he'd come back with something, a promise or an answer. There were two or three times when he stopped the car and tried to talk to soldiers about some problem he'd spotted. In her dreams his body came back to life and did such things. Her father's corpse, standing by a tank with foreigners pointing their guns at it; raising its hands to remonstrate with them, the drill-holes like moles on its face and neck.

Her mother was different. She had a better survival instinct. But he would never listen to her.

Her father's corpse, hunting through its looted office, dripping blood on the desks and chairs. She'd gone with him; she couldn't remember why. The thieves had been through the whole university. All the computers were gone. There was dust and broken glass everywhere. They'd even ripped the air conditioners out of the windows.

After a while people stopped going out. What had become of the city? Gas lines and bombs and kidnappings and crazy foreign mercenaries shooting at drivers who got too close behind them on the road. They're using this place like a playground, said Baba. They think it's their sandbox to play in with their big metal toys. He'd seen some pilot casually fly his helicopter under the crossed swords of the Hands of Victory. Though he'd hated Saddam, this made him shake with anger. She couldn't understand why; there seemed to be much worse things happening. The university was closed, and while things were so dangerous there was no chance it would reopen. At first Baba tried to do some work at home, reading and writing. Then he stopped. He was worried about money. They sold the car, then Mama's jewelry. Her father's corpse and her uncle, two zombies manhandling the washing machine down the stairs.

After a long time, the university reopened. At first the family was very happy, because Baba was to be paid a salary again. With no car he had to get a ride with a colleague, and every morning he'd put on his suit and sit at the kitchen table with his briefcase, waiting for the man to arrive. Soon her mother was frantic with worry. The death squads were killing academics. First a lecturer from the Sociology Department, then the head of the College of Humanities. There seemed to be no reason. One of the dead was an old philology pro-fessor, a man whose only passion was ancient Aramaic manuscripts. Even Baba was shaken by that. 'Akh laa!' he muttered, the telephone receiver still in his hand. 'How could it happen? That one would never hurt a fly!' No one seemed to know who was behind it: SCIRI, the Interior Ministry, Mossad. Laila begged him to be careful. 'Don't worry,' he told her. 'None of it has anything to do with me.' He said the dead men were probably involved in politics or the black mar-ket, but he didn't look as if he believed it. Mama shouted, telling him to think about his family and not to speak out in public. He would often say things against the Americans, against members of the Governing Council. He just spoke however he pleased, as if it was a free country.

He took so many risks – with his job, his loose talk – but in the end it was the stupid neighbor who broke him. Mr Al-Musawi was having problems with his TV reception. He accused their family of moving some electrical cable so that it ran near his aerial. It wasn't true, of course. They'd never touched any cable. Al-Musawi and Baba would shout at each other over the wall, the neighbor demanding the power-line was moved back to its old place, father retorting that they never had any electricity anyway, so what did it matter? Baba probably shouldn't have insulted him. All the man wanted was to see his football or his variety shows or porn movies or whatever it was. When there's a war, people cling on to little luxuries. Such things can become very important.

They couldn't prove Al-Musawi was behind the raid, but another neighbor told Mama it was certainly him because he had a cousin who worked as an interpreter for the Americans. All he had to do was give their name. The soldiers came into the house and made the whole family kneel on the floor while they went into all the drawers and closets and threw everything around. They were shouting at Baba about being a terrorist, and wouldn't listen when he told them he was nobody, just a teacher of history. Where are the weapons, they kept asking. He was begging them at least to treat his books kindly, but they were sweeping them off the shelves and taking whole handfuls of his papers and dumping them on the floor. Everyone was crying but somehow that was more upsetting than anything, seeing the papers he kept so neatly strewn all over the tiles. 'You think I'm a terrorist?' he asked in English. 'Look at this!' It was so silly. He was waving a DVD, some black-and-white American movie they'd watched the night before, about a scout leader who becomes a politician in the Senate. 'You think this is what terrorists watch? You think so?' They put a hood over his head and took him away.

He was gone almost two weeks. It was a terrible time. At first it was impossible even to find out where he was. There were horrific stories about what the Americans did in their prisons. As bad as Saddam, said one neighbor, before Mama angrily reminded him there were children in the room who could overhear. Finally one of her uncles had to take money in an envelope to some man at the Interior Ministry to get him out. He came home, unshaven and tired but saying he was OK. 'Nothing happened,' he told Laila, as she clung to him, weeping fiercely. 'It was just a little cold and dirty.' But he wasn't the same afterwards. He and Mama talked in low voices in the bedroom. He shuffled around the house like an old man.

That was when Mama started talking about leaving. When the phone was working, she spent long hours talking to her brother in America, ignoring Baba's pleas to think about the bill. Laila and Samir weren't allowed out, even to go to school. Samir had been asked by a classmate whether he was Sunni or Shi'a. He was so little, he didn't even know the answer – before the war that kind of thing had never been a problem. Now it made their mother paranoid. She saw kidnappers everywhere. So they were stuck at home, watching TV when there was electricity, drawing and reading when there wasn't. Along the street people were putting up signs saying their houses were for rent. Every day they seemed to hear about some-one else who was leaving for Syria or Jordan. Baba said he didn't want to leave, that Iraq was his country and it was his duty to stay and make it a decent place to live again.

Then, one Friday afternoon, he went out and didn't come back. *Her father's corpse, waving goodbye at the door.* The colleague he'd gone to visit said he'd never arrived. As it got dark, Laila tried to comfort her mother, who was crying uncontrollably. One by one the uncles arrived, bringing their families so they wouldn't be left alone. The house was crammed; the whole clan was sitting by the phone, waiting for news, turning the air blue with cigarette smoke. That night no one slept. They assumed it was a kidnap, and some middle-man would get in touch to demand a ransom. Instead, the next morning, there was a call from the police to say Baba's body had been found dumped by the side of the road. On a garbage heap, they said. Her darling father, in the trash like a dead cat.

This time they couldn't blame Al-Musawi. He'd taken his stupid television and left with the others. Someone drove to the morgue to get the body. Laila stayed with Mama and Samir, too numb to move from the couch.

They buried him immediately, bribing a guardian for a plot in the overcrowded cemetery. Laila wasn't allowed to go. Three weeks after the murder, Mama told her to pack her things. Two suitcases had been bought at the market, a black one for Samir and a pink one for her. They were going to America, to stay with Mama's older brother Hafiz. For how long, she asked. Until it's safer, was the reply. Samir clung to Mama's dress, pleading not to be sent away. She soothed him, telling him she'd follow as soon as possible, when she'd found a tenant for the house. She hugged Laila and told her to look after her brother. Then they got into the car, where Uncle Anwar was waiting to drive them across the border to Jordan. In Amman, they got a plane to the United States, sitting in their seats with their documents around their necks in big plastic wallets. At the other end, Uncle Hafiz and Aunt Sara were waiting.

It had been her first and only time in an airplane and she fell asleep on her cot in Wadi al-Hamam thinking about it, the novelty of the microwaved food, the movie playing on the little seatback screen. Samir had been so young he got carried away with excitement. She'd hissed at him that it was wrong to be so happy after what had happened to Baba. He began to cry and the other passengers stared. The stewardess tried to cheer him up with coloring pencils and a little toy bear.

When she woke she wasn't sure where she was. There was the sound of a helicopter flying overhead, a familiar dry heat in the air. Would there be electricity? Then she heard other people moving about and opened her eyes. No, not home at all. On the marine base. She brushed her teeth in the shower block, feeling shy at being half dressed around so many strangers, all these women towel-drying their hair, putting sunscreen on their faces. She scuttled in and out as fast as she could, then slipped into a pair of black combats and a T-shirt and walked over to the canteen to get breakfast. The sun was already high in the sky. The hills looked almost white in the fierce light.

Uncle Hafiz was sitting at one of the Formica tables, smoking and talking to his friends, the deputy mayor, the chief of police and the imam. They were already behaving like important men, puffing themselves up, taking their space. The chief of police was a limo driver. The imam had a beauty salon in Ventura. Uncle waved to her, but didn't invite her to sit with him. Decorum had to be observed. She took a tray and ate alone, trying not to make eye-contact with the people at the other tables. Again, she wondered whether she should find the person in charge and say she wanted to go home.

After breakfast it was time for a briefing. All the Iraqis crammed into the main hall, where a petite civilian called Heather intro-duced herself as the 'Simulation Coordinator for Echo Sector' and gave a PowerPoint presentation. She wore sweats, a high ponytail and a baseball cap, and carried her phone on a lanyard round her neck; her high-school sports-coach look was completed by a pair of silver running shoes. She was accompanied by 'REDFOR Control', a grumpy-looking uniformed officer called Lieutenant Alvarado. Heather was fizzing with excitement. Alvarado looked like he'd rather be cleaning the toilet block. Heather more than made up for the lieutenant's lack of enthusiasm, announcing in a helium voice that she was 'stoked to be part of Operation Purple Rose'. She wanted all the 'non-combatant role-players' (which was them) to know that they were 'playing a critical role in the nation's security'. She hoped they would all 'give a hundred and ten per cent at all times'. Laila sat there, trying to project the evil eye in a beam aimed at Heather's forehead.

The job of the villagers of Wadi al-Hamam was to help American troops understand what it would be like when they deployed to Iraq. They'd do this by playing realistic roles, some pro-American, some hostile. They'd each been assigned an individualized character with a name, biography and back story. Heather said she wanted them to think about how their characters would react in various situations, so they could be as truthful as possible when interacting with the soldiers. This was, she said, a 'fine grained simulation'. They should all consider themselves 'tiny moving parts, like cogs in a watch'.

Laila wasn't sure she wanted to be a tiny moving part, unless it was lodged in Heather's windpipe. She was even less sure when she opened the envelope containing her character details. She was a country girl called Rafah, who'd lived in Wadi al-Hamam all her life, but wanted to train as a nurse. She hated the Americans because her father had been killed in a checkpoint shooting. In the game she would be sympathetic to the insurgents and help them whenever she could. As she read the paper, her hands shook. Why had they given her a dead father? Had Hafiz told them about Baba? She went to Heather and asked to be given a different biography. Heather looked at her strangely. 'It's only for the simulation, honey. It's to help you play your part. Look at the alignment graph – you'll see you have a strongly negative attitude to the US as a liberating force. Just go with that.'

'But I don't want to be this Rafah.'

'It's not something we can change at this stage.'

'Why not?'

'I'm sorry, but I can't have this discussion with you. We need you in this role. You'll just have to live with it. And, while we're talking, if I could make a suggestion, I think it'd be best if you didn't wear so much eye make-up. We like our civilian role-players as far as possible to adopt an ethnically traditional look. You brought your veil with you, right?'

'My veil?'

'Your, uh, head-covering and your robes and whatnot?'

Laila replaced her earbuds and walked away. Go on, she thought. Fire me, bitch. See if I care. Uncle Hafiz came over and tried to speak to her. She watched his mouth move for a while, soundtracked by Arcade Fire. Eventually he threw up his hands and waddled off, presumably to do something important and administrative like rearranging his mayoral props on their shelves inside his shipping container. She spent the rest of the day hiding from everyone, reading a Neil Gaiman book in the shade cast by the minaret of the fake mosque.

That evening the villagers hung out in the hall and watched TV. On the news was a story about Nicky Capaldi. They showed pictures of him coming out of a police station and getting into a big black Suburban; he was wearing dark glasses and looking annoyed. She couldn't believe it: apparently he'd been questioned about the disappearance of a child. They showed some concert footage and a few shots of him at an awards show, then cut to a photograph of the missing boy. Laila was shocked. Obviously Nicky had nothing to do with it. His management had released a statement calling on the abductor to bring the kid back, and a disappointed-looking sheriff came on saying they'd eliminated him as a suspect. There was even a shot of the main street near her house, which was full of news vans and photographers. She wondered if Samir had been there.

Still thinking about Nicky, she went to the dormitory and wired up her record player. Ignoring the strange looks she got from the other women lounging around reading and writing letters, she plugged in a pair of big padded headphones and lay down on her cot to listen to the first side of the Ashtar Galactic Command record.

It was like no other music in her collection. It started with a quivery electronic drone, the kind of noise made by the equipment you saw on old science-fiction movies, with big metal dials and wavy lines going up and down on little screens. It was joined by a scraping of guitar strings and primitive drumming that sounded like it had been recorded inside a shoebox, a relentless dull thud that went on and on without changing at all. Sometimes there were other noises, bangs and clankings, little bursts of feedback or sounds like stringed instruments being dropped on a hard floor. Very low down in the mix, almost at the edge of hearing, there were voices whispering half-intelligible words: *We speak in the names of all sentient beings in the thirty-three sectors of the Universe, in the name of the Ascended Masters and the Conclave of Interdimensional Unity . . .* The effect was scary and boring at the same time, like a crazy person sitting next to you on the bus. The first time she played it she thought it was the worst music she'd ever heard. That was probably why she put it on the deck again. Surely nothing could be that bad. Why would anyone make music that sounded so . . . unmusical? No one would buy it. Probably no one ever did. The Ashtar Galactic Command wasn't exactly a household name.

Listen. We repeat, listen . . .

So she'd listened. She had nothing better to do. On the second, third, fourth plays, she started to hear weird things – chanting, crying and screaming, people gurgling as if they were being strangled. The record seemed to be some kind of jam session, just a bunch of musicians playing and letting a tape run. And while they played, something truly strange had been going on in the room, a party maybe. Something. Often the background noise was obscured by more musical sounds, electronic runs and trills that seemed to have been played by someone following the beat of a completely different drummer to the one banging away on the record, as if the players could hear something she couldn't, something significant that she really wanted to hear, that she *needed* to hear, if only to satisfy her curiosity.

Lying in the dormitory, she shut her eyes and listened to a passage that was now as familiar to her as Nicky Capaldi's first album. The pulse of the drums was joined by a high-pitched whistling and a sinister rumble that rose up and up until it sounded like a rocket taking off. Out of the rumble came a bass, which was doubled by a guitar and some other instrument which might have been a keyboard. Cocooned inside her headphones, her eyes tight shut, she felt as if she was inside a capsule, heading out into space.

There was a howling sound, like a dog. There was a child's voice, calling out a word, perhaps a name. There were horse's hooves, an engine, a man coughing, bare feet running across sand. There was gunfire.

A whole world.

The next day the villagers of Wadi al-Hamam started work. It was a strange routine. Every morning they gathered in the hall to hear about the day's schedule. Sometimes a patrol would be due to pass through and they had to man their imaginary homes and businesses, so they could be searched and questioned and occasionally shot at with bizarre-looking laser-guns. Usually the soldiers just walked around with shit-eating grins on their faces saying *Salaam alaikum*. This seemed to be the main plank of their counter-insurgency strategy. When violence was on the menu the villagers had to wear special harnesses over their traditional ethnic clothing, so the laser-guns could register hits. When you were shot you had to lie down and place a card on your tummy, showing details of your wound. Sometimes a make-up artist would come and sprinkle on some blood, for extra realism. Then the medics would run over and treat whatever injury was on the card, or just put you in a body bag and carry you away. There were score-keepers who tallied up the net effect on the hearts and minds of Wadi al-Hamam, and, depending on how things had gone, they would be told in the next day's briefing whether they felt more or less pro-American.

Laila's role was mainly to stand in the shipping container labeled CLINIC, though sometimes she had to come out and mill about on the main street, looking hostile. The soldiers would arrive, sometimes just a few in an armored vehicle, sometimes a whole convoy of humvees accompanying the major, a little man in a neatly pressed uniform who looked more like a sales clerk than a soldier, a sort of middle manager of warfare. When the major came, his troops would fan out and point their guns in various directions while he gave out ballpoints and toothbrushes as morale-boosting souvenirs. Then they would all surround the mayor's office while he took a meeting with Uncle Hafiz. The meetings usually ended with Uncle Hafiz announcing some new bribe for good behavior, a tube well or sanitation project or girls' school. Sometimes the major would make a speech, which was translated into Arabic by a female interpreter who spoke some Maghrebi dialect no one could understand.

Most of it was easier than Laila expected. The stressful part was when the soldiers conducted raids. The villagers had to assemble in various locations, which were supposed to represent their houses. Even though this wasn't where she actually slept, it was too close to reality to feel like a game. She still had nightmares about Baba, and one night was shaken awake by the woman in the cot next to her, who'd been disturbed by her moaning and thrashing about. Everyone was very understanding, but she didn't want their sympathy. When there were night raids she tried to stay in the background, listening to her iPod until it was time to be hooded and cuffed.

One day, about three weeks into the exercise, some soldiers shot all the customers at the café, and Heather announced that in response Wadi al-Hamam would mount its first riot. The major came, looking worried, handed out pens and MREs, and bustled into the mayor's office to consult with Uncle Hafiz. The villagers gathered outside, pumping their fists in the air and shouting 'Down with America! Down with George Bush!' Laila felt ridiculous, pretending to be angry about something that hadn't actually happened, but some of the others were getting really into it, yelling in the faces of the soldiers and ad-libbing all sorts of colorful Arabic insults. Back home she'd seen many demonstrations, of unemployed men or activists from the religious parties, and they were nothing like this, but she supposed Wadi al-Hamam was supposed to be a country place, so perhaps it was realistic enough. It certainly spooked the soldiers, who looked like they wished they had real ammo in their guns.

Mixed in with the demonstrators were insurgents, who'd come out to make trouble. Unlike the ordinary villagers, they were played by American soldiers, who swathed themselves haphazardly in robes and yashmaghs and bandanas and generally looked as if they were attending a frat-house toga party. As planned, when the riot got under way one of them set off an IED, killing a lot of people. The troops responded by killing a few more. Cutting short his meeting, the major fought his way back to the Forward Operating Base. Then everyone broke for coffee and pastries.

Later Heather came bouncing down the main street in her humvee to give notes and explain what would happen next. Apparently, Wadi al-Hamam's hearts and minds had now been definitively lost, and until the end of the rotation they should do their best to make

BLUEFOR's lives as difficult as possible. The insurgents chuckled and high-fived each other. Laila moved as far away from them as she could.

The insurgents lived in a shipping container at the edge of town and passed their days (most of their ambushing was done at night) sullenly shooting hoops, using a plastic crate they'd nailed to a board on the side of the mosque. Since it wasn't a real mosque, most people didn't have a problem with it being used for recreational purposes, though one or two of the villagers seemed to think it was disrespectful, and the imam took it very badly. For his role as local religious zealot, he'd designed himself a fantastic fake beard, a long silky chin-covering which he donned every morning in a complicated procedure involving a big mirror and a tube of spirit gum. Swathed in his clerical robes he looked very impressive, and when the beard was fixed to his chin he tended to behave as if he really was a respected spiritual leader, lecturing the village women on modesty of dress and giving fiery speeches through the speaker attached to the minaret. One afternoon there was a wail of feedback, and he began railing against the presence of the hoop, declaring it an insult against God (peace be upon Him) and a hateful symbol of the arrogance of the invader. He would tolerate it no longer, he said, and called upon all believers to take a stand against ignorance and join with him in tearing it down. Filled with righteous fury, he propped a stepladder up against the building and began to climb, only realizing his miscalculation when he saw he was surrounded by toga-clad men pointing M-16s at his chest. He climbed back down again. After that everyone gave the insurgents a wide berth.

All the insurgent role-players had served tours in Iraq, so they knew what they were doing when they sneaked around, ambushing BLUEFOR soldiers and planting bombs. They were never rude to the villagers, but they weren't friendly either; they just kept themselves to themselves. There was one man Laila found particularly frightening. He was very tall and black and walked with a stoop, cradling his gun as if it were a child's toy. He never smiled, and when any of the villagers got too close to the insurgents' bunk-house he'd raise his weapon as if he intended to shoot. The imam claimed he'd told him he would slit his throat if he ever touched the basketball hoop again. 'He would do it, too,' he said. 'I could see it in his eyes.' As they were debriefed after the riot, this soldier threw back his head and howled like a coyote, which made his buddies fall about laughing. Heather looked annoyed, but didn't say anything. Nor did Lieutenant Alvarado. Laila realized they were intimidated too.

As soon as the soldiers had gone for the day, Laila always made a point of changing back into her ordinary clothes. Most of the villagers seemed happy to have the chance to dress as if they were back home in Iraq. Several had made remarks to Uncle Hafiz, ask-ing whether he minded his niece looking like a vampire. Though he'd always defended her before, at Wadi al-Hamam he seemed far less happy about her rebelliousness. I'm the mayor, he told her. You should think of the dignity of my office. No one else said anything directly to Laila, for the simple reason that she avoided talking to them. Her one friend was called Noor. She was in her early twen-ties, hardly spoke English, and before she became a role-player had worked in some shitty part of East LA packing TV dinners for a food company. She had come to the desert with her mother, father and two brothers. Sometimes she and Laila would listen to music together. Though Noor was older, she knew very little about American life; Laila liked playing the role of educator, telling her the names of the bands, explaining the meaning of slang words they heard on the TV. Most of the women Noor had worked with on the packing line were Hispanic, so she'd learned some Spanish; she taught Laila how to say *pendejo* and *chinga tu madre*, and tried to persuade her to listen to Ricky Martin songs. Noor liked pretty things, girly things – pink accessories and stuffed animals and sparkly nail polish. Laila was determined to change that, but Noor was stubborn.

'I don't understand you,' she said to Laila one day.

'What do you mean?'

'You're a beautiful girl. You could make something of your looks. Why dress like this? All this black?'

'I like it.'

'But what about your family? Do you think of them? Why do they allow it?'

'I do what I want, OK? Just because I don't dress like a Muslim Barbie.'

There was a reason, of course. For the black clothes, the music. When Laila had first arrived in the US she'd felt lost. All she could think about was her father. She couldn't sleep, and didn't eat, even when Aunt Sara tried to tempt her with her favorite dishes. She remembered with shame how she used to behave, pushing her plate away, telling her aunt that the biryani didn't taste right, the burek was too salty. What she meant was that they didn't taste like Mama's cooking. She couldn't understand why her mother hadn't come to America. She'd been so keen to leave Iraq. When Laila could get through on the phone she'd try to persuade her to hurry. 'I'm scared for you,' she'd say. 'I miss you so much.' But somehow Mama always made excuses. Laila shouldn't worry. She was fine. She'd come soon.

'When?'

'Soon.'

'Promise?'

'I promise.'

But she didn't come. And gradually the tone of the phone calls changed. She started saying how things were getting better in Baghdad, how the city was safer, with fewer explosions and more regular electricity.

'So do you want us to come back?'

'No, darling. Not yet.'

'Well, then, when will you come here?'

'One day.'

What did she mean, one day? Auntie Sara and Uncle Hafiz were kind and patient, but often in that first year Laila would wake up screaming in the middle of the night. Once she even wet the bed, like a baby. Jamila would sit up with her and Laila would cry on her shoulder and confess how much she missed her mom. Why wasn't she coming? Jamila said it was to do with visas. Uncle Hafiz had a friend, some bigshot Republican who'd arranged things so she and Samir had a temporary right to remain in the country. This bigshot was also helping them with their applications for permanent residence. But with Mama there were complications. Baba had joined the Ba'ath Party so he could get a promotion. His widow was listed as a 'sympathizer'.

'So we'll come back,' Laila pleaded, sobbing into the phone.

'No, darling. That's not a good idea. There's nothing for you here anymore.'

Gradually San Diego came to seem normal. The city was exciting; a life which had once been contained inside the rectangle of the TV screen was now spilling out all around her. There were rollerbladers and convertibles and bikinis and big-gulp drinks. School was tough. She'd never had to sit in a class with boys before and the other girls were so intimidating that at first she didn't say anything to anyone. People thought she couldn't understand English and spoke to her slowly, making hand-gestures and exaggerating the words. Most kids thought she lived in a tent and rode camels. She couldn't believe the Americans were making a war in a place they didn't seem to know a thing about. When she tried to explain, even the clever ones just wanted to talk about suicide bombers and their stupid 9/11, as if the people in New York were the only ones who'd ever died in the whole world. She lost her temper once and shouted at some football players, who were taunting her in the school cafeteria. 'We weren't savages! We had television! I saw *Cosby Show*, *Saved by the Bell*!' She couldn't understand why they found this so funny.

Though she was angry, she was jealous too. She wanted to be an American girl, to be confident and loud and know why it was funny to have seen *Cosby Show*. The nicest girls at school were the misfits, the ones who wore black and seemed at least to have been bruised by life, instead of being unwrapped like pink cakes every morning before school, fresh and stupid and untouched by human hand. She'd always loved music, so she began to find out about the bands the misfit girls liked, with their lyrics about feeling empty and crying on the inside and being scarred and shattered and wanting to die. She too was an angel without wings. Her heart was in a million pieces. For the first time in her life she had an allowance, and, since her uncle and aunt felt sorry for her, they didn't stop her buying big boots and plucking her eyebrows and ringing her eyes with black so she looked like a panda bear. Aunt Sara was appalled, but Uncle Hafiz liked the idea of bringing up a modern teenager. In some ways he even encouraged her; the henna tattoos and briefly purple hair were proof they were an American family, not stupid immigrants who didn't appreciate the freedoms of their adopted country.

The whole emo thing was fine while they were still in San Diego, but Uncle's sudden decision to bring them out to the ass-end of the universe meant she and Samir had to deal with redneck kids who called them raghead and Saddam and sand-nigger. And though the goth clothes and the overwrought music had begun to seem a little ridiculous, they were hers, and she'd found them by herself, and no one could ever take that away from her.

The weeks went by. The first rotation ended and the clerical major and his troops were deployed to Iraq. Laila and the others watched them leave, then she spent a week back home, trawling the thrift store and hanging out with Samir, who was distant and sullen and kept disappearing to his room to take calls from some girl. Together they watched a lot of TV. One afternoon, still in their pajamas, they sprawled in front of a talkshow, watching the presenters discuss the latest twists in the Raj Matharu case, speculating whether the parents were responsible for whatever had happened to their son. They didn't say anything about Nicky Capaldi, though the blogs were reporting that he was in rehab in England and had vowed never to tour America again unless he received a formal apology from the government. So far the White House didn't seem to have made that a priority. Fans were getting up a petition, but she didn't feel like signing. While the TV presenters swapped theories, she opened Samir's laptop and they watched a YouTube interview with the Matharus, who wore pastel shirts in complementary colors and held hands and did their best to counter the rumor that they were Satanic pedophile child-traffickers.

'So you think they did it?' asked Samir, throwing peanuts up into the air and trying to catch them in his mouth.

'No.'

'I do. That woman looks like a crack whore.'

'You wouldn't look so good if your child was missing.'

'I wouldn't be having no stupid assburgers kid in the first place.'

'Well, if you did.'

'I just wouldn't. That's all.'

She was almost relieved when it was time to go back to the village.

The major in charge of the new BLUEFOR rotation was very different from the last one. He looked like a cartoon soldier, an injection-molded plastic warrior, flat-topped, bug-eyed and steroidal. He made a big show of force on the first day, driving into the village at the head of a convoy, blaring the theme from *Lawrence of Arabia* out of speakers mounted on his Bradley. But, despite his confidence, his troops were still incompetent, sheepishly drawling their mispronounced greetings and shooting randomly into crowds. Before long the hearts and minds of Wadi al-Hamam had been lost once again, and Heather was instructing the villagers to stone him when he came by to inaugurate the imaginary new cement factory.

One day Uncle Hafiz starred in a beheading video. They shot it inside the mosque because it was the most sinister spot in town. All the insurgents wanted to take part, so Lieutenant Alvarado held a casting call and whittled them down to the six he thought looked most terroristical. The video was for Al-Mojave, a fake TV channel broadcast to the troops in their mess hall, which provided their main feedback on the progress of the simulation. The Al-Mojave reporters would sometimes show up and interview the villagers about how pro-American they were feeling. They particularly liked Noor, who had a good line in wailing and angry denunciations. Uncle Hafiz had been collaborating with the occupier, so he'd been kidnapped from his office in a dramatic dawn raid. He'd spent the day watching Vietnam movies with the insurgents while the flat-topped major directed fruitless house-to-house searches. Uncle Hafiz's death (reported Al-Mojave) would be a major setback for BLUEFOR, since it called into question their ability to provide security in their sector. As far as Laila was concerned, they couldn't provide snacks and dips for their sector, let alone security, but she supposed this was the sort of thing they needed to find out before they went to Iraq and did it for real. She and Noor watched the beheaders get ready. They were even more ridiculously dressed than usual; one of them had lost his dishdasha and was wearing a Little Mermaid beach towel wrapped around his waist. Uncle Hafiz was willing to help them sort out their keffiyehs, but was hampered by the fact that his hands were cuffed behind his back.

'Girls, please come help.'

So they tugged and tucked. Much against her will, Laila found herself assisting the tall black insurgent wrap a length of cloth around his head. He looked imposing, and even more scary than usual, like a Berber dressed to cross the desert. To her surprise he smiled and said thank you. It was the first time he'd ever spoken to her.

'You're Laila, aren't you,' he said. His voice was surprisingly high-pitched, almost girlish.

'Yes.'

'Like the song.'

She must have looked blank. He did an impression of someone playing a guitar and hummed a few notes of a riff.

'Not an Eric Clapton fan, then.'

'Not so much.'

'Me neither. I like that one, though. Everyone likes that one.'

He smiled again, waiting for her to say something. She stared awkwardly at the ground.

'Come, Laila,' said Uncle Hafiz sharply. 'Come away. Everything is ready now.'

The tall soldier ignored him and stuck out his hand for a dap shake. 'I'm Ty.'

She took it, felt it twist and swivel in a quick series of moves, ending in a fist bump.

'Yeah, that's right,' he grinned. 'That's the way.'

Lieutenant Alvarado clapped. 'OK, ladies, let's get this done.'

Uncle Hafiz knelt down on the floor. Ty put a hood over his head.

'Allahu Akbar!' said one of the insurgents.

'Too soon!'snapped Uncle Hafiz, his voice muffled by the hood.

Since he was best at fiery rhetoric, they'd drafted in the imam to play the insurgent leader. He started off in formal Arabic, apostrophizing Allah the most Gracious and most Merciful and addressing a call to the young men of the Islamic lands never to relent in their fight against the Crusaders and the Jews. He reminded them that there were only two choices in life, victory or martyrdom, and tried to lead his followers in a chant of 'death to the Crusader Bush', temporarily forgetting that none of them understood a word he was saying. Lieutenant Alvarado, who was holding the camera, started to make 'wind it up' gestures. The imam ignored him, launching into a new description of the hypocrisy of the invader, who dared use his serpent's tongue to talk of human rights and dignity when he was the greatest torturer in the history of the world. Alvarado lost patience.

'Just cut his head off already!'

'Allahu Akbar!' shouted the insurgents. Ty started to saw at Uncle Hafiz's neck, slicing into a blood bag, which spurted realistically down his shirt. Uncle Hafiz fell over on to the ground.

'Cut,' said Lieutenant Alvarado. 'That's a wrap.'

Everyone got up. Ty uncuffed Uncle Hafiz, who insisted on looking at the finished product before he'd let Lieutenant Alvarado pass it for broadcast. He seemed pleased with the result. 'Very realistic,' he said. 'Very bloodthirsty.' Contentedly he turned the camera screen toward Laila. 'See what they did to me? Animals!'

One of the insurgents wanted to know if he could get a copy to send to his mom. Lieutenant Alvarado suggested maybe a postcard would be more appropriate. Ty came over to Laila, wiping the blood off his hands. 'That was pretty cool,' he said.

She shrugged. 'If you like torture and violence.'

'True. Say, you're the one with all the vinyl, right?'

'How did you know?'

'C'mon, we've been living here for weeks. You want to bring it over sometime, play us some tunes?'

'I don't think so.'

'I got some records in my storage unit. Soul music, mostly. Old school.'

'I don't know.'

'Come on, I won't cut your head off.'

Laila didn't find that funny. Uncle Hafiz put a protective arm around her shoulders. The imam shot Ty an angry look. Ty took a step toward him. The imam pretended he'd gotten something in his eye.

After that, Ty always said hello whenever Laila walked past. Sometimes when he was shooting hoops with his friends, he'd throw the ball to her to catch. He never offered to play records for her again, but she could tell he liked her.

'How old do you think he is?' she asked Noor one day.

'I don't know. Twenty-two perhaps? Twenty-three? Why?'

'No reason.'

'You like him!'

'Don't be silly.'

'But he's a black man, Laila. Your uncle would go crazy.'

'God, Noor! I didn't say anything. You have a one-track mind.'

One afternoon she was sitting outside the clinic, waiting for BLUEFOR to turn up on a routine patrol. Ty walked by, wearing his Berber headscarf. She called out to him.

'Are you going to ambush them?'

'No. Not on the list today. We're firing some rockets at their base tonight. Should be cool.'

'OK.'

'Must be kind of weird for you, all this.'

'What do you mean?'

'Playing war.'

'Isn't it strange for you too?'

'But you grew up there, right? Before you came to the States?'

'Yes.'

'So, isn't it weird? Living in this place, watching all these doofuses pretending to attack your people?'

'It's just life, you know?'

He laughed. 'That's one way to think about it. Where you from?'

'Baghdad.'

'I was there. Not for long – I was in the north, mostly. You know Tikrit?'

'Of course.'

She couldn't have explained why she asked him the next question. It just popped out. 'Did you kill anyone?'

He stared at her for a long time.

'Yes.'

'Iraqis?'

'Who else would I be killing?'

She could feel his eyes on her as she walked away.

That night she lay awake and thought about what he'd said; he hadn't sounded happy or sad or remorseful or proud. Just blank. She groped for her flashlight. Noor had found a gossip magazine with a picture of Nicky Capaldi in it. She ducked her head under the covers and started to read. He was out of rehab and leaving a charity event in London. *BACK ON THE SCENE! Nicky C. 'tired and emotional' leaving the Artists Against Anorexia bash at Shoreditch House* . . . She tossed the magazine aside. The girl he was with was as skinny as a rail. Maybe she was part of his charitable work.

The next day she saw Ty again. He waved, but didn't stop to talk. Just then the imam bustled up, a grave and clerical look on his face.

'I must talk to you,' he said. 'Seriously.'

'What is it?'

'My dear, I am like your older brother. I see what is happening with you and I don't like it. You are decent girl, so I know you will accept my advice when I say it is very bad to make conversation with – men like this.'

'I was just saying hello.'

'It does not matter. Please listen to me. I am only concerned for your welfare. There is so much immorality these days, particularly in this place. These soldiers, they are very bad people. Like animals.'

'I thought you supported the war.'

'Please, don't interrupt while I am talking to you. You are fine young girl. I have spoken to your uncle about you.'

'Why?'

'As you know, I make good business with the hair. I have several young girls working for me, but – I will speak frankly – they are whores. Sluts. I see them leaving for their nightclubs and discos, wearing short skirts and other small clothes. It make me very angry. It is why I am severe with you. It is only because I respect you. You are good Muslim girl, not some American prostitute. This is what I say to your uncle.'

'OK. Whatever. I think I need to go now.'

'But you are prey to many influences. He feels this also. These homosexual singers, with their long hair and make-up. I say to your uncle, he has not been strict enough with you. I have offered to help in your education.'

'You've what?'

'I think at the bottom you are a very good girl. But you must wipe off this make-up and dress modestly. And I forbid you to talk to these soldiers. They're immoral, particularly the black ones. They're no better than monkeys.'

It was pretty much the freakiest speech anyone had made to her since the president of the math club had written her a poem for Valentine's Day and tried to recite it in class. She didn't wait to hear any more, just turned and ran back to the women's dorm, where she knew the imam wouldn't follow her. She hadn't felt so angry since the soldiers came and took Baba. Who did this man think he was? How dare he tell her what to do? Beneath all his pious words was this strange, slimy tone. *I will look after you, I will help you with your education . . .* She knew what he had on his mind, and it was disgusting.

After that she made a point of spending as much time with Ty as she could. He brought her a disco record he'd found somewhere, a band called Rufus and Chaka Khan. They listened to it loud, sitting on the roof of the clinic container, blasting the music out into the desert as the sun set over the mountains.

'I'll be honest with you,' said Ty. 'I know I can be kind of an ass-hole. But I find it hard being around Hajis.'

'What.'

'Sorry. I know that's a bad word to you people. It's not like I'm racist or anything. It's just – well, when you're out there you got to watch your back the whole time. You got to treat everyone as a threat. It kind of eats into you.'

'So you think we're all terrorists?'

'Not you. Well, maybe that imam dude. He'd like to put the hurt on me.'

'You know he's a hairdresser?'

'Get the fuck out of here. For real?'

'Ty, why don't you like us? What have we done to you?'

'It's not logical. I mean, we're on a damn marine base. Safest place in the world. I'm not going to have to go back there, just train other idiots to do it. But I can't relax. I just want to switch off, you know? Just get a good night's sleep.'

'Did something happen to you?'

'When?'

'In Iraq.'

'Yes. You could say that.'

'Something bad?'

'Pretty bad.'

'Are you over it?'

'No.'

'Me neither.'

She thought of telling him about Baba. He'd probably have understood. Instead she played him the Ashtar Galactic Command record. He told her it was the worst music he'd ever heard, 'worse than Arab music, even', and though she probably should have been offended, she laughed. He told her they were going to do a big ambush that night, and asked if she wanted to watch. She did, so he took her to the bunkhouse and produced a helmet covered in frayed desert camouflage. Clipped to the front was what looked like a pair of binoculars, a black metal device with twin eyepieces feeding into a single lens. Some of the other insurgents watched as he placed the heavy helmet on her head and adjusted some straps so it didn't slip down over her eyes.

'You ain't going to let her borrow that, are you, Ty?'

'Why not?'

'What if she loses it?'

'She ain't gonna, are you, Laila? Kill the lights, Danny.'

Someone flicked a switch and the room went dark. Ty flipped the binoculars so they came down in front of her eyes, then pressed a button on the side. Suddenly she was in a glowing green world. She could see everything clearly: the guys lying on their cots, the jumble of kit-bags and drying laundry, even the pornographic posters on the walls.

'There ya go. Night-vision, baby!'

'That's incredible! It's like a computer game!'

'Thermal too.'

'Yeah,' chortled someone. 'You can see Ty's got his dick out.'

'Shut your mouth, Kyle.'

At midnight, following Ty's instructions, she sneaked out of the women's dormitory and climbed a low hill at the edge of town, which gave her a view over the road. BLUEFOR were due to do a round of punitive house-to-house searches, a favorite tactic of the flat-top major now he'd more or less given up on Wadi al-Hamam's hearts and minds. The sky was clear, dusted with stars. Laila flipped down the goggles and watched the insurgents taking up positions, green figures sprawling flat on the ground, assembling a rocket launcher behind a building. They'd buried an IED in the road, primed to explode when the rear truck ran over it, trapping the convoy in what Ty called 'the kill zone'. He'd warned her to be very careful where she sat, explaining that if she didn't go exactly where he said, she could get caught in crossfire. Though the insurgents weren't firing live ammo and the bombs were just whizzbangs, it was still dangerous. She had to stay far up on the ridge, away from the fighting. Luckily the goggles were fitted with a zoom, like a digital camera. She zipped up her hoodie against the chill and played with it, expanding bits of the scene, raking the empty desert with her high-tech gaze.

The darkness was alive with motion. So this was how Iraq looked to them; this was how her house looked when they flew overhead in their helicopters. She lay on her back for a while, then stood up and turned a slow three-sixty rotation, ruling the world, dominating it. Out in the emptiness, away from the town, was a single glowing shape. She couldn't tell what it was, even with the zoom doubling its size. Elsewhere she could see a conga of bright lights, the BLUEFOR convoy driving down the main road toward the village. She watched it come, getting steadily closer as the insurgents settled into their positions, ready to do whatever violent thing they had planned. Suddenly all of it felt very distant, just a boy's game. Cowboys and Indians. Kick the can.

She turned back to the glow. What was it? An animal? She couldn't tell how far away it was. How many 'clicks'? This was how she looked to the soldiers, a little point of thermal light, a grid reference to be targeted with a bomb or a drone or a shot from a sniper rifle. Press a button, squeeze the trigger. Snuff her out like a candle. Suddenly the strange glow seemed more important than watching the ambush. Taking a last look at the approaching convoy, she scrambled down the hill and started walking toward it.

She walked for ten minutes. Behind her she heard a loud boom, then the sound of gunfire. Turning around, she saw flashes, intense bursts of energy. She turned away again and carried on walking. In front of her was the shape. It was definitely alive. It seemed too small to be a human being.

She put her hand up to her mouth when she saw what it was. He was just standing there, as if he'd dropped from space. A child. A little glowing boy.

1942

He knew how they must look. The very picture of hick cops, him and the sheriff standing on the porch with their bellies stuck out and their mouths open, watching the show.

The convoy came down Main Street like there was a fire: a truck full of soldiers and an olive-drab Plymouth staff car, which coasted to a halt at the foot of the steps. The man who got out wore civilian clothes: a gray fedora, wingtip spectators and a fancy suit with wide peaked lapels. To Deputy Prince he looked more like a pimp or a fag movie actor than a guardian of the nation's security. He certainly wasn't a Fed, that was for sure. When he got up close to shake hands, the stink of cologne could have knocked an elephant on its ass.

'Office?' said the man. Too busy for pleasantries.

'You expecting Tojo or something?' Sheriff Grice gestured at the troops in the truck.

'Excuse me?'

'Seems like you come equipped to fight a war. Ain't no Japanese Army out here.'

'There's such a thing as the home front. I thought the news might have reached you.'

And with that, the man pushed right past them into the building. He ducked under the counter, walked through to Grice's office and sat down in his chair. He did just about everything but put his feet up on the desk. The sheriff looked like he was about to split his skull.

'I'll need your full cooperation,' said the man, swiveling from side to side on Grice's chair.

'That a fact?'

'And your discretion.' He jerked a thumb at Prince. 'Is this boy trustworthy?'

'Reckon so. Ike's got a good record with the department. And he's not much on talking.'

'You a native, son?'

'My father was, sir.'

That got him. That always got them. Wrong way round. Instead of some guy having an adventure, tasting a little dark meat, he now had to think about a white woman doing it with an Indian.

'Seems I got myself a regular Lone Ranger and Tonto combination,' he snorted, turning his flash of anger into a joke. 'Well, let's get down to it. We have to check out everything, no matter how slight. My office received a communication from a Miss Evelina Craw, said she suspects you have a German spy in the area. Says he's transmitting messages.'

Grice grinned. 'Sounds to me like you've had a wasted journey. Miss Evelina's not the most reliable source. She's talking about Methuselah. He's a crazy old bird lives out at the Pinnacle Rocks. Or under them, I should say. Been out there twenty-some years. He's no more a German than I am.'

'Under them?'

'Dug out a cave with his own two hands. He bought a silver claim off Miss Evelina's daddy, back when he owned the Bar-T, but everyone knows there's not a cent of silver or anything else out there. Oh, there was, up in the Saddlebacks, but that was all mined out years ago.'

'Get to the point, sheriff.'

'The point? You should probably just turn round and go back to Los Angeles. Miss Evelina's got too much time on her hands.'

Outside, the men in the truck were smoking cigarettes, upending canteens. The official, whoever he was, hadn't thought to bring them in out of the sun.

'I see,' he said, examining a scuff on the toe of his wingtip. 'Methuselah. You have his real name?'

'How about you tell me your name first?' Grice was openly angry now.

The man looked blankly at him. 'You may as well call me Munro. The rank's captain.'

'Captain Munro. What are you a captain of?'

'Being a pain in the ass, it seems. Don't be obstructive, Sheriff Grice. Yesterday you took a call from your boss, saying to afford me every assistance. You remember that call, right? Every assistance. That's you affording me, not the other way around. So, if you could just tell me the man's name, we can wrap this thing up sooner rather than later, and I can let you go about your no-doubt-urgent official business.'

Grice's face was a mask. 'He's called Deighton. I had someone check the claim papers when Miss Evelina first brought it to my attention. There weren't nothing to it. She's an old woman. Never married. She gets ideas.'

'Well, my information is this Mr Deighton has radio equipment. He may or may not be a danger, but if he's transmitting, then it's a matter of concern.'

'What in hell would he be transmitting?'

'That's what we're going to find out. If you and your boy would care to show me the way, we can leave right now.'

As Ike Prince well knew, it was Grice's afternoon for going over to the Barrington place and solacing himself with the widow. He had no interest in driving all the way out to the Pinnacles and rousting out Methuselah. But they got into Munro's car, Ike riding shotgun beside the uniformed driver, the sheriff grumpily sitting in the back, as far away from Munro as he could get.

It was a long hot silent journey.

As they left the highway and started down the rutted track toward the Pinnacles, Prince looked out of the window. Overhead a white contrail bisected the sky like a scar. Since the start of the war, the military seemed to be all over the desert. There were barbwire fences and trucks on the roads and signs saying NO TRESPASSING BY ORDER. Day and night you could hear the distant boom of ordnance from the bombing range on the far side of the Saddlebacks. Sometimes there came a sound like rolling thunder and you'd look up to see a silver shape moving too fast to be a conventional plane. The airforce were testing some kind of new super-aircraft. Secret technology. Mysterious lights at night.

No one ever asked Ike Prince what he thought of the war, or the mystery lights, or anything much at all. And if they didn't ask, it wasn't his place to say. About Methuselah, for example. About why the old man chose to live in a hole under the rocks. He knew more about Methuselah than Methuselah knew about himself.

When she got sick and realized she was going to die, his mother had said to him, *Remember who you are*. He was a little boy then, but he remembered, so when they came and took him off to the orphanage, he was stronger than some others. He might have been a half-breed orphan, but he had an inheritance: he knew his father's true name.

Not that he boasted about it. Some things grow more powerful when kept in the dark.

Everyone in the high desert knew the story of Willie Prince. It was a dime-novel story, a radio-serial story: the last real manhunt of the Old Frontier. It was also an Indian story, and any Indian story always has two versions. The white version told how Willie Prince, a whiskey-crazed brave, kidnapped a child and was chased for almost a week over the desert, until he turned and made a stand on the Pinnacle Rocks and got shot down like a dog. Most people didn't know there was any other. Maybe a few old ladies on the reservation told it over their quilting. And him. How Mockingbird Runner fell in love with a white man's woman, how that white man was consumed with jealousy and came after him with a posse, how he ran in the old way, outpacing them as easily as a mule deer outpaces a tortoise, until he came to the crossing-place, the sky-hole between this land and the Land of the Dead. How he fooled the white man into thinking he was a corpse, by swapping his bones with the bones of a dead coyote. How he escaped to live a long and happy life in Snow-Having, far to the west.

Some people remembered, some didn't. Few knew the name of the jealous white man, or that afterwards he was driven insane by the guilt of what he thought he'd done. Very few indeed knew he came back to the rocks to dig for Willie Prince, trying to cross over and take his place in the Land of the Dead.

No one but Ike – no one living – knew Willie Prince ever had a son.

It wasn't his place to say any of that.

Finally, the Pinnacles rose up through the dust, three spires connecting earth and sky. When Ike saw them, fear landed on his shoulders and wrapped him like a cloak. He knew why he had avoided the rocks. And why they tugged at him, like a thread caught on a cactus spine.

They got out of the car and at once a wind rose up. The dust was in Ike's eyes and nostrils, working its way between his teeth. Munro crammed his hat lower on his head and gave an order to his NCO, who deployed the soldiers. The wind whipped the running men's pant-legs around their ankles, sent little curls and whirls and vortices of sand scooting up off the ground.

Sure enough, there was a radio antenna perched about twenty feet up on the rock, a kite of metal rods with a length of wire spooling down into the mouth of a man-sized hole. There was junk lying about on the ground around it, tools and scrap and lumber. An ancient Model T, rusting and half filled with sand, was parked by a mound of what looked like mine tailings; its seats, all busted springs and sprouting horsehair, were propped up on some bricks under the overhang to make a sort of couch. There was a washing line with a faded denim workshirt and a pair of longjohns pegged to it. There was a woodpile and an ax. From down in the hole came the sound of a crackly swing band. It sounded like one of the FM stations out of Los Angeles.

Sheriff Grice crouched down in front of the hole. 'Deighton, you in there?'

There was no reply.

'Mr Deighton, come out. We need to talk to you.'

Munro made another sign to his NCO, who barked an order. The soldiers unslung their rifles and pointed them in the general direction of the hole.

Grice looked around testily. 'Take it easy,' he muttered. 'He's just an old man. He's probably deaf.'

He shouted louder, and still got no response.

'Deighton, come out!'

The swing music stopped. A man's voice rose up out of the cave, weak and cracked, hard to hear.

'What do you want?'

'We need to talk to you.'

'Go away. This is private property.'

'It's the police, Deighton. Come on up here.'

'Go away.'

'Don't play games. Come on out. We'll have a talk and then we'll be on our way.'

There was some banging and scraping and a ladder was propped up against the lip of the hole. A grizzled head poked out and took a look around. As soon as he saw the soldiers he ducked back down again.

'Deighton. It's alright. We just want to talk.'

Grice was trying to sound soothing. The old man hollered up from his pit, his voice hard to hear over the wind.

'The hell you do!'

Grice walked back to Munro, tying a handkerchief over his mouth against the dust. He pointed up at the antenna, dimly visible in the haze. 'You can see. It's just a crystal set or something. He's no threat.'

'We'll still need to search the place.'

The old man shouted on, calling them devils, saying that if they were trying to take away his knowledge (whatever that was) they'd have a fight on their hands. Then he broke out in a terrible, racking cough. Ike listened to him suffering down there, wondering what kind of den he'd made, in what filth he chose to live.

Munro sauntered forward, peered in, then stepped smartly back again.

'Jesus, he's got a gun.'

As if to confirm it, there was a sharp crack, which sounded to Ike like a .30-06 rifle round.

'There's no need for that!' shouted Grice. 'You're being a fool.'

Munro conferred with his NCO and called one of his men forward.

'We'll gas him out.'

There was only one thing Ike's mother ever told him about the man she'd been married to. One thing that stuck in his mind. As a kid in the orphanage, Ike daydreamed he'd meet and fight the burned-face man. Even now he was grown, twenty-one and in uniform, it still went around in his head. His monster was down in that hole. The thing couldn't be put off forever.

'Wait,' he said. 'I'll talk to him.'

The others turned, frankly amazed to hear him speak.

'Let me go down there. I'll bring him out.'

'Hell you will!' said Grice.

Munro was amused. 'No, let him. Go on, boy, be my guest. You flush him for us.'

Grice barred Ike's way. 'You ain't going down there like some hunting dog. Feller's got a squad of his own men to take his orders.'

'I don't mind, sheriff,' Ike reassured him. 'I want to do it.'

You either went after your monsters, or they came after you.

As he walked to the lip of the hole, he could sense the depth of the place, hear the silent thunder booming. He called out Deighton's name, then crouched down and called again, this time in the People's Language.

'Skin-Peeled-Open,' he called. 'Can you hear me?'

There were many things he knew.

At that moment the wind died down. The man replied, 'Who is that? Who's speaking to me?' He said some other words in the People's Language, but, to his shame, Ike could not understand.

'I'm Ike Prince,' he said in English. 'My father was Mockingbird Runner and my mother was Salt-Face Woman.'

There was a silence. Then the ladder was pushed up again to the lip of the pit. Ike climbed down.

It was not a filthy den, but a cluttered little parlor, lit by a gas lamp. There was a chair and a table and an army cot. The floor was swept, the walls smooth as plaster. The man himself looked rat-like, wizened. His face was not terrifying to look upon. One side was smooth scar tissue, the other scored with deep lines. A two-sided man. A man facing both worlds. He was clutching an ancient Spring-field service rifle. When he spoke, his voice was a strangled rasp. Ike found he was not afraid. How could he be, of such a husk? He knew then there would be no fight, no glorious taking of revenge. All he could feel was contempt.

'Why did you say that name to me?' Deighton wheezed.

'You didn't expect to hear it again.' It was a statement, not a question.

'You're Eliza's son?'

Ike nodded. He surveyed the room. The aerial wire led to a radio set, an ordinary device in a big walnut cabinet, the kind of thing designed for a rich man's house. Deighton had it mummified in cloths to protect it from dust and wired up to some device with a coil and a crank handle, which he supposed was a generator. There was paper everywhere, sheaves of it on every surface, bulging files stacked against a wall.

'What's all that?'

'Knowledge.'

'What do you mean, knowledge? What is it you think you know?'

'I'm its keeper. I'm rescuing it from the dark.'

'You live in the dark, old man. Put that rifle down.'

Deighton lowered his gun. 'I'll kill you if you touch it,' he said plaintively.

Sheriff Grice's voice boomed into the space.

'What's going on down there?'

'All fine, sheriff. I'm just persuading him to come out.'

'I won't. I'll die first.'

'Look at yourself. You're already dead.'

The local kids swapped legends about Methuselah's cave. Treasure, a maze of tunnels. There wasn't anything of the kind, just that little room, like a burrow. A rat's nest of paper. There was every kind of junk down there. Mining tools, spools of copper wire. The old fool had crates stenciled *Dupont Explosives: Special Gelatin* shoved under his bed and tin boxes of number six blasting caps jumbled among the coffee and canned food.

'Eliza had a son,' he said.

'That's right.'

'I mistreated her.'

Ike shrugged. 'Kind of late to be saying sorry.'

'But you're her son. She had a son.'

Ike wondered why he had ever been scared to face an old fool who lived in a cave. That's all this feller was. Now he'd seen him and it was done. He could climb back up into the world and get on with life.

'I just felt like taking a look at you and I did. They want you to come out. You better do it.'

'What's your name?'

'Ike Prince. Not that you need to know.'

'Ike Prince. Just that? Don't you have another?'

Ike understood what he meant and it made him angry. He had only the one white name.

'You better come out or they're going to throw tear gas down in here, force you.'

'Only if you'll take care of this.' Deighton gestured at his stack of files. 'If it belongs to anyone, it belongs to you. My life's work. I studied the People, Ike Prince. That's why your mother was there. To study.'

'Are you stupid? I don't want your old papers. I don't want anything from you. You know you were tricked? You been down here in a hole all these years. Where you wanted to put my father, down in a hole. But he tricked you. You took his place. He's alive and you're dead.'

There were tears in the old man's eyes. He hurried over to his stack of files. 'Please,' he begged. 'What I said about your father. Saying his name to those men. I never meant for it to happen. I was jealous. A jealous husband. Please, the knowledge belongs to you. If you don't take it, it will all go into the dark.'

It was pathetic, him holding out his box of scribblings, like it was the Queen of England's crown jewels.

'I'll tell them you ain't coming out.'

Ike left the old man standing there, holding his box. He climbed the ladder. At the top, Grice and Munro were waiting. 'He won't listen,' he said. 'You should use the gas.'

One of Munro's men doubled back to the truck and returned with a metal canister. Sheriff Grice shook his head. 'I don't think it's a good idea. He don't sound like he can breathe too well.'

Munro was trying to brush the dust off his suit. 'Well, sadly for you, I don't much care what you think. I haven't got time to negotiate with some crazy old man.'

He gave the sign and a soldier sidled up to the hole, pulled the pin on the grenade and dropped it in. There was a hissing noise and smoke started billowing up. They stepped back, avoiding the plume, which streamed in the wind across the dry lake.

There was a noise like thunder.

The concussion knocked them all off their feet and they squirmed to take cover beneath the cars as a rain of rocks and small stones pelted down. Ike knew what had happened. He'd known it would probably happen when he told them to throw down the gas. As the rain of stones fell, he was laughing. Now he could go and live in the world. Be a good policeman, do his duty. The lid was closed on the past.

Of course, when they'd all picked themselves up and bandaged Munro's head and driven the three wounded soldiers to the hospital and Grice was started on the long process of reporting and form-filling and sorting out who to blame, Ike ended up being the one to go down and scrape up the pieces. Splintered furniture, a lot of charred papers covered in Deighton's cramped, tiny handwriting. Of the man, he couldn't find anything much at all. Just a few fragments of bone.

2009

Raj smiled up at his father, his deep brown eyes as alien and inscrutable as stars. 'Look,' he said, pointing at a delivery van. Jaz gripped the little blue sneaker more tightly as his son hopped closer to the door, trying to get a better view. A miracle: that was the word Lisa used. God and Lisa were close these days.

'We're going far,' he told him. They always went far. For several months, walking had been their main occupation; all through the winter, even when it was tough to push the stroller through the snow. Lisa would phone from the office and ask where they were. Out, Jaz would say. He'd make up fictitious errands, trips to Whole Foods, the dry cleaner. He'd tell these lies standing on corners in strange parts of the city, where bass blared from passing cars and men hung out in front of check-cashers and bodegas.

He got Raj into his second shoe and carried the stroller down the steps. 'You want to ride?' he asked. Raj shook his head. Hand in hand they set off down the hill, making toward the river. There was a bookstore in Chelsea he wanted to visit; no matter that there were a dozen closer places to buy a book. He and Raj would walk. Sooner or later they'd find their way across one of the bridges into Manhattan. They'd stop for a snack, sit on a bench in a park. The trip could use up most of the day.

At least it was warm. June had been wet and chilly; whole days of rain. They'd trudged the streets under twin yellow ponchos, Raj's hair plastered against his face in wet black licks. Today the sky was gray and a humid pall lay over the street, cloaking the bodies of passers-by in a sheen of sweat; the dog-walkers, the neighbor carrying some kind of cake from her car to her house, its large pink box held ritually in front of her like a religious relic or an unexploded bomb. The neighbor nodded hello and grinned, campily widening her eyes in what was probably supposed to be an expression of fizzy excitement. *Oh that a day should have such cake in it!* As she fished in her purse for her keys, she stole a quick, voracious glance at Raj. Jaz knew her. Carrie-Anne or Carol-Ann. Her husband was a urologist. So ingratiating now, but a few months before she'd ignored him whenever they passed on the street. Yeah, he thought. Eat shit, lady. Try and pretend you never thought what you thought about me.

They walked past the coffee shop next to the subway stop. It had once been his regular spot, but he hadn't been in there since the previous August. One morning on the way to work he'd been standing in line when a woman tapped him on the shoulder. As he turned to see what she wanted, she spat in his face. Murderer, she hissed. Pedophile. God hates you. He'd been too shocked to react. By the time he worked out what had happened, she was gone, out on the street, the glass door rattling in its frame behind her.

The guy behind him had seen everything. 'She spat on me,' Jaz said, disbelieving. 'Did you see that? She spat on me.' The guy shrugged and got interested in something on the floor. Jaz cleaned himself with wadded napkins. No one would catch his eye. Eventually, the girl behind the counter asked, in an odd sarcastic tone, if he wanted anything to drink. Then he realized: everyone in the place knew who he was. It explained the peculiar atmosphere, the invisible bubble of indifference which seemed to be separating him from the other customers. He left immediately and didn't go out of the house again for three days. During the months of Raj's disappearance, he got used to how people reacted when they recognized him: the silent disgust; the animal recoil. He'd tell himself they didn't know him, that their anger was directed at something else, some personal mental darkness his presence in the checkout line or subway car was forcing them to confront. It didn't help. He was jostled on the street, found it hard to get service in stores. Once someone threw a soda can out of a car, which sent a great fizzy arc of orange on to the sidewalk in front of his feet.

★

They had been crushing, lonely months. Lisa had gone to stay with her parents in Phoenix. His old friends seemed distant, busy with their lives. One evening he walked halfway across the Williamsburg Bridge, judging the height of the mesh fence that separated him from the water. He was trying to remember what was supposed to happen. Didn't you die on impact? You were unconscious as soon as you hit the water. Reasons to do it, reasons not to. After a while he turned and walked back.

The story running in his head had a sickening weight. *He'd made it happen.* He'd wanted Raj to disappear. It was all he'd been thinking about as they drove from LA to that awful place – how nice it would be to have his life back, the old times when he and Lisa ran around the city like latchkey kids. Then Lisa broke the string on Raj's charm and his evil thoughts were set free to do their work. The lunatics on the internet were telling the truth – he'd murdered his son. Through force of will, bad magic. A kind of spoon-bending.

He'd stopped speaking to his parents. At first they'd wanted him to pay for a guru to come from India; some Punjabi godman his mom had been sending money to. It will be guruji and three four followers only. They will need hotel, meals. He'd lost his temper, told her she was pagal if she thought he'd pay to be exploited by some village swami. 'But you can afford it,' she said. 'You're rich. It is for your son.' One evening she called to say his father wanted to speak to him. Papaji hadn't been well. When he came on the line, his voice was shaky. 'Beta, it is God's will. That is all. If you will not go for the guru, try and give your wife another child, a son whose mind and body is sound. Do it quickly. Help her forget her pain. In the end it may be for the best.' All this, just two weeks after Raj had vanished. As if he were trash, genetic waste.

Back then they were staying in a business hotel in Riverside. Air-con buzzing, a slew of room-service trays. Lisa was barely present, just a catatonic hump in the bed. He put the phone down on his dad and got in beside her, running a hand over her back, her hip, smelling the unwashed animal reek of her. She groaned and reached out pale fingers, scrabbling for something on the bedside table. The TV remote. On it went, the daytime yabbering. Mufflers, double-glazing, great new taste. There were days when it drove him crazy and he went to sit in the antiseptic restaurant to be spied on by the waitresses; and other days when he'd give in and watch with her, trying to follow along as Gavin crashed Deana's car and Petra woke up from her coma.

As he sat in bed he found himself obsessing – not just about what had happened in the park, the tiny forgotten details on which it all hinged, which way he'd turned, what he'd heard behind him on the path, but about the day before, when Lisa had left him alone with Raj at the motel. Something had happened to her. Sure, she'd gotten drunk, but he had the sense that she'd been somewhere, somewhere a long way away. She'd been out of touch for almost twenty-four hours. She could have driven two hundred miles or more. Day by day he became more convinced that this journey had some bearing on Raj's disappearance. If she knew something and wasn't saying and because of it Raj was . . . When he got back to New York he planned to open her credit-card bill and look for charges from Las Vegas or Palm Springs. It wasn't that she was lying to him. She wasn't saying anything at all. She'd withdrawn completely. It made him feel powerless. He'd sit in the chair by the window, angrily staring at the shapeless blob bundled up under the covers, like a predatory animal waiting outside a burrow.

'You didn't do anything wrong,' he said to her on the seventeenth day, adopting a soothing tone. It was an experiment, a probe. 'Whatever you did, it doesn't matter. What's happening isn't your fault.'

'You don't know.'

'So tell me.'

She just shook her head. He kept pushing, but she said nothing. After a while he realized the medication had put her back to sleep.

When he found her on the bathroom floor, he was sure she'd tried to kill herself. Frantically he dialed 911, then saw that her eyes were open. Within minutes the room was full of hotel staff and paramedics. There seemed to be nothing wrong with her, except that she wouldn't speak. She refused to tell them whether she'd taken anything, and they drove her to a hospital and kept her there overnight while they ran toxicology tests. The results were negative.

The doctors diagnosed a 'psychotic break'. Her dad flew in and tried to take charge. Louis wanted his little girl sent to some expensive clinic in Colorado. He was a guy who liked to throw money at a situation; it made him feel he was in control. Airlifted, he kept saying, like she'd been wounded on a battlefield. Jaz disagreed and they had a stand-up finger-pointing argument in the hospital Starbucks.

'We're her goddamn family.'

'And what am I?'

'Jaz, I don't mean that. But this is my daughter we're talking about. And both of us know you haven't exactly been good for each other.'

'What do you even mean by that?'

'I mind my business, Jaz. But Jesus Christ, she's my daughter. I know when she's not happy.'

'So you're saying this is *my* fault?'

'Who the hell knows whose fault it is? But she's up there in the – you know – in the fucking nut ward.'

Then he began to cry. The tears were streaming down his face and he was just repeating oh hell oh damn over and over and Jaz took him out to the parking lot so the people in Starbucks couldn't see.

Price was still in the picture then. That slick asshole. Some Phoenix real-estate guy who'd given his card to Louis at the golf club. For those first few weeks Jaz didn't care where Louis had found him; he was just grateful for the help. The press briefings, the phone ringing off the hook; Lisa couldn't handle any of it, which meant it was all on him. He was offered medication by a hotel doctor. He said no and then changed his mind; getting to sleep was near-impossible. When exhaustion finally dragged him under, he'd dream he was digging with his hands in the ground under the Pinnacle Rocks, or else just scratching at himself, opening up sores and abscesses. The pills buried all that, at first.

The cops took them back to the scene. A wagon-train of news crews trailed their Escalade, raising dust. It was a world bleached out by sunlight. The ink on the Amber Alert notices was already crackling to brown, on its way to pale yellow and that final bone-white which seemed to be the ultimate state of all things out there. Silence and death. Jaz climbed up on the rocks, looking around and shading his eyes as instructed, to re-create the moments after Raj was taken. Standing in position, framed by long lenses, he felt phys-ically nauseated at the vast emptiness of the place. He bent over, propping himself up on his knees. Soon there would be nothing left of Raj but a few blank sheets of paper pinned on park notice boards. When the last journalist forgot about him, he and Lisa would vanish too, erased from communal memory.

The police thought the abductor had been watching them. He or she must have driven behind them into the park, trailed them up the path as they walked to the rocks. They were hoping it was just a woman who wanted a kid. The young detective with the mus-tache said if that was the case, maybe she'd give him back once she realized he wasn't – he stumbled over the phrasing, trying *mentally*, *psychologically*, settling for the unmodified *normal*. Then there were the other possibilities. A cellar; a vacant lot; the back of an unmarked van. Jaz had never given much thought to the thrill people got out of serial killers. The movies, the fat paperbacks. Duct tape and chainsaws and needles and masks. Suddenly all that Halloween glitter bore down on him as a sick weight. It was evil, debased.

Now that he was sensitized to obscenity, it seemed to jump out at him everywhere. He didn't even have to leave his hotel room; like the haggard Latina with her cart of cleaning supplies, it just shoved its way right in. The newspaper hanging in a plastic bag from the door handle was full of it; a little girl shot at a Baghdad checkpoint; ten shoppers blown up in a street market. *No, uh, por favor. Tomorrow, maybe. Come back tomorrow.* But what was new? The war had always been going on somewhere. It just changed faces and locations. There wasn't anything you could do. So why did he sit on the floor with the *Weekend Edition* spread out around him, tears streaming down his face? Why was that the only thing that made him feel clean?

There were gestures of friendship. People called from New York, asking how they were, offering help. Lisa's cousin Eli started a blog, asking for information, giving updates on the search. Lisa wouldn't speak to any of her friends except her old friend Amy, who now lived in Chicago. He called Amy to ask if she could fly out, offering to pay for her ticket. I think she needs someone, he pleaded. Someone who's not me. Amy promised to see what she could do, and two days later arrived in their fetid room, opening curtains, forcing the two of them to clean up. She was the one who helped them find another place to stay, where it was quiet and the balcony didn't look out on to a freeway. On her last night, the three of them had a meal in a Mexican restaurant. It felt almost normal. As she left for the airport, Lisa hugged her and wouldn't let go, clinging, clawing at her back with her fingers.

When the accusations started, he didn't know how to respond. It seemed outlandish. The first hint of trouble came at the second reconstruction, the one after he'd been hypnotized and remembered the car parked next to theirs at the rocks. A lot of people had turned up, not all of them journalists. There were pickups parked among the news vans. Sunshades and coolers, bored kids come to see what there was to see. He and Lisa were walking along the path. They'd been induced to push a stroller with a strange little boy sitting in it, a deputy sheriff's son. A voice called out 'What did you do with him, Lisa?' That was all. He turned around angrily, but couldn't see who'd spoken. Lisa was looking at the ground, her knuckles white on the stroller's plastic grips.

Things seemed to slide from there. The local TV stations were giving a lot of airtime to Raj's abduction. At first the tone was sympathetic, but by the end of the second week they seemed to be hunting for new things to say. The commentators were bored, punchy; they stopped dispensing clichés about how 'unimaginable' they found the family's 'plight' and began to dissect the way they behaved at press conferences. *They're kind of a cold couple. Very aloof. Very New York.* One morning they were propped up in bed, channel-surfing. On the local breakfast show, two women in pant-suits – the presenter and a guest identified as a psychologist – sat on a couch and aired their opinions. As they watched, the pair began to speculate about whether he and Lisa had killed Raj themselves. 'I don't know what it is about that woman,' said one, 'but I don't care for it. She seems, you know, not quite normal. A normal mother would show some emotion.'

An hour later Lisa had a full-blown panic attack. She was rigid, gasping for breath. He tried to rise and fall with her, but she wouldn't come down. Breathe, he said. Breathe in and out. He tried to say them, the words you were supposed to say. They had no effect. He kept saying the words. It was no good. In the end he dialed front desk. Help, he said. For some reason he was whispering. Just come and help, OK. Because I can't help her.

The hotel doctor filled her so full of sedatives that in the middle of the night he thought her heart had stopped. She was too still. He fumbled for the light switch, freaking out because his wife was lying dead next to him and he couldn't find the fucking switch. This was his fault, this on top of everything else. They'd wanted to take her to a hospital and he'd said no. She was dead because he hadn't let them take her to the hospital. He shook her violently. She turned over and groaned. After that he couldn't get back to sleep. Slowly, the sliver of sky visible through the blinds turned from black to gray.

The next day he screamed at Price. What the hell are you doing? My wife shouldn't have to hear that shit. It's defamation. It's your job to protect us. Price told him it wasn't so easy. He didn't speak out of malice, but Jaz and Lisa hadn't been helping themselves. Problem was, they weren't likeable characters. They came off – not to him, mind you, but to some folks – as snobs. You couldn't put all the blame on the media. They were just going with the story the Matharu family had been offering them. He fished in his jacket pocket and produced a page torn out of a magazine, a feature written by an ex-film-producer who'd taken to following high-profile trials and investigations. *They are*, the man wrote, *like a plaster-of-Paris couple, something that can be painted to look exactly like life.*

'Buddy,' he said, 'we got to change the story. First of all, you need to get out, show your human side. You go to church?'

'I'm not a Christian.'

'Not practicing?'

'Mr Price, just go do your job. Tell them we're not snobs or whatever they need to hear to get this bullshit to stop. Everyone, including you, seems to be forgetting about our son. Raj, his name is. Remember him? The little boy who went missing? He's the story. The only story.'

'Sir, this is me right here, doing my job. I'm telling you, go to church. You'll get the right result.'

'I'm a Sikh, Mr Price. And my wife's a Jew. You probably don't know what a Sikh is, but surely you know about the Jews. The ones who killed Jesus?'

'There's no need for that tone.'

'Man, I thought my people were ignorant. You really are a fucking hick.'

The insult hung in the air. Jaz shrugged. 'I can't deal with your crap anymore. You don't understand a thing about me or my family. You're fired. Now get out of here before you drive me completely insane.'

Price balled his fists, then picked up his briefcase and left, muttering something about a lawsuit. Jaz followed him into the corridor, shouting after him to bring it on. Price called him an elitist bastard, told him he 'wasn't surprised folks felt the way they did'. He stalked off down the hall, double doors flapping behind him.

The next morning Jaz called Louis to talk about the clinic. Lisa was sitting up in bed, groggily watching him. Hunched furtively over the phone, he felt like he was selling her out to the Gestapo.

'I don't know, Louis. Maybe it's the best thing. At least she could get some rest.'

Lisa's voice was freighted with suspicion. 'You're talking about me.'

'In a minute, honey.'

He should have taken it outside. But she'd been asleep. And he hated going outside. The hotel wanted them to leave, because of the disruption they were causing other guests. People had been jostled in the lobby. There were reports of damage done to cars in the parking lot.

Louis put Patty on the line.

'I hope you know what you're doing,' she said. 'Because I sure don't. You know your problem, Jaz? You say one thing, then do another. You were all "oh I can take care of her". Now you find it's too much trouble so you're putting her in a clinic? Just throwing my daughter in a clinic. Unbelievable.'

She wasn't interested in hearing that it had been Louis's idea. She thought Jaz was showing a 'dark side' of himself. The answer was obvious. Lisa should be back at home with them. Jaz didn't have the strength to take offence. He drove Lisa to Phoenix. While she arranged her things in the guest-room, he stood up in the kitchen and drank an awkward coffee with Patty and Louis.

'Well, then,' said Louis. 'Bon voyage.' Like he was sending him off on a journey.

Jaz sat outside in the car for a few minutes, his mind blank. Then he started the engine and headed for the airport.

Going home to New York probably made things worse. Fleeing, one newspaper called it, running the story beneath a long-lens photograph of him walking through arrivals at La Guardia. Dark glasses, wheelie-case. An image of well-heeled callousness. Suddenly #matharus was a trending topic. The internet was calling him a murderer. Everyone on earth seemed to have an opinion. He knew he should shut it all off – the TV, the net, the constant babble of voices. But somehow he couldn't. He wanted to know what the world thought of him, to look it in the face. He read the articles, the blogposts, watched the webcammed talking heads, immersing himself in the appalling churn of rumor like a yogi standing in a freezing river. It seemed he and Lisa were now the worst people in America. Someone found his email address and sent obscene taunts, describing all the things that would happen to him when the public found out 'the truth'. A journalist called his unlisted cell number and asked him point blank if he'd killed Raj.

'My son is missing,' he told the man flatly. 'I need help finding him. That's all.'

Should he have been angry? He couldn't feel anything. Perhaps he was taking too many pills. Two minutes after the call and he couldn't even remember what the guy's voice sounded like.

Late at night he watched movies on his laptop, the kind of romantic comedies he usually saw only on planes. He tried to make his life as much like plane travel as possible. He slept in an armchair he'd dragged into Raj's room, wearing an eye-mask and a pair of bulky noise-cancelling headphones. It was like staging his own extraordinary rendition, grabbing himself out of one time and place, hoping to land in another. Emotional teleportation.

Lisa called, crying over something she'd seen on Facebook. He was annoyed. Louis had promised to stop her looking at it. 'Why did you go online?' he asked her. 'You knew what you'd see.'

'He's dead, isn't he? Some pervert has got him.'

'Don't say that.'

'You think he's alive?'

'Yes, I do.'

'You don't know.'

'No, I don't know. But I believe.'

'I don't understand.'

'I'm feeling positive. I think it'll come out right. That's all I'm saying.'

'No, you're saying you *believe*. That's not the same. *Your* belief, Jaz? What's that worth? I don't even know what the word means to you.'

He couldn't understand why she was so angry. Did she mean religion? That never used to be part of their lives. Religious belief wasn't some precious commodity. It was everywhere. On a good day he thought of it as something like smoking – a bad habit that society was gradually breaking. On a bad day it seemed more a type of low-level mental illness. People who had it could be irrational, violent. His parents, for example, still trying to use God to control the family. As a scientist, he could term it an evolutionary throwback, perhaps with some residual social function – that was the kind of explanation he gave at dinner parties when asked about Al-Qaeda or Sarah Palin. So the honest answer to Lisa's question was probably *nothing*; his belief was worth nothing at all. But that wasn't what he'd meant. He'd only been trying to reassure her.

That night he went back to the Williamsburg Bridge, to a spot partway across, a kind of cage where he could sit back against a spray-tagged slab and watch the cyclists tear past. If he was a man of faith, maybe he would have found consolation? Or at least had a plan. A road map; some picture of the future. The cold was seeping through his jacket, so he got up and walked into Manhattan, wandering aimlessly downtown into the Financial District until he found himself outside the building on Broad Street where he used to work. He stood there for almost an hour, looking up at the mosaic of lighted windows, thinking about the Walter model and causality and guilt. If the world was made of signs, why couldn't he read it? He had to be some kind of fool. All he could say for sure was that everything was connected – Raj, Walter, the desert. A bloom of paranoia grew up in his mind; he felt as if he was being watched by someone on one of the upper floors. Binoculars or a rifle-sight. He walked away, trying to measure his pace. It took all his concentration not to break into a run.

It didn't feel like coincidence when he got a call from Fenton the next day. 'Were you watching me?' Jaz asked. Fenton said he didn't know anything about that, but Jaz should listen up. He was sorry to have to do it, but they were letting him go. There was a long silence, while Jaz failed to formulate a reaction. He'd forgotten this part hadn't happened yet.

The package was generous. Fenton said he felt bad, but things at the firm needed to move on and because of Jaz's 'family troubles' he wasn't in a position to contribute. The old ham managed to sound as if losing 'such a valued colleague' was a personal blow. Jaz appreciated that he was trying to be kind. He even offered to engage a private detective to help search for Raj.

'I can't accept that from you, Fenton.'

'Don't be so hard-headed, Jas-win-der. I mean it. It's the least I can do.'

He sounded sincere enough, but he didn't repeat the offer. Now the deed was done, neither of them knew what to say.

'I'm sorry to do this on the telephone, but the idea of you having to drag your ass downtown . . .'

'I understand. Thanks.'

'Well. Then . . .' Fenton's voice was uncertain. 'Goodbye.'

He sounded relieved to end the call.

So there it was. He was free. Now there was absolutely nothing to distract him from the pain.

He spoke to Lisa every day on the phone, but it was more ritual than real conversation. She seemed better than before; camped in her parents' spare bedroom, she was beginning to pay some atten- tion to the world around her, even managing a few weak jokes at her mother's expense – about the floral wallpaper she'd chosen for the house, the fussy little pouches of pot-pourri hanging over the closet door handles. The calls were never long. Jaz felt as if they were going through the motions with each other, priests of a faith they no longer believed in.

'How are you?'

'I'm doing OK. You?'

'Fine. Are you sleeping?'

'I have the pills.'

'What else are you doing?'

'Mom wants me to help her in the garden.'

'Does anything actually grow out there? It's like *Dune*.'

'You'd be surprised. She's got this cactus thing going on. She has plans for a wishing well.'

'Nice.'

'Isn't it?'

'I spoke to the contractor. He knows we don't want to go ahead with the remodeling.'

He waited for her to say something.

'So you don't have to worry about any of that.'

'I'm tired, Jaz. I should go rest.'

'What time is it there?'

'Time?'

'Is it still light where you are?'

'Yes.'

'I miss you.'

'Sure.'

'Come home. You should be at home.'

'I don't know.'

'I do.'

'At least here I'm not too far if –'

'Sure.'

'Look, I really am tired.'

'OK. I'll let you get to bed. I love you.'

'I love you too.'

Click.

Afterwards, after one of those calls, the house would feel like a huge parquet-floored coffin. He'd look around without recognizing anything. So much stuff, so many tennis rackets and dinner plates and tastefully framed prints. Were they really his? He stopped sleeping in Raj's room; the accusatory stares of the stuffed animals were too intense. Retreating to the master bedroom, he lay awake at night. He could sense the mass of clothes and shoes stacked behind the looming closet doors, threatening to spew over him in a tidal wave of wool and sea-island cotton.

He wanted to begin again, to be unformed, a fetus floating in warm amniotic fluid. One day, walking through SoHo, he went into a Japanese store that specialized in generic clothes and bought himself jeans, a gray T-shirt and a pair of white tennis shoes. He changed into them in the store and stuffed his other clothes into a plastic bag. He felt unburdened, glad to be free of their irritating particularity, their trace of the past. Later he gave the bag to a homeless guy outside the Astor Place subway. He kept walking until it got dark, a generic man in motion through the streets of his generic city. Finding himself outside an anonymous business hotel in Midtown, he checked in. He rode the elevator to his floor, slotted the keycard into the holder by the door, and when the lights clicked on switched them off again. Unusually for New York, the window opened. He lay down on the bed in the twilight, listening to the traffic noise filtering up from the street. There was nothing to remind him of his own life. It was just the sound of a city, any city; an ant colony in which he was an ant who'd followed a pheromone trail to this place in which he was programed to rest. He slept better than he had for weeks.

He took the room for a second night, then a third. On the fourth morning he was sitting in the chair by the window, watching the workers in the office building on the other side of the street. The office workers sat at their desks and stared at their screens. They moved through the space carrying files and sheets of paper. Rarely did they speak to each other. It wasn't clear what they were doing. He liked that; it was soothing to watch them work at their abstract task, to feel that they would carry on for as long as he cared to watch them, until they were claimed by death, downsizing or simple entropy. Dimly he realized his phone was ringing. He thought about answering it, decided not to, then, prompted by some obscure sense of duty, picked up. At first, he didn't understand what the voice was telling him. Who are you? From where? I don't – oh, yes. Yes? What? Are you sure?

It was the San Bernardino County Sheriff's office. Raj had been found. Alive.

He tried to process the information. His son was safe. A little dehydrated, but apart from that . . . No, they couldn't say right now where he'd been. Out in the desert. On military land. Yes, he'd understood correctly. No, they didn't know why. Of course, he heard himself say. I'll leave now. I don't know how long. Soon as possible. I'll let you know when I have an exact time. He ended the call and phoned Lisa. She sobbed incoherently. Thank God, she kept saying. Thank God, who has answered my prayers.

He checked out of the hotel and took a taxi to JFK. As they went into the Midtown Tunnel he was gripped by a sudden powerful anxiety. He'd misunderstood. This was just wish fulfillment; it couldn't be real. As soon as he could get a signal again, he phoned the sheriff's office. In the background he could hear what sounded like a party. 'You'll have to speak up, Mr Matharu,' said the deputy sheriff, in the tone of a man whose back had lately been slapped a lot. 'We got a bunch of folks here. Everyone's come in to celebrate.'

'So you found him.'

'Yes, sir, we did.'

'And he's alive?'

'Like I said. Safe and sound. He's a tough little guy, your son.'

'I know you told me already, but – could you say it again? Just go through what happened?'

The sheriff repeated the details. Raj had been found on a marine base in the middle of an exercise. No one could work out how he'd got there. He was ten miles from the nearest public road. The kidnapper must have dumped him, though why he chose that spot and how he got a car there were complete mysteries. The Marine Corps perimeter security was considered state of the art. Heat sensors, motion sensors, aerial surveillance: the whole nine yards.

At JFK he bought a ticket for Las Vegas. At the gate he paced up and down, unable to sit still. The ground staff hand-searched him twice, suspicious that he was traveling without luggage. The flight seemed interminable. Around him people read or watched movies. He sat and listened to the rumble of the engine, willing the pilot to fly faster. A police driver was waiting for him at McCarran, a young man with a wispy mustache and a misspelled sign. They drove down I-15, the evening sunlight turning the desert a dazzling orange-gold. He phoned Lisa to find out the news.

'Are you there?'

She was sobbing. 'Yes. Yes, I am.'

'Is he OK?'

'He's back, Jaz. He's really back.'

They drove on. The gold land was triumphant, a revelation of glory.

The media were waiting outside the office, the familiar mob

scene – reporters taking calls in the parking lot, television lights on ten-foot stands. When he got out of the car they surged forward with mikes and cameras, calling out his name. 'How does it feel, Jaz? How does it feel?' The driver hustled him through the doors into the quiet of the lobby.

His hand was shaken by smiling uniformed men, who ushered him in to some kind of conference room. A long table, plastic-backed chairs, fading public-information posters on the walls and, at the far end, Raj, sitting on Lisa's lap. As Jaz came into the room, the little boy looked up and smiled. Together they looked like some religious image, Yashoda and Krishna, Madonna and child. Jaz fell on his knees and embraced them both. He felt his son's hot damp breath on his cheek, smelled his hair, the soft skin of his face. He was real. It was actually happening. He exhaled and the air came out of him in a long stream, like a balloon deflating. Lisa's hand rubbed a soothing circle on his back as he cried.

Two days later, when they boarded a plane for New York, the other passengers applauded, peering into the aisles to get a glimpse of them. For the next week the storm of publicity was even more intense than when Raj disappeared. The Matharu family were now a great American story of triumph over tragedy. They were inspirational. Everyone wanted to get close to them, to warm their hearts over the sentimental fire. Though they were offered huge amounts of money to tell their story, they declined every interview. 'All I want,' said Lisa to a particularly pushy reporter who'd followed her into the women's bathroom at JFK, 'is for all the people who wrote such lies about us to have the decency to apologize.' Of course none of them did.

For a while, denied access to the central characters, the media made do with the supporting players. They made much out of the young Iraqi girl who'd found Raj. She was interviewed on evening talkshows. Everyone found her delightful. She was generally agreed to be the right kind of immigrant, a credit to America. More than one commentator quoted Emma Lazarus on the poor and huddled masses yearning to breathe free; an anonymous benefactor even offered to pay her college tuition. The British rock star Nicky Capaldi made a mumbling appearance on the BBC, sporting a mountain-man beard and singing an incoherent song called 'the boy on the burning sands'. He 'identified with Raj', he told the interviewer. 'In a lot of ways, the boy on the sands is me.'

After a man claiming to be a film producer called his cell, asking whether he could buy the family's life rights for a film, Jaz switched off his phone. He no longer felt the need to follow what the world was saying. He wanted to be private again. One by one, their friends phoned to congratulate them. There were some awkward conversations, as people who'd not spoken to them in months, and who'd obviously thought the worst, tried to establish the fiction that they'd been loyal and supportive all along. The only person Jaz was really happy to hear from was Amy. He and Lisa skyped with her, holding up Raj to the webcam so she could see his face. She cried and reached out toward the screen, as if for a moment she thought she'd be able to touch him.

They didn't go out much, preferring to stay at home, ordering in food and watching the maple outside the front window shed its leaves. Sometimes they'd take walks in Prospect Park, the three of them hand in hand, bundled up against the wind, sunk in a silence that was both companionable and eerie, as if a spell had been cast and sound had been snatched away. Sometimes Jaz would try to start a conversation, pointing out familiar things as if they were exotic and new, but he kept coming back to the conclusion that there was nothing to talk about, that somehow the months of pain and separation had exhausted words. Frequently he or Lisa would begin to cry. It would break out without warning. He'd be watching her fold laundry, red-eyed, then turn back to his book, only to find its pages were damp to the touch.

The wider world moved on from their strange little story. There was a presidential election to think about, and their neighbors were imagining change they could believe in, canvassing and putting up posters. For a while, their lives acquired a thin mem-brane of normality, like a scab. Then, another jolt of weirdness tore it back open. Jaz had been watching the financial crisis as if through the wrong end of a telescope; events which a few months previously would have dominated his life – the collapse of Lehman Brothers, the plummeting Dow – seemed to be taking place in an alternate reality, unconnected to his. He didn't go online to check his own portfolio, though he knew it must be taking a huge hit. Let it all go to hell, he thought. All those giant abstractions, the gambles on thin air. Here were the falling leaves, the smell of his son's skin. With his severance package, he wouldn't need to look for work for at least a year – longer if the family lived frugally. He wondered whether the Walter model had predicted the chaos. If Cy and Fenton were still making money in the midst of the carnage, they'd be hailed as heroes. Fenton's ego would be completely out of control.

It didn't quite work out like that. A former colleague phoned to tell him that Fenton's firm had gone under. Upstairs in the spare room, surrounded by boxes of junk to take to the Salvation Army, he listened as the man, who now worked for one of the ratings agencies, told him how things stood. No one from Fenton's office was answering calls. According to rumor, the Walter fund had been leveraged to an unprecedented degree, borrowing to take long positions on the mortgage market. When the crash came and their line of credit dried up, the business unraveled.

In the following days, Jaz was called by lawyers and administrators, hopeful he'd help them sort out the mess. Politely, he declined to get involved, even when he heard that Cy Bachman had disappeared. The police were interested. He'd taken a case of disks and documents with him. There was some question of criminal prosecution.

A thought occurred to him, which he tried his best to suppress. What if Walter had precipitated the crash – or, if not precipitated, then nudged it along, influenced it in some way? He dismissed the idea. The problems in the mortgage market were vast, systemic. They had nothing to do with Bachman's model. But, though he knew it was irrational, the thought kept nagging at him. Had Bachman gone live with his second, high-speed version of Walter? In Bachman's company, Jaz had glimpsed something mystical and frightening. He remembered Cy's expression as they peered into the display cases at the Neue Galerie. He'd seemed like a man drunk with his own power. What temptations had Walter put in his path? Why had he chosen to run away?

For a few days, the press took up the story, reporting sightings of the 'fugitive financier' in various global business hubs. Then the election took over again, its frenzied culture-war tribalism leaving no room for anything else in the national consciousness. Barack Obama was elected without the Matharu family's presence – Jaz and Lisa were too nervous to stand in line at the local polling station, not wanting to be recognized and harassed – but they mailed in ballots and gave money and stayed up late to watch the images of celebration. When they switched off the TV and went to bed they could hear car horns and whistles in the street. Jaz went to check on Raj. To his surprise the little boy was awake, and standing up by the window. He ruffled his hair.

'It's loud, isn't it.'

Raj looked up at him. 'Beep-beep!' he said.

Jaz couldn't believe what he'd just heard.

'Raj? That's right! The cars! They go beep-beep!'

He swept his son into his arms and rushed back into the bedroom, gasping and sobbing like someone who'd just been pulled out of a river. It took Lisa several minutes to understand what had happened.

'He spoke! Raj spoke! He could hear all the car horns. He said "beep-beep".'

'Are you sure?'

'Positive.'

'I knew it! I knew something was changing. The other day – he said something the other day when we were in the park. Some guy was walking this enormous Great Dane and he said "doggie". It wasn't very clear, but I'm sure that's what he was saying. It wasn't just humming or babbling.'

'And you didn't tell me?'

'I wasn't sure.'

'You didn't think I'd want to know?'

'I said I wasn't sure. And, to be honest, Jaz, I didn't think you'd believe me. I didn't want you telling me it wasn't true. But it doesn't matter now, does it? It doesn't matter.'

They went to bed half angry at each other. The next day, as they ate a silent breakfast, Raj pointed at the maple outside the window. 'Tree,' he said. And again. 'Tree.' That morning he repeated his word dozens of times, making it into a song, rising and falling, stretching the vowel out like a siren. As the days passed he added other words, giving names to things in the kitchen, out on the street.

beep-beep
tree
juice
birdy
carrot
night-night

They took him to see a pediatrician, who confirmed that he'd made an 'unusual leap forward'. She encouraged them to hold conversations with him and said she had 'high hopes' for the future. It might be that Raj's condition was less serious than they'd previously thought. If he carried on progressing, they might be able to 'revise their expectations upwards'. Lisa was so happy that she danced down Park Avenue, twirling and skipping like a musical star. Jaz couldn't remember the last time she'd looked so beautiful. He clutched Raj's hand tightly, the sunlight glittering in his watery eyes. It was such a fine day. A beautiful day. They decided to walk for a while before hailing a cab. Somewhere in the seventies, on a quiet, tree-lined block, they passed a church. Lisa suggested they go in.

'Why?'

'I want to say a prayer.'

He must have looked confused. She laughed.

'We've been blessed, Jaz. We ought to recognize it.'

'But –'

'Yes, I *know* it's a church. But it's all one, isn't it? Many routes to the same truth.'

She took Raj's hand and pushed open the big wooden door. It was a Catholic church, whose altar was dominated by a lurid crucifix on which a milk-white Jesus hung in spasms of eye-rolling agony. Lisa and Raj walked toward it, their footsteps echoing off the marble floor. Jaz hung back by the door, next to a table of flyers advertising canned-food drives and schemes to sponsor African children. Self-consciously he read a poster advertising an organ recital, trying to appear as if he belonged in the space. Lisa seemed to hesitate in front of Jesus, then turned to a smaller altar in a side chapel. She dropped change into a box and chose a slender taper, lighting it from one of a cluster already set before a plaster image of the Virgin Mary. Then she helped Raj kneel down and lowered herself beside him at the rail, clasping her hands together. It was strange to see her like that; fervent, histrionic. He half expected some priest to emerge from a backroom and shoo her away – the defiling Jew in the house of Jesus – but nothing of the kind happened. A couple of old ladies appeared, dabbed their fingers in the font, made little genuflecting crosses at the altar, as if someone or something was there to respond.

apple
go
Raj
mommy
vroom-vroom
Jesus

As the weeks went past, Raj's development seemed to gather pace. He'd always avoided eye-contact, and had disliked touch, wriggling out of cuddles, whining or screaming if he was patted or handled. Now he often met his father's gaze, looking back out of some unfathomable depth that Jaz found unnerving. He'd sprawl on the rug in the living room and make up games, lining up his toys in familiar ranks, but also talking to them, addressing them by names and designations Jaz strained to catch. There was something unprecedented about this playing, a connection to the world which had never existed for him before.

The police had admitted they were making no progress in identifying Raj's abductor, and it was obvious that their investigation was winding down. The Marine Corps had reviewed their security footage and found nothing unusual. There were no tire tracks in the vicinity where Raj had been found. It was, one of the detectives remarked, 'as if the kid had materialized out of thin air'. Jaz phoned them every week or so, but there was never any news. He got the impression he was making a nuisance of himself. His son was safe – that was miracle enough. He ought to be content, to give thanks, as Lisa did. But there were too many questions to be answered. The little boy happily lining up plastic dinosaurs on the kitchen table had been through something extremely traumatic. Until his father knew what that was, there would be a blank, an unknown on the map of their family. *Here be dragons.*

This was the wheel that kept turning in Jaz's mind. Raj had come back and Raj had changed. Or, rather, Raj had *come back changed*. There was something different about him. It wasn't just that he'd begun to speak. Some new spirit was animating him, driving his engagement with the world. Jaz was happy about it. Of course he was – this was better than he'd dared hope for. He just wished he could understand how it had come about. Half jokingly he'd tickle his son, asking him, 'What happened to you? Where did you go?' Half jokingly. Only half. The other half was steeled for some terrifying revelation.

What happened to you?

Where did you go?

Are you still my son?

One evening Lisa asked him if he'd be happy to watch Raj while she went to a meeting.

'What kind of meeting?'

She looked embarrassed, made a vague gesture with her hand.

'It's sort of like a book group.'

'Sort of like?'

Eventually he wheedled the truth out of her. It was a Jewish studies class. A group met weekly to read religious texts, 'from a contemporary women's perspective'.

'I know what you think,' Lisa told him. 'But it's not like that.'

'I didn't say anything.'

'You know exactly what I mean. Anyway, it's not what you're thinking. They're a really interesting bunch. I'll be back around ten.'

dog
big dog
house
my house
my daddy
mine

The group became a regular part of Lisa's life. She started going every Wednesday, cooking food and taking it with her in a covered dish. At home, she started to drop Hebrew and Yiddish words into conversation, particularly while chatting on the phone to her new friends: *schlep*, *meshuggeneh*, *goy*. Standing on the stairs, eavesdropping. Was he the goy? The outsider?

Then she announced she'd found a job. He hadn't even known she was looking. She just dropped her car keys on the kitchen counter and told him the news. She was going back to publishing, as an editor for a small imprint that specialized in esoteric and mystical books.

'And you didn't think to discuss this with me?'

'Well, I wasn't sure I'd get it. And then when they offered it to me, I wasn't sure I'd say yes. But then I did.'

'You said yes.'

'I said yes.'

'So who'll look after Raj?'

'Don't you even start that! You're not working. You don't seem to want to work.'

'Hang on, it's still my money that's supporting us.'

'I didn't mean that. I know where the money's coming from, and for the moment we don't need you to get a job. I'm not criticizing,

Jaz. I get it. We've been through a terrible time and we both need to regroup. But why shouldn't I have this? Give me one good reason.'

'It's just – well, it affects me. And Raj. And you just went ahead and did it?'

'Do you want me to turn it down?'

'No, but –'

'But what?'

'It's not even like it's a reputable publisher.'

'By reputable, you mean mainstream? Oh, come on, Jaz. Why not just come straight out and give your little speech about science and testable hypotheses and all the rest of it?'

'I'm just trying to talk about Raj.'

'Well, so am I. Unlike you, I want to work. Five years, Jaz. Five years I've spent at home with him. Why can't you give me this?'

'OK. It's not like I don't want you to have a life. I just – well, I wish you'd talked to me about it before you agreed. We're supposed to be a family.'

Eventually they came to an arrangement. She'd work. He'd stay home with Raj, at least for six months. At the end of that time, they'd see how things stood. The unspoken variable was Raj's condition. If he carried on improving, then all kinds of things might be possible. Daycare, school. They'd never allowed themselves to think like that before. The idea of making plans for the future was so alien that it induced a kind of panic in Jaz. Weren't they just offering hostages to fortune? What if they opened up their horizons again, and it didn't work out? After Lisa left for her first day in the office he sat at the kitchen counter with Raj, who was drawing a picture, a red crayon held tightly in his small fist. Raj looked up at him, aloof and self-contained. The picture on the pad was almost recognizable; some kind of aircraft, or perhaps a rocket.

that car
that house
go daddy
go
more juice

flying
go flying
give more juice daddy

A new routine began, the routine of walking. Twice a week they walked to see Dr Siddiqi, the speech therapist. She was young and attractive, her thick black hair falling over her shoulders in a shiny wave, or tied back in a loose ponytail, so that stray strands fell across her face. She didn't wear a wedding ring. Jaz would read a magazine, or watch as she worked with Raj, who seemed to like her as much as he did. She'd make up little routines and situations, asking questions, offering and receiving objects, giving praise when he successfully completed some new routine. Though he was developing a vocabulary, he had trouble with what she called the 'pragmatics' of conversation. When to ask for something. When to say hello, or thank you, or sorry. After the sessions, she'd make time to talk to Jaz, describing Raj's progress while the little boy played, or just sat rocking solemnly on a stool by their feet. Jaz felt a strong need to open up to her, to tell her secrets. He described the lack of progress in the investigation, his own suspicion that the abductor was someone who worked on the marine base, perhaps one of the Iraqis who helped out with their strange war games. He wanted to say more. About Raj, about himself.

'I can't imagine what you've all been through,' she said one day. He flushed with pleasure. From anyone else it would have been a banality.

Mummy's book
Give mummy's book
Go here daddy
Where are you daddy
Waiting
Where are you?

One evening, while Lisa was at her study group, he found Raj standing in the living-room doorway, staring at him. There was something about the way he was watching, a self-contained intelligence that Jaz found suddenly terrifying. The question formulated itself: *What are you?* Not *What are you doing?* Or *What are you thinking?* Or even *Who are you? What* are you. What are you if you're not my son? He poured himself a drink, told himself to get a grip, then spent the rest of the evening trying not to be in the same room as the boy, half hiding in the study, but keeping the door open in case there was an emergency. When he heard Lisa's key in the door, he almost rushed to be by her side. She scooped up Raj and cuddled him, luxuriating in the touch that she'd never been allowed before. She seemed to sense nothing out of the ordinary.

Later, as they got ready for bed, he tried to speak to her.

'Do you think it's normal, how Raj is behaving?'

'More normal than he's ever been before.'

'I mean – I don't know what I mean.'

'You think he's slipping back?'

'No, not at all. It's just – I can't help feeling something's off about him.'

'Of course there is.'

'Not that.'

'Something . . .'

He couldn't find the words. Lisa looked at him quizzically. Then she came and hugged him.

'I know, Jaz. I think we just have to trust in – you know. Just trust.'

'Do you ever think maybe it's not him?'

'What do you mean?'

'That it's not Raj.'

'What are you trying to say?'

'It's nothing. Don't worry about it. I'm just tired.'

He realized that if he pushed it, he'd begin to scare her. He was scaring himself. The thoughts he was having weren't normal. They weren't appropriate. A voice in his head was whispering, softly, insistently – *this is not my child, this is not my child, this is not my child . . .*

So he went for walks, pushing Raj in front of him, willing the voice to shut up and leave him alone. Lisa was thriving. The house was littered with manuscripts and proofs of books with words in the titles like *golden* and *pathway* and *revelation* and *light*. She was talking openly about enrolling Raj in regular school. 'He'll be ready soon, I think,' she said. 'He's actually quite gifted.' One day Jaz found a stack of papers on the kitchen counter, details of expensive specialized IQ tests – the Otis-Lennon School Ability Test, the Stanford Binet Intelligence Scales. He asked why she had them.

'I think,' she said, 'we have to prepare our minds for the realization that the up-side may be just as extreme as the down.'

'I don't understand.'

'Our son is very special. He's not an ordinary child.'

'A few months ago he wasn't even talking.'

'Jaz, come on. Can't you see it?'

'See what?'

'Wow, you're really a prisoner of your own negativity.'

'I'm just saying –'

'I know what you're saying and I wish you'd stop. I can't be around this energy. It's draining, Jaz. It really is.'

The next morning his old assistant phoned with the news that Cy Bachman had been found dead. Walkers had discovered his body on a mountainside in the Pyrenees, an apparent suicide. Lisa phoned Ellis, who sounded, she said, absolutely distraught. They talked for a long time, while Jaz hovered in the background. According to Ellis, the failure of the Walter model had been a personal disaster for Bachman. He'd left without telling Ellis where he was going, though the site of his death, near the Spanish border town of Port-bou, hadn't come as a surprise.

Feeling empty, Jaz took Raj to see Dr Siddiqi. Instead of letting the session start as normal, he told her he needed to talk. She settled herself in a chair opposite him.

'What can I do for you?'

'I know I should be happy about what's happening. What's happening with Raj, I mean. But I'm – I have a lot of questions. There's so much we don't know. To be honest, I'm scared.'

'Scared?'

He stared down at the carpet, suddenly ashamed by what he'd just admitted. Guiltily he glanced over at Raj, who was sprawled on the floor, surrounded by plastic farm animals. The boy was watching him intently.

Dr Siddiqi waited patiently for him to continue. He could feel Raj's eyes on him, a physical sensation, two little fingers pressed into the back of his neck.

'Look, Ayesha. I know this is strange, but I can't really talk with him in the room. Is there anyone who can look after him for a few minutes?'

'Are you OK?'

'No, not really.'

She called a junior colleague, who took Raj into another office.

'So, Jaz, what is it? Talk to me.'

'This is insane. I know. And I know I shouldn't be feeling like this. There's probably a name for it. A syndrome. I've been under a lot of pressure. We all have. As a family. What I mean to say, is, I realize it's probably something wrong with me, not him. But ever since he came back there's been something different about Raj. He's not the same kid.'

'It is unusual that he's made all this progress, just after having gone through such a trauma.'

'No, I mean he's not the same kid. It's not Raj.'

'I'm not sure what you're saying.'

'It looks like him, smells like him. It has his body. But it's not him.'

'You're saying you don't believe this is your son?'

'He scares me.'

'Why? He's a little boy.'

'He looks like a little boy. For all I know, maybe he is a little boy. I don't know what he is. But he's not Raj.'

She looked at him carefully.

'Jaz, have you been sleeping OK?'

'Sure. Well, not brilliantly. But not too badly. Why?'

'Anything else unusual?'

'Like what?'

'Anxiety?'

'Yes.'

'Any other disturbing thoughts? About your wife, for example?'

'No.'

'Have you been – hearing anything? Anything unusual? A voice, for example. Have you felt that people are talking about you behind your back?'

'A voice?'

'Yes. For example, a voice telling you things about Raj.'

'No. Not exactly.'

'Not exactly?'

'No. I mean no.'

'That's good. But you say sometimes you feel afraid of Raj. Have you ever had the impulse to – defend yourself against him?'

'You mean, hurt him?'

'Yes, I suppose that's what I mean.'

'You think I'm going insane?'

'I'm not saying that. But you've come in here and declared to me that you think your son isn't your son.'

'You think I'm a danger to him?'

He stood up.

'Please sit down, Mr Matharu. Jaz. Please.'

She was holding her hands out. Suddenly he wanted to embrace her, to take handfuls of her long hair and pull her close to him, to kiss her full blue-black lips, to push his tongue between her teeth. He took a pace forward, checked himself.

'I'm scared,' he said again.

'Jaz, I know you've been under incredible pressure. I must ask you again, do you ever have violent feelings toward your son?'

'No.'

'That's good. That's very good.'

'I just want to – know. Someone had him. Do you think it's possible they – I mean – do you think he could have been replaced?'

'Replaced?'

'By a double. Something that's like him in every way, except it's not him.'

She frowned, and placed her hands back in her lap, a neat, deliberate gesture, the gesture of a woman composing herself, putting up her guard. He imagined her naked, a sheen of sweat across her back, her breasts. He felt wild, disturbed. If only she'd come to him. If only she'd touch him, it might be OK.

'No,' she said. 'I don't think that's possible.'

2008

Every moment is a bardo, suspended between past and future. We are always in transition, slipping from one state to the next. She'd had doubts over the years, wondering if *this* was where she really was, if this person *Dawn* even existed, or was just a momentary confluence of forces, a ripple on the pond. She'd pause as she made a bed or wrapped a scuffed water glass in a paper sleeve, sure there was something she'd forgotten, braced to find herself back in the dome on the night of the last ritual, falling away from the clear white light.

She shouldn't have taken that New York woman up to see Judy, except the woman was so drunk and in such trouble already that it seemed like the best option. Judy had to help lay her out on a daybed, while Dawn told her what had happened, how some bastards off the base had gotten her out back of Mulligan's and were fixing to run a train on her.

'And she's got a husband, you say?'

'God knows what he's doing, letting her go drink on her own in that place. Even with him it might not be so good, not in Mulligan's. He's from Pakistan, wears boat shoes. They got this retard kid.'

'As in touched? You think he's got vision?'

'Hell, Judy. He's a retard. He ain't got no more vision than a dog. Look at the state of her. Sand all over her clothes.'

The woman – Lisa – babbled a little before she passed out. Take it away, she muttered. This isn't what I ordered. Judy rolled her eyes, said you and me both, lady, and then got down to why it was so urgent for Dawn to drop everything and drive out. She needed a favor.

'It's not for me.'

'Jesus, Judy. I already brought you more pain pills. And the chocolate milk you asked for.'

'That's it. The chocolate milk.'

At least it wasn't money. And this time Judy could remember making the call, which was something. She said her man was roaming around. He'd called her to say he needed chocolate milk and she was tweaking so hard she couldn't handle getting behind the wheel.

'You got to drive me, Dawnie.'

'You're kidding.'

'I'm serious. It's important.'

'Fuck his chocolate milk.'

'He needs it.'

'He called you to say he wanted chocolate milk? You sure he actually called you.'

'Swear to God. He'll get so mad if I don't bring it. He likes to put it on Cheerios.'

'And he's out in the desert.'

'He's cooking.'

'Is that it? You ain't got none left?'

'He needs chocolate milk, is all. I wouldn't call you if it wasn't a matter of life and death.'

And like she always did – out of pity, or the old suspicion that this world was a distraction and it didn't matter either way – Dawn gave in. They left New York Lisa passed out on the daybed covered in a sheepskin and got back in the car. Most of the journey was off-road, Dawn's old Nissan rattling across the dirt, bushes looming up in front of the headlights like ghosts.

A straight line across nothing.

As Dawn drove, she stole glances at Judy, squirming in the passenger seat, picking at some scab on her hand. The two of them, after so many years, still driving on into the dark.

She'd turned up – when? Sometime in the early nineties. The motel was doing OK and Dawn thought she'd put to rest the suspicion that she was dead – and then along came Judy to show her she couldn't be certain of any such thing. They'd pulled up outside the motel in a Corvette Stingray sprayed several shades of primer, a patchwork of black and red oxide and gray. Somehow Dawn knew who it was before she knew. The driver stayed in the car. The woman got out and walked round to the office. She opened the door and the electric bell played its little tune.

Judy's face was lined, and she didn't look crisp or perky anymore. She looked, truth be told, like Maa Joanie: a middle-aged woman in denims and a white shirt (still that white shirt!) with graying hair and the thin lips of a person who'd had to say no too many times in her life. They stared at each other over the counter, old and tired and eaten up by trouble and abuse, and it was like a faded version of the first time, a photocopy of a photocopy, redone so many times that what had once been clear and hopeful was now just a smudge.

Do not cling to life. Even if you cling, it's not in your power to stay. And do not fear, though the visions may be terrifying. Try to recognize the clear light of reality. Concentrate.

'Judy.'

'Hello, Dawnie. Looks like you made this place real nice.'

They embraced awkwardly. Judy felt thin and brittle in her arms, her spine a ridge, her shoulder blades two attenuated wings. The Corvette's engine penetrated the thin office walls, a low sinister rumble that set the bug screens buzzing. Dawn peered through the window. She couldn't see at first who was in the driver's seat. Then he got out to smoke a cigarette. His long jaw. The sour scavenging expression. She would have known him anywhere.

'You with him?'

'That's right. He came and found me.'

As they watched, Coyote stalked around the car, scratching himself. He finished his cigarette, ground it into the dirt with his boot, then got back in and pulled away. The tires kicked up gravel against the metal siding.

'He dumping you here?'

Judy's laugh didn't sound too light-hearted. 'He'll be back later. I heard you were living in town again. I wanted to say hi.'

'Are you back for good or just passing through?'

'We'll be here a while, I reckon. We got ourselves a double-wide in that lot on Three Mile Road. It's just for now. We'll find something better by and by.'

'Not out at the rocks?'

'They made that part of the National Monument, so I heard.'

'With a trail and signposts and everything. They even put a barrier round the Indian marks. You want a drink? There's soda, and a bottle of schnapps in the kitchen.'

'Schnapps sounds just fine.'

They sat on folding chairs under the car port and drank and watched the road. Judy didn't say much about where she'd been for so many years and Dawn didn't ask. It was the kind of conversation where more gets said in the silences than in the words. Coyote had spent some years south of the border. Belize. The Yucatán. Places with old gods. He and Judy had lived for a time in New Mexico, up in the mountains where you could walk for days without seeing another soul. They'd been in cities too. Judy skated over her dark times and Dawn skated over hers. Instead she asked about the others. After the split, they'd been scattered to the winds. Judy had news, but not a lot. Maa Joanie was dead of cancer. Clark Davis had passed too, shot to death in a 24-hour diner in Reno. And Wolf? Judy shrugged when Dawn mentioned his name. He went West, she said. Dawn knew what that meant. It was the last anyone in this world would ever hear of him.

Turned out Coyote was into some shit. A month or two later, the trailer on Three Mile burned down and for a while he and Judy were living in their car out back of the Taco Bell. After the fire he lay low for a while, but soon enough he was up and running again, driving an ancient RV out into the desert, brewing up his poison. In between times he propped up the bar in Mulligan's, spending money, holes in his clothes, the stink of ether on his fur. Dawn had been around enough tweakers to know what that meant.

Overnight it seemed like his meth was everywhere. You saw tweakers all over town. Caved-in faces and rotten teeth. Starting fights in the diner, riffling through the dumpster behind the Circle K. They'd steal anything. Scrap metal, patio furniture. Once Dawn

spotted a guy pedaling furiously down Main Street with a grave-
stone balanced on the handlebars of his bike. After someone swiped
the pool robot and half the chairs, Dawn got a .45 at the pawnshop,
kept it in a desk drawer in the office. No dinky little woman's gun
for her. Anyone came round she intended to put a hole in them,
stop them doing whatever they were doing.

Mostly the tourists never noticed, which was lucky for business.
They just drove out to the park, took pictures of themselves at the
designated viewpoints, drove home again. Soon Coyote's crystal
was running all over the desert, into every trailer and jackrabbit
homestead, turning the people into hungry ghosts: mouths the size
of a needle's eye, stomachs like mountains; nothing could ever fill
them up. Meth soaked its way along highways and train tracks,
through drains and power-lines and TV cables, into the very fabric
of the houses where the tweakers lived. Meth in the air vents, in the
furniture, caking the walls of the microwaves where they cooked
their children's food.

Judy was using. She'd stay up nights, riding the shoulder of her
high, smoking cigarettes and talking on the phone, or sometimes
just talking, without anyone to hear. She and Coyote moved into a
weird old house some way out of town. It was all made of wood,
beautifully finished, but though Dawn could see it was a nice place,
she didn't like it. With its dome roof and hippie angles, it reminded
her of the Command. Sometimes she'd end up driving out there on
a small-hours mercy mission, with oxy or booze or bandages to
patch Judy up after a cut or a fall. Often she just needed someone to
listen to her. She'd reminisce about men she'd known, places she'd
been, how she wished she'd had a kid. She'd talk about Clark like he
was still around, in the room even. Then she'd get paranoid, accusing Dawn of telling lies about her, bringing the cops round. Coyote
kept a lot of guns in the place, automatic weapons for use in case
the black helicopters landed and he needed to make a stand. Dawn
was always nervous about Judy out there on her own, surrounded
by all those guns. Once or twice she tried to talk to her about death,
about how she was afraid they were both still caught up in an old

lie, compelled to wander because they couldn't recognize the inner light of reality.

'Evil past actions are very potent, Judy. The cycle of ignorance is inexhaustible.'

'Don't come on to me with all that mystical shit. I had it with prophecy.'

'It's not the same.'

'Sure is. You just can't see it yet.'

Coyote avoided her. He was as slippery as ever. She caught up with him one night in Mulligan's and told him flat out he was killing Judy with his filthy chemicals. Not just her. Everyone. He was poisoning everybody. Why was he causing so much harm?

He just laughed. 'What you care?' he asked. 'You ain't even sure any of it's real.'

He knew how to get her. She turned and left, his howl of triumph in her ears.

Somehow Judy struggled on. She didn't die. She took up hobbies. Basketry. Needlepoint. Quilting. All the varieties of warp and weft. After a few years the meth craze passed its peak, headed on to other towns. Coyote diversified. He was moving money through LA and Vegas. He had something going with computers, claimed he could tap into the New York Stock Exchange and tinker with all the ups and downs. That was bullshit, had to be. He was small-time. If he was such a bigshot, how come he was out in some no-account place in the desert? He had friends on a reservation down near Yuma who were making big bucks from gambling. He started driving down to see them once or twice a month, coming back with whole crates of gadgetry, things he said arrived through air-conditioned tunnels from across the border. It was hard to say what he was doing and Dawn doubted he knew himself. He said he was part of the communications revolution. There were boxes of calling cards in the house. Cellphones, police-radar detectors. It was a compulsion, an addiction. Coyote never saw a fence he didn't want to tunnel under. He had to mess with stuff, connect things together. He had a rage for transformation.

And so it went on. They all grew older. Things changed, sometimes quickly, sometimes so slow you didn't even notice it happening.

Up ahead Dawn could see a light.

Coyote's battered old RV was parked at the edge of a dry lake. A couple of lamps were running off a generator, illuminating a patch of ground by the door. He reclined on a folding chair, a gas mask slung round his neck, drinking Jack and Coke mixed in a plastic bottle. When they drove up he pulled out a couple more chairs and they gave him the chocolate milk and then sat and smoked a joint, each thinking their own thoughts.

So, Judy said, when she couldn't contain herself any longer. You got any for me to try?

Just before sunrise, Dawn drove Lisa back to her car and watched her fumble with the keys. In convoy they drove slowly up the hill to the motel. She hoped that would be the end of it, but when the boy disappeared, she knew she was probably responsible. Not in any way you could explain to a cop or a reporter. She hadn't done anything wrong. But by taking Lisa out there, she'd got her family involved. They were mixed up with Coyote, mixed up in the paths and flows. Whatever was happening, Dawn didn't want any part of it. It wasn't her concern. She knew now – knew for sure – that she was still in the dome, descending through the realms of existence, heading toward the horror. All was not lost. At the edge of consciousness, she was beginning once again to catch the drone, the high white sound of reality.

2009

Do not seek to know what is above you. Do not seek to know what is below you. Do not seek to know what is before you. The problem with modern people – one of the problems – was that they'd forgotten how to be humble. You could ride the subway, crammed together with all the other morning commuters on their way into Manhattan, and something in the book you were reading would make you pause and look around. Then you'd see the faces, ordinary faces that on other days (or in the old days, the days *before*) you'd not have thought twice about, men and women blandly confident of their importance in the scheme of things, assured that as inhabitants of a global city, citizens of the most powerful country on the planet, they were the inheritors of certain rights, among them the right to know the world in its totality, or if they chose not to know (for they had other claims on their time, such as working and being entertained), then for others to know on their behalf, so that an explanation could potentially be made to them, or if not to them, then to an expert who would receive it and act in their best interests. They looked so ugly to her, all the morning people, because when Raj went missing she'd seen the flipside of their self-assurance: the outrage when something unknowable reared up before them, not just unknown for now, because they or their designated expert had yet to enquire into the matter, had yet to google the search term or send the email or write the check for the correct amount to the relevant company or government department, but unknowable in principle, inaccessible to human comprehension. Their fear made them dangerous, murderous even, for in their blind panic they'd turn on whoever they could find as a scapegoat, would tear them into pieces to preserve this cherished fiction, the fiction of the essential comprehensibility of the world.

Lisa knew the true face of the morning commuters, for they'd come at her, ripped at her flesh with their talons. She'd seen them, and ever since, the work of her life had been to recover herself, to function in subway carriages and department stores and checkout lines among people who'd hated her, who'd wanted her to die so their world could carry on feeling moral and meaningful. The lesson she'd learned (this was another part of the work, to see what had happened as a lesson, as something from which she could gain, instead of a wound that went almost to the bone and would probably never heal) was that knowledge, true knowledge, is the knowledge of limits, the understanding that at the heart of the world, behind or beyond or above or below, is a mystery into which we are not meant to penetrate. Before, in her old life, she'd not had a name for it. Then Raj had disappeared and been returned to her and after that she'd found a name, but kept it to herself, because she felt embarrassed in front of her husband and her clever secular New York friends. Now she could call it God, and say it out loud; she could ride the subway into Manhattan replete in her understanding, confident that though the world was unknowable, it had a meaning, and that meaning would keep her safe and set her free. Had anyone suggested the conviction she felt might have anything in common with the conviction she derided in the other passengers, she would have reacted angrily, violently, because *her* feelings, *her* self-knowledge, had been earned, authorized by suffering, while theirs was mere ignorance.

She felt like she'd been destroyed and rebuilt again. She felt, if she had to give a name to her feeling, *symbolic*, as if she now stood for something greater and more significant than herself, stood for the knowledge of limits, was – no, not God's representative, nothing so grandiose or egotistical – just one of His signposts, a person in the crowd whose life story pointed toward Him, showed the way out of the vanities of this world and into reverence for the unknowable, impenetrable beyond.

So much of this had been unclear to her before she joined the group. Esther, in particular, had been gentle and compassionate in leading her along the path. She'd had questions – that was why she'd sought them out in the first place, a half-dozen women more or less like herself, professional, college-educated, in their thirties and forties. They'd gather once or twice a month, usually at Esther's place. It was, Esther joked, much like a hundred other book groups meeting all over Brooklyn, except they had something more on their minds than whether they'd been entertained or moved or convinced by the doings of a bunch of made-up characters. It felt good to be surrounded by these new friends. None of them were preachy or overbearing. They were just ordinary down-to-earth Jewish women, coming together to discover more about their shared culture. Of course Lisa knew they accorded her a special status. There was an aura around her, a little frisson of glamour. They'd ask, shyly, how she'd coped when the media frenzy was at its height. They'd use her as an example of suffering, dig out apt quotations to share.

Esther thought Lisa ought to write a book about the witch-hunt, about being a mother in the spotlight. Lisa, better than almost anyone alive, knew how it felt to be a woman hounded by the misogynist news media. It ought to be a passionate book. A polemic. It could really make a difference to other women going through the same thing. Lisa toyed with the idea, but she didn't really have the stomach for it. Not just for the writing, for what it would mean to spend days in front of a laptop, forcing herself to think back to the bad days – the hotel in Riverside, the buzzing air conditioner, the TV and the dirty room-service trays – but for the whole process of turning herself inside out. She'd had enough of being discussed and picked apart. Now that her son had been returned to her, she wanted to luxuriate in him, and she wanted to do so in private, without interference or observation, without being judged.

Esther was understanding. We all have a right to a private life, she said. You more than anyone. Esther understood the beauty of silence, the silence in which a still small voice could make itself heard. Lisa admired her for that. In the first days after she and Jaz got Raj back, they'd barely uttered a word. It was as if they both had the same fear, that something fine and fragile was being woven around them – a magic cocoon, a crystal web – and loud voices or sudden movement would shatter it. They lived like medieval peasants, cowering from signs and portents. They hid from the FedEx man.

They were, the two of them, so very delicate, so bruised. She'd hoped – and she was sure Jaz had felt the same – that, like a broken bone, they'd eventually knit back together, filaments of new love reaching across the distance between the kitchen table and the sink. They'd been through so much. It would be absurd to split up. And she couldn't deny how hard he'd tried for her. When she'd fallen down, he'd picked her up. When she couldn't cope, when they were forcing her to walk back up to those terrible rocks, pushing some strange child in the stroller; when she was lying on the bathroom floor, paralyzed, catatonic, trying to abdicate all responsibility, trying to stop breathing, to stop her heart pumping blood around her body, Jaz had tried his best to look after her. He'd tried to say the right words. But (and this was what lay over them like a miasma) he'd failed. He hadn't been able to pull her round. When it came down to it, his love and care hadn't been enough.

They were different. Of course it had always been that way, part of what had attracted them to each other. A mutual fascination, loving contact with someone new and strange. Not *exotic*, though, never that. She believed she'd always made the effort to see Jaz as an individual, not a representative of anything. After they brought Raj back, Jaz's parents had taken the train up from Baltimore. Thank God, they'd said, pressing their palms together, and for once she'd been able to agree with them. But his mother had taken it too far, standing in their kitchen with her eyes shut, her hand on the top of Raj's head, muttering in Punjabi. Lisa had felt like snatching her son away. It's their culture, she told herself. It's just their culture. Jaz came from that, but he wasn't that. Her problem with him was purely personal.

For her it was enough to have Raj back. He seemed to be unhurt. He was proof that by loving, by holding on tight, what was lost would be returned. But Jaz seemed unsatisfied. He wanted an explanation. He worried over the evidence like a dog with a chew toy, phoning the police so often she was sure he was making a nuisance of himself. He spouted endless theories. One evening she came back from work to find him poring over a large-scale map of the Mojave Desert, drawing circles with a compass. Beside him was a yellow legal pad, scrawled with notes and calculations: how far a toddler could walk in an hour; the location of the nearest public road.

'It's so frustrating,' he said. 'The area where they found him is just a blank. It's military land, so the mapping data's classified.'

'I'm sure the police have all the information they need. What can you find out that they can't?'

'They're not doing anything. They aren't making it a priority.'

'They have other problems, Jaz. Other cases.'

'But what happened to him? What do you think happened?'

'Does it matter?'

He looked at her pityingly. 'How can you say that? He's our son. Someone had him. Someone took him away from us. How can you live, knowing that person's still out there, ready to do it again?'

'I don't know, Jaz. I just don't think it's our job anymore.'

Sometimes it seemed to her that there was only so much energy in a relationship, so much electricity in circulation between two people. As she grew stronger and more confident, Jaz seemed to wane. He lost weight. He'd pad through the house in sweats and a T-shirt, looking like a ghost. She found his listlessness irritating. 'What's happened to you?' she asked him one night, when she came home, loaded with Barneys bags, to find him collapsed on the couch, watching a true-crime show in a litter of crusted cereal bowls and the previous day's *Times*. Raj was playing unsupervised in her office. He'd upended a box of pins and clips, creating a chaos of sharp points on the rug. She bustled around, clearing up, angrily berating Jaz over her shoulder as he yawned and thumbed the remote. 'You're like a stranger. You should go back to work. You were better when you were working.'

'I don't know what I'd do,' he said. Just that. As if he'd come to the end of something and hadn't the will to go on.

Esther was blunt. 'Do you still love him?' They'd met for a coffee. Lisa had brought Raj with her, and he was being an angel, sitting quietly at the little café table eating an ice cream. A good little boy, dressed in a new blue-and-white matelot top. She glanced at him uneasily, trying to work out if he was paying attention.

'Esther, what a question!'

Her friend arched an eyebrow, making light of her curiosity. 'It's not a stupid thing to ask. If you love him, the rest will take care of itself.'

Lisa considered the matter. 'Yes,' she said. 'I think I do.' Yes, dimly. Yes, for old times' sake. Here was Esther, blowzy big-chested Esther, with her chunky amber jewelry, her silk headscarves wrapping up hair still thin from chemo, her children already at Brown and U Penn and her unapologetically fat husband, Ralph, who was always blowing in through the door with something gift-wrapped in his hands, who'd always just happened to be passing a deli or a book store or a bakery that sold the most delightful little macaroons. Ralph was so plainly thankful to have his wife alive that going to the office every morning was a painful separation and it was all he could do not to crush her to his big barrel chest when he came home again at night. Their home was a temple, their family table an altar. It was hard not to make comparisons.

She smoothed Raj's hair. He allowed her to do that now, without flinching.

'I wish – I wish he'd let it go. It's like he's still out there, wandering in that awful desert.'

The previous night they'd had a terrible fight. She'd found Jaz staring at Raj in the way he now had, a deep silent interrogation. He was squatting on the floor, watching the boy play, with a kind of forensic attention, as if every maneuver of his pack of plastic dinosaurs might yield up vital information. He spoke without even looking up.

'Do you think he was – you know.'

'Jaz.'

'There was no physical evidence.'

363

'Not in front of him.'

'That's not definitive, though. The fact that they couldn't find anything. I mean, he was away for months. It could have healed.'

'For God's sake, shut up! I don't want to talk about it. And it's not appropriate in front of him.'

She scooped Raj up and half dragged him into the bathroom, slamming the door behind her. Once inside, she sat on the toilet with the lid down, hugging him tightly. He complained a little, tried to squirm out of her grasp. Jaz knocked tentatively on the door.

'Go away,' she called out. 'Just go away. He's back. Why isn't that good enough for you?'

Of course she had the same questions. Where had he slept? What had he eaten? What was the first thing he saw when he woke up in the morning? Did they touch him, bathe him, smooth his hair? Was there one person? Two? There must, she thought, have been a woman. A couple. What was that woman thinking when she unbuckled him from his stroller and ran with him down the dusty path? Was she desperate? Angry? Insane? Each question bred more, doubling, quadrupling, a vertiginous recess of uncertainty. The only way to deal with such a pit of questions was to close the trapdoor, to refuse to look down. That was what Jaz didn't understand. God had given their son back to them. It ought to be enough.

When the job came up at Paracelsus Press, she'd not taken it seriously. The offer came through Paula, one of the other women in the group. She was a nutritionist, friends with Karl, the publisher. They were looking for an editor. She'd immediately thought of Lisa. Instinctively Lisa found herself saying that it didn't really sound like it was for her. Paula looked mystified. Why ever not? She'd have thought it was a perfect fit. Lisa looked through the list, and, among the titles on color therapy and dowsing, found a lot of books that were serious and considered. She was curious enough to set up an interview. Karl turned out to be a typical Lower East Side character, a rakish old communard with a graying ponytail and a little ebony stud in his left ear. He'd started off in the underground press, branching out into book publishing when the dream of a revolution in consciousness began to subside in the mid-seventies. He'd run Paracelsus out of his apartment for many years, but with the internet (a miracle, he said, a boon) it had rapidly grown into one of the leaders in its sector. They'd had hits with an Iyengar yoga manual and an illustrated version of the Bardo Thodol, and he wanted to plow the money back into the business. Over a meal at a raw-food restaurant in the East Village, he told her he was looking for someone to work on a series about world religion, a collection of the mystical texts of the great traditions presented in a way that was neither too popular nor too scholarly, a route for general readers into the various intersecting currents of faith. She could work out of their offices on 9th Street. She said yes straight away.

Jaz sneered. If she wanted a job, why couldn't she find one with a *serious* publisher? That word. One of Jaz's words, like *reasonable, rational, pragmatic*. He read out titles in a scoffing voice. *The Solar Seal: A Manual for Lightworkers. UFOs and the Manifestation of Spirit.* Was that really the sort of crap she wanted to foist on the world? Sure, she admitted, some of their titles were aimed at a fringe audience. But she was going to be working on something substantial, something she really cared about. He could say what he liked, but she wasn't going to be embarrassed anymore about what she believed.

'And what do you believe?'

'That my son was returned to me. And that I owe a debt.'

'To who? To the police? The people who found him?'

'I can't talk about this with you.'

'Because it doesn't make sense.'

'I know what happened. I kept my faith with Raj and he came back to me.'

'Lisa, you were catatonic. Suicidal. You told me you knew he was dead.'

'But he came back.'

'You don't even remember. I thought – look, the idea that Raj was found because of your magical thinking is – you know it's insane, right?'

'So because I want to do something more than sit in my own filth, eating chips and making up conspiracy theories, I'm insane?'

'Conspiracy theories?'

And so it went on. It was tiring, desperately tiring, but eventually he agreed. He didn't want to work and she did. They had enough money. He'd look after Raj during the day when she was at the office. She hoped it would bring him closer to the boy. She was happy when she heard about the walks. It seemed healthy. A father and son thing. She had no idea they went so far, until one day she looked at the wheels of the stroller. They'd been worn down almost to the metal.

The job was absorbing, though she was glad she didn't need to live off her meager pay-check. Her first commission was a book on Tibetan Buddhism, to be written by a Rinpoche in California, an American who'd studied for many years in the Himalayas. Karl was already pressing her to start work on the second volume, about medieval Christian mystics. She enjoyed being around him, working amid the heaps of papers in the little office, listening as he chatted to Teri, the other editor, and Mei Lin, who did the books. Karl was quickly becoming almost as important an influence as Esther. She grew to look forward to their one-on-one conversations, the lunch meetings over Thai or Japanese food, the sandwiches from the local vegan café. Karl was a positive force. It was his own description, but when you got to know him, it didn't seem arrogant, just a statement of fact. He meditated. He rode a track bike. He brewed his own kombucha, scary-looking fungal cultures housed in mason jars in the office storeroom. He was enthusiastic about the history and landscape of East Asia, particularly Laos and Cambodia, which he described in passionate detail. Though he was much older than her, in (she guessed) his sixties, his body was lean and wiry. She began to wonder, idly, what it would be like to hold him, to run her hands over his thighs, his chest.

She felt as if she'd turned a corner. Every day her life seemed to get a little better. When Raj started to talk, she told her colleagues it was an affirmation, proof that they were all protected by a higher power. At the book group she and Esther and the others said prayers of thanks. She began to allow her imagination to range farther. Raj was – it didn't seem too much to use the word – a miracle. Every day he seemed to achieve something new. With a learning curve (even the doctors said this) so much steeper than normal, anything was possible. He might even turn out to be a genius, an extraordinary mind that had started life locked away from the rest of the world. She wrote off for school prospectuses, scrutinized entry requirements for gifted and talented programs. Only Jaz seemed untouched by the new possibilities. He winced when she voiced her (perfectly reasonable) wish that he be tested by an educational psychologist, to prepare him for entry to one of the elite elementary schools in the city. That (of course) provoked another fight. Why couldn't he give thanks, like she did? Where was his joy? He told her he didn't give a damn about being 'out of touch with his light' and stormed out of the house. He didn't come back until late that evening. He smelled sour, like stale red wine. She assumed he'd been sulking in some bar.

At other times they were united. Their friends came back. A few, at least. There were some she couldn't forgive, others who still seemed alienated by the drama of the previous year. But there were the beginnings of a social life. They found a babysitter in the neighborhood and experimentally went out to dinner, leaving Raj in her care. It was a success. They began to buy listings magazines, looking at what was on in the city. Amy came to stay, with her new boyfriend, a very nice Nigerian doctor. Lisa cooked a dinner party, invited Esther and Ralph and another couple. Before they sat down to eat, she asked everyone to join her in a short prayer. Jaz looked stricken. The others understood. At the end, Adé boomed out a loud amen.

Afterwards, as they ferried dirty plates and glasses into the kitchen, Jaz hissed at her.

'Well, that was embarrassing.'

'Why? Why would you be embarrassed?'

'You're forcing it on people. Rubbing it in their faces.'

'Rubbing it in your face, you mean.'

'Try to understand, Lisa.'

It turned into an argument about Raj. What was possible. What the future looked like. She accused him of being willfully blind to the good things that were happening. Sometimes, she told him, she felt he didn't believe in his own son. He said he didn't even know how to answer such a charge.

She was triumphant. 'Because you know it's true.'

'No, because your accusation makes no sense.'

'You really ought to get your head out of the sand.'

'God, Lisa. You think I'm the one with my head in the sand? Yours is buried so far – look, I'm trying hard to be positive here. In fact I'd say I was optimistic. Cautiously optimistic. Raj seems to be doing well. But think of what actually happened. Anything could come up for him. Repressed memories, trauma. Until we know who had him, what he went through, we won't be able to say for sure.'

That night, she lay awake in bed, listening to sirens dopplering in the distance. Barricaded by pillows, Jaz had wrapped himself in the quilt, hunched up into a rigid, accusatory ball. She'd tried to dismiss his point about trauma, telling him he had only to look at how well Raj was doing to know it wasn't an issue. But in truth it did worry her. She had to admit she wasn't as certain as she wanted to be. About damage to Raj, about a lot of things. For a long time she'd been obsessing – not, like Jaz, about the day of Raj's disappearance, but the night before, her drunken odyssey into town. She'd been out of control that night. She was never out of control. Perhaps someone had put something in her drink. It was a sleazy bar, the kind of place where that sort of thing probably happened. She had only the vaguest memory of being in the woman's car, the headlights lighting up the dirt road, the house they drove to, with its odd bulbous roof, its triangular windows, the animal-skin rugs lying on its polished wooden floors. The alcohol swimming in her head had dissolved everything into shadows. Only the stone hearth and the woman in the rocking chair had substance. She remembered collapsing on to a bed which smelled of dust and cigarette smoke, feeling a rough Indian blanket under her cheek. The two women were standing over her, talking.

'What about her?'

'Leave her, she'll be OK.'

'What if she wakes up?'

'She's got so much booze inside her, she ain't going to move a muscle until morning.'

Why had that stuck in her memory? Had they left her? Where had they gone? How long had she been unconscious in that strange house? The trapdoor was open, the questions hatching and swarming, like maggots turning into flies. Raj had been spirited away into that teeming darkness. They'd said something about her, about Raj. What had they been saying about Raj? Shut the trapdoor. Draw the heavy bolt across it. There were places into which one shouldn't trespass.

The call from Raj's speech therapist came completely out of the blue. She'd met the woman, of course. She was expensive. The best. They'd been very happy with her work.

'I'm sorry to bother you, Mrs Matharu.'

'That's quite alright. What can I do for you?'

'I'd really prefer to have this conversation face to face, but – well, it's a difficult matter. I wanted to speak to you as soon as I could. Your husband came to see me.'

'Alone?'

'No. He brought Raj in for his appointment earlier today. But he asked if he could see me without Raj. Without Raj being in the room.'

'Why ever would he do that?'

'I don't know why he chose me. Maybe because I'm – well, he may have thought I'd understand. This isn't my area, of course. But I found what he told me – alarming. He has ideations. He seems very scared.'

'Ideations?'

'He's got the notion that Raj isn't your son. It's unusual, but not

369

totally without precedent. He told me he believes Raj – the real Raj – has been swapped for an identical double. A twin. I don't know why he chose me to confess to, but I believe this thought has been in his mind for some time. He knows it's not normal. He knows there's no logical explanation. He's very troubled by it.'

'I still don't understand.'

'I asked him how he knew about the substitution. How he'd noticed. What had changed. He told me absolutely everything was just like Raj, except it was clear to him that it wasn't the same boy. This Raj is identical in every respect to your son, but in some essential respect he's not the same boy.'

'But that's crazy. It doesn't make any sense. He really thinks this? That someone's swapped Raj for a double?'

'Maybe, with the kidnap, the trauma . . .'

'You're telling me he's gone insane. That's basically what you're telling me.'

'I certainly think there are grounds for seeing a psychiatrist. Strong grounds. You've both – your family has undergone a great deal of stress. It's possible that this is merely a reaction. Perhaps with rest, maybe some kind of medication, it will all be resolved. This is very tricky, Mrs Matharu, and, as I say, I'm not qualified to make a diagnosis. You really need to see a specialist. Your husband has assured me he doesn't want to harm Raj. He's not hearing voices, or experiencing compulsions. He says he's no danger to the boy.'

'Oh God! He's out with him now. What should I do? Should I call the police?'

'I don't think that's necessary. As I say, he claims he's not going to harm him. Why don't you wait and talk to him yourself? I'm sorry to be the bearer of bad news. This must be very distressing. If you need a recommendation, maybe I can call around and get you a name . . .'

Lisa sat at the kitchen counter, twisting from side to side on a high stool. She felt stalled, short-circuited. She poured out the contents of the bowl into which they habitually threw spare change.

She lined up coins to make patterns and moved them about with her forefinger, a game with no clear rules. Finally she heard Jaz opening the front door and the sound of coats and boots being removed in the hall. Raj came barreling in. She scooped him up, held him tight.

She didn't know how to start. Jaz started chatting, asking about her day. They'd booked the sitter. They had plans to go out to the cinema. What did she want to see? He seemed completely normal. She watched him. Did he seem more tense than usual? Did he seem frightened?

'I had a call from Dr Siddiqi.'

'Oh yes?'

'Jaz, I don't understand. She said you'd told her Raj wasn't our son.'

Suddenly his face collapsed. He looked hollow. She knew then that it was true. Involuntarily she put her hand up to her mouth. He was shaking his head, holding out his open palms in a gesture of pacification.

'Look,' he said. And again. 'Look.'

'What's going on?'

'I know it's not logical. But surely you of all people should understand.'

'I should understand? Why?'

'You believe in – all this stuff.'

'All what stuff?'

'You told me you thought it was a miracle.'

'A miracle that he came back. I don't think he's being – what? Impersonated? I don't even know what you think is happening. What did you tell that woman?'

'I can't – not while he's here. Raj, go play in the other room.'

Raj looked from one to the other, confusion flickering on his face.

'Go on, darling. Go play. Why not find your dinosaurs? You can take them to the living room.'

Raj obeyed. Jaz sank down on to a chair, put his head in his hands.

'Lisa, I know how weird this sounds.'

'You have no idea. What exactly did you say to her? She told me you need to see a psychiatrist. She told me she didn't think you intended to harm our son. She had to say that – she didn't think so, but she couldn't be sure.'

'I'd never do anything to him. I swear.'

'So what's going on? It's Raj. Can't you see that? There's nothing wrong with him. Nothing's changed.'

'I can't put a finger on it. It's as if – as if something's wearing his skin.'

'You're terrifying. I can't believe I'm hearing you say this.'

'I know how it sounds. I'm scared too, Lisa. I don't know what's happening.'

'You need to talk to someone.'

'A shrink?'

'Yes, a shrink. God, you've been with him all this time, wheeling him around the city. Wherever it is you go. Anything could have happened.'

'I swear I'd never hurt him.'

'But you don't even think it's him. You think it's something wearing his skin.'

'Lisa, I'll see a shrink. Whatever you want. If it's me, my mind or whatever, I'll get it sorted out. But don't you ever think it's strange, the way he's changing? He's completely different.'

'Yes, he is. He's better. I don't understand why you find that so hard to accept. It's what we've been praying for, and now you won't even believe it.'

'I need to know what happened to him. I can't stand not knowing. There's something different about him. And yes, I don't feel like it's him. I can't tell you why. Haven't you noticed the way he looks at you?'

'Looks at me?'

'At both of us. Like he's ancient. Like he knows all our secrets.'

'He's a little boy, Jaz. He's just a little boy. I want you to sleep downstairs tonight. I don't want you near us.'

'That's ridiculous, Lisa.'

'Ridiculous. Really?'

'You don't have to do this.'

'Stay away, Jaz. I don't know what I'm going to do yet. This is too weird. You have to give me space.'

'Look at him, Lisa. That's all I ask of you. Really look at him.'

She took Raj upstairs. As she got him ready for bed, brushing his teeth and helping him into his pajamas, she could hear Jaz roaming about downstairs, slamming doors, angrily rattling about in the kitchen. After a while the sound of the TV came filtering through the floor, some cop show, the volume turned up high.

Before she went to sleep, she wedged a chair under the door.

Next morning Jaz hung around in the kitchen doorway as she phoned Karl and told him she couldn't make it in to work.

'You don't have to do that,' Jaz said. 'I'm not some kind of maniac.'

'I'm not leaving him with you.'

'I promise, Lisa. I'll go to a shrink. Find one. Make an appointment. I'll go.'

That day she didn't let Raj out of her sight. She sat at the kitchen table with her MacBook, looking up psychiatrists, psychoanalysts, therapists of various kinds. Dr Siddiqi had emailed a couple of names, and in the end it was one of them she phoned. She prayed silently for guidance before she went into the study, where Jaz was lying on the floor, doing stretches.

'That couch has destroyed my back.'

'I'm sorry you had an uncomfortable night.'

'OK.'

'I need to know you're not a danger.'

'I see.'

'I can't take the risk.'

'I'm not –'

'I know, you're not a danger. I found you a psychiatrist. Here's his name, and his number. You can see him Thursday afternoon. I thought you'd prefer a guy.'

'You did? OK.'

'You want to see a woman?'

'No, it's fine. I'll see this –' He looked at the paper. 'Dr Zucker-man.'

She was relieved. That night, she and Jaz slept in the same bed, though she pulled the dresser partway across the door, so if he got up and moved it, he'd make a noise. He looked angry.

'What if I have to go to the bathroom?'

She shrugged. 'Then you'll wake me up.'

'OK, whatever you want.'

In the morning she phoned Karl, trying to let him know something serious was happening, without divulging details. She'd tell him. She'd already decided that. But she wanted to speak to him face to face, preferably over lunch. He'd be sympathetic. He might even be able to help.

'I can't come in. It's – a personal situation. I'm so sorry. Yes, I know about that. I'll call him and reschedule. He can't? I see. That's tricky.'

Jaz was standing behind her, so close that when he spoke it made her jump.

'Come on, Lisa. You can't do this forever. I haven't hurt him. I won't hurt him. I never would.'

'Jaz! I'm sorry, Karl, could you hold the line a moment? What the hell, Jaz?'

'Go to work. I'll look after him.'

The meeting was important, and Karl seemed mystified; not annoyed exactly, but certainly not as understanding as she'd hoped. As she slid her papers into a bag, she reasoned to herself that Jaz had been with Raj several days a week for months, without any problems. It would probably be fine. As she left for work, the two of them stood on the stoop and waved her off.

It'd be fine.

At lunchtime she phoned Jaz's cell. 'Where are you?' she asked, straining to hear in case there was traffic noise in the background. She'd asked Jaz not to go out with him. Just stay home, she'd said. I'll be back early anyway.

His voice was breezy. 'Oh, we're at home.'

'Everything OK?'

'Peachy.'

Something about his tone didn't sound right. After she rang off, she sat at her desk for a few minutes, the wrong feeling working its way down into her chest, her gut. Without a word to Karl or Teri, who were looking at some cover designs, she grabbed her bag and went out on to First Avenue to look for a taxi.

She got back home just in time. Jaz and Raj were already outside. Raj was wearing his little yellow rain poncho. The trunk of the car was open. Jaz was stowing a bag inside. She shoved some bills through the taxi driver's window and ran to the front of the car, placing herself between Raj and Jaz.

'Where the hell are you going?'

'I have to do this, Lisa. Don't stop me.'

'Where are you taking him?'

'Where do you think? We have to go back there. Unless we find out what happened, we'll never be able to move on.'

'You were just going to abduct him? Drive off, without telling me?'

'You think I'm insane. There's no way I could explain to you.'

'You can't take him.'

'If we don't go today, we'll have to go sooner or later. You can't keep denying it forever.'

'I'm calling the police.'

'There's no need for that.'

'There's every need. You've gone insane. You're abducting our son.'

'Come with me.'

'You're sick, Jaz. You need help.'

'You know you have questions. Come with me. We'll find out together. We'll solve this. There's an explanation.'

They'd been raising their voices. Lisa was aware of a neighbor standing watching them from across the street. She waved her hand, trying to look jaunty, unconcerned.

'Come inside, Jaz. Please. We can talk inside.'

'Only if you'll agree to come with us.'

'OK, OK. Anything you say. Let's just do this inside.'

'Raj, Mummy's coming too! We're going on an adventure! Isn't it exciting?'

An hour later they were on their way to JFK, inching through the afternoon rush-hour traffic. Jaz was at the wheel. She was sitting in the back with Raj, who was strapped into his booster seat, swinging his legs and counting off the vehicles in the other lane.

'Blue car,' he said. 'Red car. Red car white car black car blue car white car.'

She felt as if she were being kidnapped. Strap-hanging on the subway, she'd sometimes see another passenger reading a Bible. Usually they were black or Latino, heading in to minimum-wage jobs in the city. Cleaners, custodians. She'd always imagined their faith in God as primarily a protective thing. Warding off debt, family illness. Their Bibles were usually well thumbed, often in foreign languages. Sometimes passages were underlined or highlighted with fluorescent marker. She'd always felt – not above, exactly, but far away from such people. Now she wished she had her own dog-eared, familiar book, something she could clutch in her hand as they made that terrible journey.

At the airport Jaz parked the car in the long-term parking lot and carried the cases toward the terminal. She wondered if she ought to make a run for it, perhaps find a cop. What should she say? Jaz was so determined. Unless she could have him arrested, committed to a mental hospital, there was no way of stopping him. She imagined herself carrying Raj, fleeing along a moving walkway. It was useless. Maybe, she told herself, by going along with this, she'd help him see how lost he was.

They bought tickets for Las Vegas and sat warily in the lounge, half watching TV. News commentators were arguing about the war. The withdrawal from Iraq. The ramping up of operations in Afghanistan. There were brief images of mountains, bleak sandy desert. It was like a premonition.

'Are we going on a plane, Mommy?' asked Raj.

'Yes, dear.'

'Are we going to see Grandma Patty and Grandpa Louis?'

'No, baby. We're just going to where you were when you were away.'

'Where's that?'

Jaz leaned forward so he could hear. 'Where you were. When you went away. You weren't with us.'

'I couldn't see you.'

'That's right.'

'I was asleep.'

'No, Raj. Not when you were asleep. When you didn't see us for a long time.'

'I went night-night.'

'No, Raj.'

'Leave him, Jaz. Leave him alone.'

Secretly she'd been sending texts. SOS messages to her mom, to Esther. *Jaz behaving manically. Forcing us to go back to desert. Please help.* When her mom called, Jaz looked over sharply. Don't pick it up, he said. Don't answer.

The flight was interminable. At McCarran they waited in line to rent a car. Neither would leave the other alone with Raj, each convinced that there would be trickery, that the other would try to sneak off. She hung around outside the men's bathroom while Jaz and Raj were inside. When she needed to pee, she insisted on taking the boy in with her, even as he complained he didn't need to go and she was hurting his wrist.

Locked in a cubicle she called Esther.

'Are you OK?' she asked. 'Has he threatened you?'

'No, nothing like that. But he says Raj isn't Raj. That the real Raj has been replaced by something else. He thinks if we go back to the rocks we'll solve some kind of mystery. He's gone crazy, Esther. I don't know what to do.'

'Why ever did you let him get you on a plane?'

'Oh, I don't know. It seemed simpler. I thought if I let him go through with it, he might see how crazy he's being.'

'You might be right. Once he gets there, he'll probably calm down. How far away is it?'

'A couple of hours' drive.'

'Do you want me to send the police?'

'I don't know. What will they do? Jaz can fool people into thinking he's normal. He'll probably have some explanation for them.'

'I could call them anyway, let them know there's a situation. It might be easier than you just grabbing one and causing a scene.'

'OK. Maybe. Oh, I don't know. Look, maybe we should hold off. I'll call you when we get there. If you don't hear from me, phone them.'

'Good luck, dear.'

'Thanks, Esther. Speak to you later.'

Jaz was waiting outside the door, suspicious, antsy.

'What took you so long?'

She didn't reply. She fitted Raj into the booster seat, then got in and waited for Jaz to settle himself. No harm can come to you, she thought. Not in any way that matters. You're a child of a loving, personal God, whose infinite care and wisdom surrounds you now and forever. This is the world you live in. A world infused with the spirit of God.

It was late afternoon. Vegas ebbed away into drab suburbs, then trailer parks and vacant lots, fronted by billboards advertising future developments, casinos, personal-injury lawyers, evangelical churches, strip clubs. Then the land rose up in its full intensity, white rock tinted pale yellow by the lowering sun. Jaz turned off the Interstate on to a two-lane blacktop. By now the land was burnished gold, the mountains in the distance a copper-red.

'We're so close now,' he said. 'Can you feel it?' It was the first either of them had spoken since Las Vegas. 'I'm sorry I did this to you. I'm sorry I scared you. But can't you feel it? Can't you feel how right this is?'

'Yes,' she said. And, to her surprise, she meant it. The alien land was beautiful. The vast emptiness all around them seemed pregnant with something, some possibility she wanted to see made flesh.

They passed through a dilapidated settlement, a few houses with a gas station and a boarded-up motel. At the edge of town was a gnarled tree festooned with old sneakers, like a flock of crows sitting on its bare branches. The road climbed a ridge, then dropped down into a basin, where some kind of commercial chemical operation was taking place, sheds and huge tanks squatting on the flat. Then they climbed again, heading straight, or so it seemed, into the huge gold disk of the sun, right into its heart. A collision course.

Up ahead on the road, they saw flashing lights. A barrier had been erected. A highway patrol car was parked askew across both lanes. They pulled up in front of it and a policeman got out. Jaz rolled down the window.

'I'm sorry, sir. You'll have to turn back.'

'I need to get to the Pinnacle Rocks.'

'Are you a local resident?'

'No.'

'Well, then, I'm afraid you'll have to turn the car around. We've got a serious incident up ahead. It's not safe to proceed.'

'What kind of incident?'

'I don't know exactly, sir. I believe there's been an explosion. Some kind of chemical release.'

'But I really need to get to the rocks. We've come a long way. From New York.'

'Is that right?'

'I've got my son here, my boy. He's very tired.'

'Well, sir, then I don't see why you'd want to be putting him in harm's way. If you get back on to the Interstate, you'll see signs for a number of motels. There's also a diversion signposted about fifteen miles back.'

'You don't understand. We need to get there. Is there another way?'

'I don't know, sir. I'm just doing my job, and I'm afraid you'll have to turn the car around and head on back in the direction you came.'

'Please. You don't understand.'

'Sir, I'm not here to argue with you. This is not optional. Turn the car around and head back the way you came.'

Jaz swung the wheel. The narrow ribbon of road stretched away from them. Long shadows scored the sides of the mountains. They drove in silence. Lisa stole glances at him. His jaw was set, his eyes unblinking.

Suddenly, without warning, he turned off the road, bumping across the sand, a great plume of dust rising up behind them. Gravel skittered against the bodywork. There was a rhythmic thwack, the sound of creosote bushes hitting the underside of the car. Lisa braced herself against the dash.

'What are you doing?'

'I'm not giving up.'

'Stop, Jaz! Please stop! It's dangerous!'

The car vibrated. Jaz swung the wheel left and right to avoid large rocks. They were gradually climbing uphill. Eventually there was a massive jolt as they ran over something and came to a shuddering halt, the airbags deploying, filling up the car like giant white marshmallows. Jaz seemed not to care, struggling out of his seatbelt and flinging open the door. He pulled Raj out of the car and set him on his shoulders.

'Come on!'

Sobbing, Lisa followed them. There was a cut above her eye. Blood was blurring her vision. Raj was babbling, a stream of wordless nonsense that rose in tone until it sounded more like a chirruping bird or a fax machine than human speech. They scrambled up a talus slope, Jaz reaching out a hand to help her over the difficult parts. Little avalanches of stones skipped down behind them. She could feel the heat exhaled from the earth. She no longer cared what happened to her. The world had reduced itself to the slippery gravel beneath her feet, her ragged breathing. At last they stood together on the ridge of the hill, sweating and gasping for breath, the three of them holding hands and looking out across the great basin below. In the distance, the only form to break the flat surface was the three-fingered hand of the Pinnacle Rocks. They could see no evidence of anything wrong. There was no cloud, no column of fire, no toxic mist. The air was blue. Ahead of them lay only a vast emptiness, an absence. There was nothing out there at all.

1775

From the daily record prepared by Padre Fray Francisco Garcés, son of the Colegio de la Santa Cruz, Queretáro, of the journey that he made in this year 1775 by order of His Excellency Don Antonio María Bucareli y Ursúa, Lieutenant-General, Viceroy, Governor and Captain-General of this New Spain, as made known in his letter of January 2nd of the said year and decided upon by the council of war held at México on November 28th of the year preceding; and by order likewise of the Padre Fray Romualdo Cartagena, Guardian of the said Colegio, in his letter of January 20th 1775, in which Fray Garcés was directed to look over the lands west of the river Colorado and treat with the neighboring nations, to determine if they were disposed and ready for receiving the catechism and becoming subjects of our Sovereign. The following passage was suppressed before the declaration of Imprimatur, confirmed by order of His Most Illustrious and Reverend Eminence, Carlo, Cardinal Rezzonico, Secretary of the Supreme Sacred Congregation of the Roman and Universal Inquisition.

154th day: In the last week I have traveled fourteen leagues on courses west and northwest, and today arrived at a ranchería of the Chemegueba nation, situated near a spring shaded by many palm trees. The men of the ranchería came forth and issued threats, and I believe I was spared martyrdom only by showing forth the image of the damned man, whereupon my tormentors were so afraid that they begged me to turn the painting round and show them once again the gentle face of Mary Most Holy. Accordingly I named the site of my reprieve, *Aguaje de Kairos*.

159th day: In the last four days I have traveled ten leagues on a westward course. My interpreters left this morning, saying that they had come to the limits of their country and here the country of their enemies begins. They begged me not to proceed farther, warning that ahead was only desolation. I was glad to see them go as I believe they are in league with the Adversary. I watched them go and indeed they were as fleet as deer.

164th day: Of food and water I have very little. Even mice and small lizards are scarce here and it is my greatest desire to find a well. I have seen no sweet water since Aguaje de Kairos. I am afflicted with visions and do not know whether they are the work of God or my Enemy, whose name I dare not write.

165th day: This day I lost my compass needle in ground riddled by cracks and fissures. I searched for several hours, digging out the cracks with my hands, but was unable to find it. My Enemy laughed at me, bidding me find my way by God's holy light.

168th day: I climbed the San Ignacio range and looked down on an immense white plain, unbroken except for a butte whose three-spired shape I considered auspicious as a representation of the Trinity. There was no sign of water or herbiage but I trusted in God and set forth toward this sign of His grace. From this high place I could see that beyond the plain was another range, and no doubt beyond that another, and my heart was filled with fear, for my hunger and thirst are such that the sound of the wind is like a running brook in my ears and the round white stones in my path have the appearance of loaves of bread.

168th day: I halted at the rocks of the Trinity. My Adversary bade me climb them and fling myself from the peak, commanding God's angels to break my fall, but I trusted in Him to give me strength to walk forward on my two feet, though I cannot sail over the earth like the heathen runners or fly through the air like my hypocritical Adversary, who cloaks himself in sunlight like the white raiment of the just. Whatever has come from God has life only when it gazes back toward Him and this I did, looking away from the Adversary's lying light, seeking the true light of God. My trust in Him is absolute, though I am sore beset.

As I rested in the shade of the rocks it seemed to me that the sky was rent asunder and a dart of longing went out from my heart, piercing the veil that surrounded God, whose love boiled over and spilled down upon me as an angel in the form of a man with the head of a lion. And he spoke to me saying that I was beloved and revealing certain mysteries concerning life and death, which as soon as they had been revealed receded into forgetfulness, for that which is infinite is known only to itself and cannot be contained in the mind of man. I received all this in silence and stillness and then the creature retreated into the sky and I was once again alone in this desert place.

Here ends the redacted passage.

Acknowledgements

This book was written in New York, Marfa TX, Sussex, Shelter Island, Spetses, Venice CA and various hotel and motel rooms in California, Nevada, Arizona and Utah.

I would like to thank everyone who traveled with me, fed me, gave their hospitality and shared their ideas. I am particularly grateful to Carole and Richard Baron, Brooke Geahan, Jonny Geller, Ehab Khalaf, Katie Kitamura, Leonard Knight, Hardeep Singh Kohli, my parents Ravi and Hilary Kunzru, Carobeth Laird, Allan Moyle and Chiyoko Tanaka, Geraldine Ogilvy, Meghan O'Rourke, Simon Prosser, Lauren Redniss, Bic Runga, James Surowiecki, George Van Tassel, Lucy Walker, Darryl Ward and Katherine Zoepf.

This book would not have existed without the support of the Dorothy and Lewis B. Cullman Center for Scholars and Writers at the New York Public Library and the friendship of my colleagues there during the 2008/9 term. My thanks go to Jean Strouse and the staff of the library.

Fray Francisco Garcés existed. He did travel through Sonora, Arizona and California in 1775–6 and wrote about what he found. However, no part of that book (to my knowledge) was lost or suppressed as heretical.